THE COLONEL'S CONTRABAND

THE COLONEL'S CONTRABAND

Adrianne Summer

Copyright © 2022 by Adrianne Summer.

Library of Congress Control Number: 2022917151
ISBN: Hardcover   978-1-6698-4741-0
        Softcover   978-1-6698-4740-3
        eBook   978-1-6698-4739-7

All rights reserved. No part of this book may be reproduced or transmitted in any form or by any means, electronic or mechanical, including photocopying, recording, or by any information storage and retrieval system, without permission in writing from the copyright owner.

Any people depicted in stock imagery provided by Getty Images are models, and such images are being used for illustrative purposes only.
Certain stock imagery © Getty Images.

Print information available on the last page.

Rev. date: 09/27/2022

To order additional copies of this book, contact:
Xlibris
844-714-8691
www.Xlibris.com
Orders@Xlibris.com
820933

CONTENTS

Chapter 1   Our Lady of Sorrows Hospital – Frederick, Maryland....1
Chapter 2   The Weld House Museum – Frederick, Maryland 12
Chapter 3   James River, Virginia 23
Chapter 4   Williamsburg, Virginia 38
Chapter 5   James River, Virginia 46
Chapter 6   Harrison's Landing, Virginia.......................................59
Chapter 7   Union Hospital – Harrison's Landing, Virginia 70
Chapter 8   Union Hospital – Harrison's Landing, Virginia 86
Chapter 9   Union Hospital – Harrison's Landing, Virginia 95
Chapter 10 James River, Virginia 108
Chapter 11 Harrison's Landing, Virginia..................................... 119
Chapter 12 Battle of Bull Run – Field Hospital – Manassas,
            Virginia 133
Chapter 13 Battle of Antietam – Baltimore, Maryland................. 142
Chapter 14 Camp Curtin – Harrisburg, Pennsylvania.................. 157
Chapter 15 Camp Curtin – Harrisburg, Pennsylvania.................. 164
Chapter 16 Weld Manor – Philadelphia, Pennsylvania.................177
Chapter 17 Weld Manor – Philadelphia, Pennsylvania 185
Chapter 18 Weld Manor – Philadelphia, Pennsylvania 197
Chapter 19 Weld Manor – Philadelphia, Pennsylvania 210
Chapter 20 Weld Manor – Philadelphia, Pennsylvania 228
Chapter 21 Weld Manor – Philadelphia, Pennsylvania 233
Chapter 22 The Weld House Museum – Frederick, Maryland 246
Chapter 23 Weld Memorial Hospital – Baltimore, Maryland 252
Chapter 24 The Weld House Museum – Frederick, Maryland 262

Chapter 25 Weld Manor - Philadelphia, Pennsylvania...................272
Chapter 26 Weld Manor – Philadelphia, Pennsylvania..................282
Chapter 27 Frederick, Maryland 294

Epilogue...303
References 305

ACKNOWLEDGMENT

To my husband –
Thank you for putting up with my dining room table office, the boxes and boxes of manuscripts hidden in closets, cabinets, and under tables all over the house. Thank you for loving and supporting me through the doubts, the frustrations, and the tears. You are the love of my life…

To my children…more than all the stars in the sky.

To my mother, father, and sisters…from the beginning and forever.

To Christine –
It is rare in this life that you meet another creative soul that feeds your inner muse.

To Melanie –
For everything. I will be forever changed as a writer because of you.

To all the mentionable, unmentioned…thank you.

Contact Me:
adriannesummernovels.com
Twitter – @AbsintheRoses
Facebook – Absinthe Rose

CHAPTER ONE

Our Lady of Sorrows Hospital – Frederick, Maryland
Saturday, April 9th

Seraphina squinted against the mid-morning sun. A twelve-hour ICU shift that should have ended at six had dragged on until ten, and she was ready to drop. Our Lady of Sorrows served the citizens of Frederick, Maryland, most in need and the least able to pay. Staffing and funding shortages were chronic, making days like today a common occurrence. She had the skill and credentials to work anywhere she wanted, for fewer hours and more pay. But she wasn't needed anywhere; she was needed here, and for Seraphina, that's what mattered most.

Fumbling around in her bag for her sunglasses, Seraphina dropped her keys.

"I got it," a male voice called out.

Seraphina put her left hand in her pocket, securing a small bottle of pepper spray between her fingers. Our Lady of Sorrows wasn't in the safest of neighborhoods. The parking lot could be dangerous, even during the day. She spun to face the man.

"Ladarius?"

"Sorry, didn't mean to scare you," he replied, picking up her keys. "You walk fast. I was afraid I wouldn't catch you."

"That's the point. You almost caught a face full of mace." Seraphina smiled, taking her keys.

"Yeah, it's dangerous to approach a woman in this hospital since they put mace in the safety week goodie bags." He grinned broadly.

Seraphina let her smile fade, not wanting to encourage him. It didn't work.

"Would you like to go to dinner?" he asked, eyes bright with anticipation.

"I have plans tonight. I can't," she replied, prayerful that would be the end of it. It wasn't.

"Tomorrow? On me? Or maybe coffee?"

She wasn't interested. The fault wasn't his. Tall, athletic, with deep brown skin, kind eyes, and a beautiful smile, he was attractive. The fact that he was an accomplished doctor made him even more so. Ladarius Cromwell was the total package, but Seraphina could care less. Love was an ill-fated endeavor for the women in her family. Three generations, going all the way back to her great-grandmother, had proven it. She didn't need to be the fourth.

"Ladarius, I'm flattered, but right now isn't a good time for me."

It wasn't. She was running late. Her cell phone had been blowing up before she'd stepped off the elevator into the parking lot.

"I understand. But a little cafeteria coffee never hurt anyone. Tomorrow? After rounds? No strings. Just coffee."

"You aren't going to give up, are you?" she asked.

"Should I?" he replied.

The yes was on the tip of Seraphina's tongue, but she didn't want to be mean or deal with the inevitable back and forth. She could let him down easy over coffee next week with the tried and true "I don't date people I work with" excuse.

"I'm off the next few days. How about Wednesday after rounds?" she asked.

"Perfect." Ladarius opened her car door, Seraphina got in, and he closed the door behind her. "Have a good weekend. I'll see you Wednesday."

Seraphina found her sunglasses, started the car, and backed out of the hospital parking lot.

Siri's automated voice came through the car speakers. "Call from V."

It was Vanessa. Seraphina debated letting the call go to voicemail but thought better of it. Her best friend was relentless. If she didn't answer, Vanessa would keep calling until she did.

"Answer." Seraphina sighed.

"Seraphina, where are you? You promised you'd be here."

"Vanessa, I'm coming. I swear. I just got off."

"I know you, Seraphina Laurent. If you aren't here in an hour—"

"Can we make it two hours? I'd like to bathe and maybe take a power nap."

"Seraphina! I swear if you—"

"Vanessa, you're worse now than when we were in college."

"And I had to get on your ass then, too," Vanessa complained.

"I'll be there. I wouldn't miss the Brown-Oakes family reunion for all the world. I am an honorary member, after all." Seraphina chuckled.

"It isn't a family reunion! It is Auntie Mary's 100th birthday party," Vanessa snapped.

"Yes, because we all have birthday parties with one hundred and fifty of our relatives."

"Just get here. And don't wear those damn scrubs!"

Seraphina looked down at her scrubs and laughed. "I wouldn't dream of it."

"Don't be a smart ass. Bye." Siri abruptly announced that the call had ended.

Seraphina smiled. Vanessa Blackwell. Not only her best friend but her chosen sister. Vanessa was as loyal as she was loving. She was always there when Seraphina needed her. They'd met in her freshman year of college. An upperclassman and the freshman dorm resident assistant, Vanessa was bossy and overprotective from day one.

"What the hell possessed you to leave Louisiana for Maryland, Seraphina Laurent?" Vanessa asked, incredulous.

"It is pronounced loran, not la-rent. And I don't know. Something told me this was where I needed to be. So here I am," Seraphina replied.

"Well, you're too damn pretty to be left to your own. That figure, those chocolate eyes, long wavy locks, and mocha skin… What are you?"

"Je suis Française Créole," Seraphina announced proudly.

"Creole? You speak French! Lord of mercy, the men here will eat you alive. It'll be all I can do to keep them from swimming around the front door like sharks who smell blood in the water. Don't go anywhere alone. Ever! And what the hell is with all those damn plants?"

Seraphina looked down at the plastic bins by her feet. "Reminders of home."

"Did you live in the jungle?"

"No." Seraphina laughed. "My grandmother is a healer. Plants bring peace and positive energy to a space."

"What's your major?"

"I'm going for my MSN in nursing. Minoring in history."

"Why nursing and not pre-med?"

"Doctors are too removed from actual patient care. I want to be hands-on, really heal people."

"Great," Vanessa snorted. "You and that avocado toast-eating, 'I only brought sandals for the winter,' environmental science, tree-hugging girl from California will be perfect for each other. That's your new roomy. My major is history. I TA in a few freshman classes. So, I'll see you around. Your room is down the hall, on your left. We can talk later about why you want to be a nurse and not a doctor."

They did talk about it. That and everything else. Fast friends, Vanessa introduced Seraphina to her family. The Brown-Oakes clan immediately felt like home. Everyone treated her like family, especially Auntie Mary. From the moment they met, Seraphina loved her, and their bond was everything now that her grandmother Eulalie was gone.

Seraphina pulled into her condo complex and checked the time. The heavy traffic had eliminated any possibility of a nap. Seraphina hurried up the stairs. She put a K-Cup in the coffee maker and made quick work of a shower. As Vanessa demanded, she donned a pair of fitted jeans, a sexy baby tee, and her favorite Chuck Taylors. With her "no scrubs" look complete, she grabbed her coffee cup and headed out.

*****

It was a picturesque Saturday in the park. Family and friends were gathered around tables under large elm trees. Barrel cookers billowed white clouds filled with the sweet, smoky aroma of barbecued meats. Welcoming music and happy voices carried on the breeze.

Seraphina could see Vanessa in the distance. Her brightly colored sundress blazed against her umber skin, accenting her long slender frame and perfectly quaffed crown of sister locks. Auntie Mary sat next to her in a wide-brimmed sun hat with matching linen slacks and blouse. Seraphina knew immediately she was underdressed. She also knew Vanessa would have something to say about it.

"Seraphina, over here." Mary waved and smiled.

Mary did not have the frail, thin frame of an old woman. She was short and a little round with salt and pepper gray hair she kept tightly curled. Her smile lit up the warm brown skin of her moon-shaped face. And her eyes, much like her, were bright and full of life.

"Happy Birthday, Auntie Mary!" Seraphina hugged her neck and took the seat beside her at the table.

"Oh, sugar, it does my heart good to see you. I was worried." Mary squeezed Seraphina's hand. "Let me see your eyes."

Seraphina removed her sunglasses. "I'm okay, Auntie, really. I wouldn't miss celebrating your magnificent life for anything."

"Jeans and a tee, Seraphina?" Vanessa raised an eyebrow.

"It's Saturday. Hey, I didn't wear the scrubs." Seraphina shrugged.

"I guess." Vanessa rolled her eyes. "What are you going to do tomorrow?"

"Figured I stay home, do some gardening," Seraphina answered.

"Gardening?" Vanessa sighed. "You need a man."

"Let me guess. Ladarius Cromwell."

"How'd you know?" Vanessa feigned surprise.

"He tried to talk to me after work today. You think I don't know your handiwork when I see it?"

"One date, Seraphina. He's educated, settled in his career, and sexy. Mostly sexy. Give him a chance," Vanessa pleaded. "He doesn't have to be Mr. Right. He could just be Mr. Right Now."

"What would you know about it, married lady? When's the last time you had a Mr. Right Now? Ladarius does not want to be Mr. Right Now, and you know it. Stop trying to plan my love life!"

"What love life? You are brilliant and beautiful. So why do you insist on being alone?" Vanessa asked, shaking her head. "Marcus is beginning to think you're a lesbian. Not that there's anything wrong with that."

"A lesbian? I have the deepest love and affection for Marcus, but he's an idiot. How are you two even married? Auntie, tell her to leave me alone, please."

"Leave the girl be, Vanessa Edwina." Mary swatted Vanessa's leg playfully.

"Auntie, if we wait on Seraphina to get it together, she'll be a forty-year-old virgin cat lady"—Vanessa pulled a patch of grass and waved it around—"but with plants instead of cats!"

"First, plants make great company," Seraphina shot back. "Second, how do you know I don't already have a man? A tall man with broad shoulders, dark hair, and ice-blue eyes."

"If that's your type, why didn't you just say so. I'll get on it." Vanessa laughed.

"You two quit." Mary silenced them both. "Vanessa, go figure out what is taking them so long with the meat."

"Yes, ma'am," Vanessa replied and left for the grills.

Mary stood and offered Seraphina her hand. "Walk with me."

"Are you sure, Auntie? Your hip?" Seraphina asked.

"That tea you made me is working wonders. We won't go far, just around the pond. There are benches there if I get tired. Come now."

As a quiet sanctuary in the middle of bustling downtown Frederick, surrounded by moss-strewn maples and open green spaces, the pond was a great place to enjoy a peaceful conversation.

"I remember when these trees were small, braving the winter cold and the summer heat. Many didn't think they would make it. Now look at them." Mary sighed. "One hundred years is a long time."

"To have lived a hundred years. The things you've seen, Auntie."

"Yes. But that's not why I brought you out here. You know Vanessa means well."

"I know she does, but I am content."

"No, you're not. Seraphina, not every man is like your father."

"Mamie Etienne said all women have wisdom, a strength in our souls that men are drawn to. It is what binds them to us. For some women, that wisdom, that strength, draws men in, but it doesn't bind them." Seraphina looked out at the ducks in the pond before continuing.

"Fortunate women leave those men behind and find others. But the unfortunate ones, Les Malchanceux, are bound to these men forever and live a life of loneliness and longing. I am an unfortunate. All the women in my family are."

"She told you this?" Mary asked.

"Yes, but she didn't have to. My great-grandfather, Jules, was the love of Etienne's life. He left for Vietnam and never came back. She was eighteen and pregnant with my grandmother, Eulalie. She loved him until the day she died. His name was the last word she spoke. Do you remember the old gray-haired white gentleman at Eulalie's funeral?"

"Yes, I do," Mary replied. "He wept quietly in the back. You could feel his grief. He kissed you on the forehead as he left. He never said a word."

"That was my grandfather, André Phillipe Dumas. He was the love of Eulalie's life. But society and the law said colored folk and white folk don't mix. So my mother was kept a secret their whole lives."

"Seraphina, baby, that is their misfortune, not yours. It doesn't mean you will end up that way."

"Oh, really? My father, where is he?" Seraphina shook, tears falling. "My mother, Noémie was dying, dying, and the coward left. Said he couldn't bear to watch her suffer. And I could? My mother loved him to the end, you know. She didn't speak one word against him, not one. Mamie Etienne said he brought sickness to her soul, and it killed her."

"And you believe that, baby? Grief is a powerful thing, sugar. People say all kinds of things when they're hurting."

"So are loneliness and longing. He didn't even come to Eulalie's funeral. It has been a year since she died. He knows I'm alone. He knew she was all I had left in the world, and even that wasn't enough to bring him back," Seraphina sobbed.

Mary held Seraphina's face in her small, deceptively strong hands. Seraphina couldn't help but wonder how many faces those hands had held over one hundred years.

"It's all right, child. Eulalie didn't leave you alone. She left you where you are supposed to be…with us. We are your family now. And somewhere out there is a man strong enough to stick to you. Maybe not Ladarius, but someone. He will find you. You are not an unfortunate or whatever ridiculousness you said. Now, you dry those tears. It's my party, and only I get to cry if I want to." Mary's eyes, weathered by the sun, sparkled with a mischief that belied her years. "I've been dying to say that all day."

Seraphina laughed and sniffled, wiping away her tears. "I'm sorry, Auntie. I've ruined your day."

"I'm one hundred years old. I think I can spare a day. Now come on, I know you haven't eaten, and I need me one of those ginger ales. Mercy, the devil would run from this heat."

Mary and Seraphina locked arms and slowly made their way back to the main picnic grounds. Long talks with Mary usually made Seraphina feel better, but not today. She knew something Mary didn't. She was an unfortunate. Her love, the love of her life… She was already bound to him.

*****

Sunday, April 10th

The sound of lawn mowers and leaf blowers roused Seraphina from sleep.

"Seriously, on a Sunday?" she groaned.

She burrowed under the covers and buried her head in her pillow in a futile attempt to hang on to the last vestiges of sleep. Giving up, she reached for her journal.

Sunday, April 10th

He visited my dreams… We were ravenous—forbidden pleasure and pain on a sea of silk. His touch consumes me like a Phoenix, and I smolder under his artic blue gaze. We watched the stars dim their light in deference to the sun. Her majesty on the horizon. He dressed quickly and quietly, donning his tunic, sandals, belt, and sword. His sword, always his sword.

He swore if we were discovered, he'd take me with him. It never ends that way. A priestess of Rome, the punishment… beheading for him, stoning for me. Our love, like our death, is sweet. It is the longing that is bitter. Longing for a touch that is only a dream.

Seraphina rolled out of bed in her boy shorts and cami and wrapped herself in a shawl. The early April mornings had been cool of late. She stepped out onto her balcony. Overlooking a meandering creek, the small space was an urban oasis where plants hung from baskets, climbed trellised walls, and grew lush in ceramic pots. The wings of the hummingbirds and bees that frequented the flowers and feeders made a calming white noise in the tepid morning air.

She clipped mullein flowers from a planter to use in a tea for Mrs. Charleston, a friend of Auntie Mary's who was in hospice in their assisted living community. Her lung cancer was making breathing increasingly difficult. Good for the lungs, Seraphina thought as she added mullein to the rue and valerian tea she made for pain relief and sleep.

Inside, Seraphina hung the flowers to dry from the ceiling hooks and took down others she'd set out earlier in the week. She removed a box of matches from a kitchen drawer and walked into the living room to stand in front of a small altar on a floating shelf. She lit a memory candle for Etienne, Eulalie, and her mother, Noémie. "*Vous me manques,*" she said quietly, blowing out the match. She did miss them. She missed them terribly.

Back in the kitchen, Seraphina pulled an oak chest from under the cabinet. It was stained black with etchings of flowers. She opened it, exposing the purple velvet-lined interior, and withdrew stone and granite pestles and mortars. Some were very old; her mother had passed them down to her. Seraphina closed her eyes and breathed deeply as she held the oldest of them.

"*Grind it very fine, to a powder, so it will dissolve easily.*" Noémie held her hand. "*Like that, yes. Just like that, ma petit.*"

Seraphina set the mortar and pestle on the counter and removed an antique ledger journal from the box. The ledger contained all the wisdom her mothers had given her. There was no organization to the pages, just handwritten notes and instructions.

As a child, the kitchen was Seraphina's favorite place in the house. She remembered dancing barefoot on the creaky wooden floors in rainbow-soaked sunlight refracted through the mason jars in the afternoon sun. She need only close her eyes to see the ancient copper cauldrons and kettles set to boil on the cast-iron wood stove and fill her senses with the scent of flowers from the garden outside. It was hard renovating the house after Eulalie's death and putting it on the market as a vacation rental. She consoled herself with the fact that the kitchen would never be the same without her mothers, and it was time to move on.

The phone rang. It was Vanessa. She knew it without even looking at the number. Seraphina answered. "It's Sunday. Whatever it is, the answer is no."

"But I need your help," Vanessa replied plaintively. "I have the first museum tours scheduled for tomorrow, a group of school-aged children and some donors. I need a docent who knows their shit. Auntie Mary will be there too. She's speaking."

"No. Vanessa, this is the first few days I've had off in months."

"I know, and I am sorry. But I'm desperate. Please. It will just be for the afternoon."

Seraphina dropped the phone from her ear, considering Vanessa's request. The last thing she wanted to do was play host to a bunch of kids, their parents, and what were sure to be some obnoxious money bags. But no matter how badly she wanted to hibernate and commune with her wisdom, they were sisters, and Vanessa needed her. The Brown-Oakes family and The Weld House had a long, rich history. It meant everything to Vanessa. The Weld House was Vanessa's life's work.

"Okay. Tomorrow afternoon. And you owe me."

"I know. Thank you, sis. I'll text you the details."

"The things I do for you. I know I am going to regret this."

"I bet you'll have a great time. Maybe you'll even meet Mr. Right. I've got some wealthy donors coming." Vanessa laughed.

"Good-bye, Vanessa." Seraphina hung up. She rolled her shoulders to relieve the tension and flipped through the ledger. "Lavender oil? I love lavender. Maybe a little jasmine?"

CHAPTER TWO

The Weld House Museum – Frederick, Maryland
Monday, April 11th

The Weld House Museum was nestled on a rise just north of Frederick, on the Monocacy River. Once a plantation home, it sat perched above rolling greens that in times past grew fields of tobacco and cotton as far as the eye could see.

Two years of meticulous curating and fundraising restored the two-story mansion to its 1860s grandeur. An impressive, pillared porch welcomed visitors into a stately foyer with a grand staircase reminiscent of *Gone with the Wind*. Richly detailed plasterwork, stained glass, and high ceilings gave the home a cathedral-like feel.

As a multi-use space, The Weld House Museum was unique. Exhibits from the home's storied past filled the parlors, libraries, and salons. A dining room turned amphitheater was open for events, and a smaller dining room and refurbished kitchen allowed for catered gatherings.

"Vanessa, these clothes are ridiculous! You didn't say anything about historical cosplay when you asked me to do this." Seraphina tugged at her petticoats.

"I didn't?" Vanessa laughed, tightening the strings of Seraphina's corset. "Everything in a museum needs to be historically accurate, including the people. The Weld House Museum is the gold standard. I've made sure of it. Be happy I am not making you wear the crinoline."

Vanessa had made sure of it. Accurate to the smallest detail, everything was original to the house. To say the museum was the gold standard was an understatement. Vanessa had even managed to get the house on the National Register of Historic Places.

"Seraphina, be still. Stop fidgeting!" Vanessa fussed, helping Seraphina with her dress. "I hope you won't be this much trouble when the designer comes to take the measurements for your gala dress. I can't wait to see what he designs for you."

"Ne me le rappelez pas. Je suis tellement fatiguée. Je veux rentrer à la maison. C'est ridicule!"

"I love it when you complain in French. You look amazing!"

Seraphina spun around and inspected herself in the dressing room mirrors. She had to admit the dress fit her well. The corset gave her breasts a better lift than her T-shirt push-up bra. She liked the tiny yellow flowers on the field of gray pinstripes.

"Yeah, I clean up good by 19th-century standards." She yawned.

"Let's go!" Vanessa said.

Seraphina followed Vanessa down the staircase into a foyer full of little smiling faces. She stood to Vanessa's right as she oriented the group.

"Good morning, everyone." Vanessa smiled. "I'm so glad you could join us today at The Weld House Museum."

"Good morning," the group answered in unison.

The third graders were arranged in groups of four, according to color-coded name tags that assigned them to parent helpers.

"My name is Dr. Vanessa Blackwell, the museum curator. This is my good friend, Miss Seraphina Laurent. We will be your docents this afternoon."

"Hello, all." Seraphina forced a smile.

"Can anyone tell me what a docent is?" Vanessa asked.

Excitedly, the children raised their hands. Vanessa picked a girl in front.

"It's a tour guide."

"Great answer, Tasha. A docent is another way of saying tour guide. Now, what is a curator? Anyone else?" Vanessa scanned the group.

Several children put up their hands. A little boy in the back frantically waved his back and forth. Vanessa pointed to him.

"A curator is the person who takes care of the museum and all the stuff in it."

"Right again. Good job, Miles. Miss Laurent and I are going to teach you about The Weld House and its important role in the history of African Americans here in Maryland. If you have questions as we go along, raise your hand. Shall we begin?"

Vanessa ushered the group into a parlor just off the main foyer. Seraphina fell in behind the stragglers.

"Boys and girls, can any of you tell me why The Weld House is so important? What makes The Weld House special?"

A sea of hands shot up. Vanessa selected the child who raised her hand first. "Okay, Mya, tell us why The Weld House is so important."

"It was the first hospital to treat Black people and to let Black nurses and doctors work there."

"Yes, that is exactly right, Mya. Someone did their homework." Vanessa winked at the girl and continued. "During the Civil War, this house was used as a battlefield hospital. After the war in 1868, Colonel Aaron Matthew Weld, a surgeon, established The Weld Clinic in this house. The room you're standing in was a hospital ward, as were the dining room and several upstairs rooms.

"In 1889, the clinic would move from this house to the city of Baltimore and become Weld Memorial Hospital, where many of you and your parents were born. If you look to the left, you will see a portrait of Colonel Weld taken in 1881. Now, if you all will follow me to the Civil War exhibit."

Seraphina hung back and studied the black-and-white portrait. There was a sadness in the colonel's eyes. She could feel it, and it unnerved her but drawn in, she could not look away. The air around her cooled. She hugged herself and shifted from one foot to the other and back again to avoid surrendering to the sudden overwhelming need to close her eyes. The tours had just started. She couldn't leave.

"Miss Laurent, will you join us?" Vanessa gave Seraphina a quizzical look.

Shaken from her growing stupor, Seraphina replied. "Yes. Certainly."

"When the museum fully opens to the public, this exhibit and others will be thoroughly interactive, with Bluetooth headsets and touchscreens. Until then, we have the next best thing: Miss Laurent. She is a walking Civil War medicine encyclopedia. We are fortunate to have her with us today. She is going to walk you through this exhibit while I check on our special guest. Take it away, Miss Laurent."

"Thank you, Dr. Blackwell. Well, first things first. Can anyone tell me what medicine means?" Seraphina searched the group for a child that had not answered a question.

"D'Andre, what does medicine mean?"

"It is what you take when you are sick," he replied.

"That is true, but it is also what we call the practice of medicine, the things we do to make people feel better. Just like you might practice a musical instrument or a sport to play it, doctors and nurses do the same with medicine, to help people. This room is filled with items that doctors used during the Civil War to do just that. Anyone want to take a guess at what's in this case to my right?"

A parent raised his hand, smiling at her. "Surgical tools."

"Yes, Mr. Palmer, surgical tools. Surgeons during the Civil War used them to perform different types of surgeries. They removed bullets and injured limbs that were too badly hurt to fix. The most interesting thing you will notice is that many of the tools haven't changed much since then. Next to each one, you will see its modern-day equivalent. This next question is an easy one. Just shout out the answer. Why do we wash our hands?"

"To clean the germs off," several children blurted out.

"Correct. But in the 1860s, doctors didn't know about germs and the need to wash their hands. As a result, a lot of soldiers died from infections. They did not have antibiotics and other medicines like we do today."

"Miss Laurent,"—a boy pointed to another display case— "what is that?"

"What Louis is pointing to is a medical bag. It is made of leather and very deep. These were especially important. Today, when you're sick, you come to hospitals and clinics like Weld Memorial to see a doctor. But a long time ago, doctors went to people's homes, and they went right onto the battlefield during the war. They used these bags to carry their medical supplies."

Vanessa returned. "Thank you, Miss Laurent. I am going to pause us there. Our special guest is here. If everyone would follow me into the amphitheater and take a seat, we can meet her. Parents, there are chairs in the back for you."

The children and parents followed Vanessa's directions and took their seats quickly and quietly.

"Now, before I introduce our guest, I believe your teacher has given each of you an index card to write a question on. You should take them out now. I will call on everyone, so there is no need to raise your hand. Is everybody ready?"

"Yes," the children replied as one.

"We pride ourselves on living history here at The Weld House. There is no better way to bring history to life than to learn it from the people who lived it. Here to speak with us today is my great-aunt, Mrs. Mary Oakes-Timmons. Let's all give her a warm welcome."

The room clapped vigorously for a moment and then settled down. Aided by her cane, Mary slowly took her seat on the raised platform. In her seafoam green hat, matching Sunday-best suit, and pearls, she looked every bit the matriarch she was.

"Good morning, children." Mary smiled, a youthful excitement in her eyes. "Y'all are so precious. Mrs. Blackwell here says y'all have some questions for me. Who's first?"

Vanessa picked a child at random. "Malachi, why don't you ask the first question?

"Were you born at the hospital? How old are you?"

"Well, that's two questions." Mary chuckled. "I was born in this house, right upstairs. Now, ladies don't usually go on about their age, but y'all are so cute I'll make an exception. I am one hundred years old."

The children gasped in amazement.

"I know. That's how I feel about it too." Mary laughed. The children giggled with her.

Vanessa selected another student. "Paulina, you have the next question."

Paulina read her card slowly, afraid to mess up the question. "Mrs. Oakes-Timmons, can you tell us about your family?"

"My family. Well, now let's see. My grandmother and great-grandmother worked as nurses here in The Weld House. My great-grandmother, Daisy, established the Negro Nursing Corp. My great grandfather, Daisy's husband, Eli Oakes Sr., was the first Black doctor ever to work at The Weld House."

A boy named Leo, excited to ask his question, forgot Vanessa's instructions and raised his hand. She called on him.

"Next question to Leo."

"Since you're a hundred years old, did you know Colonel Weld?"

"Good question. Vanessa, you've got some smart cookies here," Mary beamed. "Sadly, no. He died before I was born. My great-grandparents, Noble and Mary Oakes, worked for the Weld Family. My great-grandfather, Eli Sr., grew up in their house in Philadelphia. They told lots of stories about him."

The children continued asking questions for a while. Seraphina could tell they were enjoying listening to Mary's stories. Before long, the Q&A was over, and Vanessa continued the tour. Seraphina stayed behind to help Mary down from the amphitheater's platform.

"Auntie Mary, you're a natural speaker. You should do an audiobook memoir."

"No, no. Don't go putting that off on me. Children are easy to talk to. It's grown folks that's hard. I see Vanessa got you in here. Made you wear that dress, did she?"

"Yes, ma'am. You know Vanessa is bossy and doesn't take no for an answer. Speaking of dress, you're looking fierce in that suit and hat. And where did you get those pearls?"

"The pearls were a gift to my great-grandmama Mary from Lady Katherine Weld before she died. I wore them on my wedding day. They passed to me when my mother died."

"And you wear them? Auntie, do you know how much those are worth?"

"I do. Jewelry is meant to be worn. A lady should always have a string of pearls. You go help Vanessa. I'll be fine. Your Uncle Filmore will be by to collect me shortly. We're going to dinner."

"Dinner?" Seraphina eyed the clock on the wall. "Auntie, it's three o'clock in the afternoon."

"Your uncle and I are old, sugar. Old folks eat early."

"I wish I could go with you, but we have another tour after this." Seraphina rolled her eyes. "You know Vanessa, always doing the most."

"Get some rest, baby. I can see the tired on you. Give me kisses. I will see you later."

Seraphina hugged Mary tight, kissing her on both cheeks. "I will, Auntie. I promise."

*****

"Seraphina, I know you've been here all afternoon, and I promised it would just be the afternoon, but—"

"No, Vanessa. No. I am tired. I cannot—"

"But I need a favor. It just came up. A courier is coming with a package that can't be left outside. I wouldn't ask, but Marcus is out of town on business, and I can't make it to the daycare to pick up Jayla by five and wait for the courier."

"Seriously, Vanessa? You drag me here in this get-up and make me deal with kids on my day off, and now this?"

"Will you wait for the package and lock up? The courier should be here within the hour. The alarm is on delay, and the door will lock behind you when you leave. Please? You can just leave it in my office."

"You are so lucky I am off the next three days. Go. I'll wait. We'll talk about your work-life balance issues later. Marcus's too."

"Thank you. Thank you. Thank you." Vanessa kissed Seraphina on the cheek and grabbed her things. "I won't bother you for the rest of the time you're off. I swear it."

Seraphina sat on a bench inside the door and watched Vanessa drive away. She vowed to hold Vanessa to her promise and not answer a single call or text she sent for the rest of her staycation.

The courier arrived as scheduled with a long rectangular box. It was damp and smashed on one side. Seraphina noted the box's condition on the bill of lading and signed for it. She went upstairs to Vanessa's office, set the box on the desk, and inspected it more closely. Then, curious and wanting to check for any internal damage, she opened it. There was a note.

Vanessa,

Here it is! The original. I trust you'll care for it. Looking forward to seeing you at the gala in October.

Cassandra Weld-Canterbury

Seraphina set the note down and finished unpacking the box. A Union blue double-breasted uniform coat, replete with brass buttons, epaulets, gold-embroidered cuffs, and a colonel's silver eagle bars, stared back at her. Seraphina smiled to herself. A man in uniform, no matter the century, always looked good.

Images of a legionnaire flooded her mind. He strode in the temple, the polished iron of his segmented armor and helmet gleaming. With his chest broad and shoulders square, he knelt before the altar, asters and roses in hand. The muscles of his bronzed legs and arms flexed their deep definition. He left the flowers on the altar and turned to face her. Removing his helmet, he revealed his sculptured face. He set his cerulean gaze upon her, hard and longing. The flowers weren't for the goddess; they were hers. She was his goddess, and he, her god. If only Vanessa knew that she had a man once, and he was glorious.

But he was her secret. Hers and Mamie Etienne's. Holding her after a particularly bad dream, Etienne had whispered, *"You've been here before, ma petite les malchanceux. Your wisdom is strong and why you see him."*

Seraphina checked the priceless coat for damage. It had been wrapped in plastic and butcher paper and did not appear to be wet. She rewrapped the coat and returned it to the box. She sent a text to Vanessa.

Package arrived. Contents in good condition. Going dark. Talk to you in a few days. Love you.

On her way out of the museum, Seraphina stopped in front of the colonel's portrait. Stronger now, the melancholy and longing in his eyes touched her deeply within. The air around her chilled, colder than before. A question settled on her, and without a thought, she answered.

"Yes."

Virginia, Peninsular Campaign
April 1862 – August 1862

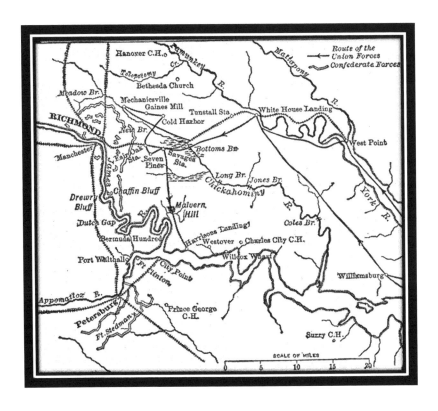

CHAPTER THREE

James River, Virginia
April 1862

The cold and a nocturnal chorus of frogs and crickets stirred Seraphina from sleep.

You left the window open, she thought.

Shivering, Seraphina reached for a blanket. There was nothing. No blanket, no bed, just the smell of damp earth and green grass. She opened her eyes to an unfamiliar darkness and a night sky carpeted with stars.

She didn't move. She'd had dreams that blurred the line between sleep and awake before, but somehow this felt different. She shut her eyes and held them closed for a moment. Then she opened them. The moon and the stars remained.

Head throbbing, Seraphina struggled to her feet. A wave of nausea and dizziness forced her to sit back down.

Staring into a vastness, cloaked in shadow, she asked herself, *Where the hell am I?*

Seraphina patted her skirts, surprised to still be wearing them. No keys. No cell phone. She searched the area around her feet and found nothing.

Okay, don't panic. Assess. How did you get here? Think. What is the last thing you remember? You were in the museum. There was a package. A courier…the courier. Did the door lock?

Thoughts spinning, Seraphina did a cursory check of her body for injuries. *Did he hit me on the head and leave me in this field? Is he coming back?*

Fear gripped her as the cold reality of her situation sunk in. She was outside, in the dark, alone, in the middle of a field with no signs of civilization and no way to call for help. Worse, no one would be looking for her, as she had "gone dark." She could scream into the inky blackness, but who would hear her? Maybe the person or persons who did this would overhear and come back to hurt her? One thing was certain; she wasn't going to stick around to find out.

Seraphina could make out a tree line some distance away. It seemed like as good a place as any to hide until morning, and when the sun came up, she'd be able to find her bearings and go for help.

*****

Sunlight poked through the canopy of trees. After a sleepless night, Seraphina stood and surveyed her surroundings. Without the ambient sounds of civilization to aid her slumber, her mind raced. She'd spent the night vacillating between fear and frustration, anger and aggravation. Now, in the light of day, all was confusion and unease.

"Where did he leave me?"

It was still too quiet, and there were no signs of the museum, its parking lot, or anything familiar. Seraphina called out. "Hello? Is anyone there?"

She waited for a response that did not come and, after a few minutes, walked back to the tree line she'd run to last night. There had to be a way back to some semblance of the world she recognized. She followed the tree line for hours. The sun was at its zenith when she reached a river bank. Gingerly, Seraphina used one foot, then the other to remove her shoes. She gathered her skirts and waded calf-deep into the river. The icy pins and needles were soothing.

"I'm lost." Her voice quivered.

A fear, bordering on panic, began welling up inside, and tears spilled over her lashes and down her face.

"Help! Help! Someone, anyone! Help!"

Greeted by silence, Seraphina returned to the river's edge and her shoes. She sat on a boulder, head in her hands, and sobbed. The sun would set again in a few hours. She was in real trouble.

****

Seraphina drank from the river, washing down the bitter taste of the edible roots and berries she'd found along the riverbank. She'd walked along the river all afternoon, hoping to stumble across a town, a road, a bridge…anything. With the sun now low in the sky, it was likely she'd spend another night in the wilderness. Everything hurt, but she wasn't cold, thanks to Vanessa's historically accurate petticoats.

"Hush now," a male voice whispered. So quietly, Seraphina almost didn't hear it.

"Hush now. You got to be quiet. Seches all in these woods. Why you out here alone? Where your people?" the man asked.

"Who are you?" Seraphina backed away slowly.

"Names Jedidiah Brown. Folks call me Jed. I won't hurt you none. You lost?"

Seraphina observed him. He was an older man with dark brown sun-baked skin, a full salt and pepper beard, and large hands. He didn't smile, but his eyes were kind. His old and more than a little disheveled clothing gave Seraphina the impression that he might be homeless.

"Yes, sir. I am lost. My name is Seraphina. Seraphina Laurent."

"How you git here?"

"I don't know. I woke up in a field last night. I don't know where 'here' is. Can you help me? Do you know where I can find the nearest road, maybe a gas station, someplace with a phone?"

The look of confusion on Jedidiah's face gave Seraphina pause. He didn't seem to understand what she'd said.

She repeated her questions. "A phone? Gas station? Road? Anything? I need to get back to Frederick, Maryland."

"Ain't no roads. A few well-worn trails, but we keepin' off them. I ain't never heard of no phone or a gas station. But I can tell you this ain't Maryland. You in Virginia."

"What?" Seraphina fell to her knees, sick. "Virginia? He left me in Virginia. Oh, God."

Jedidiah rushed to her side. "We cans help you, but you got to be quiet. Ain't been no rebels this way in a while. Figure we close now. Come wit me."

Seraphina offered a silent prayer and followed. She didn't really have a choice. He knew a lot more than she did about where they were and how she might get out of this mess. His ignorance of her questions and constant reference to confederate soldiers led her to believe he was an overly dedicated Civil War reenactor. They were in Virginia, after all, and based on her clothing, it would be easy to assume she was a reenactor too.

The two walked for what felt like an eternity. Seraphina never took her eye off the river. She was already lost, and it was the only landmark she knew. Jedidiah seemed to be following it too. The question of where they were going was on the tip of Seraphina's tongue when she saw them: a family huddled together under a large tree. Seraphina swallowed her question in disbelief.

"Seraphina,"—Jedidiah smiled, taking the older woman's hand—"this my family. My wife Addie, my grandbaby, Daisy, and her baby, Lula."

"My Lord, Jed!" Addie exclaimed.

"I know, Addie," Jed replied. "Had the right mind to leave her. Lookin' like she do. Her marse got a whole army after her."

"Leave me? What master? What is going on here?" Seraphina rubbed her temples. "All I need you to do is point me in the direction of the nearest phone, and I will be out of your hair."

"There she go talkin' that nonsense again." Jedidiah shook his head. "Told her ain't nothin' like no phone here, gas neither. She didn't know she was in Virginia. Her mind ain't right."

"Nonsense? Okay, this is too much. This isn't funny." Seraphina stepped away from them. "Where am I? Who are you?"

"You in Virginia," Addie answered. "We headed east. Union taking in runaways at Fort Monroe."

"Runaway what?" Seraphina asked, unsure she wanted the answer. If these folks were actors, they were good, very good, authentic from the tops of their heads to the soles of their dirty feet. Vanessa would be impressed.

"Slaves, child! Lord, what they done to you?" Addie moved closer, cupping Seraphina's face. "You run away alone?"

"I didn't run away. I was kidnapped. I was closing the museum, and I think the man that brought the package abducted me. I woke up in a field last night."

Terror growing within, Seraphina closed her eyes. "Wake up, Seraphina. Wake up. You're asleep. The man hit you over the head. You're concussed. This isn't real."

"Mama, she don't know if she sleep or woke?" Daisy asked, concerned.

Jed gave Addie a worried look. "She plum touched, Addie. What we gwine do wit her?"

"Keep her. If we don't, they catch her, and she be dead fore long. Come, child." Addie motioned for Seraphina to sit on the ground next to her.

"I am not crazy." Seraphina started to cry. "This isn't real. This isn't real. What year is this?"

"1862," Daisy answered.

"Oh, God!" Seraphina whispered, falling.

*****

Seraphina sat silently under a large tree, eating a stale biscuit and more of the wild berries she'd found. She hadn't uttered a word in two days. Her constant ramblings about museums, cars, phones, and kidnapping only reinforced everyone's belief that she was nuts.

She'd come up with three possible explanations for what was happening to her. One, she was in a coma. Two, she'd had a psychotic break. Or three, she really was in 1862 Virginia. One, two, or three, none of the options were good ones.

"Your mind right now, but your spirit is troubled." Addie sat down next to Seraphina.

She was a short, stocky woman with a round face and bright eyes. High cheekbones, ruddy skin, and the ringlets of salt and pepper hair that slipped from beneath her blue turban hinted at an indigenous story yet to be told. Her calloused hands bore the burn scars of kitchen work and years of hard labor. But one would never know it from her cheerful disposition.

"What happened to you? Where you come from, child?" Addie asked.

Not sure what to say, Seraphina stared off into the distance. The truth, at least the whole truth, wasn't an option. The last thing she wanted to do was provide further evidence of her insanity. She needed to be guarded.

"My name is Seraphina Laurent. I don't know how I got here. I woke up in a field, in the dark. There was a man…but I'm not sure. I lived in Maryland, but my family is from Louisiana."

"I can sees by your hands and clothes, you never done no hard work. You awful pretty. You the master baby? He keep you in the house?"

Seraphina was mortified. Addie was asking her if she was the bastard byproduct of rape and suggesting she was useless. She would have to go with it. Seraphina swallowed hard.

"My master, André Phillipe, was my grandfather. He was a doctor. I worked with him, just like my grandmother did."

"Make sense why you looks and talks like you do. You sleep so fitful. Cry in strange words. I got to rock you like a baby to settle you. You been through something awful."

Seraphina thought about it. Awful was an understatement. If she dared to believe it, she was a runaway slave in 1862 Virginia. She pushed the notion aside and turned her attention to something else Addie had said.

"*Strange words.*"

She cried in strange words. And then it hit her.

French. I cry in French in my sleep. Great! One more thing I'll have to explain.

"French. I speak French, Miss Addie. My grandfather was French. I tend to fall into it whenever I am upset or scared."

"French? Well, now."

"I know I must seem odd to you, Miss Addie," Seraphina offered in response.

"Like a fish walking on dry land." Addie chuckled.

Seraphina smiled. Daisy, who until now had been sitting quietly, nursing Baby Lula, laughed too.

"Miss Addie, where are you from?" Seraphina asked, deliberately changing the subject.

"Virginia, round Richmond. Jed work in town at Marse woodshop. He hear Mr. Lincoln say we be free if we git to the Union side. Marse say it ain't so, but Daisy read it in the papers on Marse desk when she in there with Little Miss. Once we sure, we run off."

"Richmond? How've you made it this far?" Seraphina questioned.

"Been hard. Freedom and the good Lord keeps us moving. Ain't far now."

Seraphina wasn't ignorant of history. The freedom Addie spoke of with such rapture and expectant joy would be little more than indentured servitude. The Union herded runaway slaves into camps not far from the Union lines. Considered contraband of war, the runaways became confiscated property, which did not have to be returned. And for their good fortune, the contraband would be put to work doing the same work for their new masters they did for the old. Seraphina didn't say a word. It wasn't her 21st-century place to steal Addie's 19th-century joy.

"Y'all, we need to git on. Don't look like no moon tonight. We stop again when it git dark," Jedidiah whispered.

Addie started to collect their things, but Seraphina stopped her.

"No, Miss Addie. You walk on. I got this. My back is younger than yours."

"Seraphina, you—"

"Walk on, Miss Addie, please."

Addie handed Seraphina the bags and hurried to catch up to Jedidiah. From the way he kept looking over his shoulder, Seraphina could tell they were talking about her.

"Seraphina." Daisy walked beside her, Lula swaddled to her hip.

"Yes," Seraphina replied.

Daisy hadn't spoken one word to her since they'd first laid eyes on each other. Seraphina figured that made sense. She wouldn't want her baby around a raving lunatic, either. She could only guess that Addie's assertion that Seraphina's "mind was right" made Daisy feel safe enough to engage. Or, she had finally worked up the courage to ask Seraphina the questions that had been burning in her inquisitive eyes for the last three days.

"How do you know what is okay to eat?" Daisy asked timidly.

"My mothers," Seraphina replied, surprised by the question.

"Mothers?" Daisy asked.

"My mother taught me. Her mother taught her. And her mother taught her," Seraphina answered solemnly.

"Can you teach me?" Daisy asked, eyes hopeful. "I can read and write. Little Miss had a teacher. So I would sit outside the door with Lula and Marse Jack and listen."

"Who are Little Miss and Marse Jack?" Seraphina regretted the question the moment it crossed her lips.

"Marse and Misses children. Lula Marse baby, too. I nurse and tend to Marse Jack and Lula. I stay in the house, like you. Mama Addie in the kitchen. Pa Jed be in town, smithing, and woodworking. Marse Jack, he a sweet baby. Little Miss frighten the devil."

Seraphina trembled with rage. Daisy's willowy frame, small breasts, and barely rounded hips meant she couldn't be more than fourteen. It was a miracle she survived the birth or was nourished enough to breastfeed two hungry infants. *The son of a bitch couldn't find any older women to rape?* Seraphina screamed inside. Of course not. Daisy was a pretty girl—a girl with her grandmother's eyes, red-brown skin, and jet black, tightly corn-rowed hair. A girl. Not a woman.

Seraphina summoned all her strength to bury her fury and force a smile on her face.

"I would be happy to teach you what I know, Daisy. It would be my privilege."

"Thank you kindly," Daisy replied warmly, bouncing a fussy Lula. "Hush now," she whispered.

"She is a beautiful baby." Seraphina gently brushed Lula's cheek. "To think you walked all this way with her. What is she? About a year old?"

"Yes, one year." Daisy beamed at the tawny, fair-haired little bundle with the trademark Brown family bright eyes. "Lula too beautiful. I don't want her to be like me, working in Marse house, birthing Marse children, and nursing Misses babies. I walk her to the end if I got to. She gwine be free."

Tears of conviction welled in Seraphina's eyes. "She will be, Daisy. She will be. I swear it. If I have to walk her there myself."

"I'm glad we found you, Seraphina."

"Me too, Daisy."

Seraphina was glad. She'd probably be dead by now if it weren't for the Browns. They were kind, caring people who'd taken her in when she needed it most.

Seraphina thought about Auntie Mary and Vanessa. They had to be worried sick. Knowing Vanessa, she'd do everything she could to find her. By now, she'd probably mobilized the National Guard. It didn't matter. No one had the power to bend time, or at least she'd thought so, until four days ago. And even if they did, how would they know to look in 1862? She was going to have to find her own way home.

*****

It was just before sundown when they stopped to rest. Addie handed out stale biscuits and jerky. Seraphina added the wild roots and tubers she and Daisy had found along the way. Other than the occasional fish, what little food they had was nutrient deficient and running low. Sleeping outside in late April with nothing but their clothing, woolen blankets, and a small fire was not suitable for any of them, especially Baby Lula. Everyone was tired, sore, blistered, and hungry. They made less and less progress each day. Getting to the Union lines meant more than freedom; it meant survival.

Jedidiah grabbed two biscuits. "No fire tonight. We too close."

"How much further, Jed?" Seraphina asked.

"Day, maybe two. I'm a go look out ahead fore it git dark."

Seraphina was glad they were nearing the end of their journey. For three days and two nights, they'd followed the river east, toward the Union lines around Richmond, keeping to the woods and brush and avoiding open roads. Most of Virginia was still in rebel hands; they had to be careful.

"Seraphina! Addie! Come look," Jedidiah called out to them.

Seraphina ran to Jedidiah's side, Addie on her heels. Both women stopped, mouths agape.

What fresh hell is this? Seraphina thought to herself, horrified.

It was an encampment, a bog, set between a river and a creek; the stench was unbearable. People were sick. From the coughing sounds, Seraphina was sure there were at least a few cases of tuberculosis and twice as many of pneumonia. Everything and everyone was covered in dirt or mud. Many had little to no clothing to speak of, and the available shelter was no shelter at all.

Seraphina had read about the camps in her study of Civil War history, but the reality was far, far worse. The UN refugee camps in Chad and the Sudan she'd worked in during her graduate program weren't this bad.

"Is this Fort Monroe?" Addie asked, eyes wide with disbelief.

"No, Miss Addie. It is not." Seraphina grit her teeth.

"Seraphina?" Jedidiah gave her a lost look.

"Who is in charge here?" Seraphina called out.

An old man with a graying grizzled beard and tired eyes that mirrored his gait stepped forward. "Nobody since the soldiers left."

"Left?" Seraphina cried, her tone oozing incredulity. "How long ago was that?"

"Some seven days ago now," he replied

"Why are you all still here? Why aren't you at Fort Monroe?" Seraphina asked.

"They come and say they movin' everyone to the camp down river at Fort Monroe. But they only take them that could work. Leave some food and blankets with the rest of us and say they be back."

Seraphina stood very still. She opened and closed her eyes, a part of her still clinging to the fantasy that this was all a dream. It wasn't.

She surveyed the area and counted roughly forty men, women, and children. They needed food, adequate shelter, heat, and medicine, none of which they would find in this cesspool masquerading as an encampment. The decision was an easy one. They needed to leave. All of them.

"Everyone listen, I know what they told us, but the rebels will be the least of our worries here. We'll die from disease, starvation, and exposure before they ever get to us. We passed an abandoned farm a couple of miles back. We'll go there. Gather everyone and any supplies that are left. We should get moving. It'll be dark soon."

"Seraphina?" Addie held her hand. "We are supposed to stay here. If we don't stay—"

"It will be okay, Miss Addie," Seraphina tried to reassure her.

"We can't leave." The man shook his head. "We got to wait. The soldiers said—"

"The soldiers said they'd be back, and it has been a week. A week." Seraphina raised her arms despairingly. "Where are they?"

"I don't know. Maybe we should move on to Fort Monroe?" Jed replied. "Maybe they send help?"

"Jed, there is no one here but me and maybe you who could make that trek right now, and I am not leaving anyone here, and you can't go alone. Listen, we can wait for the soldiers to return. We just can't wait here. We will die here."

"What we gwine do there?" A woman asked, bouncing a baby on her hip.

"It is a farm. We can shelter in the house and barn. It is still early. If we're fortunate, we may find some food and other things the army hasn't taken. I can gather herbs to treat your little one's cough. We'll make do."

"You can do that?" the woman asked, a hopeful tone in her voice.

"Yes. Yes, I can," Seraphina answered.

"You ain't no slave," the man's words a statement of fact, not a question.

"No. I am not. My name is Seraphina. And I am here to help. Please. We really need to leave. We won't be too far away for the army to find us when they return."

Folks gathered around, confused and unsure, waiting for direction. Seraphina waited a moment for any further objections and then gave the order. "We are leaving."

*****

Seraphina drifted in the dulcet place between sleep and awake. She could feel the creaky wooden floors of her grandmother's kitchen beneath her feet. Images of a Creole queen with tawny olive skin, brilliant green eyes, and long pewter hair carried on the scent of herbs and flowers. The sound of French lullabies sung softly in time with the rocking of a porch swing drew Seraphina further into the dream.

"Seraphina, va chercher la menthe, le brandy et le rhum pour Mamie."

"Qui, Mamie."

Careful not to disturb the drying herbs hanging from the ceiling, Seraphina retrieved the bottles of rum and brandy from the pantry. She set them on the butcher block table next to her grandmother and collected fresh mint from the windowsill planter.

"Why mint?" Seraphina observed closely.

"En français, Seraphina." Eulalie smiled at her.

Seraphina sighed. "Must everything be in French? No one speaks French anymore, Mamie."

"We are Creole. Notre langue c'est le français. Tu comprends?"

"Qui, Je comprendre. Pourquoi on utilise la menthe?"

Eulalie pointed to a stone pestle and mortar. Seraphina bruised and ground the leaves into an aromatic paste.

"Tu vois?" Eulalie lifted the mortar to Seraphina's nose. "C'est parfum apaisant."

Seraphina breathed in the soothing scent. She watched as Eulalie mixed calendula oil, cattail powder, and the mint paste into hot beeswax and poured the wound-healing mixture into small aluminum tins.

Eulalie set them aside and dusted the dried beeswax from her hands. "Come, little one, we have much to do. Qu'est-ce que c'est?" She placed a handful of berries in Seraphina's hand.

"Mayhaw," Seraphina replied.

"Comment le prepares-tu?"

Seraphina recited what she'd been taught, "It is for ailments of the heart. You soak them in vodka or brandy for four weeks…turn the bottle daily. Strain the tincture when finished."

"Bon. Comment le prepares-tu?"

Seraphina examined the furry leaf in Eulalie's hand. "Slippery elm."

"Bon. Comment le prepares-tu?"

"Dry the bark and grind it to a fine powder for a tea. It is good for stomach problems. Make it coarser for a poultice to use on the skin for wounds and rashes. Why do I have to learn this, Mamie? There are doctors with real medicine."

"Seraphina, ma chérie you sound like your mamie did at your age. Doctors are good for what doctors do. They're fixers, not healers. Knowledge is the beginning of wisdom, not the end of it. Medicine has forgotten this. Healing comes from wisdom. Nature is wisdom. A wise woman is a powerful woman. Tu comprends?"

"Oui, je comprends. I miss her, but it is hard to remember her."

Eulalie kissed Seraphina on the forehead. "Ma chérie Seraphina, your wisdom and your spirit are strong like your mamie. Stronger. Now, I want you to repeat everything…en français."

"Seraphina, we low on bandages," Addie said, a half-empty wicker basket on her hip. "What you want to do?"

Yawning, Seraphina sat up. Dreams of her grandmother were always an eclectic mix of the senses.

"I'm sorry, baby. I didn't mean to wake you." Addie brushed Seraphina's cheek.

"It's okay. I need to get up. Wash the bandages and dry them in the sun. Do it twice. Then we can use them again. Have Daisy bring some warm alfalfa broth for Cherub and have Lizzie add more hot water to his basin. He needs more steam to help him breathe."

Addie turned to leave. Seraphina stopped her. "Thank you, Miss Addie. I appreciate you. I couldn't do this without you."

"Look at all you do," Addie beamed. "I send Daisy and Lizzie."

The move to the farm was a good decision, but not without its challenges. A carpenter, Jedidiah managed to make the house and barn livable. Addie made what food they had stretch daily. As the house cook, she was accustomed to making the little the slaves were given go a long way. Everyone worked hard, adults and children alike. For a modest farm with a two-room house and a barn about the size of a one-car garage, it took a lot of hands to keep it running.

Death had culled their numbers by more than half. Seraphina treated the sick and injured as best she could, but it was difficult without medicine and sterile equipment. Thankfully, missionaries from the US Sanitary Commission arrived a few days after they moved to the farm with desperately needed rations and supplies. Due to an outbreak of smallpox and typhoid at Fort Monroe, the Union representative with the commission ordered them to remain on the farm until further notice. That was two months ago.

Seraphina stretched out on her pallet, breathed deeply, and got to her feet. She was tired but keeping busy was the only way to distract herself from the despair that threatened to consume her. She missed home. Over the last few weeks, she'd managed to piece together a few memories from the afternoon in the museum. She remembered the portrait, its longing, and a question to which the only answer was yes.

But unlike the movies, there were no magic books, enchanted runes, or tablets etched with sacred incantations to show her the way home. Alice had no looking glass. Dorothy, no ruby slippers. There was just her and everything her mothers taught her.

Seraphina washed her hands in a basin. It was time to check in on her favorite patient, a year-old little boy named Robert, whom she fondly referred to as Cherub.

"How is my little Cherub today?"

"Doing good. He sleeps at night now," his mother replied.

"Good. Keep nursing him. Lizzie will bring more hot water and mint. You keep him breathing in the steam for a little while longer. Swaddle him and keep him close at night. That way, he will stay warm and not breathe in too much smoke from the fire. When you hear his breathing get strange, give him some coffee like I showed you, but not too much."

"Thank you, Miss Seraphina."

"You're welcome, Rhea. And look…Lizzie, you've perfect timing."

Lizzie filled Cherub's basin with hot water from the outdoor kitchen. "Miss Seraphina, you need to rest."

"I know, Lizzie, I will. I promise."

Addie, Jed, Daisy, and Lizzie were always after her to rest. Lizzie was the most persistent. A ten-year-old orphan girl with window-wide brown eyes, rich umber skin, and industrious nature, Lizzie reminded Seraphina of Vanessa more and more every day.

"The sun is going down, Lizzie. Get back to the house. How much lamp oil do we have left?"

"Not much, Miss Seraphina. Mrs. Astor and them missionaries ain't been by," Lizzie replied.

"We'll only use one lamp tonight. Go to bed. I'll follow you in a minute."

CHAPTER FOUR

Williamsburg, Virginia
May 1862

The deafening roar and thunderous rumble of artillery had ceased. Aaron straddled a chair and removed his jacket. For the first time in as many weeks, he could sit in his tent and hear himself think. The Army of the Potomac under General George B. McClellan had laid siege to Yorktown for a solid month with nothing to show for it. And if the report in his hand was to be believed, General Grant had barely escaped disaster in Tennessee some two weeks ago with losses in the thousands.

As Surgeon in Chief, it was his job to ensure the division field hospitals were ready for the battles to come. The problem was, he wasn't sure they were. A lack of skilled and knowledgeable physicians and supply chain problems were sure to plague them the further they marched into Virginia. To combat this, he'd hand-picked three highly skilled medical officers and ordered all supply and ration surpluses to be doubled.

A fresh-faced young lieutenant with blond hair, blue eyes, and a mirthful grin stepped through the tent flap. "Permission to enter, Colonel. Lieutenant Weld reporting."

"Thomas!" Aaron stood and embraced the Lieutenant.

"Brother, it is good to see you." Thomas smiled.

"You too, Little Brother. How's Lucy?" Aaron asked.

"As well as any new bride whose husband has left for war. I could have floated here on a river of her tears." Thomas sighed.

"I am sorry, Brother," Aaron offered sincerely.

"There is nothing to make apologies for. This is war. I am needed. It is my duty, and she understands that."

Aaron opened the tent flaps. "I will have Noble show you to your quarters."

"No need. He's already unpacked me. That man is worth his weight in gold." Thomas chuckled.

"We are fortunate. Noble is more than a valet. He's family."

"I know Mother, Solomon, Mary, and Eli are missing him," Thomas mused.

"Indeed. I am sure Mary and Mother have the boys anxious for Noble's return." Aaron motioned to the small writing table in the corner. "Have a seat, Thomas."

Aaron removed a flask and two glasses from a small chest.

"This is serious if we need Scotch."

Aaron filled their glasses and sat down. "Speak of this to no one."

"My confidence is yours, Brother," Thomas replied.

"The war is not going well. Confidence in General McClellan is wavering."

"I know. Grumblings can be heard as far north as Boston. He'd better prove himself capable soon." Thomas tipped his glass to savor his Scotch. "What is the state of things now?"

"Graver than the grumblings let on, I am sure," Aaron replied. "Yorktown and Williamsburg left us with few casualties, but they were by no means victories. None of the men are confined to bed, and maladies are minor. Boredom, however, is pervasive."

"When do we move again, Brother?"

"A week? Maybe two. Enough time for Major Blacksmith and Second Lieutenant Marks to join us."

"Adam and Lucas? Both commissioned? And Lucas, a second lieutenant no less. You know how to pick the litter, Brother. I should have held out for colonel, but first lieutenant is good too." Thomas laughed.

Aaron sipped his Scotch. "I need capable hands. McClellan is under orders to move on Richmond. I expect the casualties of such a campaign to be high."

"You know who else needs capable hands? Mrs. Meredith Miller. She sends greetings from Philadelphia and asked that I inquire after you." Thomas smiled, handing Aaron a letter from his coat pocket.

"I speak of war, and you speak of women." Aaron set the letter aside.

"For reasons beyond me, Brother, for you, they are one and the same. You're a widower. She is a widow. A young one. It only makes sense. Marry her. She'll warm your bed, give you another son or two." Thomas drained his glass.

"I have a son. You may remember your nephew, Solomon? I have no desire to marry."

"Meredith is quite eager. Tell me, what did you do to inflame her passions so?"

"No good deed goes unpunished. No good deed," Aaron groaned.

"It must have been a very good deed. Not that I'm surprised. Women love your dark, brooding nature." Thomas grinned.

Aaron hardened his jaw. "Benjamin was ill for a long time. As his physician, it was my responsibility to care for him. As our cousin and his friend, it was my duty to see to the welfare of his family. Meredith has mistaken my kindness and concern for something more. As has everyone else."

"Duty and responsibility…fig leaves. Aaron, you forget I am your brother. I know you better than anyone. What are kindness and concern, or dare I say it, compassion, if not something more?"

Aaron stared at Thomas unblinking, barely containing the urge to throttle him as he did when they were children. A wife had the right to her husband's heart, to his love. After Elizabeth's death, he swore he would never love another woman. Not like that. The pain and helplessness of her death had a crushing familiarity. He didn't know how or why, but he'd felt it before. He did not—he would not—feel it again. Kindness, compassion, and concern were all he had to give. All he would ever have to give.

"Let us get back to the matter at hand, Lieutenant Weld," Aaron bit sharply.

"Indeed, Colonel Weld," Thomas mocked laughingly. "But, if we are going to roll around on the ground like children, I need your assurance that I will only get boxed on the ears for bad behavior and not court-martialed for striking a senior officer."

Aaron let an unwilling smile break his lips. "Thomas, you are incorrigible."

Savage's Station, Virginia
June 29th, 1862

It was late afternoon, and the shelling had continued non-stop since midday. The fighting was fierce. Aaron wondered what they would run out of first, munitions or men. From the condition of his field station, he feared it would be the latter.

The walled tent was at capacity, and the injured lay side by side, like sardines in a can. Stewards splinted fractures, packed wounds, and administered narcotics to prepare men for transport to the field hospital.

"Place him here. Remove his coat," Aaron ordered.

The stewards placed the soldier on the makeshift operating table and removed his jacket. He was ashen and non-responsive but alive. Aaron removed the packing and pressure dressing from his shoulder. A geyser of arterial blood broke through the surface of the wound.

"Damn!" Aaron cursed, applying pressure once more.

"Colonel!" Major Blacksmith shouted, to be heard above the artillery.

"Major!" Aaron shouted back.

"We are falling back to the James River. General's orders. We must move these wounded."

"Fuck!" Aaron groaned. "I've got men with open fractures and deep flesh wounds that need surgery. I cannot move them."

"We must, sir," Major Blacksmith insisted. "We are no longer in a safe position."

The major's words proved prophetic as a shell hit its mark. The earth shook violently. Aaron and the major stumbled.

"Colonel! Colonel!" Thomas called from the tent's entrance, the screams of men and whining of horses at his back.

"Lieutenant?" Aaron called back.

Thomas took a moment to catch his breath. "No injuries. Just a horse and cart. We need to move. Now!"

"Lieutenant Weld, muster every able man and set them to quick march south toward the river. Major Blacksmith, call all but two ambulances back from the front lines and evacuate all men unable to walk but whose injuries can wait for treatment at the field hospital. Send a messenger ahead to alert Lieutenant Marks and Major Lynch of the incoming wounded. Go!" Aaron barked.

"Colonel, what will you do?" Thomas asked.

"I will remain here and tend to those who cannot evacuate. I will join the rear guard and enlist their assistance in moving the remaining men. Once I've stabilized those, I can."

"No," Thomas objected. "Colonel, let's move all the men and take our chances. We will lose some, but that cannot be helped."

"Lieutenant, you have your orders." Aaron gave Thomas a hard look.

Thomas turned to Major Blacksmith. "Adam, leave us."

The major did as he asked. When Thomas observed he was a sufficient distance away from them, he shouted, "Aaron! We all retreat, and God willing, we won't lose too many, or I remain with you, and you can bring me up on charges for disobeying a direct order."

One look at his brother's face, and Aaron knew. Thomas wasn't leaving. From childhood, Thomas was stubborn and loyal to a fault. He never left Aaron's side. Orders or no orders, it was foolish to think he would do so now.

"Okay, Thomas. Have Major Blacksmith muster the men. Return here to assist me."

Thomas nodded without a word and left.

*****

James River, Virginia
July 1st, 1862

The battle was close. Seraphina could feel the ground tremble beneath her feet. The smell of gunpowder floated on the wind. Musket volleys masquerading as fireworks could be heard in the distance.

The Union was marching south of Richmond to the James River. Injured men had begun arriving at the farm two days ago, heralds of the danger and darkness to come. From the soldier's stories, they'd been overrun by rebels in the swamp and bid a hasty retreat. In the chaos, some of the injured were separated from the others. A few made their way to the farm purely by chance.

"Private Lawson, I think you're going to be okay. Your breathing is better. I don't see any signs of infection. You should be able to head back in a few days." Seraphina smiled at him.

"Thank you. I promise I will return to settle my debt," he replied.

"Private Lawson, you have no debt here," Seraphina reassured him. "Rest."

A soldier lying a few feet away began to cough. Seraphina made her way over to him.

"Lean forward, Corporal, so I can have a look at your back," Seraphina ordered him.

Addie dropped a basket of clean bandages next to them. "They hateful, awful men. Kill us in our sleep and take all we have, but they too sick to move."

Seraphina touched Addie's arm. "I know having the soldiers here upsets you. That's why they are in the barn and not in the house with all of us."

"Should let 'em die with the rest, Seraphina. They too many of them. Too many."

"They'll be gone soon, Addie. I promise. Go back to the house."

"And leave you here? No. Nothing good is goin' come of this." Addie walked away.

"The old woman is right," the corporal replied.

"About what, Corporal Mills?" Seraphina asked, changing his bandage. "That you're a hateful, awful man? Of course, she is. You should be dead, and both heaven and hell have seen fit to leave you here with me. That says a lot."

The corporal burst into a hearty laugh. "My name is James. Call me James."

"Stop laughing!" Seraphina scolded him. "You'll break your sutures."

"Why you treat me so good? Seeing as I'm white and awful?"

"I'm a nurse. I took an oath to help the sick and the awful, no matter their color."

"Right kind of you." James grabbed Seraphina's hand. "I wouldn't hurt a hair on your pretty head, but the rebels… You need to get on from here. And like the old woman said, let us die."

Seraphina ignored him. "I'll tell you like I told Lawson. Get some rest."

"Miss Seraphina, that's what they call you, right?"

"Yes."

"Miss Seraphina, you get on from here." James gave her a pleading look. "After me and Lawson, don't take in no more strays. Hell take me if you don't listen."

"Thank you, James. I will."

"Get on from here." James's words were a tempest on the fathomless sea of fear and despondency she'd been adrift on since this all began.

Where? Where am I supposed to go? What am I supposed to do? Why am I even here?

Seraphina left the barn.

CHAPTER FIVE

James River, Virginia
July 6th, 1862

Aaron reigned in his horse at the end of the fence line. The farm was as the men described. A modest house and barn, tucked behind a grove of willows, easily missed if one was not looking for it.

At first glance, conditions on the farm appeared good. A young woman with a baby swaddled to her back stood on a makeshift ladder, picking from one of the fruiting trees adjacent to the house. An old man stooped over, pulling weeds from a garden. A girl, with a toddler in tow, was struggling across the yard with what looked like a large pail of water. There were no apparent signs of famine or squalor, and the few people he saw did not appear ill. Satisfied, he urged his mount on and waved for the wagoner and other men following him to do the same.

He had not come to do a health inspection. He'd come looking for a doctor and his wounded men.

Soldiers with treated wounds were wandering into camp at Malvern Hill, days after the fighting at Savage Station. They alleged a Black woman on a farm just off the river was taking in wounded men and that a few of their fellow soldiers were still there. The hospital camp desperately needed medical practitioners, so he decided their claims warranted further investigation.

A large, aged man came from behind the barn, carrying firewood. A girl followed on his heels with all her little arms could bear.

This farm is full of nothing but children and old women and men, Aaron observed.

Upon seeing Aaron, the man set down the wood and approached warily. The child with him did the same, careful to remain behind him.

"Name's Jedidiah Brown," he stated proudly. "Y'all need help?"

"I am Colonel Weld. And yes, Jedidiah, I could use your aid. I was told there is a woman here caring for wounded soldiers. Is that true?"

Aaron noticed that both Jedidiah and the girl lowered their heads, reluctant to answer his question. He dismounted to appear less menacing, hoping to set them at ease.

"I mean her no harm. I would like to speak with her."

"Miss Seraphina in the barn. The hurt men in there too," Jedidiah answered solemnly.

The girl's eyes grew wide. She gripped Jedidiah's hand tightly and buried her head in his side. She was frightened of him, afraid of what he might do, and rightly so. Aaron could only imagine the horrors and atrocities the child had seen white men commit in her short life.

Aaron dropped to one knee. "What is your name?"

"Lizzie," she replied, never lifting her gaze.

"A beautiful name. Lizzie, I want you to take me to the woman helping the soldiers here. I will not hurt her…or you."

Lizzie peered at him from behind damp lashes, and Jedidiah nodded at her. Lizzie nodded in return.

"Good. Jedidiah, would you please help my men water the horses? Lizzie, I will follow you."

Lizzie walked Aaron to the barn, careful to keep her distance from him. She pushed open the side door, and her strength surprised him.

"She there." Lizzie pointed. "In the skirt with the stripes."

Aaron's jaw dropped. The men had spoken the truth; she was a Black woman.

"Thank you, Lizzie. You can go back to your chores now."

Lizzie ran into the arms of an elderly woman sitting in the corner of the barn. The fear in the woman's eyes at the sight of him was palpable, even from a distance. He nodded in her direction and approached the table where the woman in the striped skirt was working.

"Are you Seraphina?" Aaron asked.

"Are you injured, sir?" she answered without looking up from the soldier she was suturing on the table.

Her voice was unlike any woman's he'd ever heard, with an accent he could not place.

"No. I am not," Aaron replied.

"I'm grateful. Would you kindly step back? You are in my light," she asked politely.

He stood aside. "I would speak with you."

"If you could give me a moment. As you can see, this requires my full attention."

To his irritation, she continued to stitch, eyes fixed on her work as if he wasn't there.

"Woman, I would speak with you now," Aaron snapped.

"My name is not 'woman.'" She looked up at him. "It is Seraphina, Seraphina Laurent."

Struck dumb by her auburn eyes, warm brown skin, and mane of sable curls, Aaron could not reply. She was breathtaking. His body shivered with recognition and need. He willed himself to calm and found his tongue.

"I am Colonel Weld."

"Weld?"

"Yes. Colonel Dr. Aaron Weld."

The look of surprise on her face at the mention of his name gave him pause but did not deter his interrogation.

"You've been treating my men? Just you?" he asked.

"Yes, Colonel, I have, and if you let me, I will continue."

Aaron eyed her closely. Her boldness vexed him, but he understood her need for concentration. He decided to let it pass for the moment.

He stood over her shoulder, careful to keep out of her light. A heady bouquet of lavender drifted up from her hair. Aaron breathed deeply, memory and yearning filling him before he stepped back.

You've been too long without a woman, he thought to himself.

Seraphina finished the last of the sutures, coated the wound with a sticky substance she took from a tin on the side table, then covered the lesion with a bandage.

"What is that?" Aaron asked. "Why does he not cry out? Have you given him morphine?"

"Morphine? The Union isn't in the habit of providing that to us. No. Blue lotus flower and willow bark tea. The flower is sedating, and the willow's bark is good for pain. Balsam tree sap has properties that help prevent infection."

"You've studied medicine?"

"I have. My grandfather was a French physician. My grandmother, a healer."

"Laurent? You were not born a slave or of a freeman. Where are you from? How did you get here?"

Seraphina rolled up the sleeves of her flannel shirt and scrubbed her hands in a basin on the table. Aaron could smell the distinct aromas of mint and a strong spirit.

"Lizzie, sweetness, be a good girl and fetch more water. Mix it like I showed you."

"Yes, Miss Seraphina." Lizzie quickly retrieved the basin and left the barn.

"Your daughter?"

"No. Lizzie is an orphan. I have no children."

Seraphina's answer set off an explosion of questions in his head. *She can't be a day over twenty-five, and she has no children? Does she have a husband? If so, where is he? Is he dead? Or, God forbid, sold? Why was she alone?* Before he could question her further, she moved on.

He followed. The curiosity of a physician's scientific mind proved stronger than the annoyance of her impertinence and avoidance of his questions.

Seraphina sat down next to another man and motioned to the older woman, who'd conspicuously kept her distance since he arrived.

"Addie, bring me the candle bush and bandages, please."

Aaron noted that, like Lizzie, the woman did as she was asked without hesitation or question. Clearly, Seraphina was the authority here and ran a tight ship.

"How are you feeling, Paul?" Seraphina asked sweetly.

"Colonel." Paul acknowledged Aaron first. "Good, Miss Seraphina. The bugs tickle a little. That broth tastes awful, but I do feel good after drinking it."

"Broth?" Aaron furrowed his brow.

"Alfalfa broth. It helps the immune—it is good for the blood." Seraphina gestured for him to look around. "You see, the men all have a good color and disposition."

Aaron could see it. The four men, even the one lying asleep on the table, all appeared to be in better health than the men he'd left at camp some two hours ago.

Seraphina unwrapped the bandaged foot. She pulled a pair of tweezers from the pocket instrument case in the haversack on her hip and removed three maggots from the wound on the ball of his foot.

"You put maggots in the wound?" Aaron asked, genuinely curious. He'd seen it done a long time ago but with deleterious results.

"His foot was becoming gangrenous. I cut away what dead flesh I could." Seraphina pointed out the surgical cuts. "I used the maggots to take care of what I couldn't."

"Ah, yes. Maggots eat the dead flesh, but what about infection?" Aaron asked, inspecting the wound.

"You have to wash the maggots. You cannot leave them in place for more than three days or place them directly on the skin. They must be put in a cheesecloth or something like it."

"I see." Aaron nodded. "The cloth is the key. What is candle bush?"

"I am going to pack the wound with linen soaked in a decoction of candle bush leaves to aid healing. You must keep it clean, and the bandage needs to be changed every two to three days. The treatment only works if you catch the gangrene early."

Aaron studied Seraphina's process intently. Her wound care skills were the best he'd seen, and he desperately needed them. Men were dying from infection at an alarming rate, and gangrene-related amputations had risen sharply in the past week.

He'd worked in Europe and North Africa during his studies at Oxford. It was common for women healers to be as skilled as their male counterparts, especially in matters of childbirth. But this was Virginia, and Seraphina was a woman. A Black woman. Tending to lost soldiers that wandered onto her farm was one thing. Working alongside white surgeons with less than half her obvious skill and education was another. Once disbelief wore off, it would be replaced with jealousy and lust. Seraphina was beautiful. No man, black or white, could deny it. Envy and appetite in a man were a lethal combination. By nature, Aaron was a decisive man, but the question of Seraphina weighed on him.

The men need her. She's already in danger. If you found her, the rebels will too. She'll be safer with you in Union hands. But how the fuck all are you going to convince Thomas of this madness? Or the others, for that matter?

"Why are you here, Colonel?" Seraphina asked, interrupting his thoughts.

"I am here to retrieve my men…and you."

"Me?"

"Miss Laurent, you will come with me to the hospital camp. I have need of you there. Instruct your people to send any wounded soldiers who find their way here to Malvern Hill. I will send the stewards from the wagons outside to stretcher and remove these men."

"What!" Seraphina shrieked. "These people have nothing! Nothing! I don't just care for your men. I care for everyone. I cannot go."

Addie hurried to Seraphina's side. "Colonel, suh, Miss Seraphina begs your pardon. She tired is all. She go. I get her things from the house."

THE COLONEL'S CONTRABAND

"You should listen to your elders, Miss Laurent," Aaron said coolly.

"Come, Seraphina," Addie pleaded.

"No. I will not leave here," Seraphina stated flatly. "And as for your men, they need rest, not a wagon ride."

Aaron stood abruptly, bringing Seraphina to her feet with him. He closed the distance between them, forcing her to look up at him.

"You needn't concern yourself with these men," Aaron bit sharply.

"I beg to differ." Seraphina pointed at the soldier on the table. "I just sutured his thigh. He's still sedated."

"Woman, you will know your place and hold your tongue. These men will do as they are ordered and you the same," Aaron shouted.

James struggled to his feet. "Forgive me, sir. Miss Seraphina here been real good to us. She don't mean no harm, just looking after us is all. We boys will return to camp as ordered. Miss Seraphina, don't you worry none."

Aaron glared at Seraphina. Her eyes were a fusion of fear and anger, but she did not back down. Everything about this Seraphina begged to be brought to heel…in his bed. He banished the thought of taming her and focused instead on the anger stoked by her open defiance.

"You will do as you are told. Collect your things. I will be outside. You men, prepare to leave." He released her and stalked out of the barn.

*****

Seraphina stared out of the farmhouse kitchen window. The wagon with James, Lawson, and the other men, rolled away. For a moment, it looked as if the colonel was going to leave with them. To her dismay, he rode back and stood sentry outside the house.

It was him. Colonel Aaron Matthew Weld. The man from the portrait. The man taking her against her will. The man taking her from everything she knew.

Why was he here? Could he be her key to getting home? After all, he was the last thing she saw before this nightmare began. She had so many questions. Nothing made sense.

"I will not leave here, Miss Addie." Seraphina hugged herself tightly.

"I knows they come. Once they see what you can do," Addie cried, folding Seraphina's petticoats into a drawstring linen bag. "The devil is never satisfied."

Seraphina sobbed. "Je ne peux pas y aller! You, Jed, Daisy, Lula, Lizzie… You're all I know, all I have."

"I love you like you was my own." Addie held Seraphina's face. "My gift from the river."

"I won't go! I won't!" Seraphina slid to the floor, head in her hands.

"Mind me." Addie shook her head. "You can and you will, child."

"I'm afraid, Miss Addie. Afraid like I was before you found me."

"Be strong. You a strong girl. If he want you to doctor folks, you doctor folks. And I pray when all this is over, the good Lord bring you back to me."

"Miss Addie." Seraphina grabbed her hand. "I will come back. I swear it."

"Come now. Best not keep the man waiting. You already kicked the hornet's nest."

*****

Everyone gathered outside the house. Seraphina observed the looks on their faces. Some were grim, others resolute, and still others sad and tearful, like Daisy and Lizzie. How many times had they seen loved ones carried off like this? Seraphina knew the answer. Too many.

Daisy, Lula on her hip, ran into Seraphina's arms. Lula, blissfully unaware, smiled and held her arms out for Seraphina. Lizzie wrapped herself around Seraphina's waist, crying softly.

"Daisy, Lizzie, it's going to be okay. I'll be back. You'll see." Seraphina tried to reassure them. "Now, don't forget the things I taught you. When I come back, we'll learn more."

Aaron was seated on his horse. Tall, raven-haired with steel blue eyes, he was younger than his picture. His tight light-blue trousers and open three-button shirt left little to the imagination. Seraphina could see the anger coiled in every sinew of his muscular frame and chiseled jaw. Addie was right; she had kicked the hornet's nest. To avoid his searing blue gaze, Seraphina set her eyes on his horse.

Like his rider, he was tall, lean, and sculpted with a jet-black mane. His coat, also black, shimmered purple in the sunlight.

"His name is Shade," Aaron replied, answering her unasked question. "Can you ride, Miss Laurent?"

Seraphina eyed a smaller chestnut gelding, with a dirty blond mane and white patch around her right eye, tied to the post beside Shade.

"Her name is Cotton Eye. She's a gentle horse. Easy to handle."

"We aren't going with the men?" Seraphina asked, exchanging a question for a question.

"No. They are going to the garrison at Malvern Hill. We are going to the hospital at Harrison's Landing. Can you—"

"Ride? Yes, I can."

"Yes," meaning she tutored Jean Carlo through a brutal semester of anatomy. He had a thing for horses. In exchange, he'd given her a summer's worth of riding lessons on his family ranch.

"Good." Aaron dismounted, lowered, and knitted his hands to assist with her mount.

Seraphina stepped back, just out of his reach. Her mothers were gone. Auntie Mary and Vanessa were gone. And now, he wanted to take her away from the only people she knew in the entire world. She would be alone…again. The ocean of despair, confusion, and fear, she'd held at bay hit like a tsunami. She ran.

"Seraphina! Seraphina! Stop! Please!" Addie cried.

"Woman, you test me!" Aaron bellowed, giving chase.

"I am not going anywhere with you!" Seraphina shouted back, tripping over her skirt. It was hard to run even without a corset and in a singular petticoat.

A crushing weight hit her midsection from behind, and for a moment, she couldn't breathe. Seraphina thought she'd fallen until she saw him.

Aaron seized her waist and carried her back to the horse. There was no saddle, just a quilted blanket where a saddle should have been.

He lifted her onto Cotton Eye and snarled at her, "Do not move. Do not speak. If you try to outrun me on this mare, you will wish you hadn't."

Seraphina adjusted her skirt to sit astride and, as ordered, did not move. She didn't make a sound.

Aaron pointed to the linen drawstring bags in Addie's hands. "Are these her things?"

"Yes, suh," Jedidiah replied. He took the bags from Addie, cinched, and knotted them together like saddlebags, and tossed them over the horse's back. Then, he stepped away, pulling Addie into an embrace.

"Addie, is it?" Aaron asked, nodding in her direction.

"Yes, suh," she sobbed, holding Jedidiah.

"Addie, no harm will come to her. You have my word. I am taking her to the Union hospital downriver at Harrison's Landing."

Aaron spurred Shade into a canter. Cotton Eye followed. Seraphina did not look back.

*****

Aaron seethed. She'd defied him. Admirably, in defense of her people and at great risk to herself, but she'd still defied him. She'd run from him, forcing him to manhandle her, something he'd never done to a woman. Then there were her people; the looks of despair and horror on their faces hollowed him.

They had ridden for the better part of an hour without a word between them. Angrily content with the quiet, Aaron was startled when Seraphina broke the silence.

"Can we stop for a moment?"

"Why?" he demanded.

Seraphina brought Cotton Eye to a halt. "I am thirsty. My back is killing me, and I have needs to tend to…not to put too fine a point on it, Colonel."

Aaron tugged on Shade's reins, bringing him to a stop, and dismounted.

Seraphina extended her hand for assistance in climbing down. Rather than take it, he lifted her off the horse and set her on her feet.

"Stay. Where. I. Can. See. You," he whispered, his words slow and deliberate.

Seraphina tilted her chin and narrowed her eyes. "Êst-ce que vous êtes toujours aussi brutal?"

"You speak French?" Aaron's mouth gaped.

"Oui. Je suis Créole. I said—"

"I know what you said. And I am no brute. I am unaccustomed to having my orders questioned or disobeyed. En anglais ou en français. We are at war. I have the right by law to press any civilian goods, property, or persons into the service of the Union. The Union has need of your services, nothing more."

"Je ne suis pas un soldat."

"No, you are not a soldat. A soldier would know his place."

"My place is an hour's ride in the other direction!" Seraphina lifted her skirt and stepped out of her boots.

"What in the devil are you doing, woman?" Aaron roared, noting her stockingless feet.

"Must you shout? It is miserably hot and humid, and I don't have the luxury of pants and a simple cotton shirt. If the sight of my bare feet bothers you, don't look. I'll be over there."

Seraphina walked off into the watery brush. Far enough away for privacy, but not so far that he could not see her.

Aaron moved closer. He watched as she washed her spiced skin, from leg to knee to foot. Free from a corset, her damp flannel shirt clung obscenely to her breasts. Her bathing ritual gave a tantalizing glimpse of what he imagined from the moment he'd laid eyes on her.

Who was this woman? A French-speaking, educated Creole in Virginia? He had never seen a woman, any woman, behave as she did, look as she did. Such women existed only in men's dreams. His resolve waning, Aaron retreated.

Dreams. The word seeped from his subconscious, carrying memories of a long-forgotten goddess who'd fueled his adolescent desires. *What is wrong with you?*

He'd been away from home for the better part of a year. It'd been at least that long since he'd had a lover. Meredith was too young. Older, married women made better paramours. All they wanted was mutual pleasure and discretion. One or two back home in Philadelphia were quite fond of him, and they were well acquainted. He would call on them. Soon.

Lost in thought, it was a moment before Aaron realized how much time had passed.

"Are you finished, Miss Laurent?" he called to her.

"Yes." Seraphina wrung out her hair and twisted it into a bun. She tied her skirt and petticoat above her ankles, braided her boot laces together, and tossed the boots over her horse's back. "Are you in a hurry?"

"Yes. I had not planned to be away this long."

"Is it far?"

"No, maybe another hour. Down river."

"To the east?" Seraphina pointed.

"Yes. We'll be lucky to make it back before sunset."

"Let Shade run a little. With all that muscle, he is built for it. Cotton Eye and I will follow."

"You are familiar with horses?" Aaron asked, perplexed by her sudden change in demeanor.

"A little. But you don't have to be to see that Shade is a beautiful horse."

"Shade? How did you know his name?"

"You told me his name back at the farm. You may not remember. You were in the middle of kidnapping me." Seraphina smiled.

"I am not kidnapping you." Aaron scowled.

"Oh yes, that's right. You are pressing me into service."

Seraphina reached for his hands, and Aaron helped her onto her horse. She settled in, dropping her legs on either side and tightening her grip on the reigns. Then, clicking her tongue, she tapped Cotton Eye with her bare heels.

"See you at sunset, Colonel."

Her laughter rang out as she and Cotton Eye took off at a gallop, the two instinctively leaning into the run. Her seat was as natural as any he'd seen on a woman. The sight of her and Cotton Eye running with abandon mesmerized him. He decided to let them run for a bit. Shade could easily overtake them when he was ready to pursue.

He'd been chasing her from the moment they'd met. Deftly avoiding his every inquiry, she remained a mystery to him. He was certain of only one thing: This would not be the last time he'd have to chase her.

CHAPTER SIX

Harrison's Landing, Virginia
July 6th, 1862

The thoughtless bliss of the run was over. She hadn't intended to outrun him or even escape. She knew both were impossible.

In the rhythmic cadence of Cotton Eye's hooves, the silent wind, and the dimming of the sky, she was chasing two things that had eluded her for months: a quiet mind and a centered spirit. Such gifts of Zen were only found in the union of nature and self.

Aaron did not stop her. And when she heard Shade's hoofbeats behind her, he did not demand she pull back. They ran free together for another half mile before she had to slow Cotton Eye to a walk.

They watered the horses in a nearby stream. Aaron complimented her on her skill and inquired where she learned to ride.

"Private lessons with my grandfather," she lied.

When she did not elaborate further, they fell into a deliberate silence for the remainder of the ride.

It wasn't long before they came to a creek crossing. Seraphina road a little closer to Aaron as they passed artillery batteries, heavy with cannon, and large groups of soldiers camped out in the open.

Aaron rode around, placing himself between Seraphina and the soldiers. He glanced at her, his eyes soft and reassuring. "You are safe."

Seraphina relaxed a little but kept close.

A large plantation mansion appeared in the distance, surrounded by a city of wedge tents and buttressed by a river. The camp reminded Seraphina more of a medieval castle and village than a Civil War camp. Gunboats patrolled the length of the river as men and munitions were loaded and unloaded on the docks. Harrison's Landing was an impressive fortification.

Seraphina remembered her love of history and how she'd always wished she could go back in time and witness events firsthand. Of course, she was thinking of Rome or Egypt. Being a Black woman, in Civil War America was decidedly not on her list. Yet here she was.

"Is this where you intend to keep me captive?" Seraphina asked.

Aaron reigned Shade around to face her. "You are not my captive."

"No? Am I free to go?"

"No." Aaron gave Seraphina a hard look. "You are not."

Seraphina returned the look. "I thought not."

A young man hurried to Aaron's side. "T-take your horse, s-sir?"

"Yes, mine and the lady's. Be sure they are groomed and fed."

Aaron got down and handed the reigns off to the stable boy. Seraphina prepared for him to assist her, but to her surprise, he grabbed her boots off Cotton Eye's back and unbraided the laces.

"May I?" Aaron held out her boot. "The ground is no place for a lady's feet."

"Yes. Thank you." Seraphina blushed at his unexpected kindness. Her insides screamed. *No! Don't you dare! Don't you dare fall for this chivalrous bullshit!*

Aaron struggled to get the boots on her feet. "They don't fit."

"No, they don't," Seraphina replied. "I removed them for comfort, not to offend your sensibilities."

"Forgive me. We have a sutler. I will have Noble get you a pair that fits."

"Noble?"

"Noble is my valet. You will meet him shortly."

"You have a valet?"

"Noble has been with my family since my son was an infant. And no, he is not a slave, to answer your question. He works for me."

She hated the way he read her thoughts. Though admittedly, it probably wasn't hard. They were likely written all over her face and, all too frequently, on the tip of her tongue. A fact that had gotten her in trouble more times than she cared to count.

"I apologize. I didn't mean to suggest—"

"No need. It is a natural assumption. But no, we Welds are a family of abolitionists." He grabbed her bags. "Follow me."

Seraphina fell into step behind him. He led her down a long row of tents. Unlike the triangular tents they'd passed on their way into camp, these were big, with rectangular walls and pitched roofs.

Aaron stopped in front of a large tent with a smaller one beside it. A middle-aged Black man in a white shirt with a matching dark-gray herringbone vest and trousers stepped out of the tent on the left. He was shorter than Aaron, with a stocky build and a neatly trimmed, black woolen beard. His eyes, a warm brown like his skin, fell on Seraphina with a look of pleasant surprise and mild trepidation.

"Miss Laurent, this is my valet, Noble. If you need anything, he will see to it. Noble, this is Miss Seraphina Laurent. She will be staying with us."

"Pleased to make your acquaintance, miss." Noble smiled and bowed slightly.

"Please, call me Seraphina. The pleasure is mine."

"Colonel. I left supper for you, not knowing when you'd be back. I will prepare quarters for the doctor. Will he be here this evening too?" Noble inquired.

"No. There is no need to prepare additional accommodations. Seraphina and I will dine in my quarters this evening."

"Yes, sir," Noble agreed, confusion on his face. "I will bring supper for you and Miss Laurent."

Aaron held open the flap to his tent and set her bags down. "Miss Laurent, please join me."

Seraphina did not move. Her mind and heart raced. What did he want? Why was he being so nice? *You know what he wants. What do they all want?* she said internally.

"Miss Laurent, I only want to talk." Aaron gestured for her to enter.

"Je ne serai pas votre pute ou votre esclave," Seraphina spat viciously.

"What?" Aaron paled.

"You heard me. I will not be your slave or whore," Seraphina repeated, her tone deadly.

"You are neither, Miss Laurent. As for the liberties I have taken, it is not my intention—"

"Libertés? Intention? You've made your intentions clear! You have stolen me from my home, assaulted my person, and are holding me against my will! And now you want me to dine with you!"

"Actions made necessary by your rebellious nature. Would you rather I turn you over my knee?" Aaron raised an inquisitive eyebrow.

"Vous n'oseriez pas!" Seraphina cried.

"I would dare, Miss Laurent. Oh, I would." He sighed. "I ask that you deny me the pleasure. Please. Sit."

Seraphina squared her shoulders and walked past him. Sparsely furnished, the tent had a standard issue field cot, a table, two chairs, three large chests, and a smaller table with a pitcher and basin on top. Seraphina sat in the chair closest to the tent opening. Aaron sat across from her, a quizzical expression on his face. A chill ran down her spine. He was going to ask questions. Questions she couldn't answer and until now had been able to avoid. Aaron wasn't Addie, Jedidiah, or Daisy. The story or non-story she'd told them would not work on him. Her only choice was to go all in on the bad hand the universe had dealt her and hope he didn't call her bluff.

Noble returned with a plate of fatback, collard greens, beans, and biscuits for each of them. He poured cups of hot tea and stepped away from the table.

"I be outside, if you need me."

Seraphina's stomach growled audibly. Food wasn't scarce on the farm, but it wasn't plentiful either. She often skipped meals so Daisy, Lizzie, Rhea, and the babies could eat their fill.

"Miss Laurent, how long has it been since you had a meal?"

"Yesterday," she replied.

"Yesterday? Yet, you fed my men?"

"Yes, of course. They were injured and in need." Seraphina held her middle in a futile attempt to quiet it. "It was nothing. Anyone would do the same."

"No. No, they would not. Miss Laurent, eat…please." Aaron slid the plate of biscuits toward her.

Seraphina took a biscuit and sopped up the soup from her plate. She placed it gingerly on her tongue, and a savory sigh escaped her lips as she closed her eyes. Embarrassed, she stopped eating.

"There is no shame in what cannot be helped." Aaron smiled. "You are hungry."

Smug, condescending son of a bitch! What would you know about it? Seraphina debated screaming the words in his face but decided on a less offensive but no less effective comedown.

"Shame?" Seraphina bit sharply. "I doubt a man of your station has ever suffered the indignities of hunger."

"No. I have not. And I will endeavor to be more grateful. Please eat," Aaron pleaded.

She was ravenous. She struggled to maintain table etiquette, lifting her fork from plate to mouth with little pause between.

"How much sleep have you had?" Aaron asked.

"Oh, a few hours over the last few days," Seraphina answered, trying not to talk with her mouth full.

"You are serious?" Aaron's eyes widened.

"People were sick and dying. I was too busy trying to keep everyone well to sleep. Which is why I need to go back."

"You are needed here."

"I am needed there."

"You are one woman. You have not slept or eaten in days. Caring for everyone? Who pray tell was caring for you?"

"I can care for myself." She stiffened

"You cannot," Aaron said flatly.

"Do not presume to tell me what I can and cannot do!" Seraphina yelled.

"I presume nothing." Aaron sat back in his chair. "You are in service of the Union Army, and I am the colonel. You and everyone else here are under my authority."

"You are my kidnapper! Je ne suis pas un soldat!"

"Miss Laurent, you will cease this deliberate impertinence. You are going nowhere."

Seraphina stared at Aaron. The anger and frustration from earlier in the day were gone. In their place was a soft blue-eyed mix of concern and compassion. It was unsettling. She preferred his ire. His irk. She could war against irk and ire, but care and courtesy…control?

"Miss Laurent, if I keep you here, which I can…you will—"

"Make your life miserable. I'll make you wish you'd never taken me from my home." She glared at him.

"No." He smiled back. "You will care for my men as you did at the farm. You are as selfless as you are stubborn."

God damn him! Seraphina screamed internally in silent frustration. She began to shake; tears dampened her eyes. Weary and famished, her body cried for surrender. The battle was over…for now. Seraphina stood abruptly. "Would you please show me to my quarters? I am… I am… I am…" Seraphina began to sob. "S'il vous plaît, montrez-moi ma chambre."

Aaron stood. Seraphina hadn't appreciated his full height until his head brushed the roof of the tent. "You stay. Finish your meal and rest. My quarters are yours."

Seraphina wiped her tears. "Colonel, I would rather not stay in your quarters. I would prefer my own."

"Not tonight. It is late. You will stay here. You will join me at the hospital in the morning. Both plates are yours. Eat them. Then sleep." He left.

Dumbfounded, Seraphina sat down. Nothing had gone as she expected. He hadn't asked her who she was or where she was from. He'd simply inquired after her needs. It didn't make sense. Did he already know who she was? Did he just not care?

Seraphina grabbed her fork and made quick work of both plates and the tea. She slipped out of her skirt and used the chamber pot in the corner, thankful she did not have to traipse around in the dark to find a secluded place in the woods. She washed her face and hands using the pitcher and basin on the chest.

She rummaged through her duffle bags for a clean chemise, her baking soda tin, hairbrush, and the lavender sweet oil she used on her hair and skin. Her beauty routine was a shameful luxury but one she clung to desperately. Addie and Jedidiah often chided her on how often she bathed.

Mrs. Astor, a wealthy older woman from the Sanitary Commission, had taken great interest in Seraphina's use of herbal medicine during her first visit to the farm. Gloria, as Seraphina came to know her, had a lot of ailments. Seraphina made her a peppermint-and-willow-bark-infused sweet oil for her arthritis and a black cohosh tea for her hot flashes. In exchange for treatments, Gloria brought Seraphina, a hairbrush, and baking soda and let her keep the sweet oil and corked bottles she did not use. Seraphina skimmed off a little to make the lavender-infused oil and other treatments she traded with the ladies in the commission for additional rations of flour, yeast, beans, coffee, sugar, and salt.

The most precious commodity Gloria provided, second only to the sweet oil, was cheesecloth. Seraphina used it to treat wounds and for makeshift tampons. A little bleached cotton or linen stuffed in a cheesecloth sack did the trick.

It was a good system of barter and trade until the war got too close, and the ladies from the commission stopped coming.

Seraphina quickly changed into her chemise, not wanting to be caught undressed should Aaron return unexpectedly. She brushed her hair, rubbed the oil into her skin, and gargled with the baking soda. Routine complete, she extinguished the lantern and fell back onto Aaron's cot. It felt amazing. After three months of sleeping on the ground, she'd have argued to the death that the cot was a close second to her expensive mattress.

Aaron's scent, male and potent, enveloped her, and she relaxed. There was something comforting about it, something safe. She scolded herself. *Safe? Have you lost your mind? And crying?*

The sounds of the camp faded away as, at last, exhaustion overtook her.

*****

Aaron watched the shadows dance on the walls of his tent as Seraphina readied herself for bed. He was relieved when she extinguished the lamp for the night. He was afraid in her desperation; she might try to run away. Fortunately, hunger and fatigue proved stronger than her determination to flee.

"She mad as a cat in a sack." Noble grinned, taking the plate in Aaron's hand and offering him a mug of coffee.

Aaron waved him off. "I haven't time for coffee now. I need to get to the hospital and find Lieutenant Weld. I just wanted to be sure Seraphina got off to bed."

Noble poured the coffee into the dying fire. "Sir, I know it not my place to tell you bout your affairs."

"Noble, I've known you too long. Speak your mind."

"Sir, you think she be safe here? Seraphina the kind of woman make men do foolish things."

"You mean me. For bringing her here." Aaron laughed.

"You are not a foolish man, sir." Noble smiled. "But you are a man."

Noble's concern for Seraphina's safety was well founded. He'd had her sleep in his quarters tonight to send a message. Most men would be dissuaded. For those that weren't, the punishment would be severe.

Aaron chuckled. "I don't deny it, but I assure you, Miss Laurent is here to work in the hospital, nothing more. She will be safe. I will see to it."

"Colonel, you a busy man. Maybe you can get one of us to stand guard?"

"You have someone in mind?" Aaron asked, intrigued.

"Marshall… I mean Private Dixon. He big. Strong too. Good with a rifle. Decent."

"You're a wise man, Noble. Go get this, Marshall." Aaron ordered. "I'll stay in the officer's quarters tonight and send for her in the morning."

*****

Seraphina opened her eyes; despair and disappointment flooded her. She was still in 1862. Every night, she went to sleep hoping to wake at home, only to be disillusioned in the morning.

"What time is it?"

The lack of clocks and timepieces infuriated her. Without the sun, the day just seemed like one long hour. The bustling activity of the camp hit the snooze on her natural alarm clock as it discouraged the birds from their morning serenade. She hoped she wasn't late. Aaron said she would join him at the hospital in the morning, and she'd slept so soundly that it felt like midday. A full belly and a comfortable cot had given her what the Sandman had failed to for weeks, a full night's sleep.

Seraphina got out of bed. She intended to request fresh water for the basin but found the water had already been replaced, and a clean rag was left beside it. The chamber pot had been emptied too. She looked around for her bags only to find her belongings had been neatly folded into a small chest with a new dress and a pair of boots inside. Who had done this? Noble? Aaron? One of them had gone through a lot of trouble to create this Christmas-like morning for her. The thought of Noble or Aaron rummaging through her things was unsettling, but she was too grateful to be angry about the intrusion on her privacy. She dressed quickly and left to look for Aaron.

Noble greeted her outside. "Miss Seraphina, come have a seat. I have breakfast for you." Noble ushered her to a tree-stump-turned-chair around the cooking fire.

"Are those eggs? And coffee? And biscuits?" Seraphina squealed with delight.

"Yes, miss." Noble smiled, handing her a plate. "The sutler has laying hens. The biscuits are from last evening, but the coffee is fresh. I reckon the way your belly was complaining last evening, you might be right hungry this morning."

Seraphina ate hurriedly, stomach growling. A moment of sadness washed over her. She thought about everyone back at the farm. They were hungry too. Hopefully, less so now that she wasn't around to eat her share.

"Don't you go getting down on me now." Noble patted her hand. "Can't nobody be sad with a plate of my biscuits."

"No. They could not." Seraphina squeezed Noble's hand. It was rough and calloused like Jedidiah's. He, too, had done a life's work of hard labor. "Thank you, Noble. For breakfast…and the new clothes."

"No, Miss Seraphina. You got Colonel to thank for that. Brought the dress and shoes himself in the wee hours this morning. Said he wanted your clothes out of them bags before you opened your eyes. You ain't got much to speak of. Didn't take long."

"Oh." Seraphina felt her color deepen. "I will have to thank him."

"Mornin', Noble."

Seraphina turned at the sound of the deep baritone voice behind her. "Mercy!"

"Now I been called a lot of things but never that." He laughed. "My name is Marshall Dixon, Private Marshall Dixon. You pretty as flowers in May, Miss Seraphina."

"Thank you." Seraphina's voice quivered.

Marshall was a considerable man, standing well over six feet, and broad-shouldered with a muscular chest and back. His rifle looked like a toothpick in his large hands. In the 21st century, every NFL team would be looking for a lineman named Marshall Dixon.

Oh Marcus, if Vanessa were here, you'd be in big trouble. Seraphina mused inwardly.

"Miss Seraphina, this is my good friend Private Dixon." Noble grabbed Marshall's hand and embraced him. "Colonel Weld has assigned him to be your escort. Where he goes, you go."

"What? Escort? I don't need an escort. I am perfectly capable of—"

"I see what you say, Mr. Noble." A broad dimpled smile warmed Marshall's reddish-brown skin. "She feisty for a little thing."

"Ne parlez pas de moi comme si je n'étais pas là." Seraphina narrowed her eyes. "I am not going anywhere with you!"

"Little sister, you ain't got to go nowhere with me. But I gots to go everywhere with you," Marshall explained.

"Forgive me, Marshall, I mean Private Dixon. I understand Colonel may have given you orders, but I will not be treated like a prisoner. Your services are not needed."

Marshall crossed his massive arms over his chest. "You ain't no prisoner, little sister. I run off from the cruelest master this side of hell; you don't know what prison is. You the colonel's woman and I got orders, that all they is to it."

Marshall was right. Her prison was a gilded cage compared to the horrors he'd suffered. But a cage, however gilded, is still a cage.

Seraphina wanted to scream. She wanted to cry. She wanted to punch Colonel Aaron Weld in his blue-eyed, chiseled face. *And you blushed like a teenager because he gave you a dress!* She chided herself.

"Fine. Let's go." Seraphina headed off toward the hospital, Marshall in hot pursuit.

"Where you goin', Miss Seraphina?" Noble called after her.

"To the hospital. It's inside the house, right?"

"Colonel said he would send for you when he was ready," Noble shouted at her back.

Seraphina turned. "Mr. Noble, the colonel said he brought me here to work in the hospital, did he not? Then that is where I am going to go. Me and Private Dixon, of course."

Marshall roared with laughter. "Lead the way, little sister."

CHAPTER SEVEN

Union Hospital – Harrison's Landing, Virginia
July 7th, 1862

Seraphina was ill. If the patients were Black, she could swear she was in a refugee hospital in the Sudan. The smell was awful, a toxic mix of body odor, bodily fluids, and decaying flesh. The number of men with insufficiently treated wounds and gangrenous limbs was shocking—no doubt the reason for the high rate of amputations. She'd seen the evidence in the wheelbarrow of severed limbs she'd passed on the way in. It had been seven days since the last engagement, and things did not look good.

"Who are you, miss? Are you in need of assistance?" a lieutenant inquired.

"No, sir," Seraphina replied. "I am here to give it. My name is Seraphina Laurent. I am a nurse. Colonel Weld brought me here to assist."

"Pleased to make your acquaintance, Miss Laurent. I am Lieutenant Marks. You say Colonel Weld sent for you? He mentioned he'd be bringing on a new nurse. He did not say…" The Lieutenant ogled her openly.

Uncomfortable, Seraphina stood closer to Marshall and attempted to draw the Lieutenant's attention back to their conversation.

"The pleasure is mine, Lieutenant. This is my escort. Private Dixon." Seraphina placed a hand on Marshall's forearm. "Would it be okay with you if I got right to work? Maybe you could give the lay of the land as it were? I'd be happy to work with some of the other Black nurses and stewards."

Still distracted, the lieutenant gave Seraphina a puzzled look. "How do you know the colonel?"

"I was living on a farm nearby. Colonel Weld sought out my assistance. I was caring for some soldiers there."

"And your escort?"

"Private Dixon was assigned to me this morning by Colonel Weld. I have not had a chance to speak with the colonel today. He wasn't in his quarters when I woke this morning."

"I'm sorry," the lieutenant mumbled and turned beet red. "I did not… We need all the help we can get. Follow me."

Confused by the lieutenant's red-faced abrupt change in subject, Seraphina fell in beside him. It wasn't until he stopped making eye contact with her that she remembered Marshall's words. She was "The Colonel's Woman." The lieutenant realized who he was leering at and immediately changed his behavior. Though she appreciated the deference the association afforded her, the implications of it were infuriating. *The Colonel's Woman, my ass! More like his captive.*

It did not take long for the lieutenant to give Seraphina the whole morbid tour. Or for Seraphina to triage the situation and devise a plan of action. She knew she needed to be careful. It had been her experience that male doctors had fragile egos, and if it were true in the 21st century, it had to be gospel now. As a nurse, she'd learned the best way to deal with doctors was to play to their egos.

"With your permission, Lieutenant? Do you think we could open the windows and air things out a bit, maybe have the stewards remove all the soiled linen and bandages from the floor? The men may enjoy a little fresh air and cleanliness."

"Yes, of course. We could use some air and housekeeping."

"May I start treating the men's wounds? Beginning with this man here? Under your supervision, of course? Or you could assign me a steward or two if you think that would be best. I can imagine you have more pressing duties."

"Few appreciate the travails of a surgeon. I will assign you a steward forthwith. You there,"—the lieutenant pointed to a young Black man passing by—"come here."

"Yes, suh," the young man answered, never lifting his eyes.

"This is Miss Laurent. You are her steward now. Do as she asks. Miss Laurent, I will leave you now for those more pressing duties you spoke of. I will send another steward."

"Thank you, Lieutenant. For your attentiveness."

Seraphina waited for him to leave before speaking to the steward.

"Good. Now we can get to it. What is your name, young man?"

"Jacob."

"Jacob, is there water for washing?"

"Not in here. In the kitchens," he answered.

"Get some in a bucket or whatever you can find. Rags and bandages too. We'll need more water, so have the kitchen set a kettle to boil. Do we have any spirits or salt?"

"Yes, miss."

"Good. Bring that too. You may need to get another steward or nurse to help you. Find me someone who can forage; I need bark from the dogwood trees. You got all that?"

"Miss, you ain't from these parts?" Jacob asked, finally looking up.

"No." Seraphina chuckled. "No, I am not."

*****

Aaron stood in front of the window, taking in the view of the river landing. The Union had converted the mansion into a hospital. The first-floor dining room, living room, and library were converted into sick wards, the parlor into a surgery, and the second floor into officers' quarters. He'd spent the night in officers' quarters to allow Seraphina to have his. He preferred to stay in camp among the junior officers but sleeping in the same tent with Seraphina was out of the question.

"Are you mad? A woman? A Black woman? You jest." Thomas shook his head in disbelief.

"I did not believe it myself, Thomas." Aaron walked away from the window and closed the door.

"You aren't seriously considering this! A surgeon? You want to make her a surgeon! They'll have you resign your commission. The other surgeons will revolt."

"Not a surgeon. A nurse. Thomas, men are dying. If you'd seen the farm, the men under her care. They were in better condition than our men here. Her wound treatments are remarkable, as is her knowledge of plant medicinals. She sedated a man and sutured his wounds without morphine or chloroform."

Thomas leaned forward in his chair. "Are you suggesting she is better skilled than the assistant surgeons we have on staff? Is that what you are saying?"

Aaron sat on the edge of the desk. "I would not repeat it outside of this room, but at treating wounds, yes. Thomas, I do not intend to have her perform surgery, only treat wounds."

"Brother, do you hear yourself?" Thomas pointed to his ear. "A woman, a Black woman, is our equal? Or dare I say, our better? I do not believe that. You do not believe that."

"Seraphina is not our equal or our better, but she does have knowledge we do not."

"Seraphina? This woman has bewitched you. Is this why you were gone so long yesterday? Did she give you some of these medicinals? Or something else?" Thomas raised an eyebrow.

Aaron winced. He'd just breathed Seraphina's name as if from practiced memory, and they weren't familiar.

"It was a slip of the tongue, nothing more," Aaron said.

"Whose tongue, Brother?" Thomas searched Aaron's face. "Yours or hers?"

"Thomas, as always, you go too far! I am in complete control of my faculties, physical and mental. Our duty is to the men under our care. Little Brother, I need you to support this."

"This is lunacy," Thomas stated flatly.

It was lunacy. Had he brought Seraphina here on impulse? Had the growing number of deaths overwhelmed him? Had he not kept sufficient distance between himself and the wounded men under his care? The questions grew in their persistence throughout the night and into the morning, but he was undeterred.

"Yes, and that is why I need you behind me. Thomas, you could sell poison to a snake. You are as charming as you are affable. I am not. I could just give orders, but this situation calls for a more…delicate approach."

"Do not flatter me, you crazy bastard! Well, do, but not right now." Thomas smiled. "You are my brother. It is as much my duty to defend you as it is to protect you. You are asking me to help you walk off a cliff. Which is what this is, you know? A cliff."

"I am bringing Miss Laurent to the hospital this morning. Observe her. Be convinced for yourself."

"Who is this Seraphina? Is she a slave? Where did she come from?" Thomas asked.

Before Aaron could answer Thomas's questions, there was shouting in the hall. A moment later, Major Lynch stood in the doorway, furious. First Lieutenant Marks stood behind him, concern etched on his face.

"Colonel Weld! Colonel Weld!" Lynch shouted.

Aaron stood. "Gentleman."

"Colonel, is it you who has beset this insolent Negro woman upon us? I would strike her if it were not for the boy and that Black buck you have following her around like a dog," Lynch howled.

Major Henry Lynch was a Union soldier in name only. He was a Copperhead, and like all Copperheads, his sympathies toward the south ran deep, his disdain for Blacks even deeper. Before Seraphina's arrival, his ill-temper and rebel leanings were a nuisance. Now, they were dangerous, and Seraphina had run headlong into them.

"Tell me, Major Lynch, what has she done?" Aaron pressed.

"She is rationing out morphine. She has removed fragments and bullets from limbs that clearly should be cut off—says some salve she has will prevent infection. She has made the men bathe, and those who could not bathe, she had bathed. She has taken over the entire hospital. The nurses and stewards, Negro and white alike, are taking orders from her!"

"They ignore us completely. We may be fighting a war for these wretches, but I will not be ordered about by the likes of any Negress wench! She needs to be whipped for her manner. I demand that you tend to this at once!"

"Lieutenant Marks, how long has Miss Laurent been here?" Aaron asked.

"A few hours," he replied. "Colonel, I'm ashamed to say it, but from what I've seen of her nursing, she is better skilled than some of our surgeons. She said you brought her here. Where did you find her?"

"Boy, to suggest any woman is the equal or better of a man is blasphemous!" Lynch interrupted. "To say such of a Negro is an outrage! I will not stand for this. Colonel, if you will not deal with her as you ought, then I shall! She needs a good whipping, and I intend to give her one," Major Lynch shouted.

"Touch her, and I will have you court-martialed." Aaron's words fell cold and steady.

"Excuse me, sir?" Lynch cried.

"No, Major, you are not excused. You will change your tone, or I will have you brought to the burling."

"You would threaten me? Have you gone mad? I will quit," Lynch shouted.

"I threaten nothing as I am your colonel. I will inform the general of your resignation."

"I will not resign my commission," Lynch blustered.

"If you will not resign, then you will take orders. You will not harm Miss Laurent in any way. You will not perform any more surgeries in this hospital. Henceforth, you will apply your talents to record keeping. You will keep records of the soldiers' names, ranks, companies, injury dates, and treatments and arrange their transport to ambulance. You will have reports ready for me daily. You will cease referring to Lieutenant Marks as 'the boy' and call him by his rank. Are we clear?"

"Yes, sir," Lynch responded through clenched teeth.

"Good. Then be about your work, Major."

Aaron left Lynch standing in the doorway. Thomas and Lieutenant Marks followed.

"Colonel, not to be impolite, but I am glad to be rid of him." Marks smiled. "As for Miss Laurent, I pray, tell me more. Who is this woman?"

Like Aaron and Thomas, Lieutenant Marks was a northerner and abolitionist. Young, he was unjaded by centuries-old traditions, and his feelings toward Blacks were quite benevolent.

"I will answer those questions in time, Lieutenant. For now, take me to her."

"She is in the surgery with the young man you assigned to guard her. I did not understand why you placed her under guard until I saw her. She is an uncommon beauty."

"Do tell, Lieutenant." Thomas grinned. "Uncommon? Are you sure? Tongues do tend to slip, I mean wag."

"Yes, sir. See for yourself." Marks pointed to Seraphina.

Thomas froze. His eyes lit up; his jaw dropped. "Aaron, you found her on a farm? Lieutenant, we must improve your vocabulary. Uncommon is an insufficient description of what stands before us."

"I did not want to be indelicate, sir." Marks smiled. "I have a very large vocabulary."

"I will say to both of you what I said to Major Lynch and what I will say to any man who dares to lay hands on her. She is not to be touched," Aaron growled

"Words aren't necessary. You declared your intentions when you kept her in your quarters last night. If that was the message you intended to be received, the point would be clearer if you stayed with her." Thomas gave Aaron a knowing glance.

"Miss Laurent is here in service to the Union Army. Nothing more." Aaron rolled his shoulders. "Please forgive my foul mood. Things have not gone as planned this morning. Miss Laurent was not to be here until later."

"She is quite the early riser." Thomas cleared his throat, trying unsuccessfully to suppress his laughter. "I dare say, if she were well bedded at night, she might not be so eager in the morning, Colonel."

Aaron tightened his jaw. "Lieutenant Weld, Lieutenant Marks, you are dismissed."

Aaron set his gaze on Seraphina. He was vexed. By showing up without him, she'd ruined his plans. He'd intended to introduce Seraphina to the officers, escort her around the hospital, and introduce her skills slowly to avoid ruffling feathers. Then there was the matter of her safety. He'd wanted to make it clear before she arrived that she was not to be molested in any way, and to do so would have serious repercussions.

"Miss Laurent," Aaron called to her, "take leave of your duties for a moment. I wish to discuss something with you."

"As you wish," she replied, her tone hostile.

"I do not make wishes, Miss Laurent. I give orders. Please come with me."

Private Dixon stood to follow. Aaron stopped him. "Please wait for her at the bottom of the staircase."

"Yes, suh." Marshall nodded.

Seraphina removed her bloodied apron. Aaron escorted her up the stairs. He stopped abruptly on the landing and pointed to an open bedroom door. The room had a large bed with braided rugs on either side. An armoire and a dressing mirror lined the walls.

"In here," Aaron ordered her.

Seraphina moved past him, and Aaron kicked the door closed behind her. He saw what he thought might be true fear in her eyes for the first time. He ignored it. He wanted her to be afraid. He needed her to be afraid. He needed her to understand the gravity of what she'd done.

"Woman, do you know what you've done?" Aaron spoke softly.

"You ordered me to be here in the morning, Colonel. If I recall, you did not say what time."

Aaron seized her and kissed her hard. Seraphina stumbled in a feeble attempt to shove him away.

"Vous êtes dégoutant...ne me touche pas—"

He cut her off with another kiss, more forceful than before. Seraphina ended her struggle quicker this time. Her body softened against his. Her lips parted, allowing him to deepen the kiss. He did, pinning her to the bed beneath him. Seraphina moaned softly. His cock hardened painfully.

She is yours. Aaron felt the words in every fiber of his being. He tore his mouth from hers. *No. Not like this.*

Seraphina looked up at him, her eyes rum-colored pools of rage, fear, and something else.

"I could have my way with you right now, and there is nothing, nothing you could do to stop me. I have no desire to harm you, but there are men here who do, who will, just like this...worse. And you won't be able to stop them. I won't be able to stop them. Do you understand me?"

Seraphina said nothing. He watched as the fear and rage seeped from her eyes, leaving only tears and something else.

"You will follow my orders, without question, without insolence. You will not arrive at the hospital before me. You will leave when I leave or when I direct you to. Private Dixon is to go where you go, always. Do we understand one another?"

"Yes," Seraphina replied quietly. "I arrived early in hopes that if I got things running smoothly, you would allow me to return."

"I cannot. You are needed here. After this morning, I am sure it is obvious. Private Dixon will escort you to my quarters. You are done for the day." Aaron stood and helped Seraphina to her feet.

She snatched her hand from his. "Your quarters?"

Aaron darkened his tone. "Yes, Miss Laurent. My quarters."

"As you wish, Colonel." Seraphina hurried from the room.

Private Dixon met her at the bottom of the stairs and followed her out the door. Aaron stood fast, steeling himself against the overwhelming urge to give chase.

Thomas appeared in the doorway. "Is that French I heard? She speaks French? Who is this woman? Or do you intend to keep her a mystery?"

"Did you need something, Lieutenant?" Aaron grumbled.

"A mystery. I see. Another question. How are you going to convince her to stay?"

"Convince her?"

"Yes. Is the plan to stake her to the ground beside you? If so, you should do so now. Unless, of course, you are convinced of your brute seduction techniques. You have the temperament of an animal caged too long, Colonel."

"Continue this mockery, and you will find out how long." Aaron glared at Thomas. "You are dismissed, Lieutenant."

"As you wish, Colonel." Thomas left.

Aaron struggled for calm and clarity. The taste of her lips lingered. Her smoldering amber eyes consumed him.

Brute seduction. Thomas was right. He'd lost control. Hadn't she called him a brute the day they met?

She's made a beast of me.

Aaron sat on the edge of the bed. Calm and clarity returned, and with them, a singular thought. *She surrendered.*

*****

Seraphina lay unmoving on Aaron's cot, choking back sobs, the tears streaming down her face.

You are needed here. Aaron's words echoed in Seraphina's ears. He was right. If she had not stopped that terrible Doctor Lynch from the brutal amputation he was going to do, the poor man would have lost his leg and his life.

It didn't matter. Aaron's anger was valid, even if his tactics were bestial. She shouldn't have gone to the hospital. The soldiers' reaction to her presence ranged from indifferent to indecent. She'd overheard questions about her origins, lewd comments about her anatomy, and thinly veiled descriptions of how they'd like her to "nurse" them. It wasn't safe. She was a Black woman in 1862 Virginia. Nowhere was safe.

The battle was over. All that was left was to negotiate the terms of her surrender. Surrender. The word felt like lead in her mouth. She'd been a strong independent woman her entire life, and now, now she had been reduced to nothing more than an indentured servant.

Worse, she'd given in. Her body had betrayed her. *And it felt right.* Seraphina's heart turned over hard at the thought. His touch, his kiss… his icy blue stare set her ablaze; all that remained was an emotion she dared not name.

Seraphina's thoughts turned to her mothers, Auntie Mary, Vanessa, Addie, and the rest of her family at the farm. She wept harder, unable to quiet her cries. *I want to go home.*

Noble called to her from the tent opening. "Miss Seraphina, you need to calm yourself now. You gwine make yourself sick. Colonel gwine—"

"I don't give two shits about what Colonel gwine do! Damn him to hell! And you can tell him I said so!"

"Child, you talking nonsense." Noble pulled back the tent opening. "I will do no such a thing. Colonel a good man! You stop this. Drink this here." Noble held out the tin cup.

"No!" Seraphina turned away.

"Child, drink this." Noble's tone was stern, but the smile never left his eyes.

Seraphina took the tin cup from him. It was warm. She breathed in the steam, a calming mix of whiskey and black tea. She drank it, savoring the slow burn.

"Thank you, Noble. Please forgive me. I am—"

"No need. You rest now. I have supper in a little while. Colonel be back. Y'all can sort it out then. Marshall and I be outside."

"Noble, he won't let me go," Seraphina lamented.

"Where you gwine go, child? My wife Mary says, if this where you are, this where you supposed to be. You need to make peace with that. When it time for you to go…you go."

Seraphina finished her tea. "Thank you, Noble."

Noble squeezed her hand. "Rest."

Seraphina stretched out on the cot. She was thankful Noble added more whiskey than tea to the hot toddy. Slumber called to her from the edge of consciousness. She closed her eyes and cried herself to sleep.

*****

Aaron stood outside his quarters, the waning sun dimming the silhouette within. He had not seen Seraphina since earlier in the day. He'd sent an inquiry to Noble via another soldier, and the report was not a good one. Noble said she was distraught. He'd had to give her something to settle her down. And even with that, she'd cried herself to sleep. Prayerfully, she was calmer now, and they could talk.

"Miss Laurent? Miss Laurent, may I enter?" Aaron called to her from behind the tent flaps.

"The quarters are yours. You do not need my permission," Seraphina replied.

"Until I provide you with your own quarters, my quarters are yours, and a gentleman never enters a lady's quarters without permission."

"A gentleman?" Seraphina mocked him. "Then you should enter."

Seraphina's feigned deference and naked hostility filled him with apprehension. He did not want to fight.

Seraphina stood and turned her back to him. He caught a glimpse of her red and swollen eyes. She hadn't been crying. She'd been weeping. His heart lurched. He'd never hurt a woman in his life, and he'd done nothing but hurt her from the moment they'd met.

"I confess, I have not behaved like a gentleman. And though undeserved, I beg your forgiveness."

"Do you intend to provide me with my own quarters, or am I to remain here indefinitely?" she asked, ignoring his request for pardon.

"Not indefinitely. I will provide you with quarters of your own," Aaron answered.

"I am grateful for your hospitality, of course. But may I ask when?"

"Tomorrow." Aaron moved toward her. "I will see to it tomorrow."

"Thank you." Seraphina increased the distance between them.

"Miss Laurent—"

"Please stop calling me that. My name is Seraphina. And don't go on about decorum. I understand if you must do so in public, but not here."

"As you wish, Seraphina."

The sound of her name on his lips, like the unexpected song of a bird, delighted him. He decided then and there to use it often.

"And do not mock me." Seraphina sniffled.

"Forgive me. Seraphina, we need to talk."

"You are never going to let me leave here. I am to be your indentured servant for the foreseeable future. And the fact that my family needs me is of no consequence. That about sums it up, right?"

"God, no," Aaron bristled. "You are not an indentured servant."

Her insults, sharp and observant, always hit their mark. She still hadn't looked at him. He found it both impressive and irritating.

"Yes, I am. In exchange for my labor, I ask that you send half of my rations, whatever they may be, to the farm. As for terms of service, you will return me to my family wherever they are, when the war is over or when I am no longer needed, whichever comes first."

Aaron sat. "Are you negotiating with me?"

"Yes. I know my family's welfare and my freedom are of no consequence to you, but they are to me. Do we have an agreement?"

"I negotiate with no man who has his back to me," Aaron answered coolly.

"I am not a man. Do we have an agreement? I would have your word, sir."

It puzzled and amused him how her speech became more like his when she was angry. She only spoke French when she was furious and unreasonable. He desperately wanted to see her face. If he could, he would know what she was thinking. And then it occurred to him.

That is why she has her back to you.

"Face me," Aaron ordered.

"No."

"Seraphina, why must you fight?" Aaron sighed. "You bring misery on yourself."

"I have been a free woman from the day I was born. You are taking that away from me. I doubt you'd go like a sheep to the slaughter if you were in my stead."

Her words were true. He would not. Never in his life had he met a woman of Seraphina's intelligence and strength, which begged the question, where on earth had she come from? Why was she alone? How had she survived? A woman by herself, unmarried, childless, living with found family on an abandoned farm. Aaron knew there was more, but this was not the time to ask.

"On your word, you will remain here? You will follow orders?" he asked.

"On my word. I will remain here. You will give your word then? You will allow me to return? And send my rations to the farm?"

"I will send full rations, and you will be paid for your work, like every other nurse…not an indentured servant."

"May I send a letter to my family when you send the supplies?"

"Yes, you may. Everything you need for correspondence is in the chest beside you."

"I am going to need some supplies of my own if I am to treat the men properly."

"Make a list. You will have what you need."

Seraphina turned to face him. "Thank you. If there is nothing else, please leave."

Aaron regarded her for a moment. The tears in her eyes hid nothing from him. He'd expected despair and anger but found a firmness of resolve and a sea of sepia-colored sadness.

"As you wish." He stalked out and walked over to the quarters next to his. The men outside stood at attention.

"Sergeant Major, tomorrow morning, I want you to move your quarters. I do not care where. I want this whole area policed and a fresh tent erected. It needn't be as large, but it must be walled. I want it close enough to mine that one could not walk between them. Be sure it has the regulars. Dismissed."

Aaron did not wait for them to answer. Instead, he returned to where he'd left Noble and Marshall standing. Private Dixon rose. "At ease, Private."

"Sir?" Noble gave Aaron a worried look.

"Noble, when the men finish, add the additional items we discussed. Private Dixon, you are not to leave this evening. I want you to sleep at the entrance to the tent."

"Sir, begging your pardon, you think she run off?" Noble asked worriedly.

"No, Mr. Noble," Marshal spoke up. "Colonel worried somebody will get in."

"And you will not allow that to happen, will you, Private?" Aaron spoke sternly.

"No, suh." Marshall shook his head. "I won't. No man touch her. Swear it."

"Good. Tomorrow, when she is ready, bring her directly to me at the hospital. Once she has quarters of her own, you only need come in the morning and stay with her until evening or until I return. Good night, gentlemen." He left.

Aaron made his way back to the hospital via the camp's avenues and boulevards. Angrily, he played their conversation repeatedly in his head.

Indentured servitude? Is that what she thinks? Negotiations? She thought to barter with me, like a prisoner! I am no jailer! This is what is best for her. She is safer here. Here...with me. If she cannot see that!

"How'd it go?" Thomas stepped alongside Aaron with an open flask. "Not well, I take it, seeing you are headed away from your quarters."

Aaron groaned. Thomas was the last person he needed to see right now.

"I am not in the mood, Thomas." Aaron took the flask from Thomas and drank.

"No, you are not. What you are in the mood for is a hundred or more paces behind you. She has you wound tighter than a drum."

"Shouldn't you be on duty?" Aaron grumbled.

"If what I saw this morning is any indication of her feelings, I dare say with a little persistence, you could have your fill."

"Stop it, Thomas! That is not why she is here. I do not coerce women into my bed. If they come, they do so willingly, without games or seduction."

"Games and seduction, Brother, are half the fun." Thomas grinned.

"To think you are a married man. Men like you end up with mistresses." Aaron laughed.

"Men like you end up with Seraphinas." Thomas winked. "Are you going to tell me about your siren?"

"Her surname is Laurent. She is Creole. Her grandfather was a French surgeon, and her grandmother a healer. She had taken refuge from the rebels on a farm with other contraband."

"A French-speaking Creole in Virginia? How the hell did she get here from Louisiana? Only a daft man would believe she is a contraband. It is obvious from the way she carries herself that woman hasn't been a slave a day in her life. What else do you know about her?"

Aaron sipped from the flask. "Nothing."

"Nothing!" Thomas gasped. "Aaron, you aren't serious?"

"I am. She hasn't been very forthcoming and is adept at avoiding my questions."

"Could she be a spy?"

"A spy?" Aaron laughed. "Spies try to blend in. Sera—Miss Laurent could not do so if she wanted to. She's too damn stubborn, too beau—"

"Beautiful?" Thomas smiled. "I confess, I find your little war amusing. You have grown quite fond of Seraphina."

Aaron rolled his eyes. "Thomas, romanticism is the folly of youth."

"May I offer a word of advice, Brother?"

"As if I could stop you." Aaron sighed.

Thomas reached for the flask. "You are not that old."

Aaron handed back the flask. "Good night, Lieutenant."

CHAPTER EIGHT

Union Hospital – Harrison's Landing, Virginia
July 1862

The plantation gardens were picture-perfect. If you closed your eyes and imagined a Southern plantation garden, you'd see this place: large willows draped in Spanish moss and shaded cobblestone paths lined with blooming shrubs, open greens, and stone benches. A tiered fountain with a large reflecting pool at its base sat center stage, with room enough to sit on its edge. A grove of Magnolia trees with winding earthen clay byways crowned the garden's edge, just before a cast iron gate that separated it from the woodlands.

Seraphina sat, book in hand, under a garden willow with Marshall and a dozen or more other soldiers at her feet. She was reading aloud.

Two weeks ago, Aaron asked if she needed anything, and she'd asked for books, any books. Four months without media of any kind had been torture. So Aaron delivered a briefcase-size chest of books, all classics.

"When we cleared the library for the sick wards, I had the books crated and stored in the attic. If these are not to your liking, there are others."

She was ecstatic. The plan to maintain her composure and thank him kindly went right out the window when she opened the chest. There were at least eight books, many leatherbound, worth thousands in 21st-century dollars. He'd given her the 19th-century equivalent of diamonds, and she'd acted like it. The satisfied smile on his face proved it.

When her elation wore off, she'd immediately begun questioning his motives…and her reaction to them. Was it a ploy? An attempt to mollify her? The reflexive duty of the paternalistic relationship between 19th-century man and woman? Or, as she'd reluctantly begun to believe, was he what Noble said? A good man.

Aaron approached from behind the garden wall. At the sight of him, those soldiers that could stood at attention, and the others tried their best to salute. Seraphina joined them.

"Colonel. To what do we owe the unexpected pleasure?" She curtsied.

She'd gone out of her way to mirror the speech and mannerisms of the other women in the camp. It felt ridiculous, awkward, and at times even comical, but four years of drama in high school had done more than round out her transcript; they'd made her a great mimic.

"Please, everyone, at ease. Be seated." Aaron smiled. "I've come to listen. Please continue, Miss Laurent."

Seraphina sat down and began to read from where she had left off. The men, as always, gave her their rapt attention. The group had grown larger every day. She never intended to have "story time under the willow." She'd come to the garden to journal, to read…to be alone. To her dismay, outside of sleep, she was never alone. If asked to leave, Marshall, her ever dutiful shadow, would reply, "No, little sister. I got orders to guard you. I gwine do just that."

One day a soldier passing by overheard her reading to Marshall and asked to listen in. Hesitant, she agreed. As it does, word spread, and now she was reading under the willow and in the sick wards. She was glad to share the gift of literature in what was a mundane existence for all of them, but she did miss "me time."

Seraphina could feel Aaron's eyes on her. Tempted, she peeked over the edge of the book and their gazes locked. A man coughed, distracting her enough to break the bond. She quickly retreated behind the book. When she came to the chapter's end, she stopped.

"Gentlemen, that is all for today. I will see you tomorrow."

A chorus of groans and gratitude greeted her announcement.

"Little sister, I can see the pictures in my head…exactly what it looks like when you read like that." Marshall smiled wistfully."

"I could teach you to read books too," Seraphina offered.

"No, lil' sis. I can read some, but if it all the same to you, I listen." Marshall grinned.

Seraphina closed the book. "Being read to is often better than reading to yourself."

"That Heathcliff is something terrible." Marshall shook his head. "The way he wants that Wer-ther—"

"It's pronounced Wu-ther-ing; Wuthering Heights." Seraphina pointed to the title of the book. "Heathcliff's soul is twisted by cruelty and pain."

"I concur." Aaron pushed off the willow he was leaning on. "Private, if you'll excuse us. I will see Miss Laurent home this evening."

"Yes, suh," Marshal replied. "See you in the mornin', little sister. I'll take your things back."

"Thank you, Private." Seraphina collected her books and handed them to Marshall. "Good evening."

"Little sister?" Aaron questioned.

"Yes, a term of endearment. Far better than Miss Seraphina or Miss Laurent, in my opinion."

"Shall we? Seraphina." Aaron opened his hand, inviting her to walk beside him.

Seraphina fell into step, and Aaron clasped his hands behind his back and moved closer to her.

In the last month, the two had enjoyed several evening and late afternoon strolls along the riverbank. Four weeks out from the last battle, fewer men were confined to bed, and most were convalescing or being transferred to general hospitals to the north in Maryland and Washington DC. As a result, the camp was more relaxed, and everyone had more time for leisure.

The first time Aaron requested she join him for a walk, she wanted to scream no, but curiosity and loneliness got the better of her, and she'd agreed. If not for the arbitrary rules of decorum, their substantive dialogues on medicine and literature could easily have carried on late into the night.

"The men are quite enamored of you."

"Thank you. I, too, find the men are appreciative."

"Appreciative? You hold yourself in too low esteem. Many have requested to remain in your care rather than be sent to General Hospital."

"That is sweet of them." Seraphina blushed.

"You nurture the men."

"What good is it to heal a man's body and neglect his mind and spirit?"

"Wise words," Aaron replied.

"Common sense. But then again, common sense isn't all that common."

Aaron laughed. "You speak with an aged tongue, Seraphina."

"My grandmother Eulalie said the same thing." Seraphina chuckled.

"Seraphina, you are a remarkable woman." Aaron stopped and looked at her. "May I ask you a question of a personal nature?"

Seraphina struggled to keep her facial expressions neutral. If she did not, he'd read her like a book. Aaron never asked questions she could not answer, keeping his inquiries to the mundane demographics of her life and sharing the same about his. This was a first.

"Only if you will not be offended if I choose not to answer."

"I will not if you will not. It is a delicate question."

"Please ask. I am not one to take offense."

"Why is a woman with your considerable attributes childless and unmarried? I would wager my life there were suitors for your hand. Did you turn them all away?"

"Turn them away? Yes and no. I chose education over marriage. It has been my experience that men are fickle and singularly minded on the benefits of marriage, not the institution itself."

"May I ask, what gave you such a low opinion of men? Have you never met a man worthy of you?"

"Worthy? Colonel, my grandmother instilled in me the importance of humbleness and warned me against the deceitfulness of pride."

"Forgive me, Seraphina. I did not mean… You are not prideful."

Aaron continued to walk, and Seraphina followed. An awkward silence fell between them.

Seraphina wanted to explain. She wanted to tell him why she'd never met a man worthy of her—why she was an unfortunate.

"Colonel, it isn't about worthiness or pride. I assure you."

"Maybe one day you will tell me what it is about, my mysterious Seraphina."

Mysterious. He'd called her mysterious. The sound of the word on his lips excited and frightened her. She'd been called many things, never that. But wasn't she? What did he really know about her? If she divulged the truth, he'd think she was crazy and have her committed. It was a dangerous but necessary deception.

"Mysterious? No. I do covet my privacy."

Aaron stopped in front of a fallen tree trunk. "Please sit."

Seraphina sat down, and Aaron straddled the log, an arm's length from her.

He regarded her for a moment and whispered, "Seraphina, there is an ocean in you. I sail, but on the surface."

Seraphina's pulsed quickened. Her body trembled and ached. She searched his eyes, trying desperately not to get lost in them. It was there. The question. But unlike the museum, the air was hot and electric. Her body screamed for the surrender of the bedroom a few weeks earlier. Could he hear it? Could he feel it? She paled at the thought. *What is wrong with you?*

"You flatter me," she whispered.

Aaron's eyes flamed. "Truth is not flattery."

"We should keep walking. I would hate to ruin my already useless reputation." Seraphina rolled her eyes.

Aaron assisted Seraphina to her feet. "Reputation?"

"Yes. Didn't you hear? Don't you know who I am? I am the colonel's contraband."

"You are not my contraband!" Aaron grit his teeth.

"No? Well, it is better than being called your concubine. The ladies use the terms interchangeably, of course, when they think I cannot hear them."

Aaron took her hand, drawing her in close. He gently tilted her head up to look at him.

"You are not my concubine or my contraband. You are Seraphina André Phillipe Laurent. Let no one say different. I will not."

Seraphina held her breath and her tears. It hurt when the women referred to her as his whore. His property. To hear him say her name. To acknowledge her worth… She backed away.

"Thank you, Aaron. Your kindness is—"

Aaron put a finger to her lips. "Truth, my mysterious Seraphina, is not kindness. Come, let me see you home, lest we ruin both our reputations."

"Reputation? Do you know what they say about you?" Seraphina smiled.

"Yes. And it is all true." He grinned.

Seraphina laughed hard. "Then I should be a very happy contraband indeed."

"Indeed." Aaron chuckled.

*****

The boy was going to die. No matter how many times he said it to her, Seraphina refused to accept it. *You don't know that, Colonel. And if he does, I will care for him until his dying breath, however futile my care may be.*

Seraphina doted on all the young men, but for some reason, Liam was special. From the moment he cried out for his mother, Seraphina had been at his side. She bathed him, fed him, talked to him, read to him, slept by his bed, and tried every remedy she had in her repertoire to heal him…nothing changed. The pneumonia was slowly filling his lungs with fluid. He was drowning.

Seraphina folded Liam in her arms and rocked him gently as she sang to him. Her rich mezzo-soprano Ave Maria filled the ward.

All was still. All was quiet. Only her angelic voice and the raspy wheeze of his dying breaths filled the room. Tears fell from Seraphina's eyes onto his face. She wiped them away and continued her sorrowful entreaty to the Mother of God on behalf of the soul clutched to her breast.

Her voice faltered as his breathing slowed, and he slipped from her arms into the arms of the angels. Seraphina closed his eyes and kissed his forehead. A sound Aaron had heard at the bedside of many a dying child flooded the space where once an angel sang.

Aaron rushed to Seraphina's side. He ordered a steward to take the boy from her. Seraphina struggled to hold on to him, screaming his name. Aaron wrested her away and carried her sob-racked body from the house into the gardens.

He sat beneath a willow tree in a secluded area of the garden with Seraphina in his arms. Seraphina clung to him, burying her head in his chest. He remarked on how small she was in his arms. She felt too fragile, to delicate, to set down. He set propriety aside, instead choosing to keep her in his arms, drawing up his knees to cradle her.

Seraphina's sobs gave way to quiet cries and then deep, silent sadness. Aaron brushed the wet tendrils of hair from her face.

"I am sorry, Seraphina. I am deeply, deeply sorry for your loss. I become ill when I see these boys fighting a man's war."

"He wasn't a soldier. Liam was a boy. A sixteen-year-old boy. A child. His poor mother. My heart grieves for her." Seraphina began to cry.

Aaron held her tighter. "He had a mother in the end."

"I just didn't want him to be alone. He was so afraid. So afraid. He called out for her. For his mother, and in the night, he'd have nightmares." Seraphina trembled. "I had terrible nightmares as a child, and I don't know what I would've done if Mama Etienne had not been there. I know what it is like…to be alone, afraid. Eulalie says souls that die like that never rest."

"He is at rest, Seraphina. Your voice opened heaven for him, as it did for us all. I have never heard anything so beautiful."

He knew nothing about her, and yet he knew everything. Liam was unlike the others because he reminded Seraphina of herself. What in her life had left her so afraid that she'd give so much of herself to be sure another soul never felt as she did?

"I confess my cowardice. I avoid the young men…the boys. I should be a father to them in those moments, but I see my son, Solomon… They haunt me."

"You are not a coward," Seraphina stated emphatically. "You are a father who loves his son. You are a husband who lost a wife and child. You are no coward."

"Solomon has grown so much. My mother writes she can no longer look him in the eye. My son is becoming a man. I pray this all ends soon. Boys need their fathers to ensure they become proper men."

"You are his father. He will be a proper man."

"Thank you, Seraphina. Who is Etienne? I've never heard you speak of her before."

"My great-grandmother. She was a healer too. What you see me do, with the plants and such, is wisdom passed down through generations of women in my family."

"My mysterious Seraphina… Where is your family?"

"On the farm, where you left them," she answered. "We've been gone for a long time. I need to be sure Liam is buried properly."

Seraphina tried to leave Aaron's embrace, but he did not let go.

"Please tell me, Seraphina," Aaron pleaded.

He could feel her body stiffen. Fear and confusion danced in her eyes. Her lips parted, but no words came out.

Aaron placed a hand on either side of Seraphina's face, imploring her to speak. "Please."

Tears spilled over her already wet lashes. "Ils sont tous morts," she replied.

"All of them?" Aaron choked.

Seraphina fell into him and wept. He could do nothing but hold her in stunned silence.

"Ils sont tous morts." They're all dead.

CHAPTER NINE

Union Hospital – Harrison's Landing, Virginia
August 1862

The twilight of August brought with it temperate afternoons and a reprieve from the oppressive humidity of summer. Perfect weather for a Sunday afternoon journaling in the garden.

August 15th, 1862

I am tired. Everything hurts. Liam... I can't stop thinking about him. Aaron has ordered me away from the hospital for a week. I did not argue. Day in and day out, I watch men die because germ theory has yet to become a science fact. My treatments are good, but they aren't medicine. After some persuasion, Aaron has agreed to require instruments to be washed between uses. I didn't argue theory, just common sense. Why would you want to put something dirty in something you are trying to keep clean? The results spoke for themselves.

I am stuck here. I have no idea how to get home or if going home is even an option. Vanessa is gone. Auntie Mary is gone. Addie, Jed, everyone. Is this my life now? Alone in a world I don't know and don't understand with nowhere to go? As selfish as it sounds, I have considered trading my soul to the devil for a bath and a flush toilet on more than one occasion. And then there is Aaron. He's been kind, compassionate, and attentive to my needs. I do enjoy his company. I would be lying if I said I wasn't happier since coming to Harrison's Landing. But who wouldn't be? Life is relatively easier than it was on the farm, even if it is lonelier. None of that changes the fact that negotiations or not, he kidnapped me, is holding me against my will, and has assaulted me on more than one occasion. I am so confused...

"Seraphina! There you are!" Emma waved from the garden gate as she made her way over.

A bubbly brunette with curious brown eyes and porcelain buttermilk skin, Lady Emma Wheeler was a Jane Austen novel come to life. A Lydia Bennet, all grown up.

Lieutenant Marks's cousin Andrew, Emma's brother, was convalescing on one of the wards. She'd come to care for him and take him home to Philadelphia once he was well enough to travel.

As if heaven sent, Emma arrived the day after Liam died. To Seraphina's surprise, they had a lot in common, and unlike the other women, Emma didn't seem to mind befriending a contraband. Seraphina was grateful. She needed the distraction and the companionship.

"I didn't see you come from the house." Seraphina smiled.

"Of course, you didn't. You're hiding again." Emma sat and removed the needlepoint from her bag. "When I was a little girl, we played hiding games. I was terrible at hiding, but I had a nose like a bloodhound. No one could hide from me."

"I believe it." Seraphina laughed.

"Marcy is going to bring us tea, but look what I've found." Emma's eyes sparkled with anticipation.

"Are those peaches?" Seraphina giggled and clapped her hands like a grade-schooler. "Where did you find peaches?"

"That sutler hoards the good stuff." Emma handed Seraphina a peach. "Let's just say he won't any longer."

Seraphina ate heartily. Every vitamin C-starved cell in her body swore to never take food for granted again.

"How have you survived on what passes for food here? And why in God's name hasn't the colonel provided you with a lady's maid or made accommodations for you in the house?" Emma fired off her questions without missing an embroidery stitch.

"Emma, we are in the middle of a war. Gourmet meals are not on the menu. Neither are luxury accommodations, and I don't need a lady's maid; I can dress myself." Seraphina took another bite of her peach, determined to savor every bit.

"It is shameful what he's done to you. When you come to Philadelphia, we must have lunch. I adore Lady Katherine. She'll have you right as rain."

"I am not going to Philadelphia. When the war is over, or my services are no longer needed, I will be returning to my family."

"My dear Seraphina, you are as naïve as you are beautiful. When you arrive... Oh, Meredith is going to..."

"Who is Meredith?" Seraphina asked.

"A family friend." Emma's smile was both frightening and gleeful.

"My dear Seraphina, the Weld's are one of the oldest, wealthiest families in Philadelphia. The colonel's wife, Elizabeth, died some ten years ago now. He never remarried. He is not even rumored to have a mistress. You, my dear, have bewitched the most coveted bachelor in all of Philadelphia. You will be the talk of the set."

"I know he is a man of means, but I think bewitched is a strong word. We enjoy each other's company, nothing more. I am sure he has his reasons for not remarrying."

Seraphina thought about it. If he had reasons, she had no idea what they were. He had not shared them with her. Was that on purpose? It would have been nice to know she was walking around with Bruce Wayne. No wonder the other women despised her so.

"He has reasons. Good ones. Illegitimate children from title threaten the stability of the family and complicate inheritance. Any woman that married him would be doing so for title and money. Of course, most do, but I hear he was quite the romantic once. A Black paramour? How bold. How delicious. The set will be beside themselves. Even more so when they see how lovely you are."

"Who is the set?" Seraphina asked, bewildered.

"Society, my dear. The colonel will introduce you; I am sure. He would not be so open with you now if that was not his intent. Widowers often have a mistress in society. No one speaks of it, but it is done."

"Mistress! I am not his mistress. Or his whore. His concubine or any other name society wishes to bestow upon me," Seraphina snapped.

"Do not be vexed, my sweet Seraphina. In this man's world, we women do what we must. We look down on each other for it, but we all know the truth. The colonel is handsome, wealthy, and clearly in love with you." Emma patted Seraphina's hand. "Take heart."

Emma gabbed on, stitching as she went. Seraphina zoned out. It was all a blur. Good reasons? Illegitimate children? Inheritance? Society? There was so much she did not know. But she wasn't as naïve as Emma thought. Aaron did not love her. She was a Black woman with no means. If he hadn't remarried in ten years, there was nothing she had that would entice him, even if he could marry her. One thing was certain. She needed to stick close to Lady Emma Wheeler. Emma knew everything and everyone. She was a gossip, but not a malicious one. She had a kind heart and a no-nonsense way about her that Seraphina found refreshing.

"Oh, look, here is our tea." Emma turned from her embroidery to Marcy. "Thank you, Marcy."

Marcy set a tray of tea between them on the grass, curtsied, and without a word, walked over to the garden gate where Marshall was standing and sat down.

"I'll pour." Seraphina tipped the porcelain teapot. "It is a lovely service. The flowers and gold work are exquisite."

"Thank you. This is my travel service. I refuse to dine on tin plates. God only knows what is in those wretched tin cups. Marcy and I have lamented the lack of comforts here. And to think the colonel gave you a valet. A valet!" Emma shook her head in disgust.

Seraphina smiled over her shoulder at Marshall. "Emma, Private Dixon is not my valet. He is my escort and my friend."

"Escort?" Emma sipped her tea. "He follows you everywhere. You must tire of it."

"At first, it was difficult, but Private Dixon tries as best he can within his orders to give me space, and he retires in the evenings. But, truthfully, without him I…" Seraphina's voice trailed off.

Alone. The word left unsaid. Without Marshall's daily presence, she would be alone.

"You are resilient. My sweet Seraphina, dine with me this evening at the officer's dinner. Please. The cigar smoke and mindless male chatter are dreadful, and the other women are, shall we say, ill-mannered."

Seraphina coughed, the tea going down her windpipe. "Emma, you know that is not possible. And why would the women be that way toward you? I find you most delightful."

"Sweet Seraphina, I, too, find you delightful. It is because I've befriended you, of course. It matters not. Once we leave this dreadful place, they'll all be back, clamoring to return to my good graces. I am Lady Wheeler, after all. Half their husbands owe their fortunes to mine."

"You don't talk about your husband very much. Why?"

"I was a bride of convenience. Robert needed a wife young enough to produce an heir, and my father needed to solidify a business partnership. It was a good match."

A good match. Seraphina was horrified. Emma had been traded. Her marriage was a business transaction, and she was the payment.

Seraphina knew she should hold her tongue, but curiosity got the better of her, and she had to ask the questions burning in her head.

"Did you have a choice? I mean, was it a good match for you?"

"Choice? No dear." Emma chuckled. "I would have preferred a younger husband, but Robert is kind and provides for my every want and need. My son, Robert the third, is the love of my life. I am not as fetching as you. I could have fared far worse."

Emma's self-deprecation saddened Seraphina. She said a silent prayer of thanks for being born in 1978 and not 1840.

"You are gorgeous in and out." Seraphina smiled.

"Seraphina, your heart is goodness and light. Is it any wonder why the colonel is taken with you? Come, come to dinner."

"Emma, even if cigar smoke and mindless male chatter were of interest to me, I am not allowed."

"If you are accompanied by the colonel, no one will question it. I have the perfect dress." Emma flashed her signature elvish grin. "Look who's come to call."

Seraphina turned her head. Thomas was approaching, Marshall at his side.

"He is handsome, isn't he?" Emma whispered. "Not so much as his brother, but a pleasure to gaze upon indeed."

"I guess." Seraphina sighed, disappointed. *Where on earth am I going to hide now?*

"Good afternoon. Lady Wheeler. Miss Laurent." Thomas bowed his head slightly.

"Good afternoon, Lieutenant," they replied.

"Your presence has been missed, Miss Laurent. But then beauty always is." Thomas smiled warmly. "The men have inquired after you."

"That is kind of them. Please tell them I am well and will return to my duties once permitted."

"I will do so. Are you well?" Thomas asked, genuine concern in his tone.

It was odd. Outside of the customary pleasantries and the obligatory small talk, she and Thomas did not converse. Much of what Seraphina knew of him came from Aaron. Thomas was a good-natured rogue, loyal to a fault, and a bit of a court jester. Above all, he was Aaron's little brother, and he loved him dearly.

"I am. Thank you for your concern, Lieutenant. Would you care to sit?" Seraphina offered. "If you object to sitting on the ground, I understand."

"Not at all, Miss Laurent. A gentleman would be a fool to pass on the attention of such a lovesome woman as yourself." Thomas sat on his knees in front of them.

"I would offer you tea, but unfortunately, the service is set for two," Seraphina apologized.

"The hospitality of your smile is enough. Thank you," Thomas replied.

Seraphina laughed to herself. *Aaron was right. You are a rogue. You and Emma would be perfect for each other. The jester and his yenta.*

"Lieutenant Weld," Emma interrupted, "Miss Laurent and I were just discussing her attendance at the officers' dinner this evening. She was unsure of her invitation. Will you or the colonel be escorting her? Or do you gentlemen plan to leave her in that dreadful tent another evening? Surely not."

"It would be my pleasure to escort Miss Laurent with the colonel's permission. I will inquire," Thomas beamed.

Seraphina looked at them both. Emma's motives were clear. From day one, she'd been on a mission to free Seraphina from what she considered the prison of Aaron's keeping. If she had to throw a rock in the pond to do it, all the better. She would enjoy nothing more than sitting back and watching the ripples. Thomas wanted something too. Whatever it was, he'd decided to play the rogue to get it.

"Thank you, but no." Seraphina feigned a smile. "What brings you here, Lieutenant?"

"May I speak plainly?" he asked.

"Yes, please do." Seraphina gave an affirming nod.

"You, Miss Laurent. I am here to speak with you. Would you join me? Under the watchful eye of your escort, of course." Thomas gave Marshall a look. "He is very dedicated."

"No." Emma glared. "Lieutenant, you may step away from me if you would like a privy word, but Miss Laurent will not be joining you outside of my presence."

"Forgive me, Lady Wheeler. I forget myself. It would be most improper. Thank you. Miss Laurent, may I have a privy word? With your permission, Lady Wheeler."

Seraphina offered her hand for Thomas to help her to her feet. Marshall began to walk toward them. She waved him off.

"It is okay. I will be just over there."

Seraphina and Thomas walked away from Emma and Marshall. Once at a sufficient distance, Thomas spoke.

"Miss Laurent, Her Majesty's jewels aren't as well guarded as you."

"Yes. Noble and Aaron chose my escort well." Seraphina chuckled. "I do adore Private Dixon. Lady Wheeler too. What did you want to talk about?"

"You. I would like to get to know you better," Thomas replied.

"Why the sudden interest, Lieutenant? You've never shown any interest in doing so before. No one has."

"True. It is a cruel and grievous error for which I humbly ask your forgiveness."

Seraphina ignored his request for pardon. It felt contrived and insincere. He hadn't paid any attention to her before because she was of no consequence to him. Something changed. The question was, what?

"You didn't answer my question," she spoke.

"My brother told me you were forward." Thomas opened his hand. "Walk with me."

Seraphina followed; her irritation evident. "Forward? Lieutenant, what is it that you want? Please tell me or allow me to return to my afternoon."

"I will come to the point. I want to know what it is about you that has beguiled my brother so. I am very protective of my brother, Miss Laurent."

"I know you are, Lieutenant. Aaron has told me as much. The two of you are very close. I am sure he's told you about me, but there isn't much to tell."

"Aaron? You two are familiar, then?" Thomas raised an inquisitive brow.

"Lieutenant, I am not in the habit of discussing my personal life with people I do not know."

Thomas's eyes lit up with amusement. "It is worse than I feared."

"Feared? You think I am a danger to him?" Seraphina asked, incredulous.

"No, Miss Laurent. My brother is a danger to himself. You are but the crucible on which he has chosen to sacrifice his reputation and our family name."

"Crucible? Sir, I am openly referred to as a whore and a concubine. Forgive me if I find myself unconcerned about his reputation or your family name."

"My brother has kidnapped you and placed you under lock and key. That you care for him at all is telling…but you do."

"I do not! I—" Seraphina fell silent. Thomas's words hit her like a slug to the chest. She did care about Aaron. *Stockholm Syndrome. I am suffering from Stockholm Syndrome.*

"Do not dismay. I am certain the affection is mutual." Thomas laughed.

"I assure you, sir, there is nothing mutual or otherwise between the colonel and me." Seraphina stuttered, holding back tears. "I am here at the service of the Union Army, nothing more. I will return home like everyone else when my service is over."

"The colonel?" Thomas smiled. "And where is home, Miss Laurent? New Orleans? All is a mystery with you."

Seraphina's blood was on fire. He was mocking her and enjoying every minute of it. Confusion and frustration threatened to overwhelm her. She was going to be ill.

"Sir, you speak of that which you do not understand. You make suppositions and draw conclusions from ignorance, arrogance as it were. Your cruelty was not in taking no interest in me then, which I can forgive, but in doing so now, which I do not."

"Miss Laurent—"

"Je me sens mal. Excusez moi." Seraphina turned her back to him and fled.

"S'il vous plaît, attendez!" Thomas called after her.

Seraphina kept walking.

*****

Dinner was being held at the Westover Landing, about three miles east downriver from Harrison's Landing. The large dining room boasted floor-to-ceiling windows overlooking the river. A long mahogany table set with silver and china stood center stage, under a gilded relief ceiling and large crystal chandelier. An Aubusson rug warmed the mahogany floors, and floral-papered walls reached to the stark-white crown molding.

Aaron tugged at his collar. He hated wearing his uniform. For him, comfort was bare feet, trousers, and a cotton shirt. He smiled to himself. Seraphina preferred bare feet too. She often removed her shoes when on their walks.

He surveyed the room from his perch in front of the hearth. Senior officers in full dress were seated on either side, enjoying an after-dinner brandy, and discussing upcoming troop movements.

Six weeks had passed since the last engagement. President Lincoln ordered General McClellan back to Washington when he refused to leave Harrison's Landing. The Union had yet to best General Lee on the battlefield, and there was talk of combining the Army of the Potomac under McClellan with the Army of Virginia under General Pope. Aaron wasn't sure what that meant for the medical corps, but tonight he was uninterested in matters of war.

Seraphina did not join him for dinner. He had hoped to include her in the evening's festivities, but when he called on her, she said she was ill and begged his pardon. He did not believe her, but he didn't push the issue. Every day she had to navigate a world where she was treated with indifference and outright disdain. It was understandable she would not want to spend her evening doing the same. Even he knew the source from which she drew the grace and poise she showed daily could not be limitless. Fortunately, the men had warmed to her, and the officers were also beginning to.

"Colonel Weld! It is good to see you this evening." Emma greeted Aaron warmly and offered her hand. "I was sorely disappointed when I did not see Miss Laurent on your arm this evening."

"As am I, Lady Wheeler," Aaron said, taking her hand and bowing slightly. "She is feeling unwell and begs your pardon."

"Yes, her color was poor this afternoon in the garden." Emma opened her fan. "She simply asked to be excused—left Lieutenant Weld standing hat in hand. It was so sudden."

"The lieutenant was with you in the garden today?" he asked.

"Yes, Colonel. He called on Miss Laurent." Emma furrowed her brow. "I had to admonish him for his bad manners. He intended to converse with her unchaperoned!"

"Did he?" Aaron questioned. "Did he speak with her?"

"Yes. Too long, in my opinion. To be frank, the lieutenant is a bit of a rogue." Emma fanned herself.

"Indeed," Aaron replied curtly. "Lady Wheeler, would you excuse me?"

Aaron made a beeline for Thomas. Whatever he'd said to Seraphina was enough to make her ill. Knowing Thomas, he'd gone too far. Why was he talking to her anyway?

"Brother!" Aaron grabbed Thomas by the shoulder. "Would you join me on the veranda for a drink? Gentleman, I need to speak with Lieutenant Weld for a moment. Please excuse us."

"Yes." Thomas looked confused. "Excuse us, gentleman."

Aaron led Thomas out of the house by his shoulder, stopping in an area far from prying eyes and dropping ears.

Aaron released Thomas's shoulder. "What did you say to her?"

"To who?" Thomas questioned.

"What did you say to her?" Aaron demanded. "To Seraphina."

"I inquired as to the nature of your relationship and attempted to pierce the veil of secrecy she keeps woven so tightly around her."

"You what?!" Aaron shouted.

"She took offense and gave me a pointed and elegant come down." Thomas chuckled. "She feigned illness and excused herself before I could apologize. In French, no less. Mother would be thrilled. Miss Laurent has a fire about her. An intelligent beauty. I understand now."

Aaron grabbed Thomas by the jacket. "You understand nothing! You had no right!"

"Right? Is my name not Weld? Do I not have a responsibility to protect our family name? Am I not your brother? Release me."

Aaron dropped his hands. "I have done nothing to tarnish our family name."

"Oh really?" Thomas sipped his Scotch. "A Black paramour? You are our father's son."

"Brother, Seraphina is not my paramour. If you refer to her as such again, you will see just how much I am my father's son," Aaron growled.

"Do it!" Thomas threw his glass to the ground and crushed the shards with his boot. "You lie! You lie to me and to yourself! You have taken Miss Laurent from her family, restricted her movements, placed her under guard, and carried on with her in public. What does that make her?"

"I am trying to protect her, Thomas."

"Protect her? Who is going to protect her from you? Or you from yourself?"

"Seraphina is in no danger from me. I am not in need of, nor do I want, your protection," Aaron whispered through clenched teeth.

Thomas backed away. "You don't even know this woman, Aaron."

Aaron stepped forward. "I know her. I trust her. I do not owe you or anyone else an explanation as to how or why."

"Aaron, you have feelings for this woman."

"I brought her here. I have a responsibility for her person. Again, you confuse—"

"I confuse nothing," Thomas stated flatly. "If your pursuits were of a carnal nature, they'd be of no concern to me. Aaron, you need to end this. Give Miss Laurent a healthy sum for her services, recompense for her time of captivity, and send her back to her family." Thomas's tone was serious. "Brother, I care for your happiness more than anyone. There are other women."

"Miss Laurent is here at the service of the Union Army, nothing more. I will discharge her from her duties when her service is over and allow her to return home, as agreed."

"Liar!" Thomas screamed. "You don't believe that bullshit! And if one pressed her, I bet Miss Laurent would confess she doesn't either."

Aaron's eyes narrowed. "You will apologize to Miss Laurent for your behavior."

"You will never let her go. You forget I am your brother; I know you better than anyone."

"You will apologize. Good night."

Aaron stormed off. An acid-like anger crept along his veins, threatening to burn through his veneer of calm. He turned over the last ten years in his mind. There had been other women. Beautiful women. Women like Elizabeth. All qualified to be the next Lady Weld, but he didn't want another Lady Weld.

Sun waning, Aaron found his way to the stables. He had an aversion to carriages and preferred to take his own horse. A stable boy walked Shade out to him, and the horse nudged Aaron with his muzzle.

"I know. I know," Aaron murmured, patting Shade on the neck. "Me too."

Shade bobbed his head and scratched at the sandy clay beneath his feet. Aaron took his mount.

"Excellent suggestion."

The colonel kicked Shade into a run and then a sprint. Seraphina and Cotton Eye had spoiled them both. The ladies loved to run. They did not ride often, but when they did, every ride ended in a chase. Seraphina was never freer, never happier than when the two were in a run.

Aaron could hear Seraphina's laughter on the wind and see the amber of her eyes in the setting sun as he and Shade tore west down the dirt road.

CHAPTER TEN

James River, Virginia
August 1862

Flames turned night into day as fire raised the house and barn. Jed looked on, careful to remain in the shadows as he waded farther out into the river. An evening in the icy refuge left his skin dusky and his bones damp. He ached for the danger of warming dawn.

The gray coats had come late in the night. The fight had been brief. Outnumbered, the handful of Union soldiers on the farm were routed. Musket fire and the screams of those left behind chased them into the darkness, cloaked in a blanket of smoke.

"Shh." Jed covered Addie's mouth.

Startled awake, she mumbled under his hand, "Jed?"

"They here," Jed whispered in her ear. "In the barn. Get the girls and babies to the river. Stay in the deep reeds. I be there."

He kissed Addie on the head and sneaked out the back door into the night.

"Lizzie. Daisy." Addie shook the girls awake. "Quiet now. Swaddle them babies. We going to the river. The grays is here."

Daisy's eyes grew wide. "Mama?"

"I know." Addie tried to reassure her. "Hurry now."

"What about Rhea?" Lizzie cried. "We have to go to the barn and get Rhea."

"Hush now." Addie touched Lizzie's cheek. "She knows to meet us at the river. Now come. Hurry."

Jedidiah struggled against the current to retrieve his fishing platform. He'd built it to cast his handmade nets deeper into the river. He hoped it was sturdy enough to get the six of them down river.

Body heavy with chill, he pulled himself onto the raft and waited. Satisfied the soldiers had not seen him, he paddled into the reeds, where Addie and the children were waiting for him.

"Rhea?" Addie asked as she joined him on the raft.

"She ain't screaming no more," Jed replied solemnly. "They got the blues and others tied up."

"Merciful Lord," Addie cried, careful to choke back the wailing in her spirit.

"Addie, Lord seen fit to cover us. We thank him for his grace and move on."

Jedidiah pushed the laden down raft out into the river, and they floated into darkness.

Union Hospital – Harrison's Landing, Virginia
August 1862

August 21st, 1862

In the two months since Malvern Hill, I've focused all my time and efforts on organizing the medical corps and training surgeons. Seraphina's work with the nursing corps has been invaluable. The overall health of the troops has improved, and mortality rates have dropped. I was dismayed to find during morning report that a soldier died last evening from camp fever. He'd presented with symptoms that should have been obvious to any surgeon, but he was dismissed back to his unit. Not a few hours later, his fellow soldiers carried his fevered body back to the hospital. I've isolated the men in his company and handed down reprimands to all surgeons involved. Camp fever can spread quickly and devastate a fighting force. We will be fortunate to avoid a full-blown outbreak. That these men, these surgeons who could not rightly diagnose camp fever, will be tested in battle—an inevitability that will come soon enough—gives me pause. Seraphina…

"Permission to enter, sir?"

"Enter, Corporal." Aaron waved the soldier in, setting his journal down on the desktop.

"Sir, the River Watch is requesting your presence."

"Are there injured?" Aaron stood and moved over to the window overlooking the landing.

"No, sir. A group of contraband has arrived on a raft. Asking for Miss Laurent."

"A group?" Aaron questioned.

"More like a family, sir," the corporal answered. "Old folks and children."

"Where is Miss Laurent?"

"I told her, sir." The corporal laughed. "Sir, she jackrabbit before I get all the words out."

"Fuck all! You did not think to share this report with your commanding officer first?"

"No, sir. Beg your pardon, sir, but since they were asking for the lady, I didn't see no harm in relaying the message. Lieutenant Weld sent me to you."

"Follow me." Aaron stalked down the hall, the corporal struggling to keep pace.

Seraphina's found family had found her. Seraphina would be over the moon, and he'd have to be the ass to bring her crashing back to earth.

*****

"Addie!" Seraphina ran; tripping over her skirts, she fell into Addie's arms.

"Sweet girl, look at you! It does my heart good to see you." Addie held Seraphina, tears streaming down her face.

"Daisy! Lizzie! Jed!" Seraphina hugged them all. "My goodness, when did Cherub and Lula get so big? Oh, I've missed y'all so much."

Marshall lumbered up the pier, breathing heavily, "Little sister, you run like a jack rabbit. Almost as hard to catch."

"Everyone, this is my ever-dutiful shadow, Private Marshall Dixon. The colonel has charged him with following me everywhere I go. Marshall, this is my family."

"Good to meet y'all folks." Marshall offered Jedidiah his hand.

"Same." Jedidiah shook it.

"What happened, Jed? Why are you here? Where's Rhea?"

Jed cleared his throat. "Rebels come, Seraphina."

"Rebels?" Seraphina gasped.

"Yes. They burn everything…the barn, the house. Rhea is dead."

"Demons. They ain't fit to be called men. They did awful things." Daisy snapped angrily.

"She just scream and scream." Lizzie squeezed Cherub tight as if to protect him from the nightmare of her words. "I cover Cherub's ears... No child need to hear his mama like that."

"My god!" Seraphina stumbled back. "I am sorry. This is my fault. If we'd have gone... If I'd stayed—"

"No! If we go, it would be just like you say. Sickness kill us long fore the rebels. It's a blessing that Colonel takes you when he did. You be just like Rhea if he didn't. No, sweet girl... The fault is with the devil. He gwine do what he gwine do."

"Listen to Addie now. Don't you worry none." Jed held Seraphina's face. "Lord see us through. We come down the river like Moses. Gwine stay in the camps now."

"Miss Seraphina, we gots to get back," Marshall urged.

"It's too late." Seraphina cut her eyes. "Here comes Pharoah now. Y'all stay here. You will not go to the camps. I won't allow it. I will talk to the colonel. You will stay here with me."

Aaron was striding down the bank with Noble. She hadn't spoken to him since her garden conversation with Thomas. If they were going to talk now, it would be better if the conversation was private.

Seraphina rushed up the pier to meet him, with Marshall following.

"Colonel." Seraphina greeted Aaron with perfunctory courtesy. "My family—"

"No, Seraphina. They cannot stay," Aaron stated flatly.

"You aren't serious?"

"Yes, I am," he replied.

"Colonel, this is my family!" Seraphina pointed to everyone at the end of the pier. "I stay here. Noble stays here. Why can't they?"

"You and Noble do not stay here. You work here. The army will be on the move soon. There will be fewer troops here. All contraband not already in the employ of the Union or unable to work must go to Fort Monroe or Washington," Aaron answered.

"Okay, then they can work here. Jedidiah is a carpenter and blacksmith by trade, and Addie is a domestic."

"And the children?" Aaron asked.

"What about them? Lizzie and Daisy are a great help. They worked with me all the time."

"And the babies? Miss Laurent, I will not take two elders and four children, two of them being infants, on a miles-long march into battle. Even you can see the lunacy of such an act."

"If they go. I go." Seraphina glared.

"Woman, you will go nowhere. We have an agreement."

"I don't care!"

Aaron stood over her. "Private, escort Miss Laurent to my quarters. She is not to leave. Understood?"

"Yes, suh. Come on, little sister." Marshall took Seraphina gently by the arm and tried to lead her away.

"No! Colonel, please! Please don't send them away. Please!" Seraphina cried.

"Private! Take Seraphina to my quarters. Now!"

Seraphina ripped herself away from Marshall and stood still. Everything fell silent, and something broke inside. Something she could not name or even describe. But the something, whatever it was, poured lava-like rage throughout her entire body. Without a word, Seraphina slowly and deliberately began the walk back to her tent.

"Little sister?" Marshall called to her from behind. "Little sister, are you—"

Seraphina turned to face him and placed a finger on his lips. "Shh."

The two walked in silence until they reached the entrance to Aaron's tent. "Marshall, I would like to be left alone. I know you cannot go far, but please, if you would."

Marshall bowed his head. "Little sister, I'm sorry."

Seraphina touched his hand. "You have nothing to be sorry for."

Seraphina turned her back to him and stepped inside. She fell to her knees and then dropped face down on the ground. Dry wretches and soundless sobs racked her body as molten fury coursed through her veins. She couldn't breathe. There was nowhere to go, nowhere to run. Five months. She'd been in this hell of all fear and no freedom for five months. To have her family torn from her again…to be alone, again.

Seraphina sat up, drew her knees to her chest, and rested her head on them. Breathing deeply, she rocked back and forth, reciting her prayers to The Virgin—a soothing practice she learned from Mama Etienne to use when she was alone and troubled by her dreams. She'd since developed more adult meditative practices, drawing on the feminine energy, but when she was in real trouble, the ones from her childhood worked best.

But this wasn't a nightmare, and she was not a child. Her life, this life, was not her own. Her life, the one the universe ripped from her, was a distant dream…gone, maybe forever.

*****

Aaron observed Seraphina's family as he came down the pier. The trauma of their ordeal was written all over their faces. The corporal who came to fetch him filled him in on the general details. Rogue rebels attacked the farm. Seraphina's family escaped under the cover of darkness. They were the only survivors.

Seraphina advocated fiercely for her family, just as she had the day they'd met, and he'd taken her from them the first time. Her pleas then were determined, defiant… Today, they were desperate. She was willing to give up every comfort and live with them in a camp rather than be parted from them. If he sent them away, orders or no, Seraphina would never forgive him. He would have to shackle her to his side to keep her from running away. Or he could do what Thomas suggested, give her a sum for services rendered and send her back to her family. Neither outcome was tenable.

"Noble." Aaron sighed. "I have need of you."

"Yes, sir." Noble walked along Aaron's side. "You want me to arrange for the family to stay in camp?"

Aaron smiled at Noble. "You are a wise man, Noble."

"No, sir, just figure like you did. Miss Seraphina settle down if her kin folk close. More hands around won't hurt none. Even if it's just for a little while."

"Indeed. Move myself and Miss Laurent into the main house. Give them her tent and take mine down. I will speak with them."

"Yes, sir." Noble nodded. "And work, sir?"

"I will speak with them first."

Aaron strolled the few feet to the end of the pier to meet the family. To his surprise, they spoke first.

"Beg your pardon, Colonel." Jed stepped out in front of the group. "We don't want to cause no trouble for Miss Seraphina."

"You have not. Jedidiah, is that correct?" Aaron asked.

"Yes, suh, Jedidiah Brown. This here my wife—"

"Addie," Aaron interrupted. "And if I recall, the little one there is Lizzie."

"Yes, suh!" Jed beamed. "This is Daisy, and the babies are Lula and Cherub."

"This is my valet, Noble." Aaron pointed to Noble. "He will get you all settled.

I understand you are a carpenter and blacksmith, Jedidiah. Is that true?"

"Yes, suh." Jedidiah lifted his chin with pride. "Been smithing and working wood since I was old enough to hold a hammer and stoke fire."

"And Addie, you are a domestic?" Aaron asked.

"A domestic?" Addie replied, puzzled. "I don't know. I run the mistress's kitchen. The men have full stomachs when I get through."

"Good. Jedidiah, you report to the infantry commander in the morning. Addie, you to the kitchens. Noble will show you where after you get settled. This will be temporary. As I explained to Miss Laurent, you will go to Washington when the army moves on. Miss Laurent will remain with the army until her service is done."

"Bless you, suh. Bless you." Jed hugged Addie.

"Indeed. Noble, I will leave you to it. I have other matters to attend to."

*****

Eager to tell Seraphina about the arrangements, Aaron stepped into his tent and froze. Seraphina was seated on the ground, drawn up and rocking. He had expected her to be angry, but not this. The sight of her at his feet shook him to his core.

"Dear God!" Aaron knelt beside her. "Seraphina."

She raised her head to meet his gaze. Her murderous look stilled him. She was unrecognizable.

"Tu es un homme vil et méprisable," Seraphina whispered, trembling.

His French was rusty, but her words were clear. She hated him.

"Seraphina, I—"

"Do you think I will stay here and save the lives of white men while my family suffers? I will burn this camp and everything in it to the ground."

"I did not send them away."

"What?"

"I did not send them away," Aaron repeated. "Your family will be in camp until the army moves."

"May I stay with them?" she asked.

"You may take leave to see your family as often as your duties permit. Private Dixon must accompany you as always, and you must return to the house before dusk."

"House?"

"Yes. I need to be closer to the other officers. You will be moving into officers' quarters with me. It is not safe for you to stay in the camp alone. I cannot protect you if you are not with me."

"May I go back to my tent now?"

"Seraphina."

"Aaron, thank you for allowing my family to stay. May I go back to my tent now?"

"Seraphina, you are ill. Please let me—"

"No. Please leave or allow me to." Tears filled her eyes. "Please."

Aaron reached for her. "Seraphina."

She turned from him, drew herself into a tighter ball, and continued to rock. Aaron fell back on his heels, helpless.

Emma. I need Emma.

Aaron bolted. A feeling he'd thought long extinguished filled his chest, and the pain was suffocating. Fear. It was consuming him. His heart raced, and he quickened his step.

Emma was seated on the home's veranda with her brother Andrew. Andrew was well enough to sit in a wheelchair now. The two would be leaving soon.

"Lady Wheeler," Aaron called to Emma from the yard.

"Colonel?" Emma replied. "You look absolutely dreadful."

"Yes, sir, you do," Andrew added. "Is everything all right?"

"No. Lady Wheeler, Miss Laurent… Miss Laurent has taken ill. I need your assistance."

"Ill? Colonel, I am—"

"Now, Lady Wheeler. It is most urgent."

"Oh my. Please take me to her. Marcy, come, let us go. I may need you. Brother, I will see you this evening."

*****

Aaron opened the tent flap. Seraphina was where he'd left her, rocking and crying.

"Lady Wheeler, this is not a malady… I thought as a woman you might—"

"My god!" Emma exclaimed. "She is in a fit! What happened?"

"We had a disagreement," Aaron explained. "She will not allow me to help her. I thought she may be more amenable to your assistance."

"Indeed! Get out!" Emma snapped at him. "I will come for you when I have things well in hand."

"Lady Wheeler, I will stay," Aaron bit back.

"If you must mill about, make yourself useful. Bring me a spirit. A strong one. And you can wait…outside."

Aaron did as she asked. When he returned to his tent, he waited outside, as instructed. He watched Marcy run back and forth between his tent and Seraphina's with items from her chest. It was an hour before Emma and Marcy emerged.

"Colonel. Seraphina is sleeping now. She needs rest, a lady's maid, and the hell out of these wretched tents."

"Thank you, Lady Wheeler." Aaron smiled, relieved. "I will see to it."

"Good. And Colonel, Miss Laurent is not a common maid. Do not treat her as such. I will look in on her tomorrow…at the house. Yes?" Emma punctuated her question with a stern look that made it clear it wasn't really a question.

"I am sure Miss Laurent will appreciate the company, Lady Wheeler. Good day."

"Good day, Colonel."

Aaron entered the tent quietly, not wanting to wake her. Seraphina lay sleeping soundly on his cot. From the look of the bottles on the table, Emma had given Seraphina a shot or two of whiskey mixed with a tincture of blue lotus flower. He recognized it as the new medication they were giving prior to surgeries to reduce chloroform use. Just one of the many medicinal remedies Seraphina had introduced to the hospital. Her apothecary was a coveted commodity.

Aaron sat on the ground next to her. He wanted to touch her, stroke her hair, hold her like he'd done after Liam's death. He suppressed the urge and rose to his feet.

"My mysterious Seraphina, you will be the death of me." He sighed and walked out.

CHAPTER ELEVEN

Harrison's Landing, Virginia
August 1862

The room was sparsely furnished but had the basics and a small window that overlooked the gardens. Seraphina suspected the room had once been a pantry or storeroom. The window was for natural light, not the view.

Seraphina guessed Emma had something to do with the upgrade in her accommodations. The image of Lady Emma Wheeler shaming the great Colonel Aaron Weld into improving her living conditions brought a smile to Seraphina's face and gratefulness to her heart. She was long over the tent life. Marshall was happy too. His pallet in front of her door was a step up for him.

Seraphina wished Addie, Jed, and the kids could stay in the house. She spent every moment she wasn't in the hospital with Addie in the kitchens, playing with the babies, reading to the girls, or taking meals to Jed. She had little time for anything else, including Aaron. But he was always present. And for reasons she could not explain, she found it comforting.

Seraphina had just finished her evening routine and slipped into her chemise when there was a knock at the door.

"Marshall? What is it?" Seraphina called through the door.

It opened, and Seraphina grabbed a blanket to cover herself. "I did not give permission for you—"

She stopped. It was Aaron. He filled the doorway, and he looked different. Gone were the uniform jacket and high boots. In their place, an open cotton shirt, bare feet, and trousers. His hair was loose and, like his body, freshly washed. Spicebush and basswood. She'd scented his soaps with them. Male and potent, the fragrance enveloped her. All that remained of the Aaron she knew was the light of his piercing blue eyes.

Seraphina was stuck. She could feel her nipples harden and a deep ache, creating dampness between her legs. She clutched the blanket closer. This was not the man she'd seen in the museum.

"I did not give you permission to enter my room. A gentleman does not—"

"I am afraid you force me into ever more ungentlemanly behavior." Aaron smiled. "I want to talk to you."

"I don't want to talk to you."

"Yes, you do," he replied. "I am humbled daily by Noble's kind wisdom, and I find Private Dixon's playful commentary on life amusing. But I know neither possess the acumen to satisfy your intellect, and it has been days. You are bored. And frankly, so am I."

He was right. She was bored, and she did miss talking to him. *So, what!* she thought to herself.

"Colonel, I am not dressed to entertain callers."

Aaron stepped toward her. "I will wait outside while you dress if that makes you more comfortable. Or you can stay wrapped in that ridiculous blanket."

"Would you say that to any other woman? Would you enter the room of any other woman as you did mine?" Seraphina asked angrily.

"No, I would not. You are not any other woman." Aaron moved closer.

"Why, because I am your concubine? Your captive? Thomas says—"

"Thomas is a fool. If he weren't my little brother, I'd…" Aaron bit his tongue. "I told you; you are none of those things to me."

"Then what am I, Aaron?" Seraphina asked. "You said you wanted to talk, talk."

"Seraphina, you will be the death of me," he replied quietly. "Give me the blanket."

"No. You kidnapped me! You are holding me hostage!" Seraphina shouted.

"I did. I am." Aaron took another step toward her. "Give me the blanket."

"No. And my family? I will never forgive you!"

"I would be disappointed if you did." Aaron brushed her cheek. "Give me the blanket."

She wanted to hate him. She hated herself for not hating him. Hated herself for wanting him. But she did. Stockholm Syndrome or no, everything in her wanted to give him the blanket.

"I can't," Seraphina whispered.

"You can," he whispered back.

"You did this on purpose." Seraphina tried to step back but found she couldn't move. "You came here on purpose."

Aaron closed the space between them. "I did. But I will not take it from you. Give it to me."

Seraphina closed her eyes and let the blanket fall to her feet. She shivered from the sudden cold and the anticipation of what surrender would bring. Aaron looked at her for a long while. A need-fueled impatience dewed her skin.

"Raise your hands," Aaron requested.

Seraphina did as he asked. Aaron slipped her chemise over her head and dropped it on the floor with the blanket. He waited again, simply gazing on her nakedness. She began to tremble. The dampness between her legs, now a pool, threatened to run down her legs. Her nipples were taut and stood erect, begging to be touched. But he didn't touch them. Instead, he removed his shirt and trousers.

"Oh." Seraphina's breath caught.

She'd never seen a cock that size, let alone had one. It would hurt, but she didn't care. She wanted every fat, thick, painful inch of it. Aaron must have heard her thoughts because he tried to reassure her to the contrary.

"Seraphina, I will not hurt you. Unbraid your hair."

Fingers shaking, Seraphina quickly loosened, and finger combed her hair. It fell down her back and shoulders.

Aaron curled a ringlet in his fingers. Lowering his head, he breathed in. "Mmm…magnolia blossoms. You always smell of flowers. Your hair. Your skin. It is intoxicating. A man cannot breathe the air without thoughts of you."

"Aaron, please," Seraphina moaned, breathless.

He tilted her head back. "Take me in your hand."

Seraphina wrapped her hand around his shaft, her fingers barely closing. The feel of him made her dizzy. She could feel his need as he grew harder and thicker in her hand.

Aaron placed his hand over hers. "I lie awake every night like this… for you."

Seraphina bit her lip. "Kiss me. Kiss me like you did on the bed."

Aaron lifted her onto the bed, and it creaked under their weight as he rested on top of her.

"Like this?" Aaron pressed his lips to hers, parting them with his tongue. He held her there until she began to gasp for air and released her.

"Yes. More," she panted, chest heaving.

Aaron kissed her again. This time he rolled her nipples between his thumb and finger, and she moaned into his mouth, the orgasm cresting without warning. He replaced his fingers with his tongue, sucking, licking, and kneading her breasts. Tears rolled down her face. "Aaron! Please! Please! I can't! I can't!"

Aaron placed a hand lightly around her neck. "You can and you will. I will have you until dawn and every day after."

He ran his hand down the length of her body. "Open your legs."

Seraphina arched against his hand, kissing him feverishly. She was on fire. Nothing mattered.

Aaron palmed her sex, exploring her tight, wet depths with one finger, then two, then three. Seraphina moaned, pleasure washing over her.

"Seraphina. My mysterious Seraphina. Have you had lovers before?" Aaron caressed her ear, coming to rest between her legs.

"No," she murmured.

"You will have no others."

Aaron impaled her in a swift and brutal stroke. Seraphina screamed as his shaft filled and stretched her unexpectedly. He paused to let her settle around him.

Seraphina thrust up to meet him, closing her legs around his waist. "More."

"Yes. Now you are ready," Aaron mouthed against her ear.

He drove deep, with a measured, insistent rhythm. Seraphina rode him from below, forcing him into an ever-increasing, deeper cadence. She could feel his breath grow ragged as she rested control from him. Pained and pleasured cries escaped her lips, and he answered with tortured groans of his own.

Seraphina draped her arms around his neck and pulled him down on top of her. Aaron rolled over, bringing her with him. He pinned her hips in place and thrust upward with abandon. Seraphina leaned over him, feeding him the sweetness of her mouth, her tongue, and her breasts. She was lost in him.

Aaron sat up, Seraphina still in his arms. He locked her arms behind her back and tugged at her areolas as wave upon wave of pleasure rocketed through her.

"Say it," Aaron kissed her neck. "I want to hear my name from your lips."

"Aaron," she breathed.

"Say it again," he pleaded.

"Aaron."

He pushed her onto her back and sheathed every inch inside her until she felt his balls touch her sensitive skin. He sucked in her mouth, harder than before. Seraphina writhed beneath him, whimpering with every thrust. Her body convulsed and fell limp as Aaron growled, his seed filling her before he too collapsed.

Seraphina could feel him pulsing inside, still firm. "Aaron."

He withdrew. "Did I hurt you?"

Seraphina slid from under him and turned on her stomach. Resting her hands beneath her head, she faced him. "A little."

"I said I would not, but I-I lost control. I should have been gentler. I am not most men."

"No, you are not. I am okay. I promise." Seraphina placed a hand on his cheek. "I wanted so much to hate you."

"I was afraid you did." Aaron kissed her.

"No. I do not. When you look at me like you are now…your eyes are so blue, I feel I'm adrift at sea."

Aaron lay down and feathered her back with his fingers. "Your eyes are the sunset, for which I curse the dawn. You, my mysterious Seraphina, are beauty's perfection."

"Perfection? That is a high bar. A woman could fall far. You are pleasing to the eye…and the body." Seraphina blushed. "What now?"

"Sleep, my mysterious Seraphina. Sleep."

"And here I thought you wanted to talk to me?" Seraphina laughed.

Aaron placed a finger to her lips. "We can talk again tomorrow."

Seraphina curled herself around him. Her finger traced the cuts and curves of his muscular chest and arms. For the first time since waking in the field, her mind did not race. The forever knot in her stomach was gone. She felt safe. Sleep came easy.

*****

Shadows danced in the flicker of the oil lamps as Thomas made his way down the narrow hallway to Aaron's quarters. He rapped lightly on Aaron's door. "Permission to enter."

A bleary-eyed Noble opened the door. "Evening, Lieutenant. Colonel ain't here."

"Where is he?" Thomas insisted. "We have need of him at headquarters."

"Beg your pardon, Lieutenant. You may not want to bother Colonel just now. I tell him you come calling when he free."

"Noble, I understand the colonel may have told you he was not to be disturbed, but I assure you this is most urgent." Thomas looked from Noble's cot to Aaron's empty bed. "How long has the colonel been gone?"

"A long time," Noble replied.

Thomas smiled. "Miss Laurent?"

"Yes, sir." Noble returned the gesture. "Her room is down the hall a ways."

"Thank you, Noble. I will impose upon the colonel. Please prepare for his return. I am afraid duty beckons."

"Yes, sir." Noble nodded.

*****

The sound of hushed, excited voices woke Aaron. Thomas was in the hall, talking with another man. Aaron and Thomas hadn't spoken an unnecessary word since their fight at the party, and although Thomas had tried to apologize for his behavior in the garden, Seraphina would have none of it. From either of them.

Aaron kissed Seraphina on the forehead and slipped from her embrace. Her body quivered in protest of his absence, so he retrieved the blanket from the floor and covered her. It was then that he noticed the blood stains on the sheet; he'd deflowered her. The swelling of pride and possession that filled him was tempered only by the evidence that he'd hurt her. They'd made love late into the night. He'd never behaved so wantonly with a woman. He'd never had a woman take to him so eagerly.

Seraphina's passion pushed him to the edge of control and beyond. It scared him. He'd vowed never to love another woman. And for ten years, quiet affairs with no attachments and no expectations had satisfied his needs. He was content—until now. Seraphina reminded him there was more, so much more.

Aaron washed up in the basin and found his clothes. He dressed quickly and stepped into the hall, not wanting Thomas to knock and wake Seraphina.

"You have need of me?" Aaron winced at the lightness of his tone.

"Yes. We do," Thomas replied.

Aaron couldn't help but notice the amusement on Thomas's face as they walked toward his quarters. Curious and jocular by nature, Aaron never could stay angry with Thomas for long.

"Would you remove that ridiculous grin?" Aaron groaned.

"Do I detect the scent of flowers and satisfaction? I have never seen your countenance as light. Or your mood. She is a wonder."

"Your lack of propriety is only exceeded by your skill as a surgeon, Lieutenant."

"I am only making an observation, Colonel," Thomas continued, beaming.

"Observe your tongue, Lieutenant. Report?"

"Pope engaged Lee and Jackson at Manassas not two days ago. He had to retreat. We are scattered to the winds. We took heavy losses."

"God damn Pope!" Aaron shook his head. "Didn't General Halleck send reinforcements?"

"Yes, the third and fifth corps. We are moving north to reinforce the Army of Virginia; General McClellan has resumed command."

"Shit." Aaron opened his room door.

"Sir. All is ready." Noble nodded.

"Thank you, Noble. I know it is early, but Miss Laurent has need of a lady's maid. See to it she has one and that Private Dixon resumes his post. I do not want her disturbed."

"Sir, I be sure to find a maid before Miss Seraphina lift her head," Noble replied.

"A lady's maid?" Thomas's ears peaked. "What next? Are you going to make her a Weld?"

Aaron ignored the question and continued to dress with Noble's assistance. What was he going to say? The truth was impossible.

"My god!" Thomas gasped. "You would if you could? You truly would."

"Does it matter?" Aaron pulled on his coat. "I cannot."

"Does it matter?" Thomas crossed his arms in frustration. "You cannot be serious, Brother. Of course, it matters."

"No, it doesn't, Lieutenant. We have more pressing matters to discuss. Gather the medical corps officers and meet me at headquarters," Aaron ordered. "I need to converse with leadership to discuss our plan of movement. Let's go."

Damn. Aaron cursed to himself as he and Thomas left. Less than two weeks ago, he'd told Seraphina her family could stay until the troops moved. Now he had to tell her it was time for them to leave. He'd planned to secure a place for them in Philadelphia rather than have them go to the contraband camps in Washington. Now, they would have to go to Washington until he could bring them to Philadelphia. The temporary nature of the situation necessitated by the war would make no difference to Seraphina. *Fuck all.*

*****

Seraphina peered out the window into the gardens. Aaron was gone. Not that she expected him to be there. He was the surgeon-in-chief; sleeping in was not a luxury afforded him.

It had been a long night of lovemaking. She wasn't sure what time in the predawn morning they'd collapsed from emotional and physical exhaustion. That was last night. Now, alone in the light of day, she felt something she never had before…vulnerable. Had she given away what little respect she had in one night of passion? Was she a fool to think she ever had his respect in the first place?

"Miss Seraphina?" Minnie cracked the door slightly.

"Minnie, are you alone?" Seraphina answered back.

"Yes." Minnie walked through the door, carrying a bucket of hot water and several clean rags.

A little more than average height for a woman, Minnie's willowy frame and sun-kissed tawny skin told Seraphina Minnie was a master's child…or the child of one. And now, now she was her lady's maid. Another gift from Lady Emma Wheeler, an unwanted one.

Minnie poured the water into the barrel bath. "You go on and wash fore the water get too cold. I take these sheets to the wash and get Noble on some tea and biscuits. I be back to help you dress."

"Minnie, I don't need tending to. I am not a child." Seraphina stepped into the barrel. The water only went up to her calves. Right now, she would give anything for a long soak in a tub. "And I am perfectly capable of doing my own laundry. You don't need to—"

"Noble said you was a proud one. Give Colonel a world of trouble." Minnie pulled the sheets from the bed. "From the looks of it…you won't be troublesome no more."

"What! You, you think he tamed me! Is that what people think of me?"

"Folk won't think nothin of it. Colonel say you to stay here today." Minnie walked out.

*****

Aaron knocked on the door to Seraphina's quarters. He'd been distracted by thoughts of her all day. Thomas had noticed and taken great pleasure chiding him about it, but he hadn't been this content in a very long time. "Seraphina, may I enter?"

"Yes," she answered.

Aaron walked through the door. "Good, it looks like Minnie laid things out for you as I asked. How are you?"

"I don't know," Seraphina replied curtly. "I may be bold, Aaron, but I am also modest. I would not share something of such a personal nature with others. I could have prepared my own bath and washed my own sheets."

"Noble is my valet. He is discreet. You need not worry. Minnie understands the nature of things."

"Understands the nature of things?" Seraphina glared at him.

"Seraphina, you misunderstand. I will try to explain. To pleasure you in my bed and then leave you to your own devices would give you and others the impression that you were nothing more than my whore. A gentleman does not behave in such a manner. You are not my paramour or my concubine. I have no intention of allowing you or anyone else to believe so."

"Everyone will think it anyway. If I had the respect of anyone, I am sure not to have it now. I doubt even you would respect me now, seeing how I came so easily to your bed."

"You did not come easily to my bed." Aaron chuckled. "My mysterious Seraphina, you don't come easy to anything. I assure you, your reputation is unblemished. You have had no other man, a fact to which I can attest. I do not think any less of you. My admiration and respect for you remain unchanged."

Seraphina began to cry. "This world makes no sense. I am lost here. At home, I know who and what I am because I define myself. Here there are rules and customs that dictate those things."

Aaron sat on the floor beside her. He was seeing a side of her he hadn't before. The bold and fearless Seraphina he'd come to know and love sat before him, exposed and unsure of herself.

"Seraphina, I fear your family has done you a great disservice. Your grandfather's attention to your academics is admirable. It is most unfortunate he was not as diligent in your social instruction. We will deal with that later."

Seraphina dried her eyes. "I should get to the hospital and set things in order for the nursing corps."

"You will do no such thing." Aaron kissed her forehead.

"Aaron, I am perfectly capable of doing my job. You aren't resting. Why should I?"

"You should because I am telling you to do so," he replied.

"Aaron, I—"

"Seraphina, you need to rest. You are upset. Last night, I let my passions get the better of me."

"I am fine. Your passions were only matched by my own."

"Seraphina, ladies do not say such things." Aaron smiled. Her passions *had* matched his own; she was a phenomenal lover.

"Ladies, ladies, ladies. What do ladies do? Don't tell me. I will behave as a lady should, dress as a lady should, and do whatever other ridiculous things a lady should in public. However, I will be who I am here, and I expect you to do the same. So do not temper your passions, for I assure you, I will not temper mine."

Aaron pulled her into his arms and kissed her deeply. "My mysterious Seraphina, you will be the death of me."

"Then I guess you will die an early, satisfying death." She grinned.

"I will." Aaron laughed. "I will."

Virginia, Peninsular Campaign September 1862 – December 1862

CHAPTER TWELVE

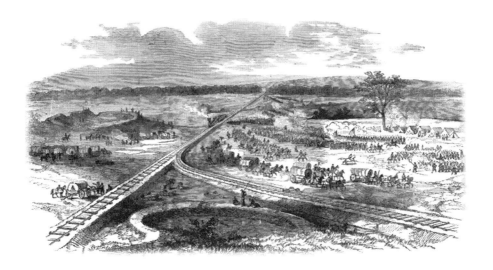

Battle of Bull Run – Field Hospital – Manassas, Virginia
September 1862

September 3rd, 1862

I had to relieve myself just now. I couldn't stand any longer. But I am so tired I can't sleep. After a two-day forced march north, we found what was left of The Army of Virginia. A forced retreat and days of vicious fighting have left a relentless river of wounded in their wake. The tidy streets and alleyways of Harrison's Landing have been replaced by a scattering of wedge tents and half shelters. The house is far less grand too. We've set up the field hospital on the edge of what was the battlefield, along a creek called Bull

Run. The hospital tent is beyond capacity, and still, they come. Covered in mud with vacant looks in their eyes, many of the men scarcely look like soldiers at all. It is enough to hollow the soul. Aaron has been on his feet for hours; neither of us has slept more than a few hours in the last twenty-four. It has been six days since the battle, and you'd think it happened yesterday from the state of things. To stay at my side, Marshall has taken on orderly duties. Noble is always after me to eat and rest, but who can think of food and sleep when faced with this carnage? Images of broken, mutilated bodies haunt my dreams. Men scream for mercy as their limbs are severed. The sound echoes in my ears like a ringing you can't escape. The stench of death and rot turns my stomach. I wade ankle-deep in bloody mud, trying to provide aid and comfort. The men reach for me like scared children. Some of them are children, like Liam. I am afraid. Afraid all the time.

*****

A triage tent was set up outside the main hospital tent for the treatment of minor wounds and to take pressure off the main hospital. It was small, with room for only a handful of soldiers at a time. A makeshift table, made from two boards over two barrels, served as the bed. Two other barrels were used as workspaces for Seraphina's pestles, mortars, and other treatment tools. She ran the triage center with the aid of two stewards, Marshall, and a small army of contraband, she'd given a crash course on finding and preparing the plants she needed for her treatments. The flow of injured men was non-stop. It wasn't uncommon for her to spend twelve hours a day or more treating the injured.

"You're going to be fine." Seraphina finished applying the soldier's bandage. "Keep the wound clean. Come back tomorrow, and I will apply more salve."

"Thank you," the soldier replied, bending his arm at the elbow, testing the bandage.

"You are welcome," Seraphina replied, wiping her brow.

Tired and a little dizzy, Seraphina was at the end of her tether. She'd long since lost track of time and couldn't remember the last time she'd eaten or slept.

"Marshall, I'm going to…" Seraphina stood and fainted.

"Somebody fetch a doctor!" The bandaged soldier shouted, gently placing Seraphina on the table.

Marshall ran to Seraphina's side. He turned to one of the contraband orderlies. "Please go find Colonel Weld. Tell him Miss Seraphina sick. I have orders not to leave her."

The orderly ran from the tent.

*****

"Suh! Suh!" The orderly rushed into the hospital tent, calling for Aaron. "Private Marshall send me to tell you Miss Seraphina in a bad way."

"Bad way?" Aaron asked. "Where is she?"

"Y-yes, Suh. She in th-the little tent," The orderly stuttered.

Aaron stepped away from the surgical table. "Lieutenant, take over here. I will return."

"Colonel!" Thomas snapped. "This man—"

"Lieutenant, take over here," Aaron ordered abruptly and stalked out of the tent, the orderly on his heels.

Upon arriving at the triage tent, he found a semi-conscious Seraphina laid out on a few planks rigged for a bed with Marshall at her side.

"She faints straight away, suh."

"I cannot treat her here." Aaron lifted Seraphina from the table. "I am going to take her back to our quarters. "Go inform Lieutenant Weld of what has happened. Tell him I will return when I have things in order, and find Noble."

"Yes, sir. Miss Seraphina gwine be all right?" Marshall asked, holding her hand.

"We'll see," Aaron answered. "Now go."

*****

Aaron made his way to the house, Seraphina in his arms. He ignored the stares and whispers of the men as he passed. A brewing cauldron of condemnation threatened to boil over when Seraphina took up permanent residence in his quarters. He'd have to confront the issue eventually, but not today.

Aaron carried Seraphina inside their room and set her on the bed. He made quick work of her skirts and blouse, then soaked rags from the basin on the table and put them around her neck, forehead, and chest.

Noble poked his head through the door. "Colonel, sir, you call for me? Marshall says Seraphina sick."

"When did she eat last?" Aaron asked.

"Colonel, I tell her to eat," Noble answered. "She nibbles a little. Says she too busy. Miss Seraphina got her own mind."

"Bring water," Aaron ordered.

"Yes, sir." Noble excused himself.

"Miss Seraphina got her own mind." Noble was right; she did. She worked as hard, if not harder than he did, without complaint. Unfortunately, he had allowed Seraphina's fierce independence and self-reliance to cloud his judgment. A lapse he intended to rectify immediately.

"Aaron, what are you doing here?" Seraphina sat up. "Where am I?"

"Marshall sent for me when you fainted in the hospital," Aaron answered.

"I fainted?" Seraphina asked, her brow wrinkling.

"You aren't eating?" Aaron asked, concerned.

"Honestly, Aaron, I just get busy and forget to eat," she answered.

"Water, sir." Noble walked in with a craft. "It's been boiled."

"Thank you, Noble." Aaron took the craft from his hand. "Please find Private Dixon."

Noble nodded and left.

"Drink this." Aaron offered Seraphina the water.

She grabbed the craft and gulped it until Aaron stopped her.

"I'm sorry. I guess that wasn't very ladylike." She smiled.

"Seraphina, you are selfless to a fault. As one responsible for your well-being, you leave me little choice but to temper your charity. You will rest until further notice."

"Aaron, I promise to take better care of myself. You need me. You and Thomas can't run this hospital alone without the triage tent."

"I don't deny it," he replied. "We will make do."

"Okay," she said. "For today. We will discuss this again tomorrow."

Aaron never allowed his countenance to betray his thoughts or emotions. If he had, the relief of her compliance would have been apparent.

"Tomorrow then." Aaron kissed her gently. "Rest. I will return later this evening to look in on you."

When Aaron left the room, Private Dixon was waiting for him.

"No need worry, suh, I back at my post. Miss Seraphina gwine be all right?"

"Yes. Private. She is not to leave this room."

*****

A serenade of crickets accompanied the bugle that bid the camp to bed as the sun's setting dropped the temperature precipitously. Aaron began the trek to the house. Seraphina had been right; running the hospital without her was damn near impossible. Her ability to anticipate the needs of both surgeon and patient was invaluable. Her smile could cure even the sourest of moods. Her presence made the wretched work bearable.

The scent of flowers and honey met him at the door to his quarters. He smiled. Seraphina bathed more than any person he knew. She had an oak barrel cut in half specifically for the purpose. The wildflower and witch hazel-infused water she rinsed her hair with and the lavender-scented beeswax butter she used on her skin gave her the aura of an earthen goddess. To his jealous irritation, the men often commented on it. A sergeant once told him, "It's like walkin' through Eden when she comes by."

Aaron opened the door. Seraphina's hair fell freely about her shoulders. Her chemise, barely clinging to her collar bones, left her cleavage bare and her silhouette visible. She was Eden, just as the soldier said.

"Why aren't you resting?" Aaron asked, composing himself.

"Great! I was afraid you wouldn't make it before the water got cold." Seraphina pointed to the barrel tub. "Take off your shirt and boots."

"You need more rest," he replied.

"I slept well this afternoon. Noble refused to let me leave his presence without eating. I have bathed, which always makes me feel better." She placed a hand on his chest. "Now it is your turn."

"You know I am perfectly capable of doing this myself." Aaron chuckled.

Seraphina looked up at him. "Take off your clothes, or I will remove them for you."

Aaron disrobed and stood nude before her. Seraphina did not move, and Aaron searched her gaze. The heat and hunger there set fire to his loins. He'd never met a woman who enjoyed love-making the way Seraphina did. The experience was all new to her, but she was not timid.

"Seraphina, ladies do not stare." He smiled wryly.

"Then it is their loss." Seraphina motioned to the barrel. "Sit."

Aaron sat down on the sheet she'd placed on the floor. Seraphina washed his face and neck. She repeated the process on his chest, back, and down the length of his arms until Aaron began to relax.

"Aaron, you need to rest more. Take your own advice. There are other doctors."

"I am a doctor. It is the nature of the work," Aaron replied.

"Did you always want to be a doctor?"

"No. I did not." Aaron smiled. "As a boy, I wanted to be a legionnaire. Alas, Rome fell before I had the opportunity."

"A legionnaire?"

"You seem surprised. I read Homer and visited Rome on holiday from my studies at Oxford. Nothing moved me more than standing on the floor of the Pantheon, bathed in light from the oculus."

"So, you read The Iliad and The Odyssey and fancied yourself a legionnaire? I mean, Odysseus was basically lost for twenty years, and Achilles was a hot head who got himself killed." Seraphina chuckled.

Aaron grabbed Seraphina's hands and brought her to eye level. "You've read Homer?"

"Now who looks surprised!" Seraphina giggled. "You know I love to read."

"My mysterious Seraphina, I know learned men who've not read the text. And you marvel at why I call you mysterious?"

"Learned is a dubious term." Seraphina rolled her eyes. "I find most learned men are dumb as rocks."

"Dumb as rocks!" Aaron cracked up. "Seraphina, I must work harder at convincing you of the worthiness of the male persuasion."

"Many have tried. Lower your head over the barrel. I need to wash your hair."

He did as she asked. The cool water was soothing, and the feel of her hands massaging his scalp was bliss. Her breasts grazed the side of his face each time her hands poured water over his head. He could feel her nipples become erect with each pass.

When she was finished, she dried his hair with a towel.

"Now. Be quiet and still. I would hate to cut your handsome face."

Seraphina worked the shaving soap into a lather with the brush, applied it to his face, and carefully shaved him with the straight razor.

She wiped away the remnants of soap with the towel and brushed her cheek against his.

"Mmm…close. Now you look rested."

Aaron brushed Seraphina's lips with his. "Thank you."

"You're welcome." Seraphina kissed him back. "Noble laid out clean clothes for you."

"I don't need them. And neither do you." Aaron pulled Seraphina's chemise down to her waist, tearing the fabric. "Open your legs."

"I want all of you." Seraphina straddled him.

"All of me?" Aaron tongued her breast, nipping and sucking one then the other.

"Yes. Please, don't tease."

Aaron placed a hand between her legs, coating his fingers in her sweet nectar. "Taste."

Seraphina greedily licked herself from his fingers. He ached at the image of his cock in her small mouth in the same way, lips stretched tightly around him. And then, as if she'd heard him, Seraphina forced him onto his back and swallowed him almost whole.

"Mercy, Seraphina. Mercy," he said hoarsely.

Seraphina's inexperienced tongue, lips, and fingers quickly found their rhythm. She sucked him deeper in her throat, harder and faster.

"Seraphina. Please," Aaron groaned.

She gave no quarter. Her eyes shot to his, a wicked, satisfied triumph behind her earthen gaze. He bit his lip, stifling a moan. He'd never had a woman suck his cock so hungrily, with abandon. All shied away at the sight of his ten-inch shaft. He could feel himself losing control. Seraphina milked him dry.

"Ne me taquine pas." Seraphina licked her lips, her eyes amber pools of fire.

"Tease? I have not begun to tease."

Aaron rolled her onto her back and pinned her hips to the floor. He buried his face in her wet heat. Seraphina screamed and tried to pull away.

"No." Aaron tightened his grip.

"Aaron," Seraphina wept.

He released her hips and dragged her beneath him. Their eyes locked.

Aaron slid his throbbing shaft in slowly, in a strained effort to maintain control.

"Seraphina, my mysterious Seraphina. A man has no right to this bliss. You are my bliss."

He thrust as hard and deeply as he could, covering her mouth to muffle her scream. Seraphina's body arched violently, glistening with sweat, trembling against the relentless waves of pleasure. Aaron let go, pouring his essence inside her again. He held her there until she became soft and pliant in his arms.

"Seraphina?"

She moaned; her eyes fluttered. He lifted her from the floor to the bed and came to rest beside her, then covered them both with a blanket.

"Aaron," she whispered.

"Yes?"

"Promise me you won't just disappear when this is over." Seraphina buried her head in his chest. "Promise we'll say good-bye just like this."

"Over? Good-bye?" Aaron lifted her chin. "You think I am going to leave you?"

"It's not what I think. It's what I know."

"Then you know nothing." Aaron sat up on his elbow.

"Just promise me," she demanded.

"I promise I will never leave you." Aaron kissed the tears from her face. "Ever."

Seraphina settled into him again. The slow rhythmic rise and fall of her breast and the airy feeling of her breath on his chest told him she'd fallen asleep.

Leave? She thought he would leave. Or did she plan to leave? Was she going to hold him to his word? And if she did, what was he going to do about it?

CHAPTER THIRTEEN

Battle of Antietam – Baltimore, Maryland
September 1862

September 20th[th], 1862

If someone had told me when we left Bull Run ten days ago that a hell worse than the one we were in awaited us, I wouldn't have believed it possible. It is awful. I close my eyes, hoping that when I open them, it will all have been a bad dream. So many are wounded that we have been forced to a gruesome triage. Those men who are likely to die from their injuries regardless of treatment are given pain relief and allowed to succumb to their wounds. Bodies lay in open trenches or are just strewn about like clothes on the floor. The gravediggers can't keep up. To add to our misery, we've got an outbreak of influenza. Staff and soldier alike are severely ill. Those that aren't, are exhausted from caring for the ones that are. We sleep in overlapping shifts. Aaron rarely returns to quarters little more than a few hours before dawn. I don't know how much longer this can go on.

*****

"Aaron, there are just too many." Thomas wiped his brow with the back of his bloodstained hand. "We need more surgeons."

Thomas spoke the truth. The piles of discarded members and mounds of turned earth grew larger daily. Aaron surveyed the carnage. This morning he'd taken a man's two legs and one arm. He'd survive, but to what end? Of what use could he be, this quarter of a man? He'd given serious thought to letting him die.

Aaron glanced across the sea of wounded to Seraphina. He'd come to rely on her, almost to the exclusion of others. She was his right and left hand.

"You must be mad!" Thomas cried. "You cannot put Seraphina in the surgery!"

"Why not? She's already there. Seraphina is more than a nurse. I have watched her. You have watched her. She performs minor surgeries on her own, using probes and forceps of every type. She has set countless fractures without assistance. She is masterful at controlling hemorrhages and repairing and suturing arteries. Her skills are far superior to many of the surgeons on our staff."

"I am aware of her abilities. Astonishing as they are, it does not change the fact that she is a woman…a Black woman."

"Seraphina's assistance will allow you to perform surgeries on your own and help us care for more soldiers, Thomas."

"The staff will not receive this well, Aaron. I told you as much at Harrison's Landing."

"Name another surgeon in this hospital who would do as well as she, and I will gladly give him the job."

Thomas was still. "None. There are none."

"Good, it is settled then." Aaron motioned to Seraphina. "Nurse Laurent, leave that soldier to another nurse. I have need of you here. Private, there is no need to follow."

Marshall stood down. Seraphina washed her hands and walked over to the two men. "Colonel, do you need assistance?" Seraphina asked.

"You are familiar with these?" Aaron laid out the surgical instruments before her.

"Yes, Colonel. The nurses and I clean them after each surgery."

"Tell me what they are used for," Aaron ordered.

"Colonel, I am a nurse, not a surgeon."

"Nurse Laurent, I order you to tell me the use of each of these instruments."

"As you wish. That is a retractor. Next to it are the metacarpal saw used to amputate the hands to the wrist, a bow, and a capital saw for cutting the large bones. Beside that are amputating knives and forceps of various sizes. Unlike some of the other surgeons who use the circular technique, you and the lieutenant use the flap technique for amputation. A single flap below the knee and a double flap above."

Aaron smiled inside, a mixture of pride and satisfaction welling within. He'd seen her reading his books. He knew she was ready…even if she didn't.

"Report to the surgery. Your training in anesthesia will begin tomorrow."

"No!" Thomas shook his head in disbelief. "There are surgeons in this hospital who could not name half of these instruments. Some of them have never heard of the flap technique."

"Lieutenant, Nurse Laurent is highly intelligent. It stands to reason she would develop an understanding of such things over time."

"Colonel, I would prefer to continue with my nursing. I appreciate your confidence in me, but I fear my presence would be a distraction and as such more of a hindrance than a help."

"She is quite right, Colonel," Thomas agreed.

"Nurse Laurent, I need every surgeon I have. That includes you. Report to the surgery. That is an order."

"Colonel, are you so blinded by her that you would suspend belief?" Thomas pointed at Seraphina.

"Lieutenant, you forget yourself," Aaron snapped.

"Do I? How did she get here? It is a long way from Louisiana to Virginia."

"It is." Seraphina narrowed her eyes. "And I do not know how. I woke up alone in a field several months ago, left for dead, I presume. I remember nothing else."

"You remember nothing? Nothing?" Thomas threw up his hands in mocking disbelief. "You have considerable training. Educated women outside of the gentry are rare, a Black woman…an impossibility."

"Maybe I am what all women, or people, for that matter, could be, given a chance to aspire to their aptitudes. I can understand why you find me so odd with such a thing not impossible but highly improbable. Fortunately for me, my grandfather, Dr. André Philippe Dumas, believed in the impossible."

"And this Dr. Dumas, believer in dreams and miracles, where is he?"

"Colonel, please, surely you can see this will not work. Even the good-natured Lieutenant has been driven rabid by the mere suggestion."

"Nurse Laurent, I will start you with the basics. The lieutenant will see to your lessons in anesthesia. Report to the surgery. You are dismissed."

"As you wish! Gentlemen." Seraphina curtsied and stormed away. Marshall jumped to attention and followed.

"Are you in your cups, man? What man in his right mind would teach a woman such things? Seraphina had the good sense to refuse you."

"And the good sense to follow orders. I am the colonel. My orders are to be followed without question. Those who do not will be dealt with swiftly and severely."

"Aaron, you are placing her in danger and your command in jeopardy. The officers will not stand for this. The prideful will be envious of her, hate her even…when they aren't lusting after her. And you, you they will resent."

"We need her skill. The men need her skill. We are physicians; our duty is to the men. McClellan hails this as a victory. If victories are measured by lives lost, then this engagement was a grand success. But they aren't, and this isn't. I trust you, Thomas. Trust me. Support me as is your duty. Protect her as my friend and brother."

"My trust and friendship are unwavering. It is your judgment that gives me pause. Permission to be dismissed."

"Permission granted."

Aaron watched as Thomas walked away. Thomas's questions and concerns were valid, and he'd shared them. Seraphina did not belong. Her very existence was an enigma, and she gave no clues. He could only surmise her guarded nature hid secrets she would reveal in time. He was content to wait.

*****

"Damn you, Aaron Weld!" Seraphina cursed under her breath, ascending the stairs to their quarters.

"You all right, Miss Seraphina?" Marshall asked, concerned.

"I am just tired, Marshall. Would you fetch some water for my basin? Please."

"You be okay while I go?" he asked.

"Yes, Marshall. I promise. I will lock the door behind you."

Marshall smiled. "Be back directly."

Seraphina flipped her barrel bath onto its bottom to prepare for Marshall's return. If he didn't do so quickly, she was in danger of filling the tub with her tears. Before her display and promotion this afternoon, she'd been defined and dismissed by most, if not all, the officers. She was the colonel's contraband and a nurse. Two positions suited to her gender and her station, even if her skill at the latter gave one pause. Aaron was throwing her into the breach. He was going to redefine her in the eyes of the men. Thomas's reaction to his decision would not be the worst or the last.

"Nurse Laurent?" Thomas knocked on the bedroom door.

Seraphina weighed her options. She could ask him to leave. She could ignore him and stay silent, hoping he would go on his own, or she could face him. Seraphina dried her face, collected herself, stepped out of the room, and closed the door behind her.

"Lieutenant, you know I cannot receive you unchaperoned. Why are you here?"

"I believe you were supposed to report to the surgery." Thomas smiled. "And you are—"

"Not there."

"May we talk?" Thomas asked.

"Talk or interrogate?" Seraphina raised an eyebrow.

"Talk. Interrogation would be fruitless." Thomas crossed his arms. "The truth of who you are lies in the words you leave unspoken."

"Is that not true of all of us, Lieutenant?"

"Maybe. I have met a New Orleanian or two, and you are nothing like them. You are nothing like anyone."

"No two people are the same. We are each unique in our way."

"There is unique, and then there is you, Miss Laurent. My brother is content with the mystery, and so shall I be, for the moment. I have more pressing concerns. You working in the surgery is wrongheaded."

"On that, we agree."

"I would like you to disabuse my brother of this notion for all of our sakes."

"Me? Convince Colonel Dr. Aaron Weld to change his mind? Now who believes in dreams and miracles?"

"I do not believe in dreams or miracles, but honey and lavender will do nicely."

"Oh, you want me to seduce him." Seraphina laughed mockingly. "I am no whore, Lieutenant."

"I do not suggest you are. Such a woman could never hold sway over my brother as you do. You, my sweet Seraphina, are a siren worthy of Homer's pen."

"If I had such power, do you think I would still be here?"

"It is because you do that you are. But I think you know that, Miss Laurent. What are women but the weakness of men?"

"Men are their own weakness. Feckless, witless cucks lead around by their dicks! Or, in your case, ego. Je suis une sirène? Only men would sail around, hear women they can't see singing, and crash headlong into rocks because their dicks are hard, Lieutenant!"

"What an opinion you have of men, Miss Laurent!" Thomas howled with laughter. "My god, the devil reached into my brother's loins and breathed life into his deepest darkest desire. Only the devil would offer a man the world at the price of his life."

"Sirens, crucibles, and devil's gifts? Vous détestez les femmes!"

"Quite the opposite. I love women. Like all Weld men, you could say 'un peu trop.' And I like you immensely. What I don't like are unexplained, unanswered questions. Talk to him. Bring him to reason."

"And if I cannot, Lieutenant?"

"Then I shall have the pleasure of your company tomorrow." Thomas grinned.

"Tomorrow then." Seraphina curtsied.

The First Emancipation Proclamation – Sharpsburg, Maryland
September 1862

Aaron kept his distance. He did not want his presence to ruin the celebratory mood. Today, President Lincoln issued a proclamation emancipating all slaves held in rebel states. At dusk, the contraband in camp gathered in a field about a mile up creek from headquarters to celebrate. Their voices could be heard in the farthest reaches of the encampment. With clapping hands and stomping of feet, they beat out an ancient rhythm, one born of misery and pain yet filled with hope and joy.

Careful not to intrude, Aaron searched for Seraphina. As the only woman dancing around the bonfire in bare feet, with her hair down and her skirts tied up, she was not hard to find. He waved to her.

The last few days had been grueling. The fighting in and around Sharpsburg and Dunker Church filled every tent with wounded. Day after day, Seraphina stood across from him in the surgery, focused on the delicate work before her.

The furor caused by her presence had calmed to a detached ambivalence. On occasion, curiosity would get the better of some surgeons, and he would find them observing her. Seraphina handled it well, but unconvinced of their disinterest, he kept her close.

Seraphina walked toward him. She had a wild and reckless energy about her. Firelight danced in her eyes. She was a burning ember fallen from heaven. In that moment, he knew he'd have to burn to keep her.

"Good evening, Colonel."

"Good evening, Miss Laurent. I did not wish to take you away from the celebration."

"You didn't. I was ready to leave. Now that you are here, I can go without spoiling Private Dixon's evening. The poor man must tire of following me around day in and day out."

"I doubt any man would tire of being your shadow."

"You are sweet, but I recall a time when you did not feel that way." Seraphina chuckled.

"Ah, you walk beside me now, but I remember spending considerable time chasing you." Aaron laughed.

An unusual silence fell between them. Aaron could sense Seraphina was not herself. Outside of the firelight, she dimmed quickly.

"You are not as excited as the others."

"No, I guess not."

"Why?"

"You and I both know that a piece of paper does not change the hearts and minds of men. There are many ways to enslave a man."

"I agree with you, yet if any freedom is better than no freedom, one would think you would find some joy in this."

"I find joy in their joy. Nothing more."

"Nothing more?" Aaron stopped and faced her. "My mysterious Seraphina, you are unhappy. Tell me what is troubling you, please."

"It is not my joy." She looked up at him. "They are my people, but I am not one of them. I am not one of you either. I do not belong. I am not unhappy. I am homesick. I long for a home that no longer exists."

"I have upset you. Please forgive me. I did not mean to. I cannot imagine."

Seraphina began to walk again. "There is nothing to forgive. You are homesick too."

"I long to see my mother and Solomon. I have been away a long time, and I know Noble misses home too."

"Noble said Solomon and his son Eli are about the same age."

"Yes. Eli is sixteen, and Solomon is fifteen."

"You don't speak of your family often. Is it because of Solomon's mother?"

"Talking about Solomon makes me miss him more and leads to inevitable questions about his mother."

"Elizabeth."

"Yes. She died giving birth to our second child." Aaron dropped his head slightly. "He is a lot like her. He has a quiet wisdom about him and has her blonde hair too."

"Is that why you haven't remarried? She still has your heart?" Seraphina asked.

"No. It isn't that. It is difficult to explain. I will always care for her; she is the mother of my son. I do not have a wife because I have had no need for one. I have a son to inherit, and his grandmother, Lady Katherine, and I are raising him."

Seraphina smiled. "You are too passionate of a man to be alone. Rumor has it you were once a romantic."

"And what of you? You, too, are a passionate woman. If you've forgotten, I can remind you later."

"I have not forgotten." Seraphina blushed. "And you can remind me now if you wish."

"After you, my lady."

Aaron escorted Seraphina up the porch stairs and through the vestibule. He marveled at how deftly she danced around the sleeping men strewn about until they reached the stairs and their room.

Aaron removed his clothing and sat on his knees in front of Seraphina.

"Undress."

"Is that an order?" Seraphina smiled at him.

"Never. A request. A plea…if need be."

"No need." Seraphina undressed, never taking her eyes from his. "The gods should smite you out of jealousy and me for wickedness. The sight of you makes me weak."

"You defy mortal man's description, Seraphina. You consume me. All of me."

Aaron grasped Seraphina's backside, wrapping her legs around him. She eased herself down until she'd taken every inch of him. The feel of her sheathed around him set him on fire. He had to restrain the beast beneath the surface. Seraphina had taken all he had to give and more, seemingly unphased by his rough handling. But tonight, he wanted to be gentle.

Aaron caressed and fondled her into a fever, guiding her hips up and down his shaft. He could feel the urgency of her need grow and her desire to ride him harder. He thrust up hard, seizing control again.

"Aaron. Please."

"Tell me how I feel. Tell me how I feel inside."

"Full. Tight. Hard. Please."

Aaron let go of her hips. "Look at me. Do not look away."

Seraphina drove him deeper and deeper still. She clinched and shuddered. "Aaron!"

Sweat beading from the effort of holding back, Aaron wrapped her in his arms and finished with a slow, easy thrust. He fell back with Seraphina coming to rest on top of him.

"Seraphina?"

"Go to sleep, Aaron. It will be dawn soon."

"You intend to sleep like this?"

"If by this you mean naked and safe in your arms? Then, yes."

Aaron waited until she fell asleep to move them to the bed. He could not wait to get her home, to his large bed, where they could make love and sleep comfortably.

Aaron ran his fingers through her hair and gently brushed her cheek. He was in love with her. She did belong…with him.

*****

Sharpsburg, Maryland
November 1862

The air was crisp but not cold enough to keep the winter sun from melting the overnight snow flurries. Aaron wound his way through the camp, returning salutes and ordering ease, preparing himself for the disapproving looks and quiet jeers he'd receive when he reached headquarters. Blowing off the morning meeting to indulge in an early morning delight would not go over well, even with Thomas and Lucas attending in his stead.

The Army of the Potomac hadn't moved from Sharpsburg since mid-September. The army's dubious success at the Battle of Antietam left General McClellan with no incentive to pursue General Lee and his army back across the Potomac. McClellan's reticence for battle made for poor military strategy, but from a medical standpoint, it was a boon for the health and welfare of the army. Antietam was bloodshed on a scale Aaron had never seen and hoped never to see again.

Aaron saluted the sentries at the door and walked in. Headquarters was busy—too busy. Something happened. *Fuck all! Where's Thomas?*

"Colonel." Noble set a cup of coffee in Aaron's hand.

"Thank you, Noble. I am not sure when Miss. Laurent will—"

"Colonel, I be sure there be food ready when she is and have Minnie tend to things."

"You are a good man Noble, good man." Aaron patted Noble on the back. "Between us, I could not do without you."

"Between us…no sir, I don't reckon you could." Noble laughed and walked out.

Aaron scanned the room for Thomas and found him. "Lieutenant."

"Colonel." Thomas stood in salute.

"At ease, Lieutenant," Aaron ordered, sitting next to him.

"I was afraid you had taken ill when you weren't at the hospital this morning. I did not see Miss Laurent either, and Private Dixon is absent from his post. Should I be concerned? Noble wouldn't say when he gave me orders to attend this morning's meeting in your place."

Aaron struggled to hold in his laughter. It was obvious Thomas had explained away his absence with an elaborate tale, and now, not knowing what it was, he'd have to play along.

"No need for concern. I trust you to handle things in my absence. Seraphina is not at the hospital because I am not there. Private Dixon was given the evening off."

"Nothing more?" Thomas's eyes danced like an excited child.

"Thomas, you are insufferable," Aaron whispered.

"Come, man. It isn't every day the great Colonel Weld is brought low…by a woman."

Aaron sighed. "Do you ever hold your tongue?"

"I do believe I suggested this as a cure to her eagerness in the morning." Thomas leaned into Aaron's ear. "But I never dreamed it would be a cure for yours. Miss Laurent truly is a wonder."

"Tell me again, Thomas, why I shouldn't have you hung by your digits." Aaron smiled.

"I am a skilled surgeon, of course. And your brother." Thomas grinned.

Aaron raised a playful brow. "Yet you tempt me."

"Telegram for Colonel Weld." The messenger stood at attention, a missive in hand.

"At ease, Private." Aaron took the telegram from the soldier and skimmed it. "Private, you are dismissed." He waited for the soldier to leave before he spoke. "Lincoln has relieved General McClellan of command."

"You jest?" Thomas gestured for the orders.

Aaron handed Thomas the orders. "I do not. He has appointed General Burnside in his stead." Burnside will march south in pursuit of Lee. We are to see the wounded to Camp Curtin."

"Camp Curtin? We have thousands of wounded."

"Find First Lieutenant Marks and bring him to headquarters immediately."

"You want to mobilize the whole Ambulance Corps?"

"Yes. They cleared the wounded from the fields at Antietam in a day. We will need them."

*****

Seraphina rolled out of bed, barely making the chamber pot. One missed period could be explained away by stress, fatigue, and poor diet…but two? And now this. By rough calculation, she had to be somewhere between eight and ten weeks. She was running out of time. None of what she needed was in season. Pennyroyal and cohosh were spring and summer plants. She might still be able to get her hands on cotton root bark, but she wasn't as familiar with it, and without Mamie Etienne's book, she wasn't sure if she could get the dosage right…or if she was too far along to use it.

"I figured, the way he be after you. Like a dog wit a bone." Minnie came through the door, bedding and wash water in hand. "You feel it yet?"

"I am just not feeling well this morning, is all." Seraphina offered unconvincingly.

"Miss Seraphina, you wit child. Ain't no shame in it." Minnie poured the water into the pitcher and basin. "You go on and wash. I'll get Noble on some tea and a biscuit. That baby ain't gwine feed itself."

"Minnie, I can't have a baby. Not here. Not now."

"Yes, you can. You healthy and strong. Man like Colonel, the baby be healthy and strong too. Now you wash. I be back to change the bed. I'll let Colonel know you ailing."

Seraphina grabbed Minnie's hand. "Please don't tell the colonel. Promise me you won't say anything to anyone."

"Why?" Minnie asked, eyebrows knitting.

"I'm begging you, Minnie. If Colonel finds out, he won't let me nurse in the hospital, and he will never let me leave here."

"Leave? Child, where you gwine go? And no, Colonel ain't gwine let you work and put his child in harm's way." Minnie patted her hand. "We speak on it tomorrow."

Minnie left Seraphina standing in the middle of the room. She placed both hands over her belly. She was "with child." Minnie had lifted the veil of denial and let in the stark light of reality. It was 1862. She was pregnant. A Black woman, a contraband, pregnant by a white man. Pregnant in a time where prenatal care, even with Aaron's resources, was non-existent. And... She had no place to go. What if Aaron decided he didn't want her or their child? What if he threw her away out of shame? Having a Black mistress was one thing; having a Black bastard was something else. Seraphina fell to her knees and wept.

CHAPTER FOURTEEN

Camp Curtin – Harrisburg, Pennsylvania
November 1862

November 20th, 1862

It was a daunting task, moving thousands of sick and wounded to Camp Curtin, and several hundred more on to General Hospital in Philadelphia and Washington. Major Blacksmith and Lieutenant Marks remained with the army under Major General Burnside's command. They pursue Lee south on the Rappahannock River, near Fredericksburg. I pray he proves more capable than McClellan. We cannot sustain losses as we did in Antietam. It is good to be working in a proper hospital again, yet I am anxious for home. It has been a year. Philadelphia feels like a distant memory. Mother's letters beseech my return. Solomon's too. I miss them terribly. A trip home is long overdue.

*****

Seraphina warmed herself over the open fire, careful to keep her distance from the soldiers milling around outside the hospital entrance. Their leering glances made her anxious. She didn't know the men. They weren't from any of the corps she'd traveled with from Harrison's Landing. If they were, they'd know who she was and act accordingly.

Camp Curtin was a world away from Harrison's Landing. The converted officers' quarters, with their single bedroom and open hearth, paled in comparison. Still, she was glad not to be in a tent in the middle of winter.

"You ain't ugly like the others? Your master spend a lot of time with your whore mama? From the looks of you, I think he did."

Seraphina ignored the man. Hoping he would grow bored and leave her alone. Most soldiers were kind or indifferent. Then there were the ones like him.

"You a nurse? They say you a nurse."

Seraphina continued to ignore him. *Marshall, where are you?*

He'd stepped away to relieve himself. It felt like he'd been gone for an eternity, but she knew it had only been a few minutes.

"I'm talking to you. Niggers done got free, think they can do what they want."

Seraphina moved to seek refuge inside the hospital tent. The soldier grabbed her arm and yanked it hard. She cried out, struggling to get free.

"You a strong one, huh," the soldier snarled. "Look here, boys. Got her like a worm on a hook."

The other soldiers with him roared with laughter. He grabbed Seraphina's other arm and forced her hand down the front of his pants.

"You a nurse, right? I got needs you can tend to."

"There isn't much there. You should be able to tend to it yourself." Seraphina shot back.

"Bitch!" The soldier struck her across the face and yanked her arm up hard, nearly dislocating her shoulder. Seraphina let out a blood-curdling scream.

"Charles, let her loose!" A young soldier came running from nowhere. "That one belongs to the colonel! He have you in the stocks for laying hands on her."

"I don't give a damn who she belong to, Willie. She get what coming to her. Y'all boys can have a turn when I'm through."

"Let her go." Marshall stood behind the man, holding a ten-inch Bowie knife to his throat.

"What you gone do with that, boy?" The man snarled.

"Follow Colonel's orders," Marshal whispered. "My orders are to keep her. If I got to make you smile to do it, then that's what I do."

The soldier shoved Seraphina, and she fell back, cold mud spattering her clothing. He spat on her. "We ain't through bitch. I see you again."

Marshall released him, and he walked away with the other men.

"Little sister, I sorry. I had business."

Marshall tried to help her to her feet, but Seraphina winced and pulled away.

"Little sister?" Marshall inspected the remnants of her sleeve. "You hurt bad. Come on, I carry you."

"No," Seraphina said flatly and got to her feet on her own.

That something, the something that had broken before, shattered like glass. An icy cold flooded her body, and she couldn't move, couldn't speak. She could only feel the hot tears against her cold skin and the searing pain in her arm. Marshall stood in front of her, his voice a distant echo.

He gently folded Seraphina in his arms, and she felt herself being carried away. She could hear familiar voices and see familiar faces, but everything felt far away.

"What happened?" Thomas burst through the door.

"She was attacked. Her arm and face need tending to. I scared the buzzards off, but little sister ain't said a word. She ain't here. I ain't never seen her like this." Marshall knelt in front of her.

"She's in shock. Did they rape her?" Thomas gave Marshall a hard look.

"Nah, suh." Marshall teared up. *"I gots to her fore that."*

Thomas ripped the tattered sleeve from Seraphina's arm. She screamed.

"Fuck all!" Thomas shouted, eyes wide. *"Where's Minnie?"*

"Oh, God! Mercy!" Noble appeared in the doorway. "Marshall, you was supposed to be minding her!"

"If it weren't for Marshall, she would be far worse," Thomas snapped. "She shouldn't be here."

"Lieutenant, when Colonel find out bout this…when he see them bruises, the devil be loosed. Won't be no reasoning with him. He'll do something terrible."

"I know, Noble. That's why I must get to him before word does. Fetch me some linens. I need to immobilize this arm. Find Minnie. I'll need help getting her out of these clothes, and she shouldn't be alone. Marshall, resume your post."

*****

Exhausted, Aaron began the long walk from the hospital to the officer's barracks. Chilled by the late November cold, his body longed for the warmth of his bed…and the woman in it.

Seraphina had not uttered a word since the assault. Not to him. Not to anyone. She was hurting, and it was his fault. He should have been with her. The camp was too big for Private Dixon to be her lone guardian. He'd assign another soldier to her detail when she was feeling well enough to venture out.

Aaron rubbed his hands together. The cold deepened the ache in his joints and tightened the skin on his lacerated knuckles. His hands weren't broken, but not for lack of trying.

"Aaron, stop!" Thomas had shouted, trying desperately to pull him off the man.

He hadn't stopped. He had felt the man's jaw dislocate over his right fist and his nose break over the left. A rage he'd never known consumed him, fueled by the visual memory of Seraphina's swollen bruises and vacant stare. By the time he'd finished, the man would spend a week in hospital. His compatriots spent a day and night in the stocks.

"Noble. How is she this evening?" Aaron stamped the snow from his boots. "Did Minnie come, as I asked?"

"Same as she was. Child ain't spoke a word. Just stare off, strange like. Minnie came. Got her to eat some."

"Bless that woman." Aaron yawned.

"I got coffee here for you, Colonel, and some stew."

"Thank you. I will look in on Seraphina, and then I will join you."

Aaron rapped on the bedroom door and stepped inside. Seraphina lay on the bed, curled in a ball, her head in Minnie's lap.

"You got her to eat?" Aaron asked.

"I tell that devil to let loose her spirit. You had her long enough," Minnie whispered, gently stroking Seraphina's hair. "Precious girl. He let loose long enough for me to get some food in her. Good thing. Ain't good for a mother to go too long without food."

"Mother?"

"Yes, suh. Miss Seraphina with child. She didn't tell you? Forgive me, suh. She asked me to hold my peace so shes could tell you herself. It been so long, I thought she had."

"How long?" Aaron demanded.

"The quickening be here soon, I think," Minnie replied. "Please don't be too cross wit her. She was scared."

"Thank you, Minnie. Please leave us."

"Yes, suh." Minnie moved Seraphina's head out of her lap and excused herself from the room.

Aaron knelt beside Seraphina, and she turned away from him. He shook inside. Not from anger but fear. Seraphina's fragility frightened him. Even more so now that he knew she was with child. If Minnie was right, Seraphina was pregnant when they left Antietam, which meant he'd sired the babe the first time they'd made love. It also meant she'd been working as hard as he, with child. His heart sank into a pool of shame. It did not matter that she didn't tell him. He should've known.

"Seraphina. Talk to me," Aaron pleaded. "Why didn't you tell me?"

"My grandfather, the French doctor I spoke of, my grandmother was his mistress. He was a kind man. He supported Mamie Eulalie in her elder years. Paid for my education too. I am named for him, Seraphina André Phillipe Laurent."

"It sounds as if they loved each other deeply."

"Yes, they did. My grandmother never married. André was the love of her life. But he never claimed her or my mother. He hid them away in shame and went on with his life." Seraphina turned to face him. "It will be the same with us."

"No, it won't!" Aaron grabbed her face. "I love you. I will never leave you or our child. I swear it!"

"You will. You'll have no other choice."

"Seraphina, I will protect you with my life. I swear it. I will not fail you again," Aaron pledged, hot tears falling.

"A man threw me to the ground and spat on me. He twisted my arm. He made me touch his… I couldn't do anything to stop him. Here, in this place, I am nothing. Less than nothing. And there is nothing you or anyone else can do about it. For the first time in my life, I'm afraid."

"Seraphina, you are not nothing. To me, you are everything." Aaron placed a hand on her belly. "You carry our child. If I could remake the world—"

"You can't." Seraphina caressed his bruised knuckles. "And you can't fight it either."

"We are leaving for Philadelphia. Things will be different there."

"Harrisburg or Philadelphia, it is all the same. I am tired. I am very tired, Aaron. I'm sorry, but I would like to be left alone."

"You have nothing to apologize for. Sleep. I will go."

Aaron dried his face and stepped out of the room. Noble greeted him with his flask.

"Thought you might need this, considering." Noble nodded. "Stew's warm."

"Noble, you are God's gift."

Aaron settled at the table adjacent to the fire. Deep in thought, he did not notice Thomas come in.

"May I join you, Brother?"

"I warn you, I will make for unpleasant company," Aaron replied.

Thomas took the seat across from him. "Seraphina is still unwell?"

"She is with child." Aaron sighed.

"You need to take her from here, Aaron. Or is it your intention to have her roaming through camp, belly swollen with your bastard?"

"Thomas, as always, you go too far."

"And as always, you are willful in your blindness. Did you doubt your virility? You know the natural order of things. Send word to Mother. Escort her home and return to your duties. She will be cared for."

"I plan to leave for Philadelphia in the next few weeks. If Burnside and Lee have not crossed swords by then, hostilities will cease through winter, I think."

"You may be right. What will you do when the child comes?"

"When the war is over, we will go abroad. France, maybe North Africa. They have need of trained physicians. And you?"

"A private practice in Boston awaits me when this terrible business is finished. Lucy and I are anxious to begin a family. I will never hear the end of it when she learns of Seraphina."

"Lucy is a lovely woman," Aaron mused. "Reminds me of my Elizabeth. Kind and quiet. The two of you are well suited."

"You have a weakness for irreverent women…like our father."

"Father said intelligence and passion in a woman are often confused for irreverence."

"A man would have no peace with such a woman. Are you not in a state of unrest now, for a woman?" Thomas laughed.

"Father was content with our mother because he understood that with such a woman, one does not make peace with words."

"If true, a man should seek to quarrel often." Thomas grinned.

"Brother, I have it on good authority that mother and father did." Aaron chuckled.

CHAPTER FIFTEEN

Camp Curtin – Harrisburg, Pennsylvania
December 1862

December 1st, 1862

I am going to have a baby…Aaron's baby. I haven't felt any movement, but I'm sure. Three months, maybe a little more. I am scared to death and confused. Not happy, not sad. I don't know. Aaron seems more concerned…worried. I have another shadow; his name is George. Corporal George Potter. Marshall is a corporal now too. George is a little smaller than Marshall, but other than that, the two might as well be bookends. I don't go to the hospital anymore. I won't touch another white soldier. I don't feel safe around any of them. I just see him, over and over again. Aaron takes his uniform off when… I just can't.

Instead, I spend my days just outside the gate treating contraband. Many have taken up residence on the nearby farms and work in the camp. I've asked Aaron to allow me to go to the farms so that I can treat more people. He refuses. Even with George and Marshall, he says no. The army won't allow any of the surplus supplies to leave the camp. It is the dead of winter. People are suffering. A man has come to the gate every day this week, asking me to come and help his sick wife. Aaron won't let me go. It infuriates me…and he knows it. If the man comes back tomorrow, I'm going. How can I not?

*****

The barn was quiet. Seraphina huddled in the back behind several bales of hay. As silently as she could, Seraphina pulled a loose board from the barn wall.

"Run!" she whispered. "Stay in the stalks until you reach the road. Go! Don't stop!"

"Come go wit us, Seraphina," a young girl pleaded.

"No. I won't fit." Seraphina pushed the board harder to make the opening wider. "And, if I go, they'll follow."

"Seraphina, they do terrible things," the girl cried.

"That's why you must go now. Take the other girls with you. Stay in the stalks. I will see you soon. I promise. Now go, please go."

The girls crawled through the space in the barn planks. Seraphina closed the wall behind them and returned to her hiding place behind the hay bales. She could hear the soldiers outside. They'd attacked without warning, rounding up the women and young girls who could not get away. The men who resisted they shot.

"Find her. She's here. She don't go nowhere without these two," the man yelled.

Seraphina fought the terror growing within. She checked her boot for the buck knife George had given her and tucked it in her skirts. She crouched down and waited. The barn door opened. She smelled the men before she saw them. A stench of filth hovered over them. Her pulse thundered in her ears as her heart began to race.

"Got her!" A man shouted, seizing her.

Seraphina kicked, clawed, and bit her way free of his grasp, then ran from the barn. Another soldier grabbed her by her hair and threw her to the ground. Seraphina scurried to her feet and kept running. A shot rang out, and she felt a bullet wiz by her head. She stopped and turned to face her pursuers.

"Remember me?" The man asked, twisting his lips.

She did. The rabid, sadistic look in his eyes was unforgettable. Seraphina struggled for calm and glared at him in silent defiance. Then, she noticed Marshall and George on their knees with a rifle to their heads. Both were badly beaten and bleeding profusely. George was missing teeth; blood-mixed dirt covered his mouth from where they'd kicked him in the face, and there was an obvious depression in his skull from where he'd been hit by a rifle butt. Marshall's leg was bent at a strange angle, and blood dripped from his face onto the ground. He had tears in his eyes. Seraphina knew they weren't for him.

"You remember. If you come easy like the other women, I won't let the rest of my men have a turn with you. Come hard, and you wish you came easy."

"Miss Seraphina, run!" George shouted.

George lunged forward, taking several soldiers to the ground with him. Marshall bolted for the fields, a volley of rifle fire at his back. He stumbled but kept running.

Seraphina tried to get away, but the soldier struck her in the back of the head, and she fell to the ground in blinding pain. The other soldiers beat George with the butts of their rifles and the heels of their boots until he stopped moving.

"Should we go after him?" a soldier asked.

"No. Let him go. We got what we came for. Tie her up and take the rest."

Seraphina watched in horror as the men dragged several young girls away. She struggled against the ropes, hoping to keep them loose enough for another escape attempt. Her fight was met with another blow to the head.

The men forced Seraphina and the girls down the road and off into a thicket of trees. Seraphina looked back; the farm was just fading from view. If by some miracle, Marshall made it back to camp, Aaron would come for her. She just needed to stay alive.

*****

At the end of a long night and early morning, Aaron was looking forward to spending time with Seraphina, even if she was still cross with him for not allowing her to go to the farms.

"Why? Why can't I go? I will have Marshall and George with me. I'll only stay a few hours. Aaron, my people need me."

"Seraphina, you are with child. You are in no condition to be of assistance. You haven't fully recovered from your ordeal. My answer is no."

"I have recovered. And I'm with child; I am not an invalid."

"Recovered? Why am I standing here out of uniform? Why are you still not sleeping through the night? My answer is no."

Seraphina persisted until he agreed to let her work at the gate for a few hours every day—a concession he made from a place of reluctant prudence. He knew if he did not let her help at all, she would defy him and do it anyway. Compromise was the coin of the realm when it came to Seraphina.

"Good afternoon, Noble." Aaron kicked off his boots and sat at the table.

"Colonel. You early. Something wrong?" Noble asked, concerned.

"No. I just want to check in on Seraphina. She did not rest well last night."

"She gone." Noble poured a cup of coffee. "Doctoring folks at the farm."

"What?" Aaron stood. "You mean at the gate?"

"No, sir, the farm," Noble replied. "That man worried bout his wife come by early this mornin'. Miss Seraphina went with him. George and Marshall follow. Didn't have much choice really, you know Miss Seraphina got her own mind."

"Own mind? She will mind if I must lock her in that room or tie her to a chair." Aaron reached for his boots. "I'll be back."

Marshall opened the door before Aaron could. He stumbled forward, beaten nearly beyond recognition and bleeding badly from a leg wound.

"Where is she? What happened? Where is George?" Aaron demanded.

Marshall did his best to stand at attention. "Miss Seraphina... He got her. It was him. The one who hurt her before. Had four men with him. I sorry, suh. Me and George... George is dead." Marshall said solemnly. "I came back to get help to go after her. I got men waitin'."

Aaron stumbled, suddenly unsteady. For a moment, the air in his lungs was scarce. Then, a soul-crushing dread threatened to bring him to his knees as his blood ran cold. Men were going to die today. Seraphina was his. They had taken what belonged to him, and he was going to take it back.

"Where did they go?" Aaron asked.

"South down the road from camp. Miss Seraphina fought. Fought like a man she did. Took two men to drag her off."

"Can you ride, Corporal?"

"Yes, suh." Marshall nodded.

"I will not pull back should your wounds hinder you. Understand?"

"With respect, they won't. Suh, little sister is ours. They steal her from me. I gwine get her back," Marshall replied.

"Get a rifle. You and your men meet me at the stables. Noble, go find Thomas."

Both men left to execute his orders. Aaron opened the chest where he kept his guns. He quickly loaded his Henry rifle and Colt sidearms and slipped his Bowie knife into his boot.

"Fought like a man she did." Hope and despair flooded Aaron at the thought. Seraphina would fight for her life. Of that, he had no doubt. But she was a woman, and no amount of fight would keep the beast from killing her or their child.

*****

Dusk veiled the sun and cast the trees in a blanket of blue and gray. The woodland path was narrow. Shade's hooves struck the ground hard, deftly avoiding fallen branches and foliage. He was a full length ahead of the men that followed and still pulling away. He knew.

Aaron could hear screams in the distance, but nothing prepared him for the sight he came upon. Soldiers had several young girls on the ground, in various stages of undress, and were rutting between their legs like wild dogs. When the men saw him, those that could, scattered into the woods. The others, too slow in pulling up their trousers, were corralled by Corporal Dixon and the other men. With rifles drawn, they herded the men together.

Aaron dismounted. "You two, after those men. If they resist, shoot them. You… Go to the farm. Fetch some women to help these girls, Corporal Dixon."

Marshall dismounted; The hard ride caused his wounds to bleed badly, but true to his word, they had not stopped him.

Seraphina wasn't among the girls they'd found. They were all too young, and there was no way Seraphina wouldn't have come to him immediately. She'd been taken somewhere else.

Aaron turned to the men. The three of them were sloven and reeked of beer, urine, and the foulest of body stench. The image of such filth touching Seraphina, rutting between her legs… All these men were dead. They just didn't know it yet.

"Where is she?" Aaron growled. "Speak."

Two of the men remained silent. The third, a stout, bearded man with dark hair and devil black eyes, smirked. Aaron retrieved the knife from his boot, walked over to the man, and slit his throat. Eyes wide with disbelief, the man gurgled his last breath and fell to the ground.

"Charlie got her!" a man screamed. "He down the road aways. Didn't want to share her with the rest of us."

"Sir, I told Charlie to leave her be. Just take the others. I swear it," the other man cried, ashen and trembling.

Aaron climbed back in the saddle. "Corporal Dixon, wait here for the others to return. If these men move or speak, kill them."

Aaron spurred Shade into a full sprint in the direction the soldier said Seraphina had been taken. He'd promised not to fail her again. He'd promised to keep her safe. He'd failed.

*****

Battered and bruised, Seraphina held him off. At one point, she managed to break free and run, but relentless in his pursuit, he'd caught her.

Desperate, Seraphina reached for the knife in her skirt and raising it, she stabbed him in the shoulder. He cried out, reaching for the blade in his back. Seraphina tried to crawl away, but he dragged her back, ripping the knife through the bodice of her dress, leaving her breasts bare.

"Aaron! Aaron!" Seraphina screamed.

"He ain't coming for you! I'm gone fuck you and sell you for my trouble," the man shouted, landing a savage blow to her head. He tore through the remnants of her dress until she lay naked and bleeding.

"Seraphina! Seraphina! Answer me!" Aaron called out, pleading for a response.

"Aaron! Please!" Seraphina called back before falling unconscious from another vicious strike.

Aaron slid from his saddle with Shade still in full gallop. He rolled to the ground and sprung to his feet. The soldier grabbed Seraphina by the hair, holding her in front of him with the knife to her throat.

"You came for your whore? What kind of white man are you? Don't you know they is the reason we in this mess? Good white men dying for nothing. Cause that's what they is…nothing," the soldier spat.

Aaron felt a deadly calm settle on him. His body relaxed, his voice quiet. "Let her go. I will not ask again."

"I let her go if I have your word me and my boys can leave? No stocks. No beatings."

"I don't negotiate with dead men."

Aaron lunged at him, and the man dropped Seraphina and ran. Aaron gave chase. He cleared the distance between them and dragged him to the ground. The man struggled to free himself from Aaron's grip, kicking wildly, scratching and clawing at the vice around his neck. With fingers wrapped around his throat, Aaron squeezed, crushing his windpipe with both hands until blood wept from his eyes and the color drained from his skin.

"My only regret is that I cannot follow you to hell and spend eternity killing you. But I will see you there."

The man's body fell limp. Satisfied that he was dead, Aaron rushed to Seraphina's side.

Cuts and bruises ran the length of her body. She was nude, the remnants of her dress strewn about. He could see impressions of the soldier's hands on her neck and arms. Aaron clenched his fist, afraid to touch her. A strange sound echoed in the trees above—an animal... wounded. The howling grew louder, deafening. It was not until Aaron saw the first of his tears fall on Seraphina's face that he realized the cries were his own.

"Curse you to hell!" Aaron screamed to the heavens. "Curse you to hell if you take her and not me!"

Aaron removed his shirt and dressed Seraphina in it, careful not to injure her further. Gently, he lifted her in his arms and kissed her bloodied lips. Seraphina did not move. Her eyes remained closed, her breathing shallow. Aaron crushed her to his chest and sobbed.

"Please. Please don't leave. Stay. Please stay, Seraphina. Please. I love you."

Aaron heard a rider approach and reached for his revolver. He set it down when he saw it was Marshall.

"Colonel, I hear a terrible sound, so I come to see—mercy no! Is she alive, suh?" Marshall cried.

"Barely," Aaron breathed.

"The other men took what they came for. Why he do Miss Seraphina like that? What kind of man do that to a woman?" Marshall asked. Tears falling, he turned away.

"A dead one," Aaron answered.

*****

Aaron sat outside the bedroom door, next to the hearth, whisky in hand. Thomas leaned against the mantel, drinking from the bottle.

"She is still so pale, Thomas. She stirs but never wakes. It has been two days." Aaron sighed.

"Aaron, it is a miracle she is alive after what that savage did to her." Thomas refilled Aaron's glass.

"This is my fault. I should have killed that animal. I should have taken her from here. If she dies…"

"Do not allow yourself to think that way, Brother." Thomas squeezed Aaron's shoulder. "Seraphina is strong. There are grown men who could not have survived that beating."

"Colonel, Lieutenant, suh," Minnie called to the men from the door.

"Yes, Minnie. What is it? Is Seraphina awake?" Aaron asked hopefully.

"No, suh. She is bleeding." Minnie spoke softly.

Aaron ran into the room and threw the covers back. Seraphina's chemise and the sheets were soaked through.

Minnie handed him the basin with the blood-soaked towels. "I couldna keep up."

Aaron inspected them. With that much blood loss, Seraphina had miscarried for sure. Now the only question was, would she bleed to death?

Aaron handed the basin back to Minnie. "Fetch more rags. We will need them."

"Yes, suh." Minnie hurried from the room.

Aaron fell to his knees. "What have I done, Thomas? What have I done? Elizabeth—"

"Seraphina is not Elizabeth. Be of good courage, Brother. She will pull through this."

"Thomas, once her condition is more stable, I am taking her back to Philadelphia to convalesce. I will not return until she is well. It may not be until sometime in the spring. Can you manage without me for that time?"

"Yes. I will send word to Surgeon General Hammond that I need a temporary replacement until you return. I doubt there will be any more engagements until the spring. Aaron, when you return, do not bring her back. You cannot protect her. There will always be men like the ones who did this. You cannot kill them all."

"I have no intention of ever returning Seraphina to this place."

"I am sorry for your loss, Brother. I truly am. I should go. I'll send for you when we have need."

"Evenin', Lieutenant," Noble greeted Thomas at the door.

"Good evening, Noble."

"May I talk wit you?"

"Yes, of course," Thomas replied.

The men moved away from the door to avoid being overheard, but the wall was thin, and Aaron could hear their conversation.

"Lieutenant, I worry. Colonel ain't well."

"I know, Noble. I know."

"Lieutenant, if she don't wake up soon or God forbid, she die… Colonel like to crawl in the grave behind her."

"Noble, let us pray it does not come to that."

"It ain't good for him to be sitting vigil at her side like this," Noble said. "He the colonel. Men need to see him. Especially after… Maybe it best you keep him with you in the surgery? Minnie can tend to Miss Seraphina."

"Noble, Aaron always says you are a wise man. He is fortunate to have you here. After tonight, I will make sure we have need of him in the surgery."

"The men? Fuck the men! And fuck you, Thomas!" Aaron raged. "The men put her here! She did nothing but help them…and they put her here! They killed our child! And, if not for you, Thomas, they'd all be dead!"

"And you'd be in the stocks facing a court martial! Brother, please."

"No, you will not have need of me in the surgery." Aaron fixed his steel blue eyes on Thomas. "And the men, the men would do well to keep their distance."

Still on his knees, Aaron crawled over to the bed. He turned Seraphina's hand palm side up and rested his head there. Noble was right. If she died, it would be the end of him. Solomon saved him after Elizabeth, and though he loved his son, this was different. Thomas was right; Seraphina was not Elizabeth. Elizabeth was his wife, and he loved her as a husband should. But Seraphina, Seraphina was his soul. It was elemental, as if she had been chosen for him by the gods. He felt guilty about the revelation when it first came to him, but it was the truth, nonetheless.

"Colonel, I have the rags and linens. Marshall got the water." Minnie walked over to the bed. "Colonel, suh, Miss Seraphina a lady. I can't tend to her with...with men folk around."

"Yes, Minnie. We will leave."

Aaron stalked to the door and slammed it behind him. He turned to Thomas. "She can't die. She just can't."

"I know, Brother. I know."

*****

Seraphina's screams could be heard in the next room. She thrashed around, fighting off an invisible attacker. Noble struggled to hold her down.

"She woke, but she ain't here, Minnie."

Minnie pushed Noble away. "Fetch Colonel. Hurry!"

"Stop! Please! Let me go! Aaron! He's killing me!" Seraphina cried, trying to break free from Minnie's embrace.

"Open your eyes, child. Open your eyes." Minnie rocked Seraphina, calmly coaxing her out of the nightmare. "You come on back to us now. It's all right."

"Aaron! He's going to kill me! Oh, God! Oh, God!" Seraphina sobbed.

Aaron came through the door. He took Seraphina from Minnie's arms.

"I have her, Minnie. Seraphina, look at me. Look at me. You are safe. I am here. You are safe now."

Seraphina wrapped herself around Aaron. He could feel the fear coursing through her veins. Her heartbeat like a hummingbird's.

"He'll come! They'll come back!"

"No, love." Aaron brushed the hair from her face. "No one is coming for you."

"Where am I?" Seraphina turned her head. Blinding pain and dizziness forced it back down.

"Camp Curtin. You have been asleep for four days. We did not know if you would ever wake. That beast beat you so severely."

"Four days? The baby! He hit me. He kicked me. I couldn't... He was too strong."

Aaron cradled Seraphina's face in his hands. "Seraphina, you miscarried two days ago. The baby is gone."

"Gone?" Seraphina went still.

"We were afraid you would die. Minnie assured me everything has passed, and the bleeding slowed. I am sorry, Seraphina."

"I killed our baby! I killed our baby!" Seraphina wailed.

"You did not kill our baby. That monster did. I should have killed him, made an example of him the moment he touched you. I should have protected you. The fault is mine."

"I should have listened to you," Seraphina cried. "I shouldn't have gone to help."

"You did nothing wrong. You tried to help someone."

"I am afraid, Aaron. What if more of them come? What if you're not here? What do I do if you are gone?"

"Listen to me, Seraphina. You are safe."

Seraphina shook her head. "No. No, I am not."

Aaron held her tighter. "I am here. You are safe. I promise. Now that you are awake, we can go home to Philadelphia. I have already sent word, and Mother is expecting us. There you will be safe and well cared for. We will leave as soon as you are steady on your feet."

"Today. Can we leave today?"

"You need a few more days before you can travel safely. Rest now."

"Don't leave. Please don't leave," Seraphina pleaded.

"I will stay. Rest."

Aaron laid Seraphina back down on the bed. She drifted off. No longer trembling, her breathing had returned to normal.

"Colonel? You all right?" Minnie asked worriedly.

"She is broken, Minnie…broken."

"Suh, it take more than this to break Seraphina. Her will is strong. You see. She quiet now. I stay wit her."

"No. I will come for you when I am ready. Thank you, Minnie."

"Yes, suh." Minnie backed out of the room and gently closed the door.

Weld Manor – Philadelphia, Pennsylvania
December 1862

December 24th, 1862

The train from Harrisburg to Philadelphia was a journey through an Ansel Adams looking glass. Snow canvased the fields and trees for miles, waiting for Mother Nature to paint her masterpiece in Spring. It was a gift of beauty I sorely needed. I feel ugly inside and out. I cry until I have no more tears, then start crying again. Our baby is gone. I was ambivalent and afraid when I found out, and now, now I am devastated and guilty. Guilty, because no matter how many times Aaron tries to convince me otherwise, I know it is my fault. Tomorrow is Christmas. I haven't left my room since we arrived two days ago. I can hear the hustle and bustle of preparations. I don't feel like celebrating. Everything is awful. Everything. The dizziness and headaches are the worst, and my cuts and bruises are hideous. The nightmares—I still see the monster. Aaron is here. He hasn't left my side.

CHAPTER SIXTEEN

Weld Manor – Philadelphia, Pennsylvania
January 1863

Seraphina sat on a settee, basking in the colored light of the library's stained-glass window. The sweet and bitter tears of memory flooded her eyes. She held out her hands and called to the light. *Mamie, everything hurts. I am lost.*

The library was her healing place. She'd discovered it while exploring. Two weeks confined to bed recovering had given her a terrible case of cabin fever. Its wall-to-wall shelves full of books were a treasure trove of first-edition prints.

Weld Manor was opulence on a grand scale. She was awestruck coming up the drive in the carriage the day they'd arrived. The greens, gardens, and fountains were magnificent.

The gardens' dormant beauty was another place she sought refuge. It was odd to walk them without Marshall. She missed him. He'd stayed with Thomas in Harrisburg. She often found herself looking for him, only to remember he was gone and miss him more.

She wasn't completely alone. Minnie had come with her to Weld Manor. As her lady's maid, she stayed on the second floor with the female staff. All male staff roomed on the lower ground floor. Minnie had settled in well and was learning a lot from Lady Katherine's maid, Sally.

Seraphina could hear voices coming from the study, just off the library. Aaron and Katherine were deep in conversation with the door ajar. Seraphina thought to leave but, curious, decided to sit and listen.

"Aaron, rarely do I concern myself with your affairs, but as Seraphina is a guest in our home, I am compelled to. Have you given any thought to how Seraphina may feel about this? Or Solomon? The boy will be home next week."

"I am a widower. Situations like this are not uncommon."

"Uncommon? Aaron, a Black paramour? Among our southern brethren maybe, but here?"

"Mother, I will not hide Seraphina away. I will make no apologies and give no explanations. Father did not."

"I am not asking you to. I am asking you to be discreet. For Seraphina's sake. And yours. You are still mourning…and so is she. The two of you have been through a lot…seen a lot."

"The loss of our child grieves me, but I am consoled by the fact that she is still with me."

"You love her." Katherine touched Aaron's cheek.

"I do, Mother, very much."

The door opened. Seraphina turned away.

"There you are! Always in the window, with your nose in a book, Seraphina."

"Good morning, Lady Katherine." Seraphina quickly wiped her tears. "I like the library. The stained-glass windows remind me of my grandmother's kitchen in the afternoon sun."

Aaron embraced Seraphina. "I must go to the hospital today. Mother has plans for you. I will be back this afternoon. You are in good hands."

"I understand."

She did, but the idea of his absence still made her anxious. This would be the first time he would be leaving her alone since their arrival.

"Seraphina. Come. Now that you are feeling better, we have much to discuss and much to do, you and I."

"Yes, Lady Katherine." Seraphina slipped from Aaron's arms, gathered her skirt, and followed Katherine into the hall.

"Où sont tes chaussures, ma fille? Où sont tes bas?" Katherine exclaimed. "Bare feet? Seraphina, a lady is never undressed. Mary informed me as to the sorry state of your belongings. How on earth did you survive on so little?"

"I managed. In a battlefield hospital, there isn't much time to worry about things like that. If it makes you feel any better, I did bathe and wash my hair regularly."

"In what? With what?" Katherine asked.

"A cut barrel with a floral scented water I made myself."

"A cut barrel! Seven months you spent like this, without complaint?"

"Complain?" Seraphina shook her head. "It was better than the three months I spent on a farm, washing in a river."

"Aaron should have sent you home months ago! Come. It is time to find you suitable attire."

Seraphina followed Katherine up the staircase.

"Vous êtes français?" Seraphina asked. "Aaron never mentioned—"

"Je suis née en France. I met Aaron's father on the voyage over. He was in France on business. We married aboard ship. It was quite the scandal—Lord Edward Joseph Weld, the heir apparent to the Weld family fortune, marrying a French woman without means or family."

"Scandal? Marrying a beautiful French woman without title?" Seraphina rolled her eyes.

"Oui. And it appears my son takes after his father." Katherine smiled.

"It does not bother you?" Seraphina asked. "That I am a Black woman without means or family?"

"Oh no, dear. I do not believe in such silly nonsense. Neither did my husband. L'amour n'est jamais facile. Tu est toute seule?"

"Oui. Love is very inconvenient." Seraphina blushed.

Silly nonsense. Lord Weld may not have believed in silly nonsense, but he was a man with a keen eye for beauty, inside and out. Lady Katherine Weld was stunning. At sixty, she didn't look a day over forty, with deep blue eyes, rich chocolate hair, and smooth porcelain skin. Beauty, coupled with a warm, caring disposition; it was no wonder Lord Weld had fallen for her.

"Aaron tells me you are a nurse. A skilled one at that. I mean no offense, but your level of education exceeds that of many women, even more so when one considers you are a Black."

"None taken. My Mamie Eulalie was French Creole. She was a practitioner of native medicine and worked with my grandfather, André Phillipe, a French doctor."

"Remarkable. You will have to tell me more, but later. We have important matters to attend to." Katherine looked down at Seraphina's feet. "Namely, your education in etiquette and decorum." She opened the bedroom door. "Sally, Minnie, are we ready?"

"Yes, my lady." Sally curtsied. "The dresses arrived yesterday. Miss Minnie and I have pressed them."

Sally was a petite homely blonde woman with a serious expression that masked her kind demeanor and did her appearance no favors.

"And her foundation garments?" Katherine visually scanned the room.

"Here, my lady." Minnie pointed to the dressing table.

"Good." Katherine clapped her hands. "Seraphina let's get you out of these…rags. And this hair?" Katherine rolled Seraphina's braid between her fingers. "What to do with this?"

Katherine and Sally set about removing Seraphina's clothing. All her pleas and attempts to fend the women off were for not, as they made quick work of it.

"Stop! I am not a child. I am—"

Katherine handed Seraphina the undergarments. "There is a basin and pitcher behind the shade. Once you are done, Sally and Minnie will corset you."

"Corset! I hate corsets. They are confining and unnecessary."

"Bon Dieu! Have you never worn a corset?" Katherine asked incredulous.

"Yes. But in the hospital, when caring for the men, it was uncomfortable and hot, so I stopped. No one noticed."

"Seraphina, my dear, you must wear a corset. When you are fitted properly, you will feel differently."

Seraphina stepped out from behind the shade. "For you, Lady Katherine. Only for you."

"Thank you, Seraphina. Sally, have Mr. Toombs fetch a coachman. Minnie and I will finish dressing Seraphina."

"Where are we going, Lady Katherine?" Seraphina queried.

"Shopping. You are going to need more than what we have here. There are teas, dinners, and other social events you must attend. Two dresses and one pair of shoes will never do."

"Dinners? Teas? Shopping? Lady Katherine, you sound like Lady Wheeler. And that is more than little frightening."

Katherine chuckled. "Emma is a lovely young woman, wise beyond her years. We had tea not too long before you came."

"She stayed a time at Harrison's Landing with her brother while he convalesced. We got to know each other. I like her. She has a good heart."

"Yes," Katherine groaned. "I understand she reminded my sons of their responsibilities when it came to you."

"She told you?" Seraphina laughed. "She is very well versed in proper etiquette and decorum. I learned a lot. Can we call on her? I would love to see her again."

"Oui. Ce serait charmant. She has inquired after you. We'll have to call on her soon." Katherine inspected Seraphina's braid again. "You must put this up. Minnie, fetch my hairpins. We'll have to add them to the list."

"Lady Katherine, thank you for your hospitality and kindness." Seraphina touched her hand.

"Think nothing of it. This is your home now if you wish it to be." Katherine embraced her.

For the first time in as many weeks, Seraphina felt a sense of calm. Aaron had said Philadelphia would be different. Maybe it would be.

*****

Seraphina wandered into the kitchen. The aroma of baking bread and spit-fired meat filled the space. After the library and the gardens, the kitchen was Seraphina's favorite place to be. A large butcher block table, like the one in Mamie Eulalie's kitchen, was set in the center, surrounded by open shelves and cupboards, with pots and pans hung from racks overhead and on the walls. The plumbed sink, wood fire stove, and ice box were recent additions, but the old hearth was still in use. According to Mary, Noble's wife and head cook, *"The ovens is nice, but the roasts still need a touch of fire and a good turn on the spit."*

The kitchen was truly the heart of the home. The staff took their meals in the kitchen. Mary always had some delectable treat to share and a story to go along with it. And the scullery maids' gossip was always entertaining. More than anything, Mary reminded Seraphina of Auntie Mary, and being near her felt like home. From the first day they met, Mary had Auntie Mary written all over her. She was short like Auntie Mary but slender, with the same warm brown skin and moon-shaped face. But her eyes carried a worn wisdom that dimmed their light. The one thing Mary had in spades was Auntie Mary's candor. She did not hesitate to let Seraphina know exactly what she thought the day they were introduced.

"Can you sew, cook…tend children?" Mary asked.

"No. I cannot sew. I can cook well enough to feed myself, and I don't have any children," Seraphina replied.

"Mercy girl, you bout helpless."

"Miss Mary," Seraphina called for Mary's attention.

"Well, look at you!" Mary exclaimed. "My, my, you a pretty girl. Turn 'round so I can see the whole dress."

Seraphina spun around to give Mary a better look. Even with the corset, the long-sleeved cotton day dress with rose floral stripes was surprisingly comfortable. Katherine allowed her to forego the hoops and wear additional skirts but made it clear that hoops were a must while entertaining and in mixed company.

"Thank you, Mary. I have never worn so many pieces of clothing at one time in my life. May I help you with anything?"

"Now, you know Sir Aaron doesn't want you working in the kitchen," Mary scolded. "Noble said you stubborn as two mules. You gwine mind me. Sit here while I knead this dough."

Seraphina sat down. The no-man's-land between belonging and not was frustrating. But she'd discovered early that beneath Mary's warm heart and infectious laugh was a firm hand. It was her kitchen.

"Noble, tell me how Colonel got a hold to you. Say you was none too happy 'bout it." Mary chuckled. "I laugh so my sides hurt."

"Looking back, I can see how one would find it funny. It is hard for me. Where I am from, I am my own master." Seraphina smiled, sullen.

"Nobody they own master. You foolish to think that." Mary tossed flour on the dough in her hand. "Man got God over him. Wives have husbands, children have mothers…nobody they own. Noble says you ain't got no family to speak of. Just those folks on the farm?"

"Yes. Addie, Daisy, Jed, Lizzie…the babies. I miss them."

"I knows you do, but the good Lord put you here. So here is where you supposed to be. Tell me why you ain't married. I figure it cause you so hardheaded, but you pretty. Some man must have come calling."

"I devoted my time to my studies. It didn't leave much time for courting. How did you and Noble come to be here with the Welds?"

"Grace of God. Me and Noble run away some twelve years ago, now. It was hard. Noble found work on the docks. We scarce have enough to eat or place to sleep. When the boss, Mr. Canterbury, find out Noble could read and write, he made him a steward. Then Lady Elizabeth died. Mr. Canterbury and Sir Aaron close. Sir Aaron needed help with the house and Solomon. Mr. Canterbury send us to work for Sir Aaron and Lady Katherine."

"What about Eli?" Seraphina asked.

Mary stopped working the dough and went silent for a few moments.

"Noble and me have three children. All boys. When they old enough to work, Marse sell them off. Say he don't need the work. We don't know where. I hurt. Hurt bad for a long time. Made Noble promise not to give me no more children. We found Eli when we run off. He was wee thing, barely two or three. He was wet, cold, hungry, and crying in a bush. We think his mama got caught and hid him away. We wait a day to see if someone come for him. No one did. Been ours since."

"Miss Mary, I'm sorry." Seraphina hugged her, crying. "I should not have asked."

"Hush now, child." Mary dried both their faces with her apron. "We Oakes is strong, like the tree. Eli is God's gift to us."

"Oakes? Your name is Mary Oakes?" Seraphina stumbled, eyes wide.

It can't be. It just can't. Auntie Mary? My Auntie Mary? First Aaron… and now Auntie Mary?"

Could she really be standing face to face with Auntie Mary's great-grandmother? It would explain the connection. Waking up in 1862 was inexplicable, meeting Aaron, even more so, but now this?

"Seraphina?" Mary touched her shoulder. "Child, what's wrong? You bout white as those linens."

"I'm sorry, Miss Mary. I am fine. Just a spell."

"Thought I was gwine have to put you back in the bed. You rest. I got to finish up supper. Hate for Sir Aaron to starve to death."

"I will retire to the dayroom with Lady Katherine. Please have one of the girls bring a tea service. Thank you."

Mary beamed. "Yes, miss."

"I am sorry, Miss Mary." Seraphina sighed. "I didn't mean it like that."

Mary dusted her hands with her apron, then took Seraphina's hands in hers.

"My hands is rough, so yours can be smooth. The branches of the tree are far from its roots, but they still part of the tree. You are a lady. We are proud."

Seraphina hugged Mary tightly. "Lady or no, I'm still going to sneak into the kitchen from time to time. Whether you like it or not."

"Two mules, child. Two mules." Mary laughed.

CHAPTER SEVENTEEN

Weld Manor – Philadelphia, Pennsylvania
February 1863

February 10th, 1863

In the last few weeks, Seraphina has settled. She and Mother do well together, and I am able to leave her in mother's care. I have taken a position at the general hospital. Physicians are needed. The work is not as grueling as on the battlefield, but the mind fatigues just the same. The wards are full of soldiers from the fighting in and around

Fredericksburg in December. They tell stories of an ill-fated charge on some loathsome place called Marye's Hill. Thomas spoke of it in his letter. Burnside has been removed from command. General Hooker has ascended to his place. I pray he proves himself better than his predecessors. We lost some ten thousand men. Ten thousand! Are we now to count the dead like drops of rain in the ocean? Thomas is taking leave to Boston; he's been assured hostilities will cease until Spring. We will both return to the army then.

*****

"Good evening, sir." The butler held the door.
The foyer was expansive. Double solid mahogany doors opened onto a tile mosaic floor framed by stark white walls and mahogany wainscoting.

"Good evening, Mr. Toombs." Aaron handed the butler his coat and hat. "Where is Miss Laurent?"

"She and Lady Weld have retired to the dayroom. Miss Mary says dinner will begin promptly at six. Mr. Noble has prepared your dinner attire, and I have left a letter from Mr. Thomas on the desk in your study."

"Thank you, Mr. Toombs."

Tall and thin, with gray eyes and white hair, Mr. Toombs was the only staff that remained from when his father was alive. He'd come over on the voyage with his parents and had been a devoted member of the Weld household for decades. *"Proper English butlers are English,"* his father would say. And Mr. Toombs was as English as the Queen.

The dayroom was set just off the foyer. Furnished to entertain a handful of guests, it was perfect for just sitting and enjoying conversation under the skylight.

The sound of Seraphina's laughter delighted him. He'd heard so little of it of late. Aaron slowed just before the dayroom door, unable to resist the urge to eavesdrop. It was for naught; his French was too rusty to keep up. He cleared his throat to make his presence known.

"Good evening, ladies. I—"

Aaron stopped. Gone were the boots, makeshift blouse, and woolen skirt of the camps; before him stood a lady in periwinkle and lace.

Seraphina stood, curtsied, and offered her hand. "Good evening, Colonel."

Aaron kissed her hand gently. "Seraphina, you are beautiful."

"Yes, isn't she ravishing? I thought the blue too bold when it arrived, but Seraphina said you would love it. I see she was right," Katherine beamed. "We had her fitted today. Seraphina chose some exquisite fabrics. She has a good eye. The other dresses should arrive next week."

"I did enjoy my afternoon with Lady Katherine." Seraphina peered over her shoulder at Katherine. "She has given me quite the education."

"Aaron, Seraphina is a natural lady."

"Of that, I had no doubt," Aaron replied, kissing Seraphina's hand again.

"Seraphina and I were discussing hosting a dinner. It would be the first of the season."

"A dinner? Mother, really?" Aaron groaned.

"Yes, or have you forgotten that you have been gone for a year? Or that you did not attend any of the Christmas and New Year's balls? We have our obligations. You know this."

"Lady Katherine, I would be more than happy to assist Mary in the kitchen."

"No," Aaron stated flatly.

"Aaron, be reasonable. I am sure Mary will need help. Noble too."

"You are not a servant in this house. Is that understood?"

"I understand, but what am I to do all evening?"

Aaron cradled Seraphina's face in his hands. "Mother will chaperone you for the evening. I am sure she will help you get acquainted. You are as well-spoken as you are enchanting. You will be fine." Seraphina pulled back. "Did it ever occur to you that I may not want to spend an evening mingling with a group of people who are sure to look down on me?"

"I want you there." Aaron tried to embrace her again, but she evaded him.

"No. If you do not want me in the kitchen or serving the guests, so be it. I will spend the evening in my room."

"You will be at dinner if I have to dress you and drag you down the stairs myself."

"Aaron Matthew Weld! You wouldn't!" Katherine cried.

"Oh, yes, he would, Lady Katherine. I will attend as is your wish. Lady Katherine will prove a great chaperone. She has been a tremendous help already. Lady Katherine, may we continue the party planning tomorrow? I'd like to prepare for dinner."

"Yes. It has been a long day."

"Thank you, Lady Katherine. Colonel." Seraphina curtsied and left.

"Aaron, I am ashamed of you! A gentleman would never treat a lady in such a manner. Threatening the poor girl. What has come over you?"

"Mother, Seraphina is willful. The woman would argue with God himself."

"So, you would molest the poor girl? Have you done this before?"

"Yes, regrettably. But I was trying to protect her. I *am* trying to protect her." Aaron sat on the couch. "And I am failing."

"Aaron, if you hold a thing too tightly, it will slip through your fingers. Seraphina is not willful; she simply knows her own mind." Katherine held his hand. "She is still very fragile. Maybe she isn't ready to make her debut."

"Mother, I am pleased you and Seraphina have come together so nicely. I hoped that would be the case. Help her adjust, Mother. Please." Aaron kissed her forehead.

"Seraphina is a wonderful young woman. She will do well. You need to apologize for your boorish behavior."

Aaron smiled. "I will do so right now."

*****

Seraphina reclined on a chaise, warming her bare feet in front of the roaring hearth.

The master suite overlooked the drive. Fit for a lord and lady, the room had every luxury. The large four-poster bed and the dressing rooms' clawfoot tub with indoor plumbing were the amenities Seraphina coveted most.

"You know if Lady Katherine catches you barefoot again, she may tie your shoes to your feet." Aaron stood in the bedroom doorway.

"Minnie, would you leave us, please?" Seraphina ordered, never taking her eyes from Aaron. Minnie left without a word.

"Are you going to turn me in?"

"On the contrary." Aaron crossed the room and knelt next to the sofa. He kissed one foot and then the other. "I rather like your feet."

Seraphina giggled and tucked her feet under her skirts.

"It is good to hear you laugh, to see your true smile."

"I am sorry I've kept them from you. I don't do so with malice. It is just when I look at you, I feel guilt. Guilt because…you told me not to leave," Seraphina cried. "You told me it wasn't safe, and I didn't listen. And because of me, our baby is dead, and I've made you a murderer."

"No. No. Our child is dead because an evil man committed unspeakable acts against you. A man I should have killed the first time he laid hands on you. I killed him, and I make no apologies for it. I would do it again. You did not make me a murderer."

"Please forgive me," Seraphina sobbed.

"There is nothing to forgive. I am the one who requires forgiveness. You do not have to go anywhere until you are ready."

"I love you, Aaron."

"My mysterious Seraphina, that is the first time you've said those words to me. Say them again."

"I love you. And I will say it forever if you like."

*****

The meeting of the Philadelphian Women's Sanitary Commission put a fine point on the definition of high society. Seraphina was bowled over by the overt display of wealth and strict enforcement of class and decorum.

The hall was large, with vaulted ceilings and floor-to-ceiling windows. Tables dressed in fine linens and floral centerpieces dotted the room. A string quartet played in the corner of the room, their soft strings barely audible above the beehive hum of the women's conversations. Several obviously important women sat on a stage draped in patriotic red, white, and blue bunting at the front of the hall.

Today the ladies were meeting to discuss fundraising efforts, distribution of donated goods, and the condition of the contraband camps. The correlation between the health and well-being of the contraband and the fighting men they supported was finally being recognized. For Seraphina, a recipient of the commission's charity, this was a fascinating look behind the scenes.

"Lady Weld, I see you've taken on a new maid. She is quite lovely. What is her name?"

The woman's large nose, nasal tone, and dark eyes gave her a crow-like appearance. *Mother Nature, you hit this one on the nose; literally,* Seraphina mused. "My name is Miss Seraphina Laurent. I am not a maid. And you are?"

"Oh?" The woman tightened her lips. "I am Lady Anne Van Bergen. I am the director of this commission."

"Well, it is a pleasure to meet you, Lady Van Bergen. I have worked in the field hospitals and have been witness to the commission's good work. You all are doing a great service."

"Lady Van Bergen, Miss Laurent is a guest. She is a nurse." Katherine smiled.

Seraphina noticed it did not reach her eyes. She was faking. *This is hilarious.*

"A nurse? A Negress nurse? I did not know such a thing existed. Lady Weld, where did you find her?"

"Je viens de la Nouvelle-Orléans. J'ai fait la connaissance du colonel Weld alors que je travaillais en Virginie." Seraphina replied.

"She speaks French!" Anne exclaimed, her shock and horror evident.

"Forgive me, Lady Van Bergen." Katherine smiled, an exaggerated cow-eyed expression on her face. "Did I neglect to mention Miss Laurent is French Creole?"

"Creole?" Anne recoiled in disgust.

"Yes, French Creole. I beg your pardon. I've so enjoyed conversing with Lady Weld that I forget myself. I am from New Orleans. I made Colonel Weld's acquaintance while working with the contraband in Virginia. Lady Weld was kind enough to open her home to me."

"Well, French women are known for their…hospitality, are they not?" Lady Van Bergen turned up her nose. "If you ladies would excuse me."

"Lady Katherine." Seraphina covered her mouth with her fan, as Katherine had instructed. "That woman was awful. Pardon my French, but she's a bitch."

Katherine brought her fan to her lips, too. "Anne Van Bergen is a terrible gossip. Worse, she puts on the most shameful of airs. The woman rules over the Sanitary Commission as if she were the Queen of England!"

"I believe the Queen would be far more magnanimous." Seraphina chuckled.

"You handled her disgraceful behavior with poise." Katherine patted Seraphina's hand. "I am so very proud of you."

"Thank you, Lady Katherine. I know the French was a little much. What the hell does she have against the French?" Seraphina asked.

"Another time. Let us mingle. There are other women here whom I'd like you to meet."

"Miss Laurent! Miss Laurent!" Emma called to Seraphina from across the room.

"Lady Wheeler!" Seraphina rushed to her side. The two embraced warmly.

"I knew it. I just knew it. Lady Weld would have you right as rain. What a lady you make!" Emma squealed gleefully. "How is the colonel?"

"Well," Seraphina replied. "And you? How is Andrew?"

"Andrew is well. I, however, am bored to tears. I cannot wait for the season to begin. Lady Weld, will you be hosting the opening soiree?"

"It is good to see you, Lady Wheeler. Yes. Miss Laurent and I have been discussing the details."

"I will await my invitation with bated breath. I must get back to my delegation." Emma hugged her. "Do call on me for tea soon."

"It is a shame what they did to Emma." Katherine shook her head. "Marrying her off to that old wretch of a man. She is so young and vibrant. She deserves a man who is such."

"Maybe the gods will have mercy and gift her with his early demise?" Seraphina shrugged. "And then there are other interests. Emma is not as unattractive as she believes herself to be."

"You, my sweet Seraphina, are a quick study." Katherine grinned. "For I have suggested as much."

"Lady Katherine, you astound me." Seraphina laughed. "Be sure he isn't too energetic. We would hate for Lord Wheeler to meet his end sooner than later."

"Dear girl, you are going to do well."

*****

Aaron paused in the foyer outside the dayroom. Seraphina sat in her favorite place under the library window, the works of Walt Whitman in her hand. He wondered what memories visited her in the colored light. What life had been stolen from her that she longed for so deeply. Could she ever truly be happy in this life? With him?

"You ladies were out early this morning." Aaron kissed Katherine on the cheek.

"Yes, the Sanitary Commission had a brunch meeting today. Seraphina was a model of grace. She held the ladies in rapt attention," Katherine gushed. "She will be the talk of the set."

"I'll be something." Seraphina stood to greet Aaron. "I am just happy the commission will be focusing more attention on the refugee camps in the new year."

Mr. Toombs entered the dayroom. "Pardon, sir, but Mister Solomon has arrived."

Katherine rushed into the foyer. "Solomon! Bien-aimé! Aaron! I hardly recognize him.

Tell me, Solomon, where is the boy I kissed good-bye at summer's end? Did you travel well? Let me look at you."

Solomon returned Katherine's overly affectionate greeting with the typical teenage lack of enthusiasm. "Hello, Grandmother."

Aaron couldn't believe it. In the year he'd been gone, Solomon had grown at least a foot. He was almost tall enough to stand eye to eye with him. His lean frame had yet to fill out, but evidence of the coming changes were there. One thing hadn't changed; he still favored Elizabeth.

"Mother, leave the boy be." Aaron chuckled.

"Mon Dieu! Solomon, what happened?" Katherine exclaimed.

"It is nothing, Grandmother," Solomon explained, struggling to fend off her efforts to examine his face better.

"Nothing?" Katherine shrieked. "Your eye and lip are swollen and blue as summer berries. Have you been fighting? Did someone attack you? Aaron!"

Aaron stepped forward. He grabbed Solomon by the chin and gave his face a cursory inspection. "What happened?"

"Michael Stewart made disparaging remarks about our family that I felt could not go unchallenged. I assure you, Father, he got the worst of it."

"You should not be fighting. I do not need you to protect me or my reputation."

"Your reputation? What of mine? Or did you think she would go unnoticed?" Solomon pointed at Seraphina. "Is that why you did not tell me?"

"Miss Laurent is none of your concern." Aaron gave him a stern look.

"Stewart said our home is a boarding house for niggers and French whores. And it is not my concern?"

"Oh my god!" Seraphina gasped.

"Solomon, mind your tongue!" Katherine shrieked.

"Solomon. Come." Aaron turned. "We will speak in the library."

Solomon did not follow.

"You defy me?!"

Seraphina stepped in front of Aaron before he could get to Solomon.

"Seraphina, it is never wise to come between a father and son," Katherine warned.

"Katherine, I am already between them," she replied.

"You will go now!" Aaron shouted.

Solomon left for the library, wisely avoiding Aaron's reach.

"He defied me!" Aaron's eyes narrowed.

"Yes." Seraphina placed a calming hand on his chest. "And we all know how much you hate that."

"I am his father," Aaron bellowed. "I owe him no explanations."

"I understand why you feel that way, but you do," Seraphina said. "What you do affects him, and you bear responsibility for that. You haven't seen him in over a year. Is this how you want to start out? Go talk to him."

Aaron stalked into the library and slammed the doors behind him.

*****

Aaron sat behind his desk, a scowling Solomon, arms folded at his chest, across from him.

"You will apologize to Miss Laurent for your ungentlemanly behavior."

"You should have told me." Solomon glared.

Aaron sat back. "I intended to. I wished to do so face to face."

"Did you think I would not find out? Find out that you have a… Is she what they say she is? A whore?"

"No. Miss Laurent is my friend."

"Friend? Father, you think me that naïve? I have never seen a woman who looks as she does. She is…"

Aaron removed two tumblers and a bottle of Scotch from the desk drawer. He poured each of them a drink and handed Solomon a glass.

"If we are going to talk like men and fight like men, let us drink like them." Aaron raised his glass in salute. "Have you known a woman, Solomon? I know there are…liberal women. I am sure you've been propositioned."

"No." Solomon sipped his drink, and his color deepened. "But one does not have to know a woman to recognize uncommon beauty."

"Her name is Seraphina André Phillipe Laurent. She is a nurse and has worked by my side in the field hospitals these many months. I have the deepest affection for her. And yes, she does share my bed, but she is not my whore, or any other foul thing they may say of her. She is a lady and a guest in this home. I expect you to treat her as such. Understood?"

"Yes, sir. Is it true? Is it true… Did you kill a man to defend her honor?"

"A man kidnapped her and beat her nearly to death. I killed him, and I would do it again. I do not want you fighting anymore. I will deal with Mr. Stewart. Now, finish your drink. You have apologies to make."

Aaron ushered Solomon into the dayroom, and Seraphina and Katherine rose to meet him. He approached Seraphina first. She held out her hand and curtsied.

Solomon took her hand and kissed it. "My lady. I pray you will forgive my lapse of manners. You are lovely, and I am pleased to make your acquaintance."

"Please, call me Seraphina. I wish we'd met under better circumstances, with proper introductions and such." Seraphina smiled. "You are forgiven. The pleasure of your acquaintance is mine."

"Grandmother, I beg your pardon for my behavior. I did not mean to offend." Solomon kissed Katherine on the cheek.

She hugged him. "There is no offense, my sweet."

"Solomon, leave us. In case you were wondering, Eli is in the kitchen." Aaron smiled.

"Thank you, Father."

Aaron watched Solomon leave. "He tests me."

"Don't be angry with him," Seraphina pleaded. "He needed to hear the truth from you."

"And now, you must hear the truth from me," Aaron said. "If you wish to leave here, I will honor my word."

"Why now?" Seraphina's eyes grew moist.

"Not for the reasons you believe." Aaron stepped forward.

Seraphina retreated a step. "And what do I believe?"

"That I find the idea of my name being associated with Blacks and prostitutes untenable."

"Am I wrong?" she cried.

"Nothing could be further from the truth. From the moment I found you in that barn, you have endured more than a man has the right to ask of a woman. And I did not ask."

"And now you want to give me the choice? Now!" Seraphina screamed.

Aaron reached for her. "Seraphina, it is not—you don't—"

"Fuck all, it isn't. Let me go!" Seraphina ran from the room.

"Aaron Matthew Weld!" Katherine shouted. "You are a proper idiot! I am ashamed of you!"

Aaron held out his hand for her. Katherine refused it and left without a curtsey.

Aaron rubbed his temples. "Mr. Toombs! Mr. Toombs!"

"Yes, Sir Aaron."

"Bring me my Scotch."

CHAPTER EIGHTEEN

Weld Manor – Philadelphia, Pennsylvania
February 1863

Seraphina hid behind the staircase in the foyer, just out of view. All the dinner guests had arrived and were congregated in the manor's hall, adjacent to the dining room—all but the one she wanted. Emma had declined the invitation due to illness.

Oil lamp sconces gave the room a soft, intimate glow. Landscapes from renowned painters hung from the walls above mahogany wainscoting. The Weld crest was emblazoned over the fireplace mantel. Ladies in evening gowns and jewels; men in black dress coats with high collars and white vests—the lavish hall was an Emily Brontë novel come to life.

"Miss Laurent? Miss Laurent? Why are you hiding?" Solomon asked.

"You all right, Miss Seraphina?" Eli asked.

"Yes, gentleman, I am fine." Seraphina stepped from behind the banister. "Solomon, why aren't you at the party? And Eli, aren't you supposed to be helping your mother?"

"Eli just wanted a peek. And I, well, I don't want to go," Solomon answered.

"Oh, well, that makes two of us." Seraphina sighed.

"Miss Laurent, you are beautiful… I mean this evening." Solomon stumbled over his words.

"Thank you, Solomon. And remember, when it is just us, it's Seraphina."

Eli snickered and nudged Solomon in the side. After a brief silent argument, Solomon offered Seraphina his arm.

"Miss Laurent, may I have the pleasure of escorting you this evening?" Solomon blushed.

"You mean I can't stay under the stairs?" Seraphina giggled.

Solomon chuckled. "I don't think my grandmother would approve."

"I guess not." Seraphina shrugged. "Then, yes, Mister Solomon, I would greatly enjoy the pleasure of your company this evening."

Seraphina waited at the door with Solomon for Mr. Toombs to announce them.

Solomon whispered in Seraphina's ear. "You're a Weld. Don't let them forget it."

Mr. Toombs cleared his throat for attention. "Presenting Mister Solomon Weld and Miss Seraphina Laurent."

Seraphina stepped into the hall with Solomon. The plunging neckline of her emerald silk dress bared her shoulders and cleavage to perfection. The deep green of the dress and the brilliance of her diamond jewelry set her auburn eyes ablaze and gave her skin an iridescent glow. A hush fell over the room as the guests stood with mouths agape. It was obvious she was not what they'd imagined. The men ogled, and the women's eyes flashed daggers as she passed.

Aaron's eyes locked with hers from across the room. She could feel the heat of his icy blue gaze on her skin. She'd told him she wasn't coming this evening. He'd tried to apologize for putting his foot in his mouth, claiming she'd misunderstood him. However, she didn't believe him, and they hadn't been together since.

"Lady Weld, please forgive my tardiness." Seraphina bowed in a low curtsey. "Solomon was kind enough to escort me this evening. He is truly a dear young man."

"Thank you, Miss Laurent. Ladies, if you'll excuse me." Solomon bowed and stepped away.

"Seraphina, you are positively radiant," Lady Katherine beamed. "I am glad you decided to join us. May I introduce Mrs. Meredith Miller? Her mother, Martha, is a dear friend. Meredith's late husband, Adam, and the colonel were cousins and the best of friends. Mrs. Miller, this is Miss Seraphina Laurent."

"I am pleased to make your acquaintance, Mrs. Miller."

"A pleasure," she replied.

Seraphina was taken aback by Meredith's icy tone. She was sure she had not done or said anything to warrant such a reaction.

"Meredith, how is your mother? I have not had time to call on her this week with all the evening's preparations."

"It has been a trying few days for mother. She is sorely disappointed she was not able to attend."

"Pray her forgiveness for me, and let her know I will be by soon." Katherine touched Meredith's hand reassuringly.

"Mrs. Miller, if you would like, I can call on your mother as well. I am a nurse. I may have some treatments that could be of help to her," Seraphina offered.

"I heard you were a nurse. A Negress nurse?" Meredith gave Seraphina a dismissive glance. "How peculiar. My mother has physicians. There is no need for you to call."

Blonde, with pale blue eyes and cotton candy lips, Meredith was the picture-perfect 19th-century woman, complete with a healthy side of racist and classist condescension.

"I find it peculiar that more women aren't afforded the chance to continue their education," Seraphina clapped back.

"Laurent? Is that French?" Meredith asked.

"Oui," Seraphina replied. "Je suis Créole française. Ma famille est originaire de la Nouvelle-Orléans."

Seraphina speaks fluent French. It is quite remarkable. We have had such the time," Katherine spoke excitedly.

"Yes, remarkable. How long do you plan to stay with the Welds? I can imagine your family would want you home."

"I expect to return to the front with Colonel Weld when the Army resumes action in the spring."

"Oh." Meredith glared. "Speaking of the Lord Weld. Lady Katherine, you must be so pleased to have your son home safe. I know we are all glad to see him."

"Yes, I am, as any mother would be." Katherine touched Seraphina's hands. "I am even happier that Miss Laurent was there to assist him."

Seraphina's insides exploded with a delight that was hard to keep off her face. Katherine was a master at 19th-century shade.

"How did you come to meet the Lord Weld?" Meredith asked. "How did you come to be in Virginia?"

"I came to help with the war effort. Nurses are sorely needed. I met the colonel when—"

"I found her. Hard at work, nursing soldiers on a farm," Aaron answered as he approached.

"Lord Weld. We have gone so long without a word from you. We would have thought you lost to us if not for Lady Katherine's assurances."

Meredith held out her hand, and Aaron kissed it lightly.

"The demands of an army surgeon are many, Mrs. Miller, especially on the front. It is difficult to find time to rest, let alone the leisure to write."

"Miss. Laurent is right." Aaron stared at her. "Any lapse in correspondence was truly unintentional."

Meredith gave Seraphina a frigid look. Jealousy. Seraphina could see its green eyes behind Meredith's smug expression.

"All is forgiven, Lord Weld. Would you care to join me on the veranda? A brisk walk before dinner?"

To Seraphina's dismay, Aaron extended his arm. Meredith wrapped her gloved hand over his in wicked triumph.

"Miss Laurent, would you care to join us?" Aaron asked.

"Thank you, no. I am afraid the night air doesn't agree with me. Please enjoy."

Seraphina watched them leave. The last thing she wanted to do was walk the veranda with Meredith Miller, no matter how delicious watching her melt into a puddle of envy might be. Meredith Miller was no Helen of Troy, but she was not unattractive. Meredith would be no competition in one hundred fifty years, but in 1862, she was all that and more. Meredith was going to be a problem.

"Seraphina, you did well. Envy is so ugly on a woman," Katherine said.

"Mademoiselle. Mademoiselle Laurent."

"Oui. Je m'appelle Mademoiselle Laurent. Qui êtes vous?" Seraphina curtly asked the gentleman. She was in no mood to socialize.

"Pardonnez-moi, we have not been properly introduced. I am Vincent Canterbury."

"Canterbury Shipping. I have heard of you." Seraphina offered her hand.

Vincent kissed it. "And I of you. If I may be so bold, the descriptions of you, Mademoiselle Laurent, fall woefully short."

"Thank you kindly, Mr. Canterbury."

"Mr. Canterbury is a dear family friend and Sir Aaron's godfather. May I trust Miss Laurent to your keeping? I have other obligations. I will see you both at dinner," Katherine excused herself.

Would you care to sit?" Vincent asked.

"Yes, thank you."

Seraphina smoothed her skirts and gently sat beside him, keeping the appropriate distance between them. Vincent was an older gentleman, a Sean Connery type with the accent to match. His eyes were warm and kind. A welcome sight, given the cold stares she had received from many of the guests.

"My business takes me to France often." Vincent smiled.

"I have never been to France," Seraphina replied.

"C'est dommage. Les jardins de Versailles sont magnifiques."

"Your French is impeccable for an Englishman."

"If you prefer Frenchmen, I will gladly play the part." Vincent's eyes sparkled mischievously.

Seraphina laughed out loud. "Why do I get the impression you have played the part for many a woman, be they French or American."

"I confess. Does this change your opinion of me?"

"To the contrary, your honesty is refreshing. I find few people here speak their mind truthfully. They hide behind arbitrary rules of decorum and tradition. I find the whole society thing exhausting."

"Mademoiselle Laurent, may I speak plainly?"

"Yes. Please do."

"These women have been groomed since birth to be what they are... not who they are. You have not. Be glad of it."

"Point taken. I will endeavor to be more gracious. You are not married. A handsome man of means like yourself should have his choice of women. Are you a widower?"

"The life of a sea merchant is not conducive to family life."

"Or, you prefer variety to monogamy."

"I could be convinced of matrimony." Vincent flashed a grin.

"Don't look to me to convince you!" Seraphina smiled.

"Speaking of decorum, we should mingle. Come, I will introduce you to the other guest."

*****

Aaron and Meredith returned to the room just as dinner was announced, and Katherine began to usher the guests into the dining room. When Aaron noticed her with Vincent, a murderous expression settled on his face. Vincent saw it too, but to Seraphina's amazement and mild amusement, Vincent boldly carried on, seemingly unconcerned by Aaron's reaction.

"Mademoiselle Laurent, would you do me the honor of taking the seat next to mine? It does not appear the Lady Weld set out place cards."

"Yes, Mr. Canterbury, I would be happy to."

Once the ladies were seated, the men took their seats. Aaron sat at the head of the table, Meredith to his right, and her father, Mr. Henry Wallace—a portly, balding old man with pot-marked skin and an arrogant disposition—on his left. Lady Katherine sat opposite Aaron at the other end of the table with Solomon on her right and another older gentleman, a Mr. Franklin, on her left. Seraphina may have been unfamiliar with many 19th-century cultural customs, but the seating around a table (and the message it conveyed) was not one of them. Meredith and her father were making a play for the Weld throne.

If the situation with Meredith was not enough to drag down her mood, things only got worse as Mary and the other servants began the dinner service. Seraphina did not want to be served by them. She felt guilty.

Tula, one of the maids from the kitchen, set a dish in front of Seraphina. She dropped her head and avoided eye contact with her.

"Don't you pay us no never mind. This here our job. You hold that head up," she whispered. "You do us proud."

"Thank you, Tula," Seraphina replied loudly enough to be heard.

"You've done something I did not think possible, Miss Laurent." Vincent grinned.

"What is that, Mr. Canterbury?"

"Bewitched my godbrother."

"Mr. Canterbury, I think Sir Aaron's intentions lie elsewhere. Maybe to his right?"

"He hasn't looked that way all evening. He has spent considerable time threatening to kill me with a look…and ravishing you." Vincent hid his Cheshire mask behind his raised goblet. "And you've been avoiding him all evening."

"I assure you, Mr. Canterbury, Sir Aaron has made it plain I am free to leave."

"So, he's made a proper idiot of himself." Vincent cracked up.

Was Vincent right? Or was Aaron just jealous? Did he want his cake and to eat it too? Seraphina stared across the table at Aaron. He was watching her, just as Vincent had said. Questions swirled, but only two answers came to the fore. One, he'd told her she could leave. And two, Meredith Miller was sitting to his right.

*****

Dinner was well into the dessert course before the conversation turned in earnest to the subject of the war. Vincent had been most pleasant company, and a welcome distraction from the master class in ass-kissing Meredith and her father were putting on. But even Vincent was not enough to keep Seraphina's attention when the subject of the refugees came up.

"I hear they are quite the burden, these contraband. They come in droves, I am told, and the army is providing for the wretches. Is this true, Colonel?"

"No, Mr. Wallace. While it is true that more and more people come every day and that the camps are full, the army affords them little, and as such, they cannot be considered a burden," Aaron answered coolly.

"Are they not being paid for their labor? And given a day's rations? Our government should not be wasting money and supplies on a lot of worthless refugees. General Butler's decision to deem them contraband of war was ill-advised. I say we send them back to their masters. I believe it is the aim of the rebel dogs to win this war by bankrupting the Union," Wallace grunted.

"I agree wholeheartedly, Mr. Wallace. And what of our men? The losses reported are staggering and, in my opinion, indicative of incompetence of leadership and the weakness of men. I say these generals and their men lack the will to win this war."

"Right you are, Franklin. Right you are," Wallace offered in agreement.

The conversation carried on in the same manner for what seemed like forever. Mr. Franklin, who Seraphina deduced was some sort of city councilman, and Mr. Wallace, her nemesis's father and local merchant, kept up their banter well after the party had adjourned to the dayroom for after-dinner drinks and conversation. Seraphina prayed they would change the topic, but she could no longer control herself when they did not.

"Gentleman, how easy it must be to cast dispersions and sit in judgment from a place of comfort and security. I can tell you these contrabands are no burden, and I can tell you that without their services to the cause, the Union would have long since lost this war. Who do you think cooks, cleans, and nurses? Who are the carpenters, blacksmiths, and burial details? It is the contraband.

"These contrabands risk life and limb for the slightest chance to live as free men. They come with nothing, walking for miles while hunted by slave raiders all the way; women are raped and whole families murdered. And you suggest they should risk all this and be enslaved, again!

"As for our men, their leaders may be incompetent, but they are by no means weak. They lay down their lives for a cause greater than themselves. Hundreds, thousands of men and boys, their noble blood given in the service of freedom. You gentlemen have no right to judge them. No right!"

"Do not forget to whom you speak or your place!" Wallace growled savagely. "I will not be lectured to by any woman, least of all ni—"

"Mr. Wallace! You are out of turn, sir!" Vincent interrupted.

"Sir, I would not presume to lecture a man of such limited intellect as yourself. I do not enjoy exercises in futility!" Seraphina shouted back.

Seraphina scanned the room. The hushed gasp and whispers of the guests told her all she needed to know: It was time to leave. She looked to Aaron. His expression was blank. Meredith stood beside him with the same look of wicked triumph from earlier.

"Ladies and gentlemen, thank you for a lovely evening. Good night." Seraphina curtsied and walked stoically from the room.

"Never in my life have I seen such a display! Colonel, such behavior… I dare say more than a scolding is in order," Wallace blustered.

Aaron set his glass down and walked over to where Mr. Wallace was standing.

"Miss Laurent has held the hands of dying men crying out for their wives and mothers, weeping for home. Born witness to unimaginable suffering and death. Stood ankle-deep in blood, limbs, and flesh for hours on end. She has served as a nurse with distinction. The Union Army and its men owe her a great debt of gratitude—a debt they have repaid with cruelty and savagery. Mr. Wallace, you would do well to remember that, as you would to remember you are in my home."

"Well, that was a distasteful bit of theatre." Vincent broke the uncomfortable silence. "Let us refresh our glasses and turn to more pleasant conversation. Shall we? Sir Aaron, care to join me?"

Aaron joined Vincent and Katherine by the hearth. The servants made a round with wine and other spirits. Slowly the awkwardness of the moment passed, and the mood lightened once more.

"Thank you, Mr. Canterbury," Katherine whispered.

"It is a rare woman who can offer both indignant and enlightened commentary on a subject. It would seem the gods have favored the Weld men."

"Aaron, my love, I have never seen you so…angry. It frightened me. It frightened everyone." Katherine touched his shoulder. "Are you okay?"

"Katherine, Mr. Wallace's behavior was inexcusable. He deserved worse." Vincent sipped his Scotch.

"Excuse me. Good night." Aaron left the room.

He thought about what Katherine said. *"It frightened me. It frightened everyone."* He wanted them to be afraid. He'd once made the mistake of not putting down a threat to Seraphina's safety from the beginning. He would not do so again.

*****

Aaron stood outside the bedroom door. He could hear Seraphina crying inside. She hadn't spoken to him in any meaningful way in days. She said she wasn't going to the party and then went anyway, without telling him. So, instead of escorting her for the evening, he'd had to spend it with Meredith. And then, to be sure he could not correct his error, she avoided him and gave all her attention to Vincent. A trespass he would later deal with Vincent for. And then, just when he was about at the end of his tether, she reminded him of who she was and why he loved her. She stood toe to toe with the cruelty and indignities of her station and passionately defended herself and her people. Her strength humbled him. Her passion fed his soul.

"Seraphina, may I enter?" Aaron called to her.

"No."

"Seraphina, I am coming in. If I must break down this door, so be it."

The door unlatched and fell ajar. Seraphina was seated on the floor, her skirts puddled around her, tears falling.

"I am sorry. I am sorry. I have embarrassed you. I have embarrassed myself. I have embarrassed Lady Katherine."

"Seraphina, my mysterious Seraphina." Aaron sat beside her.

He lifted her head and gently kissed away the tears on her face. "You spoke the truth with eloquence and dignity. I could not be prouder of you. Wallace is a pompous ass. He knows nothing of war or sacrifice."

"And Meredith Miller?"

Aaron sighed. *You knew this was going to happen. You are a proper idiot.*

He should have gone to see Meredith the moment they returned from Camp Curtin. He was so focused on Seraphina that Meredith and her intentions toward him never entered his mind. He'd tried to broach the subject on the veranda, but Meredith deftly avoided any real conversation on the topic, and the middle of a dinner party was not the place to force the issue.

"My cousin, Benjamin, Meredith's husband, suffered a prolonged illness. I was his attending physician. She and I became close during that time."

"I don't care about that. You are a man; she is a woman… You are both widowers. It is understandable. Do you love her? Is this why you told me I could leave? Because you wish to be with her?"

"No. I care for her, but I am not now, nor have I ever been, in love with her."

"She wants to marry you. And you know it. She intends to be the next Lady Weld. Something I cannot be. Of course you would choose her. The Weld name—"

"God damn it, woman! What must I do? What must I do to convince you my heart is yours and yours alone? I swear there will never be another."

Aaron got up. He kicked the door closed and locked it, and then he pulled Seraphina up from the floor. "You will be convinced."

He unpinned and unlaced her dress, kissing and sucking her silken skin as he exposed it. Her skin warmed beneath his lips. He could taste the sweetness of the honey butter on his tongue.

"Lie down," he commanded.

"Aaron, we are not alone. There are guests downstairs."

He seized her and dropped her on the bed. "I do not care. You will be convinced. And if need be, so, shall they."

Aaron stepped away and stripped until he stood before her nude, his member painfully erect. Seraphina slid off the bed onto her knees.

"No."

Aaron put her back on the bed and laid a savage kiss on her lips. Then, he kneed her legs apart.

"Touch yourself."

Seraphina massaged her sex, and Aaron could feel her body begin to shake.

"Give me your hand. Let me taste you."

Seraphina placed her hand in his mouth. He licked the slick dampness from her fingers one by one, savoring the flavor.

"This is mine. Mine and mine alone. Say it."

"Stop. I am going to scream, Aaron. Please. We are not alone," Seraphina pleaded breathlessly.

"Scream, I care not who hears. Say it."

Seraphina bit her lip. "Yours and yours alone."

He pinned her hands over her head with one hand and rolled her nipples between his fingers with the other.

"Oh, please. Please, Aaron."

"These are mine. Mine and mine alone. Say it."

"Yours and yours alone," Seraphina panted.

He kissed her again. Hard like before. He bit at her lips, caressing them.

"Whose cock do these belong to? Who do these belong to?"

"You. You. Oh, God. You," Seraphina cried.

"Turn over."

Aaron moved to allow her space to do so. He put love bites down the length of her back, drinking the beads of perfumed sweat from her skin. He wrapped her hair around his hand and pulled hard, exposing her neck.

"Look at me. Do not look away. Speak my name. Tell me you're mine."

"I am yours, Aaron."

"You will be convinced. I love you. I will never leave you. I will be yours, and you will be mine, in this life and the next."

Aaron buried himself deep inside her, swift and severe. Seraphina screamed. He drove harder, forcing her onto her belly. She shuddered beneath him, her walls spasming around him. He chased his own release without restraint. A groan, primitive and primal, escaped him as he collapsed on top of her.

It was a moment before he regained his composure. Finally, he moved to free her, rolling her over to face him. He ran his hand down the length of her body and kissed her on the forehead.

"Where did you come from? At times, I think you cannot be real. It is impossible that a man should deserve such a gift."

"I am very real. Would you think me mad if I told you that your soul conjured mine to your side from across space and time?"

"No. I would not. Because my soul is yours."

"And mine yours."

CHAPTER NINETEEN

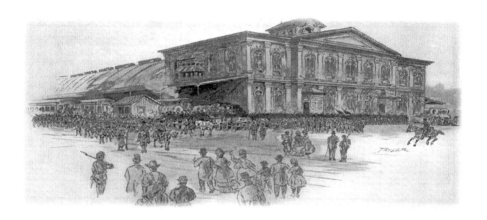

Weld Manor – Philadelphia, Pennsylvania
March 1863

March 8th, 1863

Last evening, I received a letter from Thomas. We are needed. He and Lucy will be coming to visit, and then he and I will return to Camp Curtin. From there, we will meet up with General Burnside in Maryland. Seraphina expects to return with me. She cannot. After what happened, I will never put her at risk again.

*****

"What has come over you? Would you scandalize this house? You entertain your needs without care of who may hear! You ravish the poor girl! Your barbarous behavior is beyond the pale. I thank God your father is not here to see this."

"Calm yourself, Mother. I will satisfy my needs as I wish." Aaron sat back in his desk chair, grinning contentedly.

It was late morning, and Seraphina was still sleeping. It was a long night. They'd indulged in every delight and done little to hide it. He'd been greeted with knowing glances and high color from the staff all morning. The only person upset was Katherine, who'd come to the study to voice her displeasure.

"Do you care at all for me? For your son? Can you not be discreet? You will end this wretched behavior at once!"

"You need not worry, Mother. You will be rid of me. Thomas and I will be returning to Maryland."

"No!" Katherine gasped. "Why? You cannot go."

"You have fulfilled your obligation many times over, Aaron. Let someone else go."

"Mother, I will not hide behind my wealth and privilege while other less fortunate souls fight to preserve our Union. I know you understand this."

"I do. But, like any other mother, I worry for my sons. We were fortunate to have you home safe this time. God may not grant us such a blessing again."

Aaron sighed. "We are needed. It is our duty."

"And what of Seraphina?" Katherine asked.

"She will remain here with you."

"Have you told her this? She believes she is returning with you."

"No, I have not, and I ask that you keep this between us for now. She will be unhappy at the news. I plan to tell her right before I leave," Aaron said.

"And Solomon? Is the boy to grow up fatherless?"

"Solomon is not a boy, Mother. He is a young man and old enough to understand."

"When do you leave?"

"April. Noble is already preparing for our departure. Vincent is coming by later to discuss my affairs."

Katherine teared up. "Fine. I will leave you to it."

"Mother." Aaron came from behind the desk. "I need you to be strong. I need you to help Solomon and Seraphina; they are going to be devastated. Please."

"I will. You just come back to me." Katherine touched his cheek. "Both of you."

"We will. I promise." Aaron hugged her. "We will."

*****

"Sir, Mr. Canterbury has arrived." The butler ushered Vincent into the library.

"Thank you, Mr. Toombs."

Aaron set his eyes on Seraphina. "Canterbury, you're early."

To Aaron's irritation, Vincent did the same.

"So, I am, Mademoiselle Laurent."

"Monsieur Canterbury." Seraphina rose to greet him. "What brings you here?"

"The colonel and I have business to discuss. It is a pleasure to make your acquaintance again."

"You are kind." Seraphina lowered her head. "I doubt anyone would wish to see me after my behavior."

"Chin up, my dear. You were the highlight of the evening. Wallace needed to be chastened."

"I am glad you found it amusing, Mr. Canterbury, but I don't think anyone would agree with you."

"Oh, they do. They will never say it, but they do. These gilded birds need their feathers pruned from time to time."

Aaron downed his drink. Vincent's shameless flirtation unnerved him. He cleared his throat. "Miss Laurent."

"Monsieur Canterbury, it seems you and the colonel have much to discuss. I should go."

"Mademoiselle, it was a pleasure." Vincent kissed the back of her hand.

"Gentlemen."

Aaron's eyes followed Seraphina as she exited the room. He poured Vincent a glass of whiskey and refilled his own.

"You are a rogue, Vincent."

"Come, you cannot fault a man," Vincent offered laughingly. "Seraphina is exquisite. A man would not be a man should he deny it."

"Deny it," Aaron replied with a hint of sarcasm.

"Even a rogue desires to settle down…eventually."

Vincent sat on the couch, and Aaron handed him the drink.

"I suggest you settle elsewhere. Maybe the widow Meredith Miller?"

"Here I thought you settled that affair."

"I am not going to remarry. Meredith is a lovely woman, and she would make you a fine wife. She is cultured enough to travel abroad. Benjamin's sons are near men. She is young enough to bare you a son."

"All excellent qualities in a wife. However, her passions lie with you. Do they not?"

"Lest your cock fail you, an extended honeymoon aboard ship should redirect her passions."

"And Wallace? Seraphina gave him quite the come down last evening."

"That horrible bastard? He cares only for money. A man of your means will be welcome."

"Now that my future nuptials have been decided, shall we discuss the reason you called me here?"

"How are things with Canterbury Shipping?"

"The Union naval blockade has cut off our access to southern textiles. Store goods are hard to come by. We are still making a profit—a small one, but a profit just the same. We will ride out the war. Come to the point, Aaron. Tell me why I am here."

"I am returning to the front."

"Good God, man, why?"

"I am needed. The war is not going well."

"Aaron, you have done your duty. Stay. I have a ship setting sail for England two weeks hence. Take Solomon and Seraphina."

"I cannot."

"You will not. You are thick-headed, Little Brother. No man will think less of you. You have done more than most. See your son into manhood. Let Seraphina warm your bed. Live your life."

"I am returning. I need you to continue to manage my affairs while I am gone. I have changed my will and named you executor. Solomon isn't old enough to manage my estate. You will turn it over to him when he is twenty-one. I have made provisions for mother, the Oakes, and Seraphina. My interest in Canterbury-Weld shipping will fall to you as recompense. I have had the papers drawn up. Here is your copy. I have left copies with attorney Van Bergen."

"Aaron, our fathers were like brothers. You are my brother. There are hospitals here that tend to wounded soldiers. Take a position here. Open your own practice. Anything."

"Vincent, I need you to do this for me. I am asking you to take care of my family. You are the only man I trust."

"If you will not be convinced of reason, I must. Have you told them?"

"Mother is of your opinion. I have not told Solomon. And Seraphina—"

"You are not returning with her?" Vincent sat forward. "Are you mad? After what has happened?"

"No. No." Aaron shook his head. "I am not. I will not. I cannot put her in that kind of danger again."

"Good." Vincent relaxed. "I am sure your decision did not go over well."

"I have not told her," Aaron replied.

"Brother, you are willing to go to war but fear telling Seraphina of your decision?" Vincent roared with laughter.

"You do not know Seraphina as I do. If the Union could unleash her fury on the rebels…this war would be over."

*****

March 15th, 1863

Lucy and Thomas arrived from Boston a week ago. I love her! A fiery redhead with emerald eyes and alabaster skin, Lucy is a true Irish beauty. Aaron told me she was quiet and demure, but that must be an act she puts on for the masses because when it is just us ladies, she is as raucous as any Irishman. We had lunch with Emma Monday, and between the two of them, I could not get a word in edgewise. Thomas loves her. That ego-driven SOB turns into a lovesick puppy whenever Lucy's around. I've caught many a tender moment between them. Heard a few too. Mary was joking the other day that the Weld house was going to need two nurseries. Oh, and Lady Wheeler is now the widow Wheeler. However, I suspect not for long. I have good reason to believe she has taken Katherine's advice. Meredith and her mother, Martha, are coming over today for tea. Martha is still ill and has been for some time. I wish Meredith would let me help. I am going to try again today to offer my assistance. However awful Meredith is, I hate for her mother to suffer needlessly, if I can help it.

*****

The dayroom was bright and airy. The window dressings light, the walls a stark white that reflected the sun coming in through the windows and the skylight. Upholstered settees, high-back chairs, small tables, and luxurious rugs furnished the room. It was perfect for teatime.

"Lady Katherine, my mother sends her regards," Meredith said. "She so enjoys your visits."

"How is Martha?" Katherine asked.

"Yesterday was a good day. Sadly, there are fewer of them as of late."

"Well, as always, if there is anything I can do to help."

"Meredith, I know you've said your mother has physicians, but I would be happy to see if any of my holistic treatments might be of help to her. If you'd like."

"No. We will not be in need of your assistance," Meredith shot back.

"Seraphina is a nurse. From what my sons tell me, a very good one. I wish you would reconsider, for Martha's sake," Katherine pleaded.

Meredith painted a smile on her face. "Lady Katherine, I will confer with my mother's physicians about the need for additional treatments."

"Good afternoon, Mrs. Miller, Miss Laurent, and Lady Katherine," Lucy greeted everyone upon entering the room.

"Lucy, your timing is impeccable." Katherine motioned for Lucy to sit and poured another cup of tea. "We were just speaking of Mrs. Wallace and her being ill."

"I am sorry she is still ill. Seraphina is a nurse. I am sure she would be happy to look in on Mrs. Wallace."

"Yes, she has offered her services before. I find it quite remarkable that you are a nurse."

"As do I at times." Seraphina sipped her tea.

So, this is how it's going to go, Seraphina thought to herself. Sparring with Mrs. Meredith Miller was the last thing she wanted to do today. She wanted to leave but could not think of any good reason to be excused.

"Seraphina, you must be enjoying your time here with the Welds. It is a shame you must return to the camps with your people."

"I didn't stay in the camps. I lived on a farm not far from the Union lines. Colonel Weld sought out my assistance for the nursing corps, and I moved to the hospital camp. He provided officers' quarters for me. The accommodations were sparse but adequate," Seraphina replied.

"You did not live in the camps?" Meredith asked, perplexed. "You will return to your farm then?"

"No. I will return with the colonel when he leaves. I confess I will miss the amenities."

Seraphina could feel the tension rising between them with every word. She guessed Katherine did too. She changed the subject.

"Meredith, how are the boys? I missed seeing them over the holidays."

"Ethan is preparing for university."

"My word, he was just a boy not so long ago. And Logan?"

"Logan is clerking in his grandfather's law firm. He sits for exams in June," Meredith glowed.

"Their father would be so proud of them," Lucy said.

Tula walked into the room with another tray of sandwiches, apple tarts, and a pot of tea. She served each of them and warmed their teacups.

"Tula, please tell Mary these sandwiches are divine, and this tart is absolutely sinful." Meredith blotted her mouth with her napkin.

"You should thank Miss Seraphina. She made them." Tula curtsied slightly, careful not to drop the tray. "Lady Katherine, if you need me, I be in the pantry."

"Seraphina, you have been in the kitchen?" Katherine asked, her exasperation evident.

"I know. I just enjoy Mary's company. And her treats." Seraphina smiled.

"Lady Katherine, Seraphina is a Negress." Meredith flashed her signature wicked, triumphant glare. "It is only natural that she would take well to such tasks."

Seraphina struggled to keep her composure. She did not want to embarrass Katherine with a repeat dinner party performance. Moreover, she did not want to give Meredith the satisfaction of knowing she had gotten under her skin. Thankfully, Katherine came to her rescue.

"Seraphina, Lucy, would you excuse Meredith and me for the moment."

"Yes, of course," the two answered in unison.

Seraphina wasted no time taking leave of the situation, Lucy on her heels. If she could have run from the room, she would have. Still, she was dying to know what was being said in her absence, so she hung around just out of sight.

"Seraphina, what are you doing? Get from behind that door," Lucy scolded.

"And miss this? Not on your life."

"Let me closer." Lucy moved Seraphina back.

"Lady Katherine is none too happy with her." Seraphina struggled to hear.

"Good. Somebody needs to pull her nose down. I thought she was going to spit her sandwich out when Tula said you were the one who made it." Lucy snickered.

"I know. I thought she might choke." Seraphina giggled.

"Seraphina, if Lady Katherine catches you out here, she'll be none too happy with you too."

"We won't stay long." Seraphina put her finger to her lips. "Shh."

Lady Katherine spoke softly, and Seraphina and Lucy leaned into the door to better eavesdrop.

"Meredith, Seraphina is not a servant in this house. She is a guest, as are you," Katherine retorted hotly.

"I beg your pardon, Lady Katherine; I did not mean any offense."

Liar! Seraphina thought to herself. It was all an act. Meredith was trying to save face with Katherine. If she were going to marry the crown prince, she had to be sure to stay on the queen mother's good side.

"You have taken every opportunity to be rude and unkind to Seraphina. I will not allow it."

"Forgive me, Lady Katherine. I am unaccustomed to socializing with Negros in such a manner as this. I assure you my behavior is merely a reflection of that and not of any malice on my part."

Oh, she's good. Seraphina rolled her eyes.

"I understand. More tea?" Katherine offered.

"No. I am suddenly feeling unwell. I do tend to indulge whenever Mary is in the kitchen. I beg your pardon, but I think it best I go."

"You are welcome to stay. Seraphina makes a tea that does wonders for the consequences of overindulgence. I will have Noble take you home when you are feeling better," Katherine offered.

"Thank you kindly, but no." Meredith collected her handbag from the seat next to her. "I have been gone long enough. I should get back."

"Let me have Mr. Toombs see you out."

"No! I mean, no, thank you, Lady Katherine." Meredith started for the door. "I will see myself out."

Seraphina and Lucy tried to move from the foyer before they were caught. Unfortunately, they failed and found themselves face to face with Meredith.

"Leaving so soon?" Seraphina smiled, feigning surprise and disappointment. "Let me help you get your things."

"No. I do not require your assistance." Meredith removed her coat from the rack. Her fingers shook as she buttoned it. Frustrated, she gave up and snatched her hat and gloves from the wall hooks.

"You are a whore! Aaron will grow tired of you and discard you like the rubbish you are."

"Meredith!" Lucy exhaled sharply.

"There is nothing for you here," Seraphina said coldly.

"Nurse? Huh! Drab is more like it! You belong in those camps with the rest of your kind," Meredith spat.

"That may be, but as long as I warm his bed, any hopes you have of being the next Lady Weld will die on a widow's vine." Seraphina glared at her.

"Bitch!" Meredith slapped Seraphina hard across the face.

At that moment, Meredith was everything and everyone who had made her feel like nothing since waking up in that field in Virginia. Seraphina moved in until she and Meredith were but a hair's breadth apart.

"Touch me again, and I will strangle you with my bare hands and drag your soul to hell!"

Meredith paled. "I will call the authorities! I will be rid of you! Aaron will hear of this!"

"Thomas!" Lucy shrieked. "Katherine!"

"Yes. He will. And you know what he did to the last person who dared to lay hands on me? When I drag your ass to hell, you can ask him," Seraphina snarled at her.

"Ladies!" Thomas came running from the dayroom. "Ladies!"

Katherine stepped into the foyer. "My god, what is going on here?"

Thomas pulled Seraphina away and held her shaking body back from Meredith. "Mrs. Miller, perhaps you should leave."

Panic-stricken, Meredith stepped back. "Lady Katherine, I thank you for your hospitality. Good day."

Lucy walked Meredith to the door, and Mr. Toombs closed it behind her.

"What happened to your face?" Katherine demanded, grabbing Seraphina's chin.

"Nothing." Seraphina pulled away, tearful.

"Meredith struck her!" Lucy exclaimed. "She hit her so hard that it is already starting to bruise."

"She struck you?" Katherine gasped.

"Yes, and I… I lost it." Seraphina began to cry. "She will go to the authorities. They will take me away."

"You didn't strike her. Meredith will hold her peace. Aaron will see to it. You have nothing to worry about," Thomas said.

"I doubt it. She hates me. She wants me out of the way. She wants Aaron." Seraphina wept.

Lucy put her arms around Seraphina and handed her a handkerchief. "Aaron loves you. He will deal with Meredith. You put the fear of God in her."

"That she did!" Thomas laughed. "Mr. Wallace owes Aaron too much. Nothing will come of this. For you anyway. For Meredith? When Aaron learns of this…"

"Owes him?" Seraphina wiped her tears.

"Aaron paid off Mr. Wallace's debts after Martha took ill and his business was in trouble," Lucy continued. "Meredith does not know this. Mr. Wallace will make sure Meredith stays quiet."

"Why would Aaron do this for him?" Seraphina asked, confused. "He clearly is not fond of the man."

"Aaron cares for Meredith," Katherine said. "He loved Benjamin. He promised to take care of her and the boys."

"Benjamin's family, the Millers—more specifically, John Miller Sr.—cut the Wallace's off after his son died," Thomas added. "He was afraid Wallace would spend all of Ethan and Logan's inheritance. Rightly so. John moved Meredith and the boys to Boston. The boys' inheritance stays with him. He provides Meredith with an allowance."

"She is only in Philadelphia because her mother is ill," Lucy said.

Seraphina thought about how awful it must be for Meredith to be of no use to her in-laws and only a means to an end for her father. In 1863 a woman's fortune rested on the benevolence of men. Empathy tugged at the edge of Seraphina's conscience. She let the feeling pass. Meredith was the enemy. Anything and anyone who threatened to separate her from Aaron was.

"Lady Katherine, I know I continue to disappoint you, and I am sorry. I make no excuses for my behavior. I think it best I remain in my room whenever company calls."

"Thomas, Lucy, dear, would you give Seraphina and me a moment."

Lucy stepped away, and Thomas followed.

"Seraphina, we will be together here for some time. Do you plan to hide in your room forever?"

"I don't know."

"I am going to share something with you, but afterward, we can never speak of it again. Tu comprends?"

"Oui. Je ne le ferai pas. Of course, Lady Katherine."

"J'étais une prostituée."

"What?" Seraphina reached for a wall that wasn't there and almost fell over.

"I was a prostitute working the ship in exchange for passage to the Americas. I was hoping to find a new life here—one where I did not have to be at the mercy of men. I met Edward one evening. We talked for hours. Instead of paying me for my time, he paid my debt in full. We married aboard ship, and a few men who were aboard remembered me. The rumors began shortly after we arrived. I understand how you feel. I understand more than you know."

"Qui est ce Edward? I mean, what did he do?"

"Edward? He threatened to sever business with all of them if they spoke of it again. And to blacklist their wives from all social engagements if they mistreated me in any way."

"And you? What did you do? That had to be horrible."

"Fisticuffs." Katherine grinned. "I wasn't always a lady."

"You got in a fight? With who?"

"Lady Ann Van Bergen, of course." Katherine chuckled. "It wasn't much of a fight. Though she did wear considerable powder on her cheeks for several weeks."

Seraphina burst out laughing. "You smacked the Queen of England?"

"Yes. It is quite the tale. How about we retire to the dayroom? We can talk about it over a good glass of sherry and the rest of those tarts."

"That would be wonderful. Katherine, you are too kind to me, and I love you for it."

"You are a wonderful girl, and you make my son exceedingly happy. A mother could not ask for more."

*****

A simple two-story Victorian, the Wallace home was modest by high society standards but reflective of Mr. Wallace's diminished wealth. Aaron knocked loudly on the door. It was too late for callers. He knew he'd have to knock hard enough to wake the butler.

It was a few moments before a bleary-eyed Mr. Sinclair opened the door.

"Lord Weld? Mr. Wallace did not say you would be calling. The family has retired for the evening."

"Where is she?" Aaron demanded, pushing past Mr. Sinclair and into the vestibule. "Wallace! Mr. Sinclair, you will fetch Mr. Wallace now! Tell him Lord Weld demands his presence."

Aaron paced back and forth to calm the volcano erupting within. Seraphina's cheek was swollen, and she would have another nasty bruise. He could not keep her safe anywhere, not even in his own home.

Mr. Wallace stumbled into the vestibule in an evening jacket he'd obviously just thrown on. "Colonel, I beg your pardon, but this is my home!"

"Is this your home? Is it, Mr. Wallace?" Aaron shouted.

"Colonel, we should talk and leave the women out of it. Come to the parlor. Let us have a drink."

"I am in no mood, Wallace. I want to speak to Meredith. I will speak with you afterward."

"Father, I heard shouting. Is everything okay? Meredith descended the staircase. "Aaron. What are you doing here?"

"Meredith, I would like to speak with you alone," Aaron asked calmly.

"Please, join me in the parlor," she requested. "I will have Mr. Sinclair pour you a drink."

"Thank you, no. I will not be long." Aaron followed her.

Meredith ushered him into the parlor and closed the door behind them.

"Meredith, please sit down." Aaron guided her to a settee and sat beside her. "Meredith, I am not going to marry. I am never going to marry again."

"May I ask why?" Meredith's voice strained with barely contained emotion.

"I have a son. I have no need to marry."

"I could give you more sons and make you a fine wife. Lady Katherine adores me. Our families are close."

"Meredith, I loved Benjamin dearly. And I care deeply for you, Ethan, and Logan. But that is all there is. I should have made that clear from the beginning and not have assumed you would understand the nature of my affections."

Meredith was young, and he, ten years her senior, should have known better. Everyone had done Meredith a disservice. Her father for marrying her off for money too young and her husband for dying too soon.

"I do not believe you." Meredith turned her back to him.

"You want a marriage and deservedly so. I cannot give you what you want."

"Cannot or will not?" she demanded.

"Why do you persist in this?" Aaron pleaded. "Any words I speak will only injure you further. There are other gentlemen who would make suitable husbands for you."

Meredith grabbed his arm. "I love you, Aaron. I love you."

"And I care for you. I hope you find someone who will return that love, I truly do." Aaron freed himself from her grasp and stood to leave.

"You are in love with her! I can see it. How can you love her? She is Negress. She is a whore."

"Miss. Laurent is not my whore. And you will not refer to her as such in my presence," Aaron snapped.

"I could have her jailed or worse for her manner toward me." Meredith shot tearful daggers at him.

Aaron froze. A darkness filled him from a place deep within, and he moved toward her, standing close enough for her to feel his breath on her forehead. Meredith stumbled. Shaken by his sudden change in demeanor.

"Hear me. You do not know on what a sword's edge your fortunes lie. Do not threaten me or mine. You will do nothing. What happened between you and Miss Laurent today will not happen again. Understand?"

"You would threaten me? For her?" Meredith cried.

"I do not make threats, Mrs. Miller."

"What does she have that I do not?" Meredith slumped in the chair. "What makes her so much better than me?"

"Good-bye, Mrs. Miller."

He could not answer her questions without hurting her further. Seraphina was everything Meredith wasn't. The list was too long to enumerate. But the answers Meredith wanted were in the questions she asked. *Seraphina would never have asked them in the first place.*

Aaron closed the door behind him. Mr. Wallace was waiting.

"There is no excuse for my behavior, Mr. Wallace. This is your home. I was wrong. I want to assure you that our other financial arrangements will continue until they become unnecessary. As for Meredith, I would suggest that you, as her father, find her a suitable husband. Canterbury may be such a man. Good evening, Mr. Wallace."

*****

Aaron walked through the hall into the library. Seraphina was there. He did not announce his presence right away, choosing instead to admire her from a distance. Her bare feet peeked out from under her skirts. The buttons of her blouse strained slightly against the fullness of her breasts. No stockings and corset meant she was nude, save for what he knew would be delicate drawers. He hardened at the thought.

"What are you doing up this late?"

"Waiting for you, my love. Where've you been? You haven't found another lover, have you?" Seraphina raised a playful eyebrow.

"Never." Aaron closed the doors behind him. "Come here."

"Say please."

Aaron sat on his knees. "Come here, please."

Seraphina walked over and stood before him. He slowly lifted her skirt, exposing her bare legs.

"Where are your shoes? Your stockings?"

"In the same place as my corset and the other medieval torture devices we women are forced to wear."

Aaron raised her foot to his lips, caressing it. "Shoes are a medieval torture device?"

"Yes," she said quietly.

"You do not know what torture is."

Aaron dropped her skirts over his head. Separating her folds, he licked playfully at her clitoris, intensifying the tongue lashing until he could taste the liquid heat pooling between her thighs.

"Now do you know what torture is?"

"Yes. No. Aaron, please."

"No?"

Aaron pulled the fat swollen nub with his lips. Seraphina moaned. "Aaron."

"Yes, there's my name. Say it again." He buried his face, jutting his tongue in and out, rubbing and sucking until slickness ran down her legs.

Aaron tried to take her to the floor, but Seraphina fought him. Her strength caught him off guard as she pinned him by his shoulders. Slowly, she slid him inside. He tore at her blouse, but before he could touch her breasts, Seraphina pushed him down again. Her nipples grew taut as they grazed his chest with each up and down motion of her hips. She changed her rhythm, bringing him to the brink, only to deny him.

"Let me," he pleaded.

Seraphina fixed her eyes on his. "No. Speak my name."

Aaron sat up, folding his arms around her. "Seraphina."

The wave came on him so quickly he could not control it. Seraphina rode it behind him, a satisfied smile on her lips.

"I guess I will never learn to be a lady."

"You are a woman…something far better."

"We should dress. I am starving."

"Later. Wait here."

Aaron quickly donned his trousers and left the room.

Seraphina took the opportunity to remove what was left of her skirts and blouse. She put on Aaron's shirt, buttoning it just below her breasts. His scent made her ache once more.

No longer warmed by the heat of passion, the room felt cool. Seraphina stoked what was left of the fireplace embers. Aaron would have to start it again when he returned. Her stomach growled. It had been a long time since dinner.

Aaron returned with a tray perched precariously in one hand, a tenuous grip on a blanket, a bottle of wine, and two glasses in the other. Seraphina rose to help him. Taking the tray of bread, cheeses, and sliced apples, she set it down in front of the fire and began to eat heartily.

Aaron stood still, drinking her in. Still swollen, her breasts filled the shirt. It stopped just below the curve of her backside, giving a full view of her long, curvaceous legs. An ache settled in his groin.

How am I going to leave? But he was leaving. Tomorrow afternoon on the late train to Camp Curtin.

"I did not think it was possible for you to be any lovelier. Yet here you sit in my shirt, and I am awestruck."

"Do you remember the first time we met?"

"Vividly. You were quite hostile."

"You kidnapped me!" Seraphina threw a piece of bread at him playfully.

"An act for which I will never be forgiven." Aaron laughed.

"I was unafraid. I knew I had nothing to fear from you. I am afraid of nothing in this life when I am with you. Do not leave me."

Aaron wrapped Seraphina in the blanket and held her close. "I love you. Promise me, no matter what happens in this life, you will remember that."

"I promise."

"I have something for you."

Aaron pulled a small oak chest down from a high shelf. It featured a carved relief of the Weld crest on the top and beautiful crowned dragons along the sides. From another shelf, he retrieved a skeleton key from inside a book and brought both to the floor where they were sitting.

Aaron unlocked the box and removed a satin drawstring bag.

"I was saving this for last Christmas…but it was not the right time. Turn around."

Seraphina did as he asked. Aaron draped a silver pendant around her neck. The medallion was emblazoned with a dragon sitting atop a gilded crown, encrusted with emeralds and diamonds.

"Aaron! I cannot accept this."

"Read the inscription."

Seraphina turned the pendant over. "Nil sine numine. S. L. Weld."

"This is my family crest. It reads, 'Nothing without the deity.' I swear before God, what I cannot give in law is yours in mind, body, and soul. You are and will always be Seraphina Weld."

"I love you, Aaron Matthew Weld. I am desperately, hopelessly in love with you."

Aaron pulled Seraphina into a tight embrace. "Thank God. I was afraid I was going to have to chase you again."

"Cotton Eye is getting faster." Seraphina kissed him.

"When this war is over, I will take you away from here. You and Solomon."

"Why wait? Let's leave tomorrow." Seraphina wrapped herself in his arms.

Aaron kissed the top of her head. "Yes, tomorrow."

CHAPTER TWENTY

Weld Manor – Philadelphia, Pennsylvania
March 1863

The morning fog was just lifting. Aaron stood on the veranda, surveying the surrounding greens and gardens. It would be a long time before he'd see them again. He, Thomas, and Noble would be leaving that afternoon. He'd chosen to wait until now to tell Solomon and Seraphina. He knew they would be angry and want to go, but he had not wanted to spend his last few weeks at odds with them.

"Father, Grandmother said you wanted to speak to me." Solomon came onto the porch.

"Yes, Solomon. Come outside."

"I see the trunks. I see the trunks. I know you are leaving. When?"

"Yes. I will be returning to the front. Today," Aaron replied calmly.

"May I return with you?"

"No. You have your studies to attend to, and I need you here to assist your grandmother."

"Grandmother does not need my assistance. Eli will be here in my place. I am ahead of every other student. I am sure my teachers would grant me leave for a semester. There is no reason I cannot join you."

"Solomon, you cannot return with me. It is too dangerous."

"There are boys younger than me at the front. I know this, for John Hanover reads us letters from his father who is away fighting in Kentucky."

"Cannon fodder!" Aaron slammed his fist on the door. "Did George Hanover tell his son that those young boys were nothing more than cannon fodder? Did he tell him of the thousands of dead, some left to rot where they fell? Did he tell him of the stench of death that never leaves? Did he tell him of the men with missing limbs because they were either blown off or cut off? Or of the poor bastards with the misfortune to suffer mortal wounds but die slowly and painfully. Did he tell him of the diseases that afflict the soldiers? Tetanus, rheumatic fever, dysentery, typhoid, smallpox, lice, and any number of infections. Did he tell him that?"

"No. He did not. But I am unafraid and wish to return with you. If Seraphina, a woman, could survive these things, then I should do as well."

"Seraphina is a unique and rare woman. She is a survivor. A fighter."

"And I am not?"

"On the contrary. You are every bit the Weld I have raised you to be."

"So, let me join you."

"No, Solomon. Let that be the end of it."

"No, it is not the end. I will not accept—"

Aaron grabbed Solomon by the collar. "Have I been gone so long that you feel you no longer have to respect me in my own home?"

Solomon pulled away. "I will not. If you wish for me to stay here, then you will tell me the reason you do not want me to go. The real reason."

Aaron was silent for a long while. He did not want to take Solomon for the same reason he did not want to take Seraphina. Fear.

"I cannot protect you. You are my only son. I need you to stay here. If anything were to happen to you, I could not live with myself."

"Father, you are afraid, and rightly so. I still want to go with you."

"No. That is my final word on the matter."

"You will take Seraphina!" Solomon shouted. "I doubt you could be as easily parted from her as from me!"

"Solomon! That is not true. I love you. I don't want to leave either of you."

"Then don't. Stay."

"I cannot." Aaron sighed. "I am needed. It is my duty. I need you to understand that."

Solomon turned on his heel and slammed the door. Aaron's heart sank. If Solomon was this adamant about going with him, how much more would Seraphina be? Her fury had no equal. Maybe he shouldn't have waited.

*****

Aaron put away the last of the papers on his desk. His train left in three hours. He set out the correspondence Mr. Toombs needed to take to the post and the instructions for the steward.

"Aaron, Solomon is really upset we are leaving. You should talk to him again. He thinks you don't believe he's man enough to handle it."

"No. He isn't man enough to handle it, and neither are you. And that is why you are both staying here."

"What? You aren't serious? When did you decide this? Were you even going to talk to me about it? When are you planning on leaving?"

"Seraphina, you have done enough for our soldiers. It is best you remain here."

"No. Aaron, I belong at your side. You need me."

"It is too dangerous. You will remain here."

"I know the dangers. Please, Aaron. I beg you to take me with you. I cannot stay here. I cannot stay here without you."

"Seraphina, I will not be moved on this. You will stay. I will have your word on this."

"I cannot."

"Damn it, woman! You test me beyond all reason! Your word, Seraphina!" Aaron shouted.

"If I have no say, why do you need my word?" Seraphina cried.

"I know you, Seraphina. The only thing stronger than your will is your word. I must have it."

"Aaron, please take me with you. I cannot stay here."

"No!" Aaron grabbed Seraphina by the shoulders. "What if you are with child?"

"Then I will return when it is no longer safe for me to work at your side."

"No! Absolutely not! It is not safe."

"Nowhere is safe! I am not safe anywhere, but I am even less safe when I am not with you!"

"I cannot protect you. You were there, lying on the ground, broken and bleeding. Four days! Four days I sat by your bedside, paralyzed with the fear of losing you. In my rage, I killed two men, one of them with my bare hands." Aaron held up his hands. "If you love me. If you truly love me, you will stay here."

"If you love me, you will take me with you!" Seraphina cried.

"Seraphina, it is because I love you that I cannot. Please understand. I need you to understand," Aaron begged.

"Liar! You promised! You swore you would not leave! You swore you would not leave me alone! Liar! Is that what last night was? Was that the good-bye? It was, wasn't it? You're leaving today, aren't you? Liar! Coward!" Seraphina screamed.

"Seraphina, please!" Aaron wrapped her in his arms.

She slid to the floor, and Aaron followed.

"Stay. Please stay," she sobbed. "Don't leave me alone. You promised."

"I love you. I love you more than my life," Aaron cried. "I will return to you. I promise I will not leave you alone in this world. I swear it."

*****

March 30th, 1863

We are in a plantation home north of Fredericksburg on the Rappahannock. Conditions are crowded, and many men lay out in the open. One could believe we had not been fighting this wretched war for some two years from the state of this field hospital. Even now, we depend on the Sanitary Commission for supplies and lack trained physicians. The surgery has become a classroom, and me a professor and surgeon. Thomas, Noble, and Corporal Dixon tell tales late into the evening. They are in better spirits than I, and it is impossible to be sour in their company. Seraphina was so distraught and angry when I left. I miss her desperately. I've written as much to say so and beg her forgiveness for choosing duty over her. This cause, the preservation of our union, will come at a great cost whether or not we prevail. I fear losing her will be a price I cannot pay.

CHAPTER TWENTY-ONE

Weld Manor – Philadelphia, Pennsylvania
June 1863

June 2nd, 1863

I received a letter from Addie last week. There are no words to express the joy it brought me to know they are safe and well. Addie says they are working and living at a Methodist church in Washington. She is serving in the kitchen, and Jed is doing the woodwork on the parsonage. Lizzie is attending school. Daisy too, when she is not too busy with Lula and Cherub. I know Aaron did this, and I will be forever grateful and love him ever the more for doing so.

Katherine is now head of the Sanitary Commission's charity board. Mrs. Van Bergen stepped down. It was quite the scandal. The Commission has established a clinic for contraband in an African Methodist church in the city. I have been placed in charge of it. The clinic is busy, very busy. Illness and poverty are no respecters of persons. Many of the poorer white families have come for help too.

I follow the news that I can in the papers. I know Chancellorsville, like Fredericksburg, was another disaster. How much blood must be shed on the same ground for men to find the battle pointless? Men are arriving at the general hospital from the front. Their numbers grow every day. I volunteer on the wards with other women of the commission when I can get away from the clinic. The men tell horror stories. I share a common bond with these men. Death has left its mark.

Vincent came to the house and asked for my help with Martha Wallace. Her condition was grave. The care she'd been receiving was awful. To think Mr. Wallace let her suffer like that is appalling. With Vincent's help, we dismissed her physicians, and I took over her treatment. She is now at Weld Manor and doing much better.

Vincent and Meredith are to be married in July. They will sail to England afterward. Martha will be accompanying them. I think they are separating. Polite society won't call it that… She's simply going abroad. But whatever they want to call it, after the way he let her languish, it is for the best. Meredith and I have come to an uneasy peace. She is gracious, as am I, but we do not speak outside of the customary pleasantries. It has been good to be busy. It helps keep my mind off how much I miss Aaron. His letters worry me, though. He needs me, he won't say it, but I know he does.

*****

It was a lazy Sunday afternoon. Martha sat in the dayroom window, needlepoint in hand. Katherine's high-back chair gave her a regal presence in the room. Seraphina soaked in the light in an armchair, reading a letter from Aaron.

"It was Ann's love of gossip and cruelty that felled her, Katherine. Good riddance," Martha quipped, never looking up from her needlework.

"Well, Lady Van Bergen won't be receiving many social invitations when the season begins." Katherine twisted her lips to mask the pleasure the thought gave her.

"And do not take pity on her, Katherine. She made her bed. On your back, no less."

"I am happy about Ann Van Bergen's demise because, under Katherine's leadership, the contraband and refugee camps are receiving better support from the commission," Seraphina added.

"Seraphina, always thinking of others before yourself. How are the rest of us sinners supposed to keep up?" Katherine laughed. "How are things at the clinic?"

"There are so many patients, some days I cannot see them all. I turn no one away," Seraphina answered.

"I know the citizens of Philadelphia will not find better care." Katherine nodded.

"The white physicians are angry, Katherine." Seraphina grimaced.

"Seraphina, they care not for you but for the money. The poor who can pay are all that matter. And though I am sure your care has diminished their salaries by a mere pittance, men have sold their souls for less."

"I've heard rumblings." Seraphina frowned. "They want to close the clinic."

"Poppycock!" Martha moved to sit next to Seraphina. "You are doing the Lord's work. God has no stomach for the groanings of wealthy men. The church's charity still rests in the will of the divine."

It never ceased to amaze Seraphina how different Martha was from her husband and daughter. She was kind, open, and frank. Moreover, she seemed unphased by Seraphina's presence. She and Katherine were dear friends. Seraphina often wondered how'd they become friends. She suspected Martha might have come from humble means too.

Martha patted Seraphina on the hand. "What is this?"

"A letter from Aaron." Seraphina reddened.

"Seraphina, if you read that letter one more time, you will wear the ink off the page." Katherine sighed.

Seraphina set the letter on the table next to the settee. "I know. I know. But I can feel him. He is…alone. I should be with him."

"You should not." Katherine gave her a stern look.

"Oh dear, Katherine is right." Martha turned toward Seraphina. "War is no place for a woman."

"War is no place for anyone, man or woman. But at Aaron's side is the place for me, war or no war. You weren't there, Katherine. You did not see. He needs me," Seraphina cried.

Katherine closed her book. "Come here, Seraphina."

Seraphina crossed the room and set to Katherine's right. Katherine placed her hand over Seraphina's.

"I have never seen two people love each other as you and Aaron do. It makes the burden of absence a misery for you both. But you cannot go to him. It is not safe."

"He needs me." Seraphina wiped her tears with the back of her hand.

"What he needs is to know that you are safe," Katherine groaned. "Now you put away the idea of leaving here, or whatever nonsense you have swirling around in that head of yours. Leave it be."

It was too late. The idea had already taken root, its seeds planted the day Aaron rode away on Shade. The idea only needed a plan and an accomplice. *Emma.*

*****

Gettysburg, Pennsylvania
1863

The plantation house was quiet. The Union had taken possession of the home and converted it into a headquarters field hospital. It was a small house, and Aaron's room was on the second floor, overlooking what he knew would be the field of battle in just a few days' time.

The late evening heat had lulled all but the insects and nocturnal creatures to sleep. Yet he, being neither an insect nor nocturnal, was still awake. The full moon cast a cool gray light on the floor where he sat beneath the window. Head down, his hair, grown three months too long, hung in his face. He stared at the letter in his hand. The scent of lavender from the flower she'd pressed between the pages hung in the air. The last letter had rose petals, and the one before that, magnolia blossoms. He wanted to go home.

"Colonel? Aaron?" Thomas knocked on the door.

"Come in, Brother," Aaron answered.

Thomas opened the door. "Seriously, Aaron? On the floor? In the dark? You are a rudderless ship. I have never seen you like this."

"How is Lucy? I take it the letter says she is well?" Aaron pointed to the letter in Thomas's hand, ignoring his comment.

"She is with child." Thomas smiled.

"Bully for you!" Aaron stood and slapped Thomas on the back. "This is truly an occasion to celebrate. I have a bit of whisky. We will drink to the future Weld."

"You may receive such a letter soon too, I think."

Would he? Aaron wondered. Seraphina didn't tell him last time. Would she this time?

"Maybe. I am sure mother is overjoyed. She's wanted another grandchild for years." Aaron laughed.

"Yes, she is, in fact." Seraphina set her bags down in the doorway. "Congratulations, Thomas."

"Seraphina!" Thomas's eyes grew wide. "How on—"

"What the hell are you doing here?" Aaron shouted.

"Aaron, we can have that drink later. Seraphina. I did not believe it possible for you to be any lovelier. It is good to see you." Thomas kissed her hand. "If you will excuse me."

Thomas bid a hasty retreat from the room, closing the door behind him.

"You gave me your word. Your word, you would stay in Philadelphia. How did you get here?"

"I did not give you my word. In fact, I refused to do so, if I recall. And Emma and I had a lovely train ride. She is affianced to a Lieutenant Malcolm Pierce now. He is here too. You may know him."

"Fuck all! What are you doing here? You cannot be here. How in the hell did you convince Emma to bring you here? Against my wishes no less."

"I've been told I am quite industrious and very determined."

"You are stubborn, fool-hearted, and defiant! Seraphina, you cannot be here. It is not safe."

"Life is not safe," she shouted back.

Seraphina closed the distance between them. She nipped at his lips and nudged his nose with hers, but he did not return her affections. He could not. He wanted her too badly.

"Seraphina, you cannot stay."

"You want me here. You can't say it, but you do. Inside, you think it selfish and shameful to want me here with you. Your sense of duty and sacrifice will not allow it."

Aaron regarded Seraphina for a moment. How many times over the last three months had he looked for her across the surgery? How many nights had he ached for her, reading her letters over and over again? He wanted her to stay. Prudence demanded he send her back, take her back if need be.

"If you understand me, why do you ask the impossible of me? You are asking me to risk your life, to keep you near me. Something I cannot do."

"Aaron, I will not leave. Either I stay, or you go."

"For me to go, I would have to resign. There are men here who have left many a wife and child behind, some never to be seen again. If we are to win this war and preserve the Union, men like me must serve."

Seraphina's autumn eyes blazed. "Then I will serve at your side."

Aaron could see his reflection in the flames. Her eyes burned brightest when she set her mind. She wasn't leaving.

"Colonel, sir…" A young soldier opened the door.

Doorknob still in hand, he stared at Seraphina. "I'm sorry, sir. Beg your pardon. I should have… I tell them you can't come just now."

The soldier closed the door without a salute.

"Aaron, you should go. They wouldn't have sent for you if it wasn't urgent. I will follow you shortly."

"No. You will remain here. Do not defy me. I will send Corporal Dixon to stand guard." Aaron slammed the door behind him. Thomas waited at the bottom of the stairs.

"You." Aaron threw his hands up. "Why is it always you that I run into at times like this?"

"Because the gods know that you need someone to talk sense into you. She cannot stay," Thomas replied. "Take her home and leave her there. Lock her in her room if you must."

"She will not leave me, Thomas."

She will not leave me. The words reverberated in his soul. She wouldn't. It was not until this moment that he truly understood what that meant. He was so busy trying to protect her that he'd missed it. She was willing to give all, to remain at his side. She loved him that much.

"Then you must leave, Aaron." Thomas shook his head. "You must leave, and take her with you."

"I will request reassignment to the general hospital in Philadelphia when we reach Harrisburg."

"You will restrict her to your quarters until then?" Thomas asked.

"As tempting as that may be, we will need her help when the army engages. I will have Corporal Dixon guard her, but she will always remain with me or in my quarters when she is not with me. She will not roam freely as she did before."

"Have you lost all reason? All common sense? You behave as a ship lost to the mercy of the wind. War is no place for a woman."

Aaron stopped. "Thomas, have you ever stood on the bow of a ship in a storm?"

"No, I have not."

"When you do, you will understand."

*****

Corporal Dixon sat sleeping, his back resting against the bedroom door. Aaron nudged him a little. He woke with a start, reaching for his knife. When he saw it was Aaron, he relaxed and sheathed his weapon.

"You're dismissed, Corporal," Aaron spoke quietly.

Marshall nodded and left.

Inside, Aaron watched Seraphina sleep for a while. The dawn sunlight creeping through the window bathed her face in an angelic glow. She was nude, save her delicate chemise. He smiled. She always waited for him like that. She was an impatient lover… Removing clothing, in her opinion, took too long.

Aaron took off his shirt, boots, and trousers. He knelt beside the bed, painfully erect.

"Seraphina." He brushed her cheek.

"Aaron."

He placed a finger to her lips. "Take this off."

Seraphina sat up and removed her chemise. She reached for him, but he backed away. "Not yet. Unpin your hair."

She did. Longer now, it fell to the small of her back.

"If all of man could gaze upon such resplendent beauty, he would be stilled, and all desire for war and death would cease."

Aaron suckled one breast and then the other, molesting each tip with his tongue. "Open your legs."

Aaron grazed her teasingly with his tongue and fingers until she was swollen and wet. "Kiss me," she whispered.

Aaron lifted his head. Seraphina grasped handfuls of his hair and gently pulled his head back. She kissed herself from his lips, sliding her tongue in and out of his mouth and licking and tugging at his lips. "Give it to me. Let me taste you."

Aaron maneuvered himself onto the bed. He fell back into the bliss of her hot mouth and the wicked twist of the tongue. He fought for control, the feeling of the tip of his cock hitting the back of her throat weakening him. Aaron wrapped Seraphina's hair around his hand and slowly pulled her away, freeing his throbbing shaft from her. He tilted her head back and sucked her mouth until it was swollen, and she begged for air.

Seraphina straddled him, her back to him; he watched as she joined his body to hers until he could go no further. Aaron drew her into him as she raised and lowered herself along his shaft, her skin dewy from the exertion. He rubbed her sex until she began to moan and quicken her pace. Aaron pushed her forward onto her stomach and drove until they were skin to skin. He stretched and filled her until her body began to shake. He held himself there and whispered in her ear. "What is your name?"

"Seraphina. Seraphina Weld," she replied.

Aaron buried his head in her hair and breathed deeply. "You are Seraphina Weld."

He pressed her hips against him with a relentless fervor. He felt her spasms of pleasure and followed her in sweet death. Oblivious to the world around them, the two lay together in quiet bliss.

"Was this another good-bye? Don't make me leave. Let me stay with you. Please." Seraphina touched his face.

"When have I ever been able to make you do anything?" Aaron smiled. "You, Seraphina Weld, have your own mind. Nothing I do will change that."

"I can stay?" Seraphina asked, hopeful.

"For now. You are never to leave my side. You are to remain in this room when you are not with me. Understood?"

"What do you mean by 'for now'?"

"I will resign my commission after the next battle. Then we will go home."

"Are you serious?" Seraphina gasped. "Aaron, you don't have to resign."

"You will not leave, and you cannot stay. Is that not the choice you've given me?"

"I don't want to take you away from your duty. I know how important it is to you. Why can't we work together side by side? You need me. The men need me."

"I do. They do. But none of that matters. I cannot lose you. I will not lose you. My honor is not worth your life."

"Do you want to resign?"

"I've given the war two years of my life in the field. I will work in the general hospital in Philadelphia."

Seraphina sat up. "You didn't answer the question. Do you want to resign?"

"No. No, I do not. I want to go home. Just like all the other men. But no. I do not want to resign."

"Then don't."

Aaron looked up at her. "Will you go home and stay there?"

"So, my choice is to take you away from your duty or remain locked in a gilded cage?" Seraphina started to cry.

"Will you just this once do as I ask?" Aaron pleaded.

"I can't," Seraphina sobbed. "What if you don't come back?"

Aaron brushed away her tears. "I love you. I will come back. I am not them."

Seraphina rested her head on his chest. "And I am not her. You cannot protect me from the world."

A solemn silence fell between them. Aaron wasn't sure what she was going to say. Seraphina was fearless. She'd endured unimaginable pain and loss. Yet, she lay beside him, ready to go one more time into the breach. He would have to resign.

"It is funny," she said quietly. "We are both afraid to lose one another. My fear draws me to you. Your fear pushes me away. Love is a sweet and bitter misery. I will return home."

"You've never called it home before," he whispered.

"I am a Weld. Your home is my home," she replied.

"I love you, Seraphina. I love you desperately, and I will return." Aaron kissed her forehead.

"You will have to escort me back. Emma cannot."

"How did you get Emma Wheeler to escort you down here?"

"Emma and Malcolm are eloping. She enjoys her lover's bed too." Seraphina grinned.

"Indeed." Aaron laughed. "Malcolm Pierce is a fortunate man. Far more fortunate than the late Lord Wheeler, I think."

"God rest his soul." Seraphina giggled.

*****

Battle of Gettysburg – Gettysburg, Pennsylvania
July 1863

Seraphina crawled over the hellscape, keeping low to the ground to avoid becoming a target. Aaron had forbidden her from joining him on the battlefield, but she did so anyway. How could she sit idly by while the world burned around her?

Cannon fire shook the earth and bled the ears. The foul humor of death induced violent retching, made worse by a fog of smoke that choked the lungs and burned the eyes. Corpses lay in piles two and three deep, the aftermath of days of ill-fated charges breaking like waves on earthen fortifications.

The battle began two days before. The number of wounded was so great the ambulance corps could not keep up, forcing nurses and surgeons onto the battlefield. A dystopian opera of screams carried on the breeze, quieted only by the gift of the god Morpheus, as morphine and rudimentary last rites were given to the injured and dying.

Artillery from both sides had bludgeoned each other for hours earlier in the day to soften one another's defenses. Seraphina lamented that all they had done was create readymade holes for the gravediggers.

A bloodied soldier grabbed Seraphina's skirt. She pulled him from beneath the mound of bodies that covered him. She tied a tourniquet on both his legs and packed his chest wound with pieces of linen from her leather satchel.

Aaron was barely visible through the haze. Seraphina called his name, waving her arms back and forth, and Aaron turned, a look of shock on his face. He mouthed words she could not hear and made his way toward her. A shell hit the ground between them. A wall of earth exploded in her face, and everything went dark.

CHAPTER TWENTY-TWO

The Weld House Museum – Frederick, Maryland
Tuesday, April 12th – Present Day

The ground felt oddly solid…and cold. Gone were the fetor and echo of war; silent sterility had taken their place. Head pounding with a painful ringing in her ears, Seraphina opened her eyes.

"Aaron?"

Nothing. Seraphina tried to sit up, rolling to her side. Disoriented and dizzy, she vomited. Her vision blurred; she couldn't make out where she was. The taste of blood and dirt mixed on her tongue, and she began to panic.

"Aaron! Where are you?"

Nothing. She closed her eyes. Aaron was there. His blue eyes filled with fear. He mouthed something to her, and he was gone. Her eyes swung open, and the flood of artificial light brought the room into view.

"No! No!" Seraphina screamed, the sound tearing through her head and chest with a searing pain.

She rolled onto her knees, and still unable to stand, she dragged herself across the floor. A trail of vomit, mud, and blood followed her. She pushed over a display case in a futile effort to stand again. It shattered. She dragged herself through the shards until she reached the wall at the base of his portrait. Hands bleeding, she reached for him.

"Ask me again! Ask me again like you did before! I will say yes! Forever yes! Please! I cannot live this life without you!"

The portrait said nothing. The air did not chill. The melancholy and longing did not call to her. All was silence, and Seraphina slid down the wall, sobbing.

*****

Vanessa and Marcus drove through the property gate into the museum parking lot. Vanessa was surprised to see a car there. It was ten o clock on a Tuesday morning, and the museum was open by appointment only until after the gala.

"Is that Seraphina's car?" Vanessa pointed.

"Looks like it, but how many green Honda Civics are there?" Marcus asked. "I told you we need a lock at the gate entrance. People will use the museum lot to avoid paying for street parking."

"Yeah, yeah." Vanessa waved her hand. "Pull up next to it."

Marcus parked next to the vehicle, and they both got out. Marcus did a cursory inspection of the vehicle and noticed the Our Lady Hospital parking decal in the window.

"Baby, it is her car. You think she had car trouble? Took an Uber or something? When was the last time you talked to her?"

"Monday". Vanessa shrugged. "I figured she was just being Seraphina. We're supposed to meet for lunch today." "I figured she was just being Seraphina. We're supposed to meet for lunch today."

"Let's go inside." Marcus walked toward the door. "Call her. Make sure everything is okay."

Vanessa entered the building's alarm code. The LED lights flickered on overhead, illuminating the room.

"Siri, call Seraphina." Vanessa paused. "Do you hear that? It sounds like… Oh no."

"Get behind me!" Marcus grabbed Vanessa.

They both walked slowly toward the sound of the ringing phone. The sound grew louder as they approached the Civil War exhibit.

Marcus opened the door. "What the hell?"

"Seraphina! What are you doing here?" Vanessa ran to her side. "Oh my god! Marcus call 911!"

"Holy shit! On it," Marcus replied, dialing.

Vanessa grasped the sides of Seraphina's head. "Who did this to you?"

"I didn't want to come back." Seraphina trembled violently. "I didn't care about slavery, the war, any of it. I love him."

"Love who?" Vanessa cried, frantic. "Who did this?"

"Oh God, this is my fault! He said just this once! Just this once!" Seraphina wailed.

"911 is on the line. They want to know how long she has been here like this?" Marcus asked.

"I don't know. She isn't making any sense." Vanessa examined Seraphina's clothes. She's wearing what looks like the costume she had on on Monday, but it's covered in dirt and…blood."

"My wife said since Monday, yesterday maybe. And there's blood," Marcus told the dispatcher. "Vanessa, is it her blood? Can you get her to calm down? Tell you anything?"

Vanessa brushed the hair from Seraphina's face. "I don't know. She won't stop screaming. Seraphina, baby, stop, stop."

"Is that vomit?" Marcus asked, horrified.

"Yes. Oh God, Marcus, her nose and ears are bleeding. Tell them to hurry!"

"The lady says they are five minutes out. What the hell happened?"

"Seraphina, who did this?" Vanessa held her face.

Seraphina stared back, her eyes hollow, her expression blank.

"I did!" she screamed.

****

The emergency room waiting area was standing room only. Crying babies and the sick from all walks of life filled the chairs and lined the hallway. Anxious for news on Seraphina's condition, Vanessa paced the floor.

"They should have taken her to Weld Memorial. Our Lady is always standing room only. God only knows what kind of care she's getting."

"Be still, Vanessa. Doctors are doctors," Mary replied reassuringly.

"Mama, you didn't see her. She was hysterical. Her eyes were wild. She was filthy. Something awful happened to her."

"I know. I know." Marcus held Vanessa close. "Baby, it is going to be okay."

"Are you the family of Seraphina Laurent?" A young doctor in blue hospital scrubs and a white coat approached.

"Yes, that's us," Vanessa replied. "Is she okay? What happened to her?"

"I am Dr. Geyser." He sat down on the bench next to Mary. "We don't know. We were hoping you could tell us. Was she in an accident?"

"We know nothing," Marcus replied. "We found her injured, screaming incoherently. What's wrong?"

"She has a concussion, her eardrums are ruptured, and she's got more than a few deep lacerations. Thankfully nothing is broken. Outside of a car accident or an explosion, I can't see any other way she would've sustained these types of injuries."

"She hasn't said anything?" Vanessa asked worriedly.

"Not a word. We had to sedate her when she first arrived. She is resting now, and I am going to keep her for a day or two. You can see her. One at a time."

"I'll go." Mary rose with the aid of her cane. "Doctor, may I follow you?"

"Of course." He offered his arm to steady her.

"Auntie, I think I should go. Since we can only go one at a time, you can wait here with Marcus, and I will come back for you."

"Sit down, Vanessa Edwina," Mary said sharply. "I know you mean well, but all you're going to do is ask a bunch of questions."

"How else are we supposed to find out what happened?" Vanessa grumbled.

"Seraphina doesn't need that right now. When she wants us to know, she'll tell us," Mary replied. "Now go home. Change your clothes. Bring a bag for her. Seraphina's going to need you, but not right now."

"Vanessa, baby, she's right." Marcus lifted her chin. "Come on. I'll bring you back. Mama, you'll be okay until then?"

Vanessa looked down at her soiled jeans and T-shirt. "Mama, she said she did this to herself."

"I doubt it," Dr. Geyser interrupted. "But, just in case, I have already sent a referral for a psychiatric evaluation. Maybe they can get her to tell us what happened."

"No. Seraphina too strong for that. You go on now. I'll stay with her."

*****

Mary stood at the bedside, looking over Seraphina, who was curled in a ball like a small child. She could see the tracks of dried tears in the remaining dirt on her face.

"Seraphina."

"Auntie. You told me. Stubborn as two mules, you said. Stubborn as two mules."

"What, baby?"

"I found him. The one who stuck to me. I found him, and now he is gone."

Mary stroked Seraphina's back. "Found who? Where?"

"I can't tell you. If I do, you'll think I'm crazy," Seraphina whispered.

"Try me."

"It has only been a day for you, but I've spent the last year and a half with the love of my life. I swear to you, Auntie, on my very life, it was real. He was real. And he loved me. He loved me. And I loved him. You don't think I'm crazy?"

"I've seen a lot in my time. Including crazy. Things happen in this life that we can't explain. Sometimes because we can't, other times because we ain't supposed to. If you believe you met the love of your life and lived a life with him, who am I to say you didn't."

"And I threw it all away," Seraphina cried.

"Hush now, child." Mary stroked Seraphina's cheek. "It's going to be all right."

"No. No, it won't. I followed him onto the battlefield. I followed him. There was an explosion. Oh, Auntie, his face. His eyes. I wasn't supposed to be there."

"What on earth were you doing on a battlefield?"

"He pleaded with me. He said, 'Just this once.' Just this once, and I didn't listen. I was afraid…"

"Afraid he'd leave like all the rest? Afraid he wouldn't come back?" Mary gave her a grave look.

"He said he would. He proved he would, but I—"

"You refused to believe him."

"Oh God! How am I going to live this life without him? How? I cannot. Auntie, my soul hurts. It screams." Seraphina pulled herself into a tighter ball and wept.

"You won't be without him. Sugar, if your love is strong enough to do this…you will see each other again. Tell your soul that. Hope on that. Rest now. Vanessa will be here soon."

"Auntie, don't tell her, okay? Don't tell anyone. Please."

"Sugar, your secret is safe with me."

CHAPTER TWENTY-THREE

Weld Memorial Hospital – Baltimore, Maryland
Tuesday, September 20th

Aaron waited alone in the hospital courtyard, a triple espresso in hand, the first of many cups of coffee for the day. If residency at Weld Memorial had taught him anything, it was how to work on little to no sleep.

The Chief of Surgery had asked to meet with him privately. A meeting request from an attending was never a good thing as a resident, even if the attending was your uncle, renowned surgeon Dr. Michael Weld.

Lulled by the solitude of the outdoor space, Aaron closed his eyes. She was there, his mystery woman, lingering in the quiet of his mind. She washed her legs and feet in the river. Her skin, bronzed like the sands of the Sahara, mirrored her copper eyes. She looked up at him from beneath a torrent of sable curls and smiled.

"Wake up, Weld! You look like shit." Michael sat down on the bench beside him.

"I'm a surgical resident, Uncle. I'm supposed to look like shit."

"Are you going to tell me what's up?"

"There's nothing to tell, Uncle."

"Like your father, you're a terrible liar. You're distracted and unfocused."

"Bullshit! Says who?" Aaron asked angrily.

"It doesn't matter who told me. It is my job as chief to know what is going on with all my residents."

"Just a little trouble sleeping. Nothing to get excited about, Uncle. I can handle it."

"When did you sleep last?" Michael asked.

"I sleep. It isn't an issue."

"A surgeon can't afford to be tired, distracted, or unfocused."

"I'll get more rest. I'll even hand off some of my more complicated cases this week. Will that satisfy you?"

"No. I'm taking you off the rotation for a week."

"What! You aren't serious?"

"I've already reassigned your cases. Finish your rounds and go home."

"Do you know what people will think? They'll think I've made a mistake or that I can't hack it."

"Can't hack it? Aaron, you can't save every patient. The only mistake you've made is thinking you can. I'm telling you to take the week off. We'll call it a vacation. People will think you are taking a well-earned rest. You haven't left this hospital in a year. Don't be sore, Aaron. It's for your own good."

"Suspension is suspension, regardless of how you try to spin it," Aaron groused.

"Come on. I'll take the elevator with you." Michael patted him on the back. "We can talk a little more."

"No." Aaron stood up. "I'll take the stairs."

Aaron tossed his half-finished espresso in the trash at the stairwell door and began the long climb to the eighth floor. Every angry step gave way to the knowledge that his uncle was right. He was tired, distracted, and unfocused. His mystery woman was blurring the lines between sleep and awake, and his life, his sanity, hung in the balance. *Get your shit together, Aaron. She's a dream...a dream.*

The Weld Estate – Baltimore, Maryland
Friday, September 23rd

The Weld Estate was set just off the main road, at the end of a willow tree-lined cobblestone drive. As a colonial mansion on a sprawling five acres of pools, ponds, garden terraces, stables, and green lawns, the home required a small contingent of staff to keep it all pristine.

Aaron killed the engine. Coming home was a Hail Mary. He'd spent the better part of the week in his apartment, doing what he'd been doing for the six months...running from nightmares and sleeping in daydreams. He was hopeful a change in scenery and a little company would help settle his mind.

Aaron entered the house through the garage. The aromas from one of his mother's culinary masterpieces greeted him at the door. It had been a long time since he'd had a meal that wasn't from a vending machine or microwave.

He opened the door onto a spacious kitchen with a large picture window that overlooked the five-acre property. His mom and his aunt sat around the kitchen island, piles of paper spread out before them.

"Hey, Mom. Auntie Ginny." Aaron set his bag down.

"Aaron! I've missed you, love. Come, give me a squeeze."

As a petite blonde with blazing blue eyes and a stunning figure, nothing about Rose Weld betrayed her years.

"I missed you too, Mom." Aaron hugged her. "What are the two of you up to?"

"Your Auntie and I are finalizing the plans for the Weld Museum Gala."

"Finalizing?" Ginny sighed, incredulous. "Your mother has changed the plans a hundred times. I'm surprised the caterer hasn't quit. Hell, I want to quit."

Ginny, a fiery, green-eyed redhead with a wickedly funny disposition, was nothing like her sister Rose. They were so different; his mother claimed the stork left Ginny by mistake.

"Auntie Ginny, you know better than to plan anything with my mother." Aaron shook his head. "Did you forget Gabe and Monica's wedding?"

"To hell with both of you," Rose scolded. "It's our family history on display. I want the gala to be special."

"Mom, I'm sure it will be. I'm starving. When is dinner?"

"Dinner is at six, as always. I had Minerva turn down your bed. It'll be so nice to have all of you home."

"All of us?"

"Yes. Your brother and his wife are coming for dinner tonight and staying the weekend."

"Gabe and Monica will be here? So much for a relaxing weekend," Aaron groaned.

"I'd take you with me, nephew, but your mother would throw a fit," Ginny quipped.

"Start the car, Auntie. I'm right behind you." Aaron smiled.

"Don't encourage him, Ginny. Aaron, love, it'll be fine. I promise. There is plenty of room for everyone. Minerva is staying for the weekend to help. And I will do my best to get Gabe to behave."

"My brother? Behave?" Aaron rolled his eyes. "Auntie, honk twice before you go."

"Will do, Aaron. Will do." Ginny laughed.

"The both of you are awful. Just awful." Rose pouted.

"I'm not going anywhere, Mom." Aaron kissed her on the cheek. "Where's Robert?"

"Don't be a smart ass. Your father is out." Rose examined his face. "You look terrible."

Aaron pulled away. "Thank you, Mother."

"You need…a wife. Someone to balance you out. It's been a long time." Rose grabbed his face. "Look at you."

"Mother, we talked about this," Aaron warned.

"Okay. Okay. Get some rest. I'll call you for dinner."

*****

Aaron fell back on the bed. He was exhausted and badly in need of sleep, but he was afraid, unsure of what a loss of consciousness would bring.

"Someone to balance you out." His mother wasn't the only member of the Weld clan who shared that sentiment. None of them understood that he was in complete control of his life and his heart for a reason. He

only knew one way to love a woman…and it always ended in heartache and loss.

Too tired to fight it, sleep found him, and so did she.

He kissed her sex, sucking her into a swollen wet heat. She tangled her fingers in his hair.

"Please," she wept.

"No," he replied, hungrily tasting every inch of her body, leaving nothing unscathed by his hot mouth and teasing lips.

"Take me," she begged, her fevered skin glistening with sweat.

The look in her eyes stilled him, hardened him…broke him. He gave in, sheathing himself until she could take no more and then pushing deeper still. His name escaped her lips in a whimper.

"Aaron."

"Yes. Yes, my mysterious…"

He fell into the ecstasy of her. A guttural groan left him, and he filled her with his seed. Her body softened beneath his with every wave of pleasure. He rolled onto his back, taking her with him.

"Don't leave." He held her close. Praying this time, he would be strong enough to keep her from leaving. He wasn't.

She looked at him lovingly, her image fading. Only the faint scent of honey and lavender remained.

Aaron stumbled from the bed into the bathroom. He took off his sweat-drenched clothing and stepped into the shower. He turned the knob to cold; icy water fell from above. The tension began to dissipate, and reason returned. After a few minutes, he shut the water off, grabbed a towel, and wrapped it around his waist. The vanity mirror reflected the circles under his crystal blue eyes and the five-day-old stubble on his face. His raven locks, grown too long, had returned to their natural curl. His mother and uncle were right. He looked like shit.

Still damp, he returned to the room and searched through his weekender bag until he found it: a vintage leather journal with an antique locking clasp and handmade cotton paper. The leather cover, embossed with the Weld crowned dragons, gave the book an almost ancient feel. It was a gift from his Aunt Charlotte. She'd given him a journal every Christmas since he was eight years old. He'd journaled ever since, pouring his thoughts and feelings onto the pages, every journal becoming his own personal book of secrets.

Aaron sat down at his writing desk and opened the book. A Montblanc fountain pen rolled from between the pages. He removed the cap from the nib and wrote.

Friday, September 23rd

Who are you? I feel you. Your scent, your touch, your taste…are real to me. I long for them. You call to me. Who are you? My mysterious…who are you? Please tell me. I cannot take this torture. Let me have you or set me free.

He set the pen down.

*****

Dinner was served in the dining room just off the kitchen. Aaron sat across from Gabe and Monica, his mother and father at the heads of the table.

"Thanks, Mom. It's been forever since I had your lobster, shrimp, and crab cakes. As always, the steak was cooked to perfection. Thank you."

"My pleasure, love. There's nothing like a home-cooked meal and a good wine to cure what ails you."

"How are things at the hospital?" Robert asked, curious. "Your mother didn't tell me you were coming."

"Good, Dad. I was able to get some time off."

"You? Take time off?" Robert raised an eyebrow.

"Mom has been after me, and Uncle Mike insisted."

"Robert, leave the boy alone." Rose waved a dismissive hand. "Now that everyone is here, we can talk about the gala."

"Sweet mercy, woman!" Robert exclaimed. "All you talk about is the gala. It's a party, not a state dinner."

"Robert Joseph, the gala is a premier event! An opportunity to show off our family history and raise money for local charities. You all will help me do it, or by God, I'll disown the lot of you!"

"Okay, Mom." Gabe sighed.

Gabe had the classic Weld blue eyes but Rose's blonde hair. He and Aaron were nothing alike. Aaron often wondered if, like Auntie Ginny, the stork had left him by mistake too.

"Well, I, for one, would love to know more about the gala. From what Ginny says, it's going to be spectacular. I'm dying to find out all the details."

"Thank you, Monica. I do hope so. It will be black-tie, of course. Actors from the local community troop in period dress from the last one hundred and fifty years will mingle with the guests during the hors d'oeuvres reception in the museum. A plated dinner will be served in the formal dining room, followed by a wine and dessert course back in the museum. Dr. Vanessa Blackwell, the curator, will speak, and your father will share a few words on behalf of the family. I've hired a string quartet to accompany the evening. It's going to be fantastic!"

"Another Weld event for the ages!" Robert bellowed.

"Rose, no one can put together an event like you." Monica smiled. "I can't wait."

"Let us come to the point, Mother." Aaron set his drink down. "What do you need us to do?"

Aaron knew Monica would agree to anything, desperate for her mother-in-law's approval. Monica was just Gabe's type: a pretty brunette with a sweetheart face and a kind heart.

"You read my mind, love." Rose leaned forward. "I'm glad you asked. I need you to come dressed as Colonel Weld."

"And there it is. No way! Not going to happen. I'll do anything else. You name it. Wash dishes, dance with decrepit old ladies, park cars—anything but that!"

"Oh, come on, bro. It'll be like Halloween, but with rich people and no candy." Gabe laughed.

Aaron shook his head. "No."

"Please, Aaron. It would make the night so much more magical," Rose pleaded.

"Son, do as your mother says. If you don't, we'll never hear the end of it."

"Bro, you must admit, you look just like him." Gabe pointed. "Same name, same face, same job. It's eerie. Monica agrees. Tell him, Monica. We were just talking about it the other day."

"Aaron, it is kind of…well, odd. I mean, have you seen pictures of yourself, I mean of him?" Monica asked.

Why did no one understand that his appearance, a novelty, and wonder for them, wasn't for him? To look in the past and see your face reflected in a man you shared so much with and knew absolutely nothing about was unnerving.

"Yes, Monica, I have. Genetic coincidence…nothing more. We all look like someone. Now the name? The name is Mom and Dad's doing."

"Truth be told, love, we didn't name you, Addie did," Rose mused. "You remember Miss Addie, don't you? Maybe not. You were too young. My God, she worked in your father's office for years and with your grandfather before that. Sweet woman, sharp as a tack, with the memory of an elephant."

"Miss Addie. She was a gem," Robert replied. "The day you were born, Addie placed you in my arms, looked me in the eye, and said, "Aaron Matthew Weld. His name is Aaron Matthew Weld." Figured it was as good a name as any, and I knew better than to argue with Ms. Adelaide Moreau."

"Wow. So, the nurse named you?" Gabe held his sides, laughing. "You learn something new every day."

"Gabe! Your brother is named after your great-great-great grandfather. Have some respect," Rose snapped, pointing her fork at him.

"No, Mom, let him laugh," Aaron said, lowering her forked hand. "Maybe he'll asphyxiate and put us out of our misery. No offense, Monica."

Monica shrugged. "None taken. He's your brother."

"Aaron, don't say things like that," Rose scolded.

"Mother, if my suffering will make you happy, I'll do it."

"Great!" Rose beamed. "I'll call the tailor and schedule your fitting."

"Mom, really? You just assumed I'd do it?" Aaron rolled his eyes.

"Oh, calm down. I had to. Your Aunt Charlotte found the colonel's original Union Army dress coat in the family home in Philadelphia about a year ago now. We figured it would be perfect but can't have you wear the original, so I am having one made. You're going to look so handsome."

"Yes. Handsome and miserable." Aaron poured himself another glass of wine.

"You could always bring a date?" Rose offered timidly.

Aaron got up from the table. "Excuse me."

"Where are you going, Big Brother? Please tell me that wherever it is, there is a woman involved. You need a woman in the worst way."

"Shut up, Gabe!" Monica punched him in the arm. "You're such a pain in the ass sometimes."

"My romantic life is none of your business," Aaron bristled. He had a woman in his life, and she was driving him insane.

"Life? You have no life, romantic or otherwise. What is this? The first time you've taken time off in what, three years? I mean, when was the last time you had a girlfriend? College?"

"Gabe!" Monica cried.

"Monica, it is fortunate Gabe sleeps with you, and we no longer share a room." Aaron narrowed his eyes. "I have a sudden overwhelming urge to practice suturing wide orifices."

"Aaron Matthew!" Rose shouted. "I forbid you from being so macabre in my presence."

"Forgive me, Mother." Aaron drained his glass. "But he started it."

"Gabriel Michael, shut the hell up! Or I'll give him the string and let him truss you up like a turkey!" Rose glared. "Monica, as badly as I want grandchildren…I pray you have daughters."

Monica laughed. "Oh, Rose… I have sisters. Trust me, my mother fared no better."

"Calm down, Rose." Robert cackled. "Gabe does have a point." Robert sipped his Scotch. "Three years is a long time. And a man, well…a man has needs."

"Robert Joseph!" Rose exclaimed. "You can take your needs and your Scotch to your den!"

"Oh, be still, woman!" Robert quipped.

"Brother, I'm just giving you a hard time. I worry, is all. You look worn out. Seriously."

"I know, Little Brother. You're still a little shit, though." Aaron kissed Rose's cheek. "Good night. I'll see everyone in the morning. Breakfast at eight?"

"Yes, my love. Do not be late." Rose touched his face.

"Good night, all." Aaron left the room.

He stopped at the base of the stairs. The air around him had a sudden chill, and his mind settled on a singular thought. *It is time.*

CHAPTER TWENTY-FOUR

The Weld House Museum – Frederick, Maryland
Saturday, September 24th

Last night was the first good night's sleep he'd had in weeks. The wine and two shots of bourbon he had at dinner did what months of melatonin had not. He'd gone for a run before breakfast and planned to take his horse, Shade, out for a ride after, but Rose had guilted him into putting off his ride and coming with her to the museum instead. As he thought, the relaxing weekend he was looking for was not to be.

Aaron followed Rose through the museum doors. The restoration committee had done a superb job. The impressive foyer and antebellum staircase were spectacular. He admired the painstaking attention to detail. In this setting, the gala would be an event to remember.

"Aaron, love, look around for a moment. I need to find Dr. Blackwell. She is dying to meet you."

"Let me guess,"—Aaron sighed— "you told her I was the spitting image of the colonel?"

Rose gave him a sheepish look. "I may have mentioned it."

Aaron wandered over to what looked like a dining room. The refinished dark hardwood, and ivory pearl floral damask wallpaper with vintage frosted glass sconces, gave the room an elegant, almost regal look. Ethereal prisms of reflected light from the feathered cut glass and pear-shaped pendants hanging from the room's grand chandeliers boasted, the gods dine here.

"In the early years, this room was used as a hospital ward. It was restored from pictures found during the renovation. Would you like a tour?"

Aaron turned toward the small voice behind him. The young lady smiled sweetly at him.

"Thank you kindly, but I don't do groups well. I kind of just wanted to look around."

"No groups. The museum is not open to the public except by appointment. I could use the practice, but if you'd prefer, we have self-guided tours. I can give you a headset that will tell you about each exhibit as you approach it, or there are interactive displays in every area too."

"Thank you. I would love a headset," Aaron replied.

"Great! I'll be right back."

He didn't really want one, but the young woman was doing her best to give him a good experience, and the least he could do was oblige. She returned with the Bluetooth interactive headset and a map, gave him a quick demonstration, and sent him on his way.

Aaron put on the headset as she instructed and proceeded to the first exhibit on the tour: Civil War Medicine. He wandered into the room. The first item on display was a surgeon's field case, and next to it was a leather haversack. A disembodied female voice came through the headset.

"Made from leather, this haversack would have been expensive and not easily parted with. Note the bag's branding."

Aaron checked the brand. S.L.W. The card on the glass case said it was found in the home during the renovation. It made no mention of who S.L.W was.

The next case contained surgical tools used for various purposes, principally amputation. The surgeon in him cringed at the barbarous nature of 19th-century medicine and lamented that many of the tools didn't differ much from the surgical tools he used to perform amputations today.

Aaron circled the room, moving from one exhibit to another. As he did, the temperature of the room dropped perceptibly. A dense cloud of smoke filled the room, like a fog rolling in on the tide. A heaviness settled in his chest. It was difficult to breathe. He reached out for what he hoped would be a wall or other solid object hidden in the haze.

The room changed. Nurses in long aprons, floor-length skirts with long sleeves, and high-collard bodices scurried between the rows of hospital beds that lined the walls. A tall man in a medical white coat, high waist flat front pants, and a pinstriped waistcoat stood in the center of the room. He looked up from his clipboard and pointed to a patient. A nurse went to the bedside.

Aaron moved closer, struggling to see their faces. The man turned around.

"Oh god!" Aaron shouted.

It was him. An older, bearded him, but him. He was standing face to face with himself. And then, as quickly as the scene appeared, it vanished. Shaken, heart racing, Aaron sank to the nearest bench.

"What is happening to me?" he whispered to himself.

"Sir, are you okay?" The young woman placed a hand on his shoulder. Are you here alone? Would you like me to call someone?"

"I am fine. Thank you. Just needed to sit down."

"You don't look well."

Aaron glanced up at the young woman. Her name tag read Jasmine.

"Jasmine, I'm okay. Really. I can finish the tour on my own. I just needed to sit down. Thank you for your concern."

She gave him a nervous look but left him alone.

Heart still racing, Aaron was just regaining his composure when Rose returned with Dr. Blackwell.

"There you are! Aaron, this is Dr. Vanessa Blackwell, the museum curator."

"Please, call me Vanessa. Wow! You really do look like him."

"And you didn't believe me." Rose clasped her hands excitedly. "Vanessa, he will be the highlight of the evening!"

Still tense and more than a little shell-shocked, Aaron offered his hand in greeting.

"Hi, Vanessa. You must forgive my mother. Planning events is like catnip for her. The museum is magnificent. You've done a marvelous job."

"Thank you." Vanessa shook his hand. "It is a labor of love. Our families and Weld Memorial share a long history."

"I'm ashamed to say it, but I've never actually been here before."

"Not surprising. After the first Weld Memorial Hospital was built, the home fell off the map, for all intents and purposes."

"The colonel, you know a lot about him?"

"About Colonel Weld, the doctor, quite a bit. About the man, not so much. Oddly we haven't found any journals or letters of a personal nature. Most of what we know is anecdotal, stories handed down through people who knew him or knew those who did. People like my great-great aunt, Mary Oakes-Timmons. Your Aunt Charlotte has given us most of the hard facts about the colonel."

"Why the sudden interest, dear?" Rose asked. "I had to twist your arm to get you here."

"I'm standing in the man's house and being fitted for his clothes. He is my namesake. And as you and everyone else like to point out, I share his rugged good looks. It is enough to make one curious…don't you think?"

"Yes, dear." Rose smiled. "I see your point."

"Good afternoon, all. Forgive my interruption. You must be the man of the hour. Signore Weld, I presume?"

"Yes, I am. And you are?" Aaron answered curtly. The last thing he wanted was to entertain strangers. He needed to get the hell out of this museum.

"Signore Francesco Bisaccia."

"Francesco!" Rose kissed the man on both cheeks. "Aaron, this is Mr. Bisaccia. You may remember him from Gabriel's wedding. He is designing all the gala costumes."

"Mom, just for this?" Aaron asked, incredulous.

"Young man, when Signora Weld calls,"—Francesco took Rose's hand and kissed it lightly—"a gentleman answers."

"You flatter me, Francesco." Rose blushed.

Aaron wasn't sure if he wanted to throw up or punch the Don Giovanni in the face. He chose instead to break up the offending scene.

"And you had to come all the way here to take my measurements? I could have sent them to you…Francesco."

"I never trust another's measurements. I would normally do this in my shop or the client's home, but Signora Weld insisted I meet you here this morning."

"Are you serious?" Aaron groaned.

"Don't be cross with me." Rose patted his hand. "I didn't know when I would be able to corral you again; you work so much. And Vanessa wanted to meet you, so I figured it was a win-win. Oh, and the coat. You will get to see the coat."

"If you would come with me, Signore Weld." Francesco gestured to a room behind the stairs.

Aaron followed Mr. Bisaccia to a small office, where a folding shoji screen and large mirror had been set up. Aaron put on the muslin mockup of the uniform and stepped in front of the mirror.

"I am going to need the leg more tapered for when I ride. Loosen the waist a bit. I need a little give for my Colt."

"Your Colt?" Rose walked into the room.

"Mother, I am quite capable of attending a fitting on my own. And yes, my Colt. I have two. You didn't find them in the chest with the coat?"

"As a matter of fact, Charlotte did. They are being cleaned and appraised prior to display. How did you know?"

"I don't know, Mother. Where else would a man keep his guns?" Aaron answered, adjusting the mock garment in the mirror.

"Finito." Chalking complete, Mr. Bisaccia stood back, inspecting his work. "You may change."

Aaron stepped behind the screen. Out of Aaron's sight, Don Giovanni began to work his charms again, as was obvious to Aaron by the sound of his voice beyond the screen.

"Signora Weld." Francesco's lips smacking indicated he was likely kissing her hand again. "It is always a pleasure."

Rose giggled. "The pleasure is mine. We will talk soon about how the preparations are coming along."

Aaron walked around the screen and placed the muslin garment between Mr. Bisaccia and his mother. "Thank you, Francesco. That will be all."

"Yes. It was a pleasure meeting you, Signore Weld." Francesco bowed and made a quick exit.

"Aaron! That was rude." Rose grinned.

"You're married!" Aaron laughed. "I was doing him a favor. Dad would have punched him in the face."

"Mr. Bisaccia is harmless." Rose admired herself in the mirror. "At my age, it's nice to be noticed occasionally." She adjusted the hem of her mini dress. "Enough of that. Vanessa would like to take you on a personal tour. If you want to go home, I'll tell her you'll do it another time."

Aaron was torn. He did not want another experience like the one he'd had earlier. He was barely holding things together as it was. But, deep down, he wanted to know more.

"No, I have time. I would like a tour."

*****

The Weld Estate – Baltimore, Maryland

The den, with its leather recliners, big screens, built-in bar, and lack of discernable design scheme, was the only room in the house that truly belonged to his father. Aaron often mused that the den was his father's homage to disorder in an otherwise well-ordered home. Or a passive-aggressive way to piss his mother off.

"Dad, you got a minute?" Aaron stuck his head around the door.

"Yup," Robert replied. "Have a drink with me. A man should have a drink occasionally."

"I'll have a Scotch. Neat." Aaron held up two fingers. "Make it a double."

"A real man today, eh?" Robert poured two glasses and handed one to Aaron.

"Thanks." Aaron slipped into the chair across from his father.

He noticed that his hair and beard were grayer than the last time he'd seen him. But his eyes, the Weld blue, soft and inviting, remained unchanged.

"You going to tell me what's going on, or am I going to have to play detective like when you were little?" Robert asked.

"Nothing is wrong." Aaron downed his Scotch and got up to pour another.

"Okay, detective. You haven't had a vacation in over a year. And when you do take one, you come home?"

"Am I not allowed to come home?"

"Of course you are. And you know what I mean. You're a single, attractive, thirty-year-old doctor. Why aren't you on a beach somewhere with a beer, trying to decide which bikini-clad woman you want to wake up with in the morning?"

"You must have me confused with Gabe." Aaron laughed.

"I wish. Aaron, there are other women."

"I know that!" Aaron raised his voice. "You think I don't know that?"

"Yes, you do." Robert sat forward in his chair. "But that isn't why you are sitting here on a Saturday night."

"Don't say it. We aren't going to talk about this."

"Charlotte is gone. And son, it isn't your fault."

"You always bring her up. Why?"

"Well, I am your father, for one. And I am a therapist, so it's kind of my thing. Are you seeing anyone?"

"No. It was three years ago. I'm good."

"Good? Three years ago, the woman you loved and were going to marry died in your arms on the bathroom floor from an overdose. You haven't had a relationship, plutonic or otherwise, with a woman since."

Charlotte. College sweethearts, he'd popped the question with a two-carat diamond ring at Christmas in front of family and friends. Six months later, he'd found her on the floor of their apartment, seconds away from death. He knew she had mental health issues, but he wasn't too concerned. She was on medication, and he was always around to protect her from her worst impulses…until he wasn't.

"Dad, a man should be able to protect the people he loves. If he can't…"

"If he can't, what? He shouldn't love anyone?"

"It's working for me, so like I said, I'm good."

"Son, you can't live a loveless life."

"I'm not a monk. I get my needs met." Aaron left the bar and came back to his chair. "This is not what I came here to talk to you about. No more armchair therapist, okay?"

"Okay, but this conversation is not over. What did you want to talk about?"

"You sit on the museum board; how much do you know about the colonel?"

"Not much. Why?"

"I was there today…just curious."

"If you really want to know about the colonel, you should talk to your Auntie Cassandra. She fancies herself a sibyl. But once you get past her tarot cards and crystals, she is a damn good historian and the authority on all things Weld."

"Dad, you should be more open. Auntie Cassandra is a free spirit. Hard to come by in this family."

"None of that mysticism stuff is real. There's no science behind it. It can become a crutch and leave many with undiagnosed and untreated mental health issues."

"If that's how you feel, Dad, no wonder she lives in Philadelphia." Aaron chuckled.

"Cassandra is my baby sister. I love her. But like you and Gabe, I can only take her…in small doses."

"How did she get to be the family historian?"

"Well, she has a doctorate in history, for starters. She's always had an affinity for old things. All that 'the future can only be found in the past' nonsense."

Aaron raised his glass. "Here's to small doses."

"Pour me one too." Gabe entered the study. "What are we drinking to?"

"Nonsense and free spirits, Little Brother."

"I'm in!" Gabe laughed.

Aaron handed Gabe the drink in his hand and poured himself another.

"I asked Dad about the colonel, and somehow, he ended up in a rant about Auntie Cassandra."

"Auntie Cassandra. Now that's a woman who knows how to have a good time." Gabe smiled.

"You would think so. The two of you are peas in a pod." Robert laughed.

"Auntie Cassandra is a mystic. Gabe, Gabe is more of a Loki, mischievous and hell-bent on destruction." Aaron smiled.

"I'll drink to that! You could use a little more mischief in your life, Brother."

"Funny you should say that, Gabe. Aaron and I were just talking about—"

"The colonel," Aaron interrupted. "We were just discussing the colonel."

"Yes, again, your Auntie Cassandra is the best person to talk to. She's a goddamn Weld Wikipedia." Robert scratched his beard. "But I'll give it a whirl. What do you want to know?"

"Why is there so little information about him?" Aaron asked.

"He was a private man, by all accounts. Stands to reason he wouldn't leave much of a personal nature behind."

"Nothing about the women in his life? I mean…the man was wealthy and good-looking."

"His wife died young, and he never remarried. Wise man, if you ask me. I would guess he probably had a mistress or two over the years. He was a Weld man, after all. We can do monogamy, but celibacy is a no-go. People didn't talk about things like that, and as far as we know, he didn't have any illegitimate children."

"The man built an integrated hospital. Employed and trained Blacks and women. He was on the civil and women's rights train before they were the cause de jour. The man journaled everything. A man this significant, and we know nothing else about his personal life?"

"Why the sudden interest, Aaron?"

"You and Mom, I swear. She asked the same question. Does it matter?"

"Well, as fascinating as all of this is, let's change from *The History Channel* to *The Food Network*." Gabe downed his Scotch. "Mother sent me to get the two of you for dinner twenty minutes ago."

"Gabe! You know your mother will have our necks if we make her dinner cold!"

"Dad, Mom has you wrapped around her little finger." Gabe smiled.

On the way to the dinner table, Aaron feigned interest in his father and brother's antics.

"The future can only be found in the past." To his father, the words were nonsense, but for him, they resonated, the answer to a question deep within.

Uncle Mike was right. His father was a terrible liar. He wasn't telling him everything. He needed to see Auntie Cassandra.

CHAPTER TWENTY-FIVE

Weld Manor - Philadelphia, Pennsylvania
Sunday, September 25th

"Aaron! It is good to see you. How long has it been?" Cassandra hugged him tightly.

Aaron leaned over to return her embrace. "Since Gabe's wedding. It is good to see you too, Auntie."

He could smell the faint scent of flowers in her jet-black hair. A short, Rubenesque woman with gray eyes, Cassandra did not wear her age as his father did.

"Come in. Your mother called." Cassandra's eyes shimmered.

"Of course she did." Aaron sighed. "She wouldn't let me leave until I told her where I was going."

"Nephew, Rose by any other name would still be Rose."

Cassandra ushered Aaron into the large foyer across the mosaic tile floor, past the staircase. Aaron stopped at the bottom of the stairs. He turned ashen, and his heart quivered in his chest.

She was there…descending the staircase. His mystery woman. A vision in silken emerald green. She smiled at him and held out her hand for him to take. Before he could reach for her, she disappeared.

"Are you okay?" Cassandra asked worriedly. "Your energy is so frantic, almost frightened."

No. No, I am not okay. I just saw an imaginary woman walk down the staircase. Aaron collected himself. "I'm good, Auntie. Just a little tired."

"Sit down. Let me get you some water." Cassandra left for the kitchen.

Aaron sat on the couch. The room felt familiar. The décor, sleek and modern, gave the space a 21st-century update, but the natural skylight, set in the textured plaster medallion and the landscape water-colored walls, rang true.

"Here. Drink this." She handed Aaron the glass and sat next to him. "Now talk to me. What's up?"

"Dad said you were the authority on Weld family history—a virtual Weld Wikipedia."

"Wikipedia?" Cassandra rolled her eyes. "Try Yale scholar. Remind him of that next time."

"Will do, Auntie. My father's backhanded compliments aside, I do have a reason for my visit."

"You mean you aren't here because you desperately missed me?"

"I do miss you. You should move to Maryland." Aaron sipped his water.

"Your great-great-great-great grandfather, Lord Edward Joseph Weld, built this house. Generations of Welds have lived here. Including you. A Weld will always live here."

"Me?" Aaron's eyes widened. "I only remember spending summers here as a child."

"Yup. You used to toddle around getting into everything. You were so cute, with those inquisitive blue eyes of yours. Your parents moved out when that palace they built in Baltimore was finished."

"Says the woman who lives in a mansion." Aaron laughed.

"True." Cassandra smiled devilishly. "Nephew, I know why you're here. That face and name of yours finally got you curious. What has your father told you?"

"Other than the story of how I got my name, Dad hasn't told me much of anything."

"Ms. Addie!" Cassandra lit up. "She is a gem."

"You know her?"

"Of course. She only worked with your father forever. You would be too young to remember. A sage, that woman. She has been vital to my oral history project and The Weld House Museum. A treasure trove of information. You should hear her version of the story about your naming."

"There's another version?"

"Yes. Your father would never tell it. He isn't a very "open" man. Anything that isn't black and white is nonsense to him."

"Nonsense." Aaron smiled. "His words exactly. You know your brother well. Says you fancy yourself a sibyl."

"I am no fortune teller. I just feel things deeply. I stay open and listen. It allows me to see things others don't. I think it is the blessing and curse of all Cassandras."

"I get it. Would it be possible to talk to Ms. Addie?"

"We've already met this week, but she loves company. I am sure she wouldn't mind another visit. I'll give her a call."

*****

Addie lived in a retirement community outside Philadelphia. The gated enclaves, carpets of green grass, man-made ponds, and attractive condos put the benefits of a well-planned, well-funded retirement on display.

Aaron knocked softly on Addie's door. After a few moments, a beautiful green-eyed woman with fair smooth skin, a lush silver mane, and an enigmatic smile opened the door. There was nothing old about her loose denim, stylish collared button shirt, and bedazzled sandals. Aaron was taken aback. Seventy-seven years later, echoes of Adelaide Moreau's youthful beauty remained.

"Ha! You were expecting a frail old woman in a polyester leisure suit. I can see it on your face. Well, I am happy to disappoint you." Addie laughed, kissing him on both cheeks.

"Yes, ma'am, I confess I was. Forgive me." Aaron reddened, embarrassed.

"Aaron Matthew Weld. The last time I saw you, you were just a little thing. Come in. Let me have a look at you."

"Ms. Moreau, you remember me?" Aaron replied.

"It's Addie, and yes. Even if I didn't, I would recognize that Weld handsome anywhere. Ms. Cassandra." Addie kissed her on both cheeks. "It is good to see you."

"The same." Cassandra returned Addie's affections. "Thank you for the invitation. I know it was last minute."

"Come. I laid a little something out for us on the patio."

Addie ushered them both outside, where what could only be described as five-star charcuterie boards and iced tea awaited them.

"Miss. Addie, you didn't have to go through all this trouble for us." Aaron sat down.

"It was no trouble," she replied, pouring him a glass of tea. "Now, Ms. Cassandra says you have a question for me."

"Yes, ma'am. My parents told me recently that you named me. I would like to know what made you—"

"Name you after your granddaddy? Not to put too fine a point on it, baby, but have you looked in a mirror lately?"

"Yes, ma'am." Aaron laughed. "But you couldn't have known I was going to have his face."

"Baby, you don't have to see the future when you know the past. Truth is, you named yourself."

"I don't understand," Aaron asked, confused.

"The day you were born, I was the first to hold you. Slid right out into my arms, as it were. You didn't cry or fuss. Just looked at me with those blue eyes, all serious and quiet, like the world wasn't new to you. My grandfather, Armand, used to tell me stories about the time great-grandma Lula spent growing up around the Weld house. Lula's mother, Daisy, and her husband, Eli, worked with the colonel after the war. Everyone said the colonel was quiet and serious, with piercing blue eyes that always seemed far away, like he'd lost something dear to him. When I held you, that memory came to mind as if Grandma Lula had just whispered it in my ear. See, you named yourself."

"None of this makes sense. With respect, that is very hard to believe."

"You already believe it, or you wouldn't be here." Addie smiled. "Your spirit understands; your mind is in the way. Let it rest for now. It will come to you. Young folks, so impatient."

"Aaron, Addie's great-great-grandfather, Eli Oakes, lived in the Weld house as a child. He and your great-great-grandfather, Solomon, grew up together," Cassandra added. "His parents, Noble and Mary Oakes, were the house staff."

"He wasn't blood. But the colonel treated them all just the same. He paid for Eli's education and sent Lula to France when she was old enough to go. Grandma Lula was my great-great-great grandmother Daisy's child by her master. She could pass as it were, and things was different for Black folks over there."

"Master?" Aaron set his glass down.

"Yes, Master. Y'all white folks crack me up, thinking slavery was so long ago. Where you think I got these green eyes from? Lula lived in France before the great war, where she met my great-granddaddy, Chandler Moreau. He was with the French Legion in North Africa. They came back to the states after the war. Listen to me go on. I'm not boring you, am I? You came here to ask questions, and I haven't done nothing but talk."

"No. No. Please continue," Aaron prompted. "Your story is fascinating. I am not bored at all."

"See Aaron, I told you…a treasure. My oral history project is going to be everything."

"Yes, Miss Cassandra seems to think people will find some interest in the droning on of an old woman."

"Do you have any children, Miss Addie?" Aaron asked.

"Sadly, no. I was destined to deliver them, not have them. I have a niece somewhere in Louisiana, I think. My brother Jules was a bit of a rolling stone. I haven't been able to find her, though. Miss Cassandra is helping me with that. Got a nose like a bloodhound, that one."

"Do you know her name? Or where in Louisiana she might be?"

"I know Jules was with a woman named Etienne. I found a letter she'd written him during the war, but the address wasn't legible, and the only other information was that she'd had a baby girl named Eulalie. Jules died in Vietnam. The letter was unopened. I don't think he knew."

"My dad says Auntie Cassandra is a damn good historian. Pardon my language. If anyone could find her, she can."

"That's because your auntie understands that the future can only be found in the past and that the past defines the present. She has a respect for what came before. She is a wise one, Miss Cassandra."

"Thank you for the compliment, Miss. Addie." Cassandra blushed.

"It ain't a compliment if it is the truth. Now, where were we?"

Aaron sat and listened to Addie talk for a long time. His mother was right; she had a memory like an elephant. A part of him wanted to ask about his mystery woman. Tell her about his dreams…his nightmares. If she knew this much Weld family history, even anecdotally, she might know more personal things about the colonel. But to ask, he'd have to admit he was seeing things. And he was not about to tell anyone he wasn't in control of his faculties.

As they were leaving, Addie kissed him on both cheeks again, but this time she paused and waited for Cassandra to walk away.

She whispered in his ear, "Le contrôle est une illusion."

A shiver ran down his spine. "You speak French?"

"Oui. Doesn't everybody?" Addie laughed. "Baby, when you are ready to ask your real question, the one I can feel weighing on your spirit, you come back and see me, okay."

Aaron could see a wisdom behind Addie's smiling, shamrock eyes. The impetus was there, but he wasn't ready. "Yes, ma'am."

*****

The library's ceiling-to-floor dark wood bookshelves, mixture of leather and upholstered furniture, and area rugs gave the space a warm and inviting feel. It was the middle of the day, but Aaron could feel a fire in the hearth and see the shadows cast by the dimming light of evening.

"You didn't change this room like the others," Aaron said.

"No. Other than a furniture update, it looks exactly like it did when the house was built. Even the books are original. Family stories say this was the colonel's favorite room in the house. He spent hours here every day, sitting in that window. Funny, since you can't see out of it."

"It was the light." Aaron placed his hand on the stained-glass window. "He could see."

"Are you okay, Nephew? You're looking a little pale again." Cassandra felt his forehead.

"I am fine." Aaron removed her hand from his forehead and held it in his. "I mean, I am a doctor, Auntie."

"That doesn't mean shit. Doctors are the worst at taking care of themselves."

"I'll give you that. Just a little overindulgence. I didn't think it was possible to get so full on a fancy meat and cheese tray."

"Good food and good company will do that." Cassandra chuckled.

"Good company is right. I think I am in love with that old woman. I could listen to her talk for hours. You are right. Your oral history project will win awards with her as the storyteller."

"I hope so. Take a nap. Your uncle Jim will be home later, and I know he's going to want to go out with you."

"Thank you, Auntie." Aaron kicked off his shoes and stretched out on the library couch. "Thank you for taking me to meet that extraordinary woman."

"You're welcome." Cassandra turned off the lights and closed the library doors behind her.

Aaron put his hands behind his head and closed his eyes. Sleep came quickly, too quickly. He wasn't prepared for the horror his mind would conjure this time. The fear coursing through his veins brought everything to life.

The stench of rotting flesh and blood-soaked earth, the percussion of artillery, and choking clouds of smoke hung over the bitter cries of the damned and the dying. She was crawling toward him, her face covered in blood and soot. He could not hear her, but he could read his name on her lips. He moved toward him, trying to stay out of the line of fire.

"No! Seraphina, go back! For God's sake! Go back!" he screamed.

And in a moment…she was gone, swallowed by a wall of earth, an empty crater in her place. It was the faint retreat of a bugle in the distance that woke him.

Aaron sat on the edge of the couch, heart-pounding, struggling to catch his breath. As the terror abated, a singular thought emerged from the chaos. *Seraphina. Her name is Seraphina.*

The library doors opened. "Aaron! Cassandra told me you were here. It is so good to see you."

"Uncle Jim?"

"The one and only. You look like shit."

"Sorry, Uncle Jim. I just woke up from a nap. How are you?"

"Good. That sister-in-law of mine driving everyone crazy over this gala?"

"You know it. You are coming?"

"Nephew, it is a wise man that avoids Rose's thorns. Ask your father." He chuckled.

James Canterbury was his father's oldest friend. A tall man with a strong build, Uncle Jim was nothing like his friend Robert. Warm and witty, he was the perfect man for his whimsical, bordering on eccentric aunt.

The Weld and the Canterbury families went all the way back to the English boats that brought them to America many generations ago.

"How's business, Uncle?"

"For the most part. The import-export arm of Canterbury Shipping is doing well, but our stock hasn't fully recovered from the '08 recession. But I didn't come home early to talk business. There are a couple of beers and steaks in this town with our names on them."

"Sounds good. Give me twenty minutes. I need to clean up."

"Jim, you're home early." Cassandra stood in the doorway. "Aaron, did he wake you? Jim!"

"Cassandra, it isn't every day my nephew comes to visit. We're going out for a bite. Get going, boy. The sooner you get cleaned up, the sooner I can eat."

"Aaron, sweetheart, forgive your uncle," Cassandra said. "Mr. Coleman has taken your things upstairs. He will see that you have everything you need while you're here."

"Roger that. Excuse me." Aaron kissed Cassandra on the cheek and headed up the stairs.

Mr. Coleman met Aaron at the top of the stairs. "This way, sir. It is good to have you home, Mr. Weld."

"Hello, Abner. It is good to be here." Aaron followed him down the hall. "I would happily stay in one of the smaller guest rooms."

"Mr. Weld, you are not a guest. Your bed has been turned down, and fresh linens are in the bath. Let me know if you require anything else."

"I will. Thank you, Abner."

Aaron shook his head. "A bona fide English butler." A rebel, Aunt Cassandra was always one to set fire to convention, but like Addie said, she deeply respected history and tradition. An English manor had an English butler, and Weld Manor was no exception.

Aaron crossed the room, past the imposing four-poster bed, to the window overlooking the drive. He'd seen the view before, in a dream. He turned from the window and tripped over what he thought was a chaise. It was, but it wasn't a real one. From his knees, he looked toward the door, a heavy feeling in his stomach. It was him standing in the doorway, but unlike in the museum, he wasn't old… He was young, the same age he was now.

Aaron fell back on his knees as the apparition of himself walked by. Time appeared to slow down as he watched the movie play out before him.

Seraphina was there, sitting on the chaise he'd just tripped over. He knelt beside her and kissed her feet. She smiled at him and laughed. But after a moment, tears began to fall. He comforted her. And then it was over.

Aaron sprung to his feet and ran for the bathroom. He splashed cold water on his face, soaking the front of his shirt in the process and masking his angry tears. It was worse now than when Uncle Mike had put him on leave. He couldn't return to the surgical suite like this: sleep-deprived and hallucinating.

He'd mastered this. He'd mastered this years ago. He had whole books of secrets devoted to this. He remembered. He remembered Aunt Cassandra and his father fighting. He remembered the hours of counseling. And then he'd learned control. Control of everything. His life. His emotions. His mind. Everything. And he never spoke of it—of anything.

"Le contrôle est une illusion."

"No! Control is not an illusion. This! This is an illusion."

CHAPTER TWENTY-SIX

Weld Manor – Philadelphia, Pennsylvania
Monday, September 26th

Aaron gave up on sleep. A headache and an overwhelming need for coffee drove him out of his titanic four-poster bed and downstairs into the kitchen. The house was quiet. A good thing because he wasn't in the mood for company. The night out with Uncle Jim helped distract him for a while, but once alone, his thoughts turned to Serafina once more.

He'd killed two men this morning. It wasn't an apparition or a movie; the knife was in his hand. He'd felt it slide across the man's neck and heard the gurgling of his last breath. Shade's hoof beats set his heart's pace. Another man's crushed windpipe and hemorrhaged eyes were real. Seraphina's broken and bleeding body was real. Never in his life, real or imagined, had he ever felt the intensity of rage and despair he'd experienced in the wee hours of this morning.

"Good morning, Mr. Weld." Alice smiled and handed him a cup of coffee. "You're early for breakfast."

Aaron could see behind her cheery façade that Alice was distraught. It'd been years since he'd spent summers at the manor. He'd forgotten what life in a house with servants was like. He'd broken the rules. The home ran on a schedule. To be early for breakfast, or any meal, left the kitchen staff unprepared.

"Forgive me, Alice. I had trouble sleeping. Don't go out of your way for me. The coffee is fine. Thank you."

Aaron made his way to the library. The early morning sun filtered through the stained-glass windows. Aaron sipped the hot liquid slowly, breathing in its earthy aroma, savoring the rare serenity of mind and body. The faint scent of lavender began to fill the space around him. He wasn't alone. Seraphina was there, seated on a small settee, reading in a kaleidoscope of colored light. Her hair, a wavy sable, was down, partly obscuring her face.

Aaron moved closer, and Seraphina stood, returned the book to the shelf, and vanished.

Aaron searched the bookcase until he found it. *Leaves of Grass* by Walt Whitman. He took the book from the shelf and opened it; dried sprigs of lavender fell from between the bindings. Aaron ran his fingers across the page as he read.

I am not to speak to you, I am to think of you when I sit alone or wake at night alone,

I am to wait, I do not doubt I am to meet you again,

I am to see to it that I do not lose you.

Cassandra tapped lightly on the door. "Mind if I join you? Walt Whitman? I would never have pegged you for a poetry guy."

"He's my favorite. Hers too. She was here."

"Her who?"

"She was here. The poems, the poems were his reminder. He pressed the lavender there to remind him of her. She always smelled of lavender and honey. The library was her favorite room. She loved this window. It is why he always sat here."

"She who? Lavender and honey? Remind him of who? Who is he? Sweetheart, you aren't making any sense."

"I see her. I see her in my dreams. Dreams so vivid that, at times, I can't tell if I am asleep or awake. And now, now that I am here in this house, it is only getting worse. I see her when I am awake."

"She who, Aaron? Who is this woman you're seeing?"

"She whispers to me in French…autumn-eyed and beautiful. I don't know who she is. Auntie, he loved her."

"He who?" Cassandra asked.

"The colonel. Auntie, I am losing my mind." Aaron batted at the tears running down his face. "I cannot live like this. She is everywhere."

"Do you know her name?"

"Seraphina. Her name is Seraphina."

Cassandra handed him a tissue. "No, Nephew, you are not losing your mind. They aren't dreams. They are memories."

"Memories?"

"Yes, memories. Ever since you were a small child, you have known things you could not possibly know—could see and feel things beyond your years. Your father did everything he could to tamp that down in you. It is why this has been so hard for you. You remember these things because you've lived them. You remember her because you loved her."

"What are you talking about? Past lives?"

"The soul is a spiritual being having a human experience. Our bodies are merely vessels that take our souls from one plane of existence to another," she explained.

"I don't believe that," Aaron said.

"It is like Addie said. You believe it, or you wouldn't be here. You lived a life before. Your soul is remembering."

"Is this why you and Dad fought when I was little? Is that why we stopped coming here for summers? You told him this, and he didn't believe you?"

"You see that chest there? On the top shelf just below the crown molding?" Cassandra pointed over Aaron's head. "Take it down. Be careful. It's heavy."

Aaron removed the ornately carved chest from the shelf and placed it on the desk.

"That is our crest. This box is beautiful. The craftsmanship is stellar. Whose is this?"

"It belonged to the colonel." Cassandra pulled two pairs of white gloves, a magnifying glass, and an old skeleton key from the desk drawer. "You will need these."

Cassandra handed Aaron the gloves and magnifying glass. "Your father and I are the only people who have seen these. We found them during the renovation. Your father thought it best for this part of the family history to remain in the family. But when the soul speaks…one should listen. And you are family."

Cassandra unlocked the chest to reveal a leather-bound folio case. The distressed corners and binding showed the folio's age. Cassandra gently untied the satin string holding the case closed and removed several sheets of aged parchment encased in plastic protectors.

"Are those letters? Journals?" Aaron asked. "I thought we donated all the colonel's journals and letters to The Weld House Project."

"We did. All but these. I think this is what you are looking for. They are faded in some spots and a little fragile." Cassandra sat on the sofa.

Aaron took a seat at the desk and put on the gloves. He removed the first sleeved letter from the chest. "Are you serious?"

"Yes. These are the letters and journals of Colonel Aaron Matthew Weld and Seraphina Laurent."

*****

April 1st, 1863

Seraphina, my love,

Duty, she is a fool's errand whose only reward is honor. Forgive me for choosing her over you. I care not for honor at this moment. I would cast all honor and duty aside for one taste of you. I am a fool, a dutiful fool. I would not have left you otherwise. The preservation of our union will come with great sacrifice, even if we prevail. Losing you is a sacrifice I cannot make. However vigilant duty remains, I love you and will return to you.

~ Aaron

*****

April 20th, 1862

Aaron, my beloved,

You are no fool. I am. I watched Thomas's and Lucy's good-bye. Sweet, tearful, loving…and know that I should have given you the same. I should have told you how much I love you; I should have kissed you with abandon and wished you well. I am the fool, for now, I can only do so with paper and ink, cold substitutes. Forgive me, my love. Come home safely to me.

~ Seraphina

*****

May 9th, 1863

Dearest Seraphina,

I have not seen nor heard a living thing in weeks. So deafening is the sound of war that a man can scarcely think. A soldier died this morning, and for reasons still unknown, I was compelled to watch death take him. The futility of all this fell upon me, such that for a moment, I was unable to breathe. How did I endure before you? I am glad to hear your family is doing well. I know how important they are to you, and as such, they are important to me. You are more than worthy of my love; I should perish if you ever doubt it. My affections for you wash over me in the rare quiet. No greater battle wages in this war than that between my duty to this cause and my love for you.

~ Aaron

*****

May 21st, 1863

My dearest Aaron,

Your words weigh heavy on my heart. My love, I fear you will become a casualty too. One not of the body but of mind and spirit. Say the word, and I will be at your side. I know your pride, your fear, and your love will not allow you to ask it but say the word, and I will be at your side. You need not endure this alone.

~ Seraphina

*****

June 10th, 1863

Dear Aaron,

It has been so long since I received a letter from you. Thoughts of you fill my days and evenings. At night I find myself lost in a depthless sea of longing for you. You are as necessary to me as air. I pray this letter finds you well. Please write soon to say as much.

~ Seraphina

*****

June 20th, 1863

Dearest Seraphina,

I long to leave this war behind and come home to you. Thoughts of you linger in my mind daily. The Army is moving north toward Pennsylvania. Another battle looms. I will write again when I can. Take care, my sweet, fearless Seraphina, take care. I love you.

~ Aaron

Aaron fell silent. Cassandra stayed in the silence with him. He recalled the myriad of phantasms, feelings, and emotions he'd had over the last few weeks and months.

"Are these all of the letters?" he asked.

"Yes and no. These are the only ones we could save. They weren't stored properly."

"How do I find her? Where is she? Why did she leave him? Why does she appear and then disappear?" Aaron pointed to the stack of letters. "I mean, there is nothing to say where she came from or where she went? Who she was?"

"Aaron, would you be open to trying something? Something I think will help."

"I'll try anything at this point, Auntie."

"Wait here."

Cassandra left for the parlor and returned with a wooden case displaying a blue-and-silver relief of the High Priestess on the top, and a candle, incense, and matches. She cleared the desktop and arranged the candle and incense, leaving a space for the spread. She shuffled and cut the tarot deck.

"Tarot Cards?" Aaron asked, skeptical. "Are you going to tell my fortune or my future? How is this supposed to help?"

"You've spent too much time with your father. He's closed you off. I am not a fortune teller. I cannot see the future, but I may be able to help you understand the past…a guide, as it were."

One by one, Cassandra laid the cards out. "Past, present, future, spirit, mind, and body. Divine Timing, The Emperor, The Empress, The Lovers, The Hermit, and The Hanged Man. Ask your questions."

"Who is she?"

"Shhh," Cassandra silenced Aaron.

He sat quietly. Cassandra's expression gave no clues to her thoughts and feelings. All he could do was wait until his aunt, his oracle, spoke.

"The nature of the soul is eternal. It moves through lifetimes until it finds its divine purpose and fulfills it. She is your soul's mate. Somewhere in time, you lost one another. Her feminine energy is strong, sensual. It comes from the earth, from nature. It is why you feel her so deeply. Your male energy is drawn to her; the bond is deep, timeless. You need her. She is your balance, and you are hers. Your souls will seek each other until they find the right place and time, the divine timing."

"So, I am destined to suffer in this hell without her until the universe decides it is the right time for us to be together? That's bullshit!" Aaron shouted. "Does the universe understand that I cannot live my life like this? That I will end up in the nut house if I keep 'seeing' and 'feeling' things that aren't there?"

"Aaron, I want to try something else, but you are really going to have to be open."

"How open?" Aaron gave her a wary look. "I don't want a lobotomy, spiritual or otherwise."

"No lobotomy, but it will be intense. I know you want to find out who she is, but I think we need to start by finding who you were. Come lie on the couch."

Aaron walked over to the couch and lay down. "No lobotomy."

"I promise. Now close your eyes. Focus on the feeling and physical sensation in your body…relax them. Breathe deeply, slowly, until you feel comfortable. Are you comfortable?"

"Yes," Aaron answered.

"Good. Now I want you to do more breathwork. Breathe even more deeply, slowly, until you feel a light, floating, almost weightless sensation."

Aaron could feel himself lifting out of the space. It scared him. He always found her here, in the place between sleep and awake, tension and relaxation.

"Now, I want you to find a place you remember, anyplace, if it makes you feel safe and serene. Look around. Find that little you, that younger you that was able to receive the light energy of the universe before the physical world cut you off. What do you see?"

Aaron began to concentrate. "A path."

"Follow it. Tell me what you see. How you feel."

The memory flooded his mind like a high tide rolling in. The uneasy feeling returned.

"She and I would wander the forest and streams. I would catch fish while she gathered plants. She wore her hair in two long black braided ropes. Her eyes sparkled when she laughed. I'd catch butterflies for her and steal chaste kisses just to see her eyes light up and hear the music in her smile. Our village was attacked, the long houses were burning, it was a freezing winter…death. Men carried her off. I ran until my lungs burst; I could not save her."

"Where are you now," she asked. "On the path."

"Her bronzed skin, always warm against the polished white marble of the temple columns. We'd make love in the gardens among the roses and aster flowers or in the grassy fields beyond the city walls. There is a crowd…angry, menacing. They are there for her. For me. She won't let me go out to face them. She lowers my shield and my sword. She takes the poison. I hold her and leave her body on the altar of the goddess. I kill everyone until they kill me."

Aaron could feel hot tears running down the side of his face into his ears. His body began to tremble.

"Aaron, you can come back up the path now." Cassandra touched him. "If you are feeling unsafe. Aaron—"

"No! It always ends that way. She stares at me from behind a silken veil. Her eyes bright, the scent of jasmine in her hair. It is forbidden.

She waits for me. For our time. Time when the world falls away. And then…and then, I can still see the flash of the sword as it severed her head and then mine. And now, now she disappears in a wall of earth, right in front of me."

"Aaron, come back! Sweetheart, come back!" Cassandra shook him hard.

Aaron snapped back and sat up. "I shouldn't have done that. We shouldn't have done that. It was all put away. All of it. Why did you bring it back? Why?"

"Aaron, slow your breathing. Slow your breathing and listen to me. Listen to the sound of my voice."

Aaron moved back on the couch. Cassandra sat next to him.

"How old were you?" she asked. "How old were you when you first saw these memories?"

"Eight. The first time."

"No one believed you?"

"No one. Dad sent me to therapy. So, I kept her to myself. I never spoke about it. I said nothing when I'd wake up in a cold sweat."

"Oh, Aaron." Cassandra cried. "How awful!"

"To what? See yourself die? No. Awful? Awful is to watch her die again and again. Awful is to see apparitions of her everywhere in this house. Awful is to love her and no one else. Not Charlotte, not anyone."

"I wanted to help you embrace who you are, who you were. I hoped if you knew she was real and you weren't crazy, you could move on."

"Move on? Auntie, what aren't you telling me?"

"The colonel searched for years, making long treks all over the south, New England, Canada, and France. When he could no longer look, he paid others to. He never stopped. It consumed him."

"How do you know all this?"

"There are other journals from later in his life."

"Why are you and Dad keeping this a secret?"

"Our name is Weld, not Jefferson. Our family never owned slaves. We were abolitionists. People will stir up controversy with the museum. Your father will not allow it, Aaron."

"Seraphina was not a slave."

"No one will care, Nephew. She was a Black woman and the colonel's mistress. For eight generations, the Weld name has been a beacon for civil rights in Maryland and Pennsylvania, and we want it to remain that way."

"He loved her. I love her. The life of a woman so significant, so rare, cannot be left to fade from memory. You're a historian, for Christ's sake."

"Seraphina will not fade from memory because you remember her. But she must be your memory and yours alone."

"If she is to be mine alone, then give her to me. I want them all. All the journals. All the letters. Everything."

*****

Saturday, October 1st

I didn't go back to work. I am on extended leave, until after the gala. Everyone is worried. Dad and Aunt Cassandra are on the same team for once. It only took me losing my shit to make that happen. I've read every letter and journal so many times that I have them memorized. The colonel and I are two sides of the same coin. At first, I couldn't believe or didn't want to believe he'd kidnapped her and kept her under guard for over a year! But then, I can. Charlotte came to mind. Isn't that what I did with her? Sometimes, you can hold on to a thing so tightly that it slips through your fingers. The colonel blamed himself for losing his grip, but in the end, it was inevitable. I read a journal entry for the hundredth time yesterday, and I stumbled on a thought I hadn't paid much attention to before. Seraphina didn't belong. He knew it the moment he laid eyes on her. He just didn't know how or why. He tried to hold on to her, to protect her, but whatever brought her to him…took her back. He would have never let her go. Hell, I wouldn't have. Maybe that is why it took her back, but I thought about what Auntie Cassandra called divine timing. A

Black woman, educated, a nurse, and a wealthy white man? Not in 1862, but now? Maybe, now? I am going to look for her. Dad and Auntie say I am chasing a ghost. I am obsessed. It isn't that. It really isn't. It is just something I need to do.

CHAPTER TWENTY-SEVEN

Frederick, Maryland

Monday, October 10th

It was six months ago today. Everything hurts. The pain ebbs and flows, but it never ends. I don't think it ever will. Every day, I struggle against the darkness. I plead for the light in my prayers. I feel like I am being punished. Poor Vanessa. For weeks, she just held me while I cried. She's pleaded with me to confide in her. I can't. I told her I couldn't tell her what had happened to me because I didn't know. I can't explain it, and I don't think I am supposed to. She's stopped asking, but I know Vanessa, and that will be short-lived. I haven't even told my therapist the truth. All she knows is that my husband died in an accident. I leave everything else out. I spend most of my days immersed in my wisdom. It grows stronger every day. Mamie Etienne said we were unfortunates, destined to live lives of loneliness and longing, bound to men who aren't bound to us. I have known a love so full, so complete that it transcended time. I chose this, hell. Me. I am no Les Malchanceux. Neither were my mothers. They chose not to break their bonds, just like I chose to be careless with mine. I pray Mamie Etienne was right about one thing: if I am bound to Aaron forever, we will be together again, if not in this life, then in the next. My soul would give all for it to be this life.

*****

The moon was full. Seraphina prepared the ritual dream bath, the way she had on every full moon since she'd returned to the present. Mamie Etienne had written the recipe for the bath as a medium for visions and looks beyond the confines of time and space. She'd added an honesty candle for clarity.

Seraphina poured the boiled dried altamisa, mugwort, rue, lemon balm, and rose petals into the bath she'd drawn. She lit the white honesty candle she'd made from bee's wax, lavender essential oil, and the seedpods from the honesty flower. She dimmed the lights, slipped beneath the surface of the water, and allowed her body to float freely.

Her whole life had changed. She'd quit her job and opened a holistic shop named Eulalie in the downtown center. The store front windows were stained glass, like Eulalie's real kitchen. Business was good. In a bittersweet irony, her best-sellers were the lavender and witch hazel-infused water rinse and the honey and lavender skin butter she'd used during her time in the past. Her blue lotus flower and willow bark pain-relieving tea was also picking up quite a following, despite the price. The Eulalie had a small greenhouse in the back and a full kitchen. She'd subleased part of the space to a yoga instructor to offset costs. It was a lot of work and a good distraction from the grief.

But tonight, tonight was about her and Aaron. Full moons enhance all wisdom. A sacred medium, water under the moon's influence, should open her to receive. She'd never tried this level of wisdom before. Her wisdom was strongest in the healing arts. All she wanted was to feel him. Even his essence would be enough.

The moment she returned, it was as if every connection in her body had been severed. She felt nothing. The thought that he'd died in the explosion sent her to bed for days. Instead, she chose to believe he was looking for her like she was looking for him. If the gods were kind and fate stayed her cruel hand, they could be together once more.

"Aaron. Aaron, where are you?" Seraphina sank further into the bath and cried.

*****

The Weld House Museum – Frederick, Maryland
Saturday, October 29th

Seraphina stared out of the car window at the museum. She'd been sitting in the parking lot for half an hour. Today would be the first time she'd been back to the museum since it happened. She promised Vanessa to be her Black Scarlet O'Hara for the gala. The museum meant everything to Vanessa, and she couldn't let her down. So, she dragged herself out of the abyss of grief and came to the very place she swore she would never go again.

She was still mourning. Aaron was gone, and the museum was an ever-present reminder of him. The last thing she wanted to do was walk through the remnants of their life together. But in truth, it was more than that. The part of her that hoped against hope that she'd get another chance, that time would whisk her away again, was terrified. Terrified that it wouldn't. Terrified that she would have to live with her mistake forever. And all that would be left of their love were a few artifacts—eternal reminders of how stupid she'd been.

Seraphina got out of the car, retrieved her makeup bag and suitcase from the trunk, and began the slow walk across the parking lot. She flashed her badge at security and proceeded to the rear entrance. She walked through the double doors into a chaotic scene reminiscent of backstage at the fashion show she'd done last year for their sorority fundraiser.

"Mademoiselle Laurent! My goddess! Bene sei qui!" Mr. Bisaccia gleamed.

"Mr. Bisaccia, it is good to see you too," Seraphina replied.

"You should grace the runways of Milan. You are too gorgeous for this…nowhere place."

"Thank you for the compliment… I think. Where do I get dressed?"

"You won't need your bags. My team is here. Tu mio dolce sarai il mio capolavoro!"

"I have no idea what that means, but let's get this show on the road," Seraphina said with feigned enthusiasm.

****

After the better part of an hour, all the other actors had joined the party, but Seraphina was still under construction.

"Seraphina! You came!" Vanessa hugged her neck. "When I didn't see you downstairs, I thought…"

"A promise is a promise. This is your moment… I wouldn't miss it for the world. You look fantastic! I hoped you go bold and not classic black. That red on you is fierce. Is that Vera?"

"It is." Vanessa did a little spin. "But enough about me, where is your dress?"

"I don't know." Seraphina shrugged. "I've been standing here in my petticoats and corset for…"

"Here it is!" Francesco hung the dress from the rack. "I took the liberty of giving the bodice a bit of Bisaccia sparkle. Emerald is your color. You will stun coming down the staircase. It isn't Milan, but a boy can dream."

"Vanessa, where did you find my…dress?" Seraphina asked, tears in her eyes.

"We found it in the attic during the restoration. It was in a trunk with a lot of other dresses. The moment I saw it, I knew it was for you. Unfortunately, it was faded, and the fabric worn. Rose had Mr. Bisaccia replicate it. After tonight, it will go on display. Oh, and this… Mr. Bisaccia."

Francesco walked over to Seraphina with a jewelry case and opened it.

"It was with the dress. We know the emblem is the Weld family crest. We just aren't sure who it belonged to. The initials don't match any of the Weld women that we know of. But you get to wear it tonight."

Seraphina touched the emerald and diamond-encrusted pendant. *You are and will always be Seraphina Weld.*

"Are you okay?" Vanessa touched Seraphina's shoulder.

"Yes. I am fine. The woman who wore this was loved."

"Girl, yes, she was! That damn thing appraised at thirty thousand. I can only imagine what it cost back then. So don't lose it." Vanessa laughed.

"Mademoiselle your face!" Francesco waved an assistant over. "Let's get you dressed. It is just late enough for you to make a grande entrée."

*****

Aaron gazed at his reflection in the window. He'd stolen away from the reception to get some air. Rose had gotten her to wish; he was the toast of the evening. Everyone wanted to meet him, shake his hand, and take his picture. It had only been an hour, and he was ready to leave. Being his past self was exhausting.

An older woman approached from behind, and Aaron caught a glimpse of her in the window's reflection. He prepared to turn and be charming.

"Well, aren't you the spitting image," Mary said, smiling.

"Yes. My name is Aaron Weld. The colonel was my great-great-great grandfather."

"I know who you are." Mary stepped closer. "You got that sadness too."

"Forgive me, ma'am, you are?"

"Mrs. Oakes-Timmons, but please call me Mary."

"You are Vanessa's great-aunt, right? It is good to meet you. I have been dying to talk with you. Unfortunately, I must get back to the guests. May I call on you later? Isn't that what they used to say?"

"Something like that." Mary laughed. "And yes, you may."

"May I escort you inside?" Aaron offered her his arm.

"Yes. Thank you."

Mary took Aaron's arm, and the two made their way back into the museum.

"You know the Welds and the Oakes go back generations... all the way back to the colonel."

"I know. I've learned so much since the museum project started. Seems the colonel and I have much in common. If I remember correctly, your father was the first Black doctor to work at Weld Memorial?"

"No. that would be my great grandfather, Eli Oakes Sr.," Mary answered. "He was the first Black doctor to work in The Weld Clinic, back before it was a hospital, of course. He grew up in the Weld house in Philadelphia."

Should I ask? Aaron thought to himself. Like Adelaide, Mary seemed to know everything about everything. Maybe she would know about Seraphina. He knew from his journals, the colonel had forbidden anyone to speak her name in his presence, but the staff always talk.

"You going to ask me that question that's got smoke coming out of your ears?" Mary stopped.

"Is it that obvious?" Aaron laughed.

"Smoke signals, sugar, smoke signals. Now, what's your question?"

"Are there any stories about the colonel having a mistress?" Aaron asked sheepishly.

"The man is dead. You ain't got to be bashful." Mary chuckled. "Well, he was white, wealthy, widowed, and male… so stories or no, odds on yes. But nobody would talk about that type of thing in mixed company."

"You got me there. What if she were Black?" Aaron winced at the tentative nature of his tone.

"Oh my, they might put you out of here, you start going on about that." Mary smiled. "I don't have any stories about a Black mistress, but it wasn't uncommon, and that would have been kept hush, hush. Why the interest?"

"Everyone keeps asking me that." Aaron sighed. "I'm just trying to learn more about him. I came across some correspondence that suggested that may be the case. Just looking for other sources."

"I guess if I had your face, I'd want to know more too. Did you find a name? I can ask other family folks. My cousin Addie might know… She's working with your Aunt Cassandra and my niece Vanessa."

"No, Addie didn't know. Her name is Seraphina. Seraphina Laurent."

"It can't be," Mary gasped and stumbled. "It just can't be. It's you."

Aaron held her arm firmly. "Mary, maybe you should sit down. Is there someone I should call?"

"Seraphina Laurent is here." Mary's voice quaked.

"Here? Like in an exhibit? Which one?" Aaron asked, frantic. "Please tell me."

"No sugar, she is here. In the building." Mary replied.

Aaron paled, and for a moment, he could not breathe or get his bearings.

"Aaron, love, you look like you seen a ghost. Don't go falling now… We both go down if you do." Mary held his arm tighter.

"Where? Where is she?" Aaron pleaded.

"Should be just inside." Mary pointed. "Wandering around greeting folks like all the other actors."

"Please excuse me." Aaron ran inside.

*****

In a moment, the guests fell into a hushed silence. All eyes were on the grand staircase. Seraphina, a vision in emerald green, descended the stairs to a stunned audience.

She was dying inside, drowning in a river of inner tears. It was too much like the last time, although the faces were kinder and more admiring, of course. But the one person's admiration she wanted wasn't there.

"Seraphina! Seraphina André Phillipe Laurent!" Aaron pushed his way through the crowd until he stood face to face with her. "Do you remember me? Do you know who I am?"

"Aaron?" Seraphina moved back slightly. Hope and disbelief shifted the ground beneath her feet, and she fell into his arms.

"Yes," he replied. "It is me."

Voice shaky, Seraphina reached up to touch his face. "How?"

Aaron placed her hand in his and pressed his cheek into the palm of her hand. "You remember me?"

"I remember everything." The dam inside broke; a river of emotion and tears spilled over.

Aaron kissed her, deep and slow, and Seraphina melted into him. The world fell away.

Aaron ended the kiss and lifted the crest pendant in his hand. "My soul has missed you, Seraphina Weld."

"And mine, yours. I am sorry. I am so sorry. Please forgive me." She clung to him.

"I will not leave you, Seraphina." He held her face in his hands. "Not in this life…or the next."

"I know, and I will never, never forget it. I love you, Aaron. And I am yours in this life and the next."

EPILOGUE

Seraphina stared at the door, her heart racing. Her life had changed dramatically in the last year. She and Aaron were married and expecting baby girl Weld in three months. Curiosity about the origins of their relationship had waned with the announcement of the baby. Only Mary and Cassandra knew the truth.

"Cassandra, are you sure? Really sure?"

"Yes. I am sure. Seraphina, we did the leg work. The DNA is a match."

"Do you think she will believe us?" Seraphina inquired, nervous. "I mean…"

"Believe us? Why wouldn't she? It's going to be okay," Aaron tried to reassure her.

Cassandra rang the bell. Seraphina grabbed Aaron's hand and squeezed it. Adelaide opened the door.

"Miss Cassandra, it is good to see you, love. Lunch is ready. And there is my handsome boy… Come give me a hug."

"Miss Addie, we brought someone with us. I would like you to meet Seraphina Laurent, your great-great niece."

Seraphina stepped out from behind Aaron and came face-to-face with her great-great-aunt. Addie, with Eulalie's tawny complexion, silver mane, and brilliant green eyes. Seraphina began to cry. "Hello, Auntie."

"Jules's grandbaby? My god. Come here, child." Addie embraced Seraphina tightly, tears streaming down her face. "Cassandra, how on earth did you…?" Addie kissed Seraphina's cheeks, wiping her tears away.

"It was a happy accident. You know I'm always interested in people's stories. Seraphina and I got to talking with your cousin Mary. Seraphina was sharing stories about her grandmother. She grew up in Louisiana."

"Auntie, my grandmother's name was Eulalie Moreau. Her mother was Etienne. Mamie Etienne never talked much about her life until late. She told me about a man named Jules Moreau. She said he was the love of her life."

"I figured it could just be a coincidence but decided to take a chance. And well…" Cassandra smiled through tears. "We can add another branch to the Brown, Oakes, and Weld trees."

"Your great-grandpa Jules died in the war. I found your Mamie Etienne's letters to him in his belongings, but they were damaged. I couldn't read the names. I thought I was going to die and never see your face. But here you are, Jules's grandbaby." Addie placed her hands on Seraphina's pregnant belly. "And who is this?"

"Auntie Addie." Aaron smiled. "This is your great-great-great niece Adelaide Eulalie Weld."

Seraphina placed her hands over Addie's. "Auntie, you don't know this, but somewhere a long time ago, you found me, and when I needed it most, you loved me."

"Je suis vraiment heureuse," Addie exclaimed.

"Vous parlez français?" Seraphina smiled, surprised.

"Je suis un Moreau. Bien sûr."

"Mamie Eulalie always said I would thank her one day for insisting on my learning French. She was right."

"Ma douce, Séraphine. Moreau women always are."

REFERENCES

Graham, Martin F. A Pocket History of the Civil War. Osprey, (2011)

Lyman, Darryl. Civil War Wordbook including Sayings, Phrases and Expletives. Combined Books Inc., (1994)

Ward, Andrew. The Slaves War. Houghton Mifflin Harcourt Publishing Company, (2008)
Straubing, Harold E. In Hospital and Camp. Stackpole Books, (2014)

Katcher, Philip. The Civil War Day by Day. Zenith Press (2007)

Wilbur M.D., C. Keith, Civil War Medicine 1861-1865, The Globe Pequot Press, (1998)
Diaz, Juliet. Plant Witchery. Hay House Inc. (2020)

Using Foreign Words in Your Fiction (writing-world.com), Cora Bresciano (2011)

10 Facts: Civil War Artillery | American Battlefield Trust (battlefields.org), (2022)

U.S. Civil War Morphine Addiction – SmartDrugPolicy, (2018)

Tarot Card Meanings: Understanding Major Arcana Cards (top10.com), Sarah Pritzker (2021)

Woman, Healer, Goddess? Famous (and Forbidden) Female Physicians in the Ancient World | Ancient Origins (ancient-origins.net), Martini Fisher (2017)

"Clipart courtesy FCIT" URL https://etc.usf.edu/clipart

Title: The "Reliable Contraband" Contributor Names: Forbes, Edwin, 1839-1895, artist
Created / Published: [between 1861 and 1876] Call Number/Physical Location: DRWG/US - Forbes, no. L23 (A size) [P&P] Source Collection: Morgan collection of Civil War drawings (Library of Congress) Repository: Library of Congress Prints and Photographs Division Washington, D.C. 20540 USA

A Bloody Killing Field in The Battle Of Williamsburg - Daily Press https://www.dailypress.com/history/dp-battle-of-williamsburg-killing-field-20130802-post.html

Benson John Lossing, ed. Harper's Encyclopedia of United States History (vol. 2) (New York, NY: Harper and Brothers, 1912) – Ruins of Chancellorsville

Benson John Lossing, ed. Harper's Encyclopedia of United States History (vol. 3) (New York, NY: Harper and Brothers, 1912) - Independence Hall, Philadelphia where the Declaration of Independence was signed.

Benson John Lossing, ed. Harper's Encyclopedia of United States History (vol. 10) (New York, NY: Harper and Brothers, 1912) - Harrison's Landing

Benson J. Lossing, The Pictorial Field-Book of the Revolution (New York: Harper & Brothers, 1851) II:433 - Scene on the James River, at Richmond

Benson John Lossing, ed. Harper's Encyclopedia of United States History (vol. 3) (New York, NY: Harper and Brothers, 1912) - Scene at Fredericksburg

Charles Carleton Coffin Drumbeat of the Nation (New York, NY: Harper & Brothers, 1915) - Harrison's Landing at Berkeley Plantation

Dodge, Mary Mapes St. Nicholas an Illustrated Magazine for Young Folks (New York, New York: The Century Co., 1886) - An Illustration of Carpenter's Hall in Philadelphia

Frank Leslie Famous Leaders and Battle Scenes of the Civil War (New York, NY: Mrs. Frank Leslie, 1896) - Harrison's Landing, James River, Va

Frank Leslie Famous Leaders and Battle Scenes of the Civil War (New York, NY: Mrs. Frank Leslie, 1896) - The Old Harrison Mansion, Harrison's Landing, Va.

Frank Leslie Famous Leaders and Battle Scenes of the Civil War (New York, NY: Mrs. Frank Leslie, 1896) - Battle of Gettysburg, Cemetery Hill

Frank Leslie Famous Leaders and Battle Scenes of the Civil War (New York, NY: Mrs. Frank Leslie, 1896) – Battle of Williamsburg

Frank Leslie Famous Leaders and Battle Scenes of the Civil War (New York, NY: Mrs. Frank Leslie, 1896) - A Street in Fredericksburg, Va

Frank Leslie Famous Leaders and Battle Scenes of the Civil War (New York, NY: Mrs. Frank Leslie, 1896) - President Lincoln Riding Through Richmond

Frank Leslie Famous Leaders and Battle Scenes of the Civil War (New York, NY: Mrs. Frank Leslie, 1896) - The War in Virginia--General Hooker's Army Marching Past Manassas.

John Gilmary Shea, The Story of a Great Nation (New York: Gay Brothers & Company, 1886) after 908 - Soldiers Outside A Few Tents.

John Gilmary Shea, The Story of a Great Nation (New York: Gay Brothers & Company, 1886) after 812, says "page 825" - Depiction of the Battle of Gettysburg.

Lester, C. Edwards Lester's History of the United States (New York, NY: P. F. Collier, 1883) - Carpenters' Hall, Philadelphia, Pennsylvania,

Pennsylvania's Emergency Men: 151st Camp Curtin Commemoration (paemergencymen.blogspot.com)

Alfoxton or Alfoxden House, Holford, Somerset, UK. Once the home of William Wordsworth
old book illustration - old book illustration - Public Domain - File: Alfoxton01.jpg - Created: 8 January 1920

"Philadelphia, Wilmington, and Baltimore Railroad Station, Philadelphia, Pennsylvania, 1861," House Divided: The Civil War Research Engine at Dickinson College, https://hd.housedivided.dickinson.edu/node/33606.

Harrison's Landing: Mcclellan's Headquarters, Harrison's Landing, James River Hatzigeorgiou, Karen J. U.S. History Images. 2011. Online. Internet. <Http://Ushistoryimages.Com>.

Title: U.S Mail boat dock, Harrison's Landing, James River, Va.— Floating houses of the contrabands erected on the freight boats, etc. Related Names: Schell, J. H., artist - Rights Advisory: No known restrictions on publication. Call Number: Illus. in AP2.L52 1862 Case Y [P&P] - Notes: Bookmark This Record: https://www.loc.gov/pictures/item/96516941/

General View of The Encampment Of The Army Of The Potomac At Harrison's Landing. —Sketched By Mr. A. R. Waud. - http://www.

sonofthesouth.net/leefoundation/civil-war/1862/august/army-potomac-harrisons-landing.htm

U.S. History Image Sources (ushistoryimages.com) Savage's Station: Abandoned

Virginia's East Peninsula, 1862
Title: Virginia's East Peninsula
Description: A map of eastern Virginia during the Civil War, showing towns, roads, and railroads, and the routes of the Peninsula Campaign against Richmond.
Place Names: Virginia, Richmond, Williamsburg,
Source: Joel Dorman Steele, A Brief History of the United States (New York, NY: American Book Company, 1885) 236 - Map Credit: Courtesy the private collection of Roy Winkelman

Maps | America Civil War - Movement of armies 1861 - https://www.americacivilwar.org/maps

Vintage Graphic of Victorian Dining Table: Black and White Illustration of Decorated Victorian Dining Room - https://antiqueimages.blogspot.com/2012/03/vintage-graphic-of-victorian-dining.html

Cover Art:
Elena Dudina – Web Designer https://www.elenadudina.com/
L. Prang & Co, and Thure De Thulstrup. Battle of Antietam / Thulstrup. Dec. 19. Photograph. Retrieved from the Library of Congress, <www.loc.gov/item/2003663827/>.

Made in the USA
Columbia, SC
31 March 2025